At age eighteen, when they become marriageable, all royal children in the Thousand Kingdoms must either go questing to rescue another royal or be hidden away to await rescue themselves. Some go the traditional route of princes rescuing princesses, but not all princes want to be rescuers...and some would rather rescue other princes.

Then there's Prince Gerald, who has no interest in getting married at all. When he refuses to choose a role as either rescuer or rescuee, his royal parents choose for him and have him magicked away to a distant tower to await a spouse.

Gerald, however, is having none of it. He recruits his guardian dragon and a would-be rescuer and soon the trio is dashing to all corners of the united kingdoms on a quest to overturn the entire system.

ROYAL RESCUE

A. Alex Logan

A NineStar Press Publication

Published by NineStar Press
P.O. Box 91792,
Albuquerque, New Mexico, 87199 USA.
www.ninestarpress.com

Royal Rescue

Printed in the USA
First Edition
April, 2018

Print ISBN: 978-1-950412-56-3

Also available in eBook, ISBN: 978-1-950412-41-9

To all those forging their own path, with thanks to Patricia C. Wrede for Cimorene

Chapter One

GERALD FOLLOWED THE steward to the study wearing an expression that would have been more appropriate if he were being led to the dungeon. The steward rapped on the door twice before opening it and stepping aside for Gerald. She gave the young man an encouraging wink, but he was too intent on bracing himself for the upcoming confrontation to notice.

He took a deep breath, visibly set his shoulders and stepped through the doorway. The steward closed the door behind him, and Gerald fought back the feeling of being trapped.

"Don't lurk in the doorway," an imposing voice scolded. "Come in where I can see you."

Gerald did as he was told, stopping and giving a shallow bow when the woman came into view. She nodded, acknowledging the courtesy, which caused the sunlight streaming in through the window to catch and reflect off her golden crown.

Gerald resisted the urge to reach up and touch his own circlet—silver—which he too late realized was probably once again askew.

"Well?" the Queen asked. "Have you made your decision?"

Another deep breath, another forceful straightening of his shoulders, and Gerald said, a hint of defiance in his tone, "I have."

The Queen's harsh expression broke into a smile. "Oh, Gerald, thank goodness. Your mum and I were about at our wits' end! There's barely enough time left to make all the arrangements. So, what will it be? Rescuer or rescuee?"

"Neither."

The smile melted off the Queen's face. "Neither! Don't be ridiculous, Gerald. You said you had made your decision."

"I have," he said, crossing his arms in front of his chest. "I've decided not to participate."

"That is not an option," she said coldly, the warmth in her voice gone the same way as the smile. "As you are well aware."

"I don't wish to marry," Gerald replied, trying to match her tone but not quite managing it. "As *you* are well aware."

The Queen waved her hand dismissively. "This is merely the first step. It may take a year or even two for you to rescue—or be rescued by—someone who appeals. Then there's the courtship, the inter-kingdom negotiations, planning the festivities...why, unless it's True Love and you two want to rush things, I doubt the wedding will happen before you turn twenty-one."

"I didn't say 'I don't wish to marry in the next three years'," Gerald said, forcing himself to keep his voice level even as he balled his hands into fists. "I said, 'I don't wish to marry.' As in, ever."

But the Queen was no longer listening.

"I really don't know where we went wrong with you," she said. "We never had this sort of problem with your older siblings or even your twinling..."

"Don't call her that," Gerald snapped. "You know how much I hate that—we're not twins, we're not even sort-of twins. We're half-siblings at best and maybe not even related at all."

The Queen looked up at the ceiling as if imploring it to give her strength. "Now you're being deliberately obtuse," she snapped back. "You know very well that the term 'twinling' has been in use for at least a century throughout every single one of the Thousand Kingdoms, and it's a perfectly apt word. You're acting like your mum and I made it up to irritate you. You're acting like a child, Gerald."

"Isn't the point of all this that I *am* a child?" he responded. "Isn't the entire purpose of this whole charade of rescue and marriage to make me into an adult?"

"It's hardly a charade. It's—"

"—a well-respected, long-established tradition to encourage young royals to broaden their horizons, explore more of the Thousand Kingdoms, find love, and forge stronger connections among the Kingdoms, yes, yes, I know," Gerald interrupted. "I still say it's a charade. It's perfectly possible to accomplish all of those goals without forcing every royal into a ridiculous marriage quest the moment they turn eighteen."

"You seem to be forgetting something very important here, Gerald," the Queen said calmly.

"What's that?"

"This isn't optional."

"You can't force me to choose," Gerald said. "Why can't you leave me be and let Lila broaden her horizons, explore the Kingdoms, forge alliances, and all that rot? *She* wants to."

"You have ten days," the Queen continued, as if Gerald hadn't spoken. She turned away without even bothering to dismiss him.

GERALD STALKED BACK to his room, quietly fuming. It's not that he *expected* the Queen to understand, but he hoped perhaps they could reach some sort of middle ground...but no.

I should have known, he thought grumpily. *When have either of them ever listened to me? Lila got all the lessons she wanted, on every topic she wanted, and all of the approval of both of them, and while they were hanging on her every word there was never an ear free to listen to me.*

It was while thinking those dark thoughts he turned a corner and came face-to-face with Lila. His scowl deepened and he was again conscious—too late—of his crooked circlet and general disarray. Lila's own circlet was straight and shining from its recent polish, and she looked every inch the royal, easily projecting their parents' attitudes of confidence and serenity.

Gerald had never gotten the knack of projecting either one.

"I heard you got summoned," Lila said. Gerald grumbled something inarticulate and tried to step around her, but Lila slid over to block him.

"Are you ever going to grow up?" she asked. "I'm tired of sitting through all these uncomfortable family dinners because you can't get your act together."

"Because they can't accept my decision," Gerald corrected.

Lila snorted. "Doing nothing isn't a decision, Gerald, it's the lack of one!"

Gerald scowled and Lila returned the expression. "You know what your problem is? You're spoiled."

Gerald gaped at her. "*I'm* spoiled? You're the one who gets everything you want! Tutors for every subject you're interested in, the best training, the best of everything! You're the heir of Andine, and I'm the afterthought."

"The *heir* gets those things," Lila snapped. "Not me. I don't get those things for *me*. The lessons, the tutors, the training, those aren't *rewards*, Gerald, they're *responsibilities*. And you have none. You want none. You don't care about Andine, only yourself."

Andine doesn't care about me, Gerald wanted to snap. But he didn't want to give Lila more ammunition. "Don't you have a quest to be getting ready for?" he asked instead and, without waiting for a reply, he dodged past Lila and ran until he reached his room and barred the door behind him.

Gerald could easily have stayed in his room for the rest of the day, alone with a book, but he forced himself to go to dinner. The monarchs only dined in state once a week, unless there were holidays or festivals or visiting royalty. The rest of the time, it was family dinners, and they were strictly enforced. The only acceptable reason for missing one was a serious illness or a trip abroad.

Unlike the morning's official meeting, there was no steward to announce him or give him an encouraging wink at the door to the dining room. He opened the door himself and tried to slink in unnoticed, but every head immediately turned his way when the door slipped out of his hand and latched with an echoing click.

There was Lila, her circlet still straight and polished, catching the lamplight and glittering against her short, dark hair; Queen Mixte, an older, softer version of Lila, with the same dark hair and the same green eyes; and Queen Danya, much paler than the other two, whose icy blue eyes had pinned Gerald in their meeting that morning.

At least James and Vani aren't here. James resembled Mixte as much as Lila did, while Vani had the same icy beauty of Danya, although her temper was much warmer than her mother's.

And then there was Gerald, whose skin tone was halfway between the Queens', whose hair was red-streaked auburn, whose eyes were hazel. Who always felt like he was unbalancing the royal tableau.

"About time," Lila said. "I was starting to wonder if you were going to go on one of your ridiculous sulks and refuse to come to dinner at all."

"I'm not that late," Gerald said mildly.

"Children," Queen Mixte said warningly, but Gerald made no move to reply to the rest of Lila's comment.

I'm going to have to choose my battles tonight, he thought as he took his seat across from Lila.

Indeed, as soon as the soup had been served and the servants withdrew, the Queens exchanged a significant glance and Gerald sighed, knowing what was coming.

"I heard about your discussion today," Queen Mixte said lightly. "I have to say, Gerald, I'm having trouble coming to terms with your objections."

"If you heard about the discussion, then Mother will have told you my objections."

"She did. But I don't understand them."

"I don't wish to get married. It seems a very straightforward objection to me," Gerald said. His tone was level, but his knuckles whitened as he gripped his spoon like a lifeline.

"You're royalty," Queen Mixte pointed out gently.

"I'm aware."

"So you must marry!" Queen Danya interjected. "Mix, you mustn't coddle the boy. He can choose his role, but he will play one of them!"

"Why must I marry?" Gerald demanded. He dropped his spoon, ignoring the clatter and the soup that splattered the table, and snapped, "*I'm* not the heir. Lila is, and she's obviously far more suited to rule, and there's always James or Vani!"

"You know very well that James and Vani are out of the line of succession," Queen Danya retorted. "They have gone to their spouses' kingdoms."

"Because you allowed it! You could have negotiated differently—"

"But we didn't."

"And what if I'm negotiated to join another kingdom?" Gerald asked, changing tacks.

"You're getting quite far ahead of yourself, Gerald," Queen Mixte said calmly. "You know very well you and Lila are both in the line of succession and you both must remain in the line of succession since our prior twinlings went abroad."

"But Lila's the heir."

"Lila's the heir," Queen Mixte acknowledged.

"So she will marry—she wants to marry!—and she will have children and she will inherit and her children will inherit after her, and I am completely irrelevant to the succession!"

"Even so. There are other purposes a royal marriage can serve. Even though you are not a crown prince, you are a prince. And your marriage can ensure many benefits for Andine. You owe your duty to your kingdom and your people. And your marriage is a duty."

"I will not marry," Gerald said flatly. "I will not argue any further, but I will not marry. Let Lila go off questing. She's clearly dying to. She'll find a spouse and be happy doing it. I will not."

The Queens exchanged another significant look while Gerald glared furiously at his soup and Lila sat back and watched the scene with a faint amused smirk.

"Honestly, brother," she interjected. "It's a marriage, not an execution. What's the harm of it? Are you afraid you'll be stuck with someone unsuitable?"

"Anyone—everyone—would be unsuitable," Gerald growled.

Lila rolled her eyes. "If they could see you now, I'm sure the rest of our cohort would be thinking the same thing about you."

"Children," Queen Mixte said again and they subsided.

Gerald didn't say a word for the rest of the meal, which lasted four long courses.

GERALD WOKE WITH the sun, as usual, and after easing himself out from under the covers to avoid disturbing the cats he always collected in the night, he quickly dressed and left his room before anyone could come looking for him. After a quick stop in the kitchen for a portable breakfast—warm rolls filled with cheese and sausage—he trotted to the stables.

His favorite little bay pushed forward to the front of her stall when he entered, and he soon had her saddle and tack on. After a quick word to the hostler, Gerald and Wisp were out of the stable and heading into the forest.

At least riding is one royal thing I do well, he thought as they trotted down the path. This early in the day it was dim under the trees, although their leaves were starting to turn color and fall, leaving gaps where the light could shine through. But even draped in shadows, the forest was a comfortable place for Gerald, and he—and Wisp—knew the path well enough that the low light caused no difficulties.

"We'll go to the second clearing," Gerald said aloud, and Wisp flicked an ear back as if she were really listening. He lapsed into silence after that, watching the small animals and birds of the forest start their own days. *I wish my life were as simple as theirs*, he thought. *Instead, I'm stuck with a half-sister-or-less who thinks I'm simple and a pair of mothers who don't understand me. I don't want to marry! It's not even the quest, as such...although I'd be horrid at that, let's not get any ideas there... But I don't want to find a spouse, I don't want to produce heirs!*

A pair of squirrels bickering loudly about an acorn caught his attention and he sighed. *I guess if I were a squirrel, I'd do all that and not think anything of it. Lila certainly isn't thinking anything of it... And I can't remember either James or Vani objecting, when they turned eighteen. Am I really the only one who wants out of this system?*

Thinking of all the many ways in which he was different from Lila, from the Queens, and from his older siblings, Gerald sunk further into gloom. *Probably*, he concluded. *The problem's not the system. It's me.*

Slowly but surely, the ride, the fresh air, and the time spent with Wisp—simple, uncomplicated Wisp, who was content to provide unconditional affection and was easily bribed with nothing more than a carrot, a bit of sugar, or a good brushing—drew him out of his gloom. By the time the sun was fully up, his stomach was grumbling for lunch. *It doesn't matter what the problem is*, he decided. *I'll have to find the solution.*

A MESSENGER WAS waiting by the stable when Gerald rode back in. "Your Highness," she said, giving a shallow bow. "Correspondence for you."

Gerald dismounted and took the scroll with a word of thanks. There was no sender's mark, and he tucked it unopened into his belt to read later, after Wisp was settled and when he was alone.

The messenger, the hostler, and the stable boys were all hovering "unobtrusively" in the area, and if Gerald opened it now, they'd all be looking over his shoulder, wondering what it said. The entire palace was aware the youngest prince was feuding with the monarchs, and his eighteenth birthday—and the deadline day—was barely more than a week away.

When Gerald was back in his room, a plate of lunch in his hand, he retrieved the scroll from his belt. He wondered about the lack of a sender's mark until he noticed the ribbon holding it closed—dark green, tied in a double bow—had a small yellow bead knotted into the center.

"Of course," he said aloud. "Who else would be writing me?"

He untied the scroll and pocketed the bead before he unrolled the message and weighed down the corners. His gaze flicked to the signature at the end and he smiled to see he was correct. It was from Erick, his cousin and one of his very few real friends.

> *Dear Meathead,*
>
> *I hear you are being as meatheaded as usual. My parents must have had a dozen urgent messages from yours in the last few weeks. Knowing you, I'm guessing they'll be getting several dozen more...*
>
> *So I want to know, why don't you just choose? No, stop making that face. Keep reading. It's not like you'll be monitored, you know. No scrying, no messages, no contact is permitted. So tell them you'll go questing, and then...don't. Or do. As you wish.*
>
> *You can travel with me! We'll be starting at the same time, remember, even though I'm three whole weeks older than you (youngin'!). You're lucky your birthday is the last day of the month; you can start right away. I've been sitting around twiddling my thumbs for weeks, waiting for the first of next month to come around.*
>
> *But look, we can start together; I'll keep you from falling off a cliff or getting eaten by a dragon, and you can keep me from starving to death.*
>
> *Sound good?*
>
> *Erick*

Gerald smiled at the idea of traveling the Thousand Kingdoms with Erick—it would certainly be fun at least for a while—but the underlying problem would still be there. He might be able to get away with not truly questing for a while, but sooner or later Erick would complete his quest and rescue a spouse, and Gerald had no illusions about his ability to survive a quest alone. Not to mention the pesky fact that eventually Gerald would be expected to return home with a spouse, too.

A false quest would delay the inevitable, but that's all it would be: a delay. Gerald started to pen a reply to Erick saying as much when the original scroll chirped and went blank. Gerald let a large drop of ink splash on the parchment and within moments it began to spread out into a spidery line of text.

The two-way parchment was Erick's own invention and he was very proud of it. The spell was keyed to the recipient, too; with this piece of parchment, only Erick and Gerald would be able to write back and forth. For anyone else, it would act like regular paper.

So, meathead? Ready to be less meatheaded?

Gerald wrote back.

It won't work.

What do you mean, it won't work? Of course it will work. No one will find out it's a fake.

Until I come home without a spouse.

Ah. You mean it won't work long term. Well...you know, you might change your mind. If you meet a few eligible princesses— or princes—or princexes—you may decide marriage isn't so awful after all.

I'm not going to change my mind.

Well, Gerald, I hate to break it to you, but your parents are not going to let you sit this out. To be honest, I doubt they're going to let you sit marriage out. Wouldn't it be better to have some fun with me first?

Maybe "better" isn't good enough.

Meathead.

Spellbrain.

Well, I tried. And if I starve to death, it'll be on your head.

Pack a lot of journey bread.

A knock on the door drew Gerald's attention away from the scroll.

I have to go

He scrawled it quickly and then lifted the corner weights. The scroll would erase itself in a few minutes unless he used the bead to archive the conversation. *I don't think this one needs to be archived,* he thought wryly.

He opened the door and blinked in surprise to see Queen Mixte standing there.

"May I come in, Gerald?" she asked.

"You never come here," he said, but he stepped aside to let her pass, too surprised to say no.

"I wanted to talk to you privately. I thought, perhaps, without you and your mother butting heads, I might be able to help sort things out."

Gerald turned away from her serene smile to pace around the room. "There's nothing to sort out. You two want me to participate in this ridiculous tradition and I don't care to. You two want me to get married and I don't care to."

"Yes, but Gerald, why don't you care to?"

He turned back to face her. She seemed genuinely interested in his response, and her expression was as calm and warm as ever. Unlike his mother, Queen Mixte never turned to ice.

"I..." he trailed off.

"Many young people are worried about marriage," she said gently. "Pre-quest nerves have rattled many a royal. But nerves can be overcome, my dear. And the reward at the end is worth it."

"But don't you get it? For me, marriage isn't a reward. Being stuck with someone, tied to someone I don't even know, a stranger, for the rest of my life? That's supposed to be a reward?"

"They won't be a stranger. That's the point of these quests, Gerald. For the royalty of the Thousand Kingdoms to become friends and more."

"It seems an awfully circuitous way to do so," he grumbled. "I mean, if you're questing, you have to go to desert after swamp after mountain, trying to find the right royal to rescue. And the one being rescued has to sit and wait and wait and wait. How many other people do they really meet?"

"Through portfolios and signposts and correspondence? Dozens."

"In person."

"I believe the average is five."

"All this nonsense to meet *five people*?" he yelped, throwing his hands up in frustration.

"The circumstances forge bonds," Queen Mixte said serenely. "The couple is much more devoted than if they met at a simple ball, where neither one would have to prove their worth or endure a wait. The rescuers form deep bonds with each other by helping fellow questers over obstacles or by working together to best a guardian. And the rescuees all have a deep well of common experience to draw on, to make them more sympathetic with each other and engender more cordial relations between kingdoms. You know all this, Gerald, and you know it works. It's worked for hundreds of years."

"I don't want to forge bonds, Mum!" he burst out. "I'm not suited for marriage. I'm not suited for a relationship. I'm not Lila! I'm not Erick, I'm not you or Mother."

Queen Mixte tilted her head and looked at Gerald as if she were actually listening. His heart lifted slightly as she asked, "Why do you think that?"

"I've never—I've never wanted to be with anyone," he said, crossing his arms defensively. "Lila's had crushes, Erick's had crushes. I've never looked at anyone and felt my heart flutter. I'm never going to. I don't want to marry someone I don't love, and I don't think I can love anyone."

"You love us. Your mother, and me, and even Lila, as much as you two bicker. You love Erick. Of course you're capable of love."

But Gerald shook his head miserably. "That's different. I don't think I can love anyone the way you love Mother, or the way James and Vani love their spouses."

"You're still young," she said gently. "You'll grow from this experience. You'll mature, and you'll find love. Everyone does."

She gave him a kiss on the forehead. "You'll be fine, my dear. But please—make a decision before your mother makes one for you."

And with that, she swept out of the room.

Gerald sat down heavily on his bed.

Even when they're listening, they don't really hear me.

Chapter Two

GERALD WOULDN'T—COULDN'T—make any decision other than the one he'd already declared. The deadline was hanging over his head and Erick's offer was looking increasingly tempting. But he was determined not to simply postpone the problem, but to deal with it in the here and now. *I can't have this looming over me forever.*

He pored through the books and scrolls in the library, examining royal genealogies and histories from before and after the Thousand Kingdoms had united. He was looking for a precedent. *If I can find another royal who has refused...then they'll see it's not simply me having a tantrum.*

But he came up empty again and again.

He wrote to Erick, asking his cousin to check *his* library. Rather than spending three days poring over books, Erick wrote a search spell and set it loose in the library. Once the dust, both literal and metaphorical, had settled—and after the furious librarian had banned Erick for life—he wrote back that he, too, had found nothing.

> *Leave off this idea. You're not going to find a precedent, and even if you do, it's going to be ancient enough your parents won't care. Change tacks. Offer alternatives. What are you going to do with your life instead?*

Gerald realized he had no idea. He hadn't thought beyond trying to avoid spouse-hunting, beyond avoiding a marriage he couldn't envision as anything other than an awkward sham.

What am *I going to do with my life?*

Gerald had never given much thought to his adult life before. He'd had the usual lessons given to royal offspring—everything from swordplay to diplomacy—but he wasn't the heir and he wasn't ever likely to use them. He was no warrior, no knight; no brilliant strategist or tactician; no silver-tongued diplomat. He was...just Gerald.

He had dabbled in other lessons, ones that weren't so usual and Lila hadn't bothered with, such as cooking and astronomy. He'd even taken a few theory of magic classes, although he didn't have the talent to turn that theory into anything real. Erick could create all sorts of spells—*Erick probably needs a bit more theory,* Gerald thought wryly, picturing the destruction his search spell had wrought in the library—but Gerald couldn't perform even the simplest conjuration. Not that magic was thought to be a suitable pastime for a royal, anyway. Erick's parents had magic in their families, and they tolerated it in Erick, but he was their heir; magic was always going to be a simple diversion. It wasn't his career.

The only thing I'm really good at is riding. I'm good with animals in general. They're much easier than people are. Gerald spent most of his time in and around the stables and kennels and mews, and when he was indoors, there was nearly always a cat or dog at his heels. The animals didn't care if he got married or not. They had no expectations, so Gerald never felt like a disappointment when he didn't live up to them.

There must be something *I can do with animals,* Gerald thought, and he disappeared back into the library.

By the time dinner rolled around, he had several pages of notes and a new enthusiasm. Everything was cross-checked and referenced and organized with headings and subheadings and bullet points. He felt prepared and ready to convince his parents—right up until he opened his mouth.

Queen Danya interrupted him as he was getting started. "It is irrelevant," she told him.

He gaped. "Plans for my future are irrelevant?"

"You can't use this as a way to get out of your obligations. As you've spent so much time telling us over the past few weeks, you are not the heir. After your marriage, you will have to take on some responsibility; we can't have you moping about the castle. And if animal husbandry is what you want to do, so be it. But there's no reason why you can't be married first."

"But..." Gerald trailed off. She was right. All his research, all his planning, didn't change anything. They still weren't listening. He was still stuck.

"You have six days to make your choice," she said.

And Gerald fell silent. He folded his notes and tucked them away. He finished his meal in silence and looked only at his food. He returned to his room and seriously began to consider the possibility of running away. But they would track him down; running away would only postpone the inevitable—and put Queen Danya in an even sourer mood.

WITH EVERY PASSING day, the air of frenetic preparation that hung over the castle increased, as did the tension between Gerald and Queen Danya. She turned hard and icy whenever she saw her youngest son, and she didn't speak a single word to him, refusing even to ask him to pass the salt at dinner.

Gerald almost thought he preferred it when she was yelling, because at least then he could defend himself by yelling back. He had no defense against the brittle, brutal silence.

Queen Mixte was too caught up in ensuring Lila had everything she needed for her quest to take on her usual role of mediator between her wife and son, and Lila was positively enjoying Gerald's squirming discomfort. "It's all your own doing," she pointed out whenever she ran into him, which was often enough Gerald rather thought she was seeking him out in order to gloat.

With preparations in full swing for Lila's departure, the regular routines of the castle had all gone to pieces. There were no lessons for either of the royal children, and all of the tutors, servants, and staff were too busy with Lila to pay attention to the other, aimless royal child.

Gerald spent as much time as he could away from the castle, riding Wisp out in the morning and not coming back until dusk, but every evening he had to come back. Even with tensions running so high, family dinners remained non-negotiable. They were icy, silent meals that Gerald endured under the disapproving glares of one queen and the distracted gaze of the other, with Lila smirking at him across the table.

By the end of the week, he was wondering if it would be better to give in.

Maybe Mum's right. Maybe I just need to mature. Maybe I'll do this and it will work out, like it does for everyone else.

But he couldn't quite convince himself.

HE SPENT EACH and every one of the remaining days refusing to make his choice and waiting for the arguments to start up again, waiting for Queen Danya to start yelling at him again. Waiting for the other shoe to drop.

And it didn't, and it didn't, and it didn't, until his nerves were so frayed he flinched whenever he saw Queen Danya, or Lila, or even Queen Mixte.

And suddenly it was the last night before his and Lila's birthday. The last night of the month. The last dinner. Lila was riding out in the morning and Gerald was waiting for the royal decree of his fate.

There was no silence to shield him now. It was a formal dinner, a state dinner, and the Grand Hall was full of royalty, nobility, servers, and entertainers. The baseline level of noise set Gerald's ears ringing as soon as he entered the room, and he felt more out of place than ever. James and Vani and their spouses had come to see Lila off and—as far as they knew—Gerald as well. Gerald didn't bother to disabuse them. He hadn't bothered to do much of anything for several days. Not even riding out with Wisp had been able to cheer him up.

As he climbed the dais to the royal table, he put on his royal face, the friendly smile that didn't reach his eyes. He kept it fixed firmly in place and he nodded whenever his siblings addressed him, and he held his tongue and waited for the other shoe to drop.

The formal nature of the dinner put Gerald several seats away from Queen Danya. He could almost pretend she was simply too far away to be able to speak to him without shouting, which would be much too low class for her to dream of doing. He could almost pretend she wasn't deliberately freezing him out like she had during the past half-dozen dinners. But pretending could only get him so far. At heart, he was too practical to engage in even those minor fantasies.

He picked listlessly at his dinner and waited for the night to end. *At least she won't yell at me in front of all these people.*

It was a small comfort, but only a small one. *I should have asked Erick for a spell. Something to hide me... Then I could have run. Too late now... Of course, knowing his spells, it probably would have blown up in my face anyway. Well, at least if I were dead, I wouldn't have to deal with this...*

He pushed another forkful of food from one side of his plate to the other, lost in his dark thoughts. An elbow in his side brought him back to the present.

"What's wrong, little brother?" Vani asked.

He tried to paste his royal smile back on. "Nothing."

"Are you nervous about tomorrow? It's nothing to worry about, Gerald, really. Everyone does it, and no one even dies while questing anymore, not since they implemented the new training programs for the guardians. And that was ages ago!"

"That's not it."

"You know, I didn't even think—Lila's going rescuing, I assumed you were as well. But are you? Or are you following James's example?"

Gerald glanced over at his older brother and smirked. "James was never going to put the effort into rescuing someone when he could laze about in a tower and make them come to him."

"And you're not lazy," Vani finished. "So you are questing, then?"

He hesitated. "I don't plan to."

"Ah. Where are you going, then? Mountain? Swamp? I hear the fire forests have gotten quite nice."

"I don't plan to go anywhere."

Her mouth dropped open. "Gerald! What do you mean by that?"

"Exactly that. I don't plan to participate. I don't want to get married."

"Men!" she huffed. "Honestly, Gerald. What's wrong with getting married? Everyone does it! And hardly anyone dies at the altar anymore," she added with a grin. "Not since they implemented the new training programs..."

Gerald rolled his eyes. "Very funny, Vani."

She brightened up. "Or—is it because you're already in love? Is it a commoner? Will there be a scandal? You know, if it's True Love, you can probably push it through despite the gap in stations."

"No," he said shortly. "I'm not in love." *I never have been and I don't think I ever will be, and that's the whole problem!*

"Well...what does Mother say?"

"What do you think?" he asked bitterly.

"Yes, well. She is rather...stubborn. But cheer up, little brother. Marriage isn't the end of the world."

Gerald did not look convinced.

The dinner lasted for hours, with half a dozen courses and then dessert, and then what felt like an endless parade of entertainers. Lila soaked up all the attention, while Gerald wanted nothing more than to get away from it all.

When the evening finally reached its end, Queen Danya instructed him to stay.

He watched everyone drift out of the hall and wished he was among them. Finally, the room was empty of everyone except the Queens and Gerald.

"Have you made your decision?" Queen Danya asked. Her voice echoed in the empty hall.

Gerald tried to summon the same defiance he had found the last time she asked him that question, but the week had worn him down. "I haven't changed my mind," he said quietly, bracing himself for the explosion.

It didn't come.

She nodded once, a stiff, sharp movement. "You may go."

He hesitated, not wanting to press his luck, but needing to know. "You're not going to make me choose?"

"You've lost that prerogative."

"So you're not going to respect my decision. You're going to choose for me."

"You may go, I said," Queen Danya repeated, her tone as cold as her expression.

Gerald glanced at Queen Mixte, hoping for a reprieve. She smiled at him but gave a tiny shake of her head. There would be no help from her.

Gerald turned and left the hall without another word, and without giving either monarch a bow.

It took him a long time to fall asleep that night. He was caught up in an endless loop of thoughts, tracing and retracing the same mental pathways as he tried to come up with a last-minute way to convince his mother he didn't need to get married.

Nothing came to him.

Worst of all, he didn't even know what she had planned for him. *I should have just decided*, he thought bitterly. *I knew they would never actually listen to me. I could have gone with Erick. So what if it would only be a short-term solution? It would have given me time to think of something better. Now...I don't know. Maybe they'll tie me to Lila's horse and make her cart me around. She probably wouldn't even mind; it would give her so many opportunities to make me miserable.*

He finally dropped off to sleep out of sheer exhaustion as the sky outside his window began to lighten.

When he woke up, he was no longer in his room.

Chapter Three

THE LIGHT COMING in through the window, the brightness that had woken him up, was falling full across his face: the window was in the wrong place.

He sat up quickly and tried to get his bearings. He was wearing the same clothes he had dropped off to sleep in, and the bed was his familiar four-poster one. But nothing else was the same.

The room was nicely furnished, with wall hangings, a thick rug underfoot, a plush upholstered chair and a sturdily constructed wooden desk.

But it wasn't his room. It wasn't his furniture. The decorations weren't to his taste. All of his personal items were gone, and there were no cats curled up on his blankets.

That's when he noticed the strangest thing about the room. It was round.

"They stuck me in a tower," he said aloud. "*Oxa, oxa, oxa.*"

Gerald got up and went to the window. The view was of sand. Unending sand. There were no trees or streams or roads or mountains or anything at all to break up the monotony of the view. It was sand, sand, and more sand, as far as the eye could see.

"They stuck me in a tower *in the middle of a desert.*"

He closed his eyes, squeezed them shut, and thought, *Maybe I'm still dreaming.* But when he opened them, he was still there. In the tower in the desert. Alone.

Gerald briefly considered throwing himself out the window, but it was only a fleeting thought, a passing fancy. *I can always do that later...let's wait until I've got the whole picture.*

He turned away from the window and began taking a more thorough inventory of the room. There was a chest at the foot of the bed, and he opened it to see piles of clothes and even a pair of boots. *Not that I'm not going to be able to go outside...* His heart clenched and he pushed that thought away and kept exploring. The desk drawers were stocked with paper, quills, and ink, although he wasn't sure how he was supposed to send any letters he might write. He shifted the rug and found a trapdoor in the floor, and he heaved it up with a grunt. His grip slipped as he tried to set it down and the heavy wood crashed against the stone floor with a resounding thump. He froze instinctively, but nothing happened. There was no reaction to the noise. *Because I'm alone,* he reminded himself.

He peered into the gap in the floor and saw a spiral staircase, lit like his room with the early morning sun. He slowly worked his way down the tower, exploring each new room as he came to it. There weren't many. A tiny bathroom, a small kitchen, and a library.

The library caught Gerald's attention until he saw that, rather than Andinian or Common, most of the books were in Yevish, which—of course—he didn't speak. *That tells me where this tower is, though. It must be right in the middle of the Yevin Desert. No one lives out here...if Mother wanted to punish me, this was a good choice.*

He left the library with a sigh and kept going, but there was nothing more to find. Just the stairs and the stone walls of the tower. He went by about a dozen windows, small ones, large enough to let in the light at regular intervals. But they stopped abruptly once he got about halfway down. *I guess this means I'm low enough to survive a jump from here. They can't have me escaping.*

He slowly made the long climb back to his room. *Nothing to read. Nothing to do. Nothing even to look at. I have got to get out of here or else I'll go crazy.*

He caught sight of the open desk drawer, with the paper spilling out and he suddenly remembered Erick's spell. A quick check of his pockets revealed he still had the yellow bead from his last letter from Erick. He wasn't sure if he could use it to key the two-way message spell without the original paper, but what did he have to lose? If it didn't work, he wouldn't be any worse off.

He tapped the bead against a sheet of parchment experimentally and began writing.

> *Erick? Is your spell still active? I hope so. I've been stuck away in a tower in the Yevin Desert. I don't suppose you want to come rescue me before you go off looking for a spouse?*

He let a large drop of ink fall on the paper under his few lines and waited, but there was no bright chiming noise and the ink didn't start spreading out into letters and words.

With a sigh, Gerald turned away from the desk. And screamed.

There was a *face* in the window.

"Honestly, Gerald," it said. "Control yourself."

"Mother," he said flatly, trying to match her own icy tone. It wasn't hard this time. "I thought scrying us was forbidden. Of course, so is using magic on someone without their consent. How *did* you get me here, anyway?"

"A sleeping draught and a simple transportation spell. Don't act so put upon. You're the one who chose not to play by the rules. Don't even start complaining about your location. There wasn't much available on such short notice."

"What do you *want*, Mother? Or are you here to gloat?"

"I assume you would like to get out of that tower at some point, Gerald."

"Obviously."

"To do that, you must be rescued. And to be rescued, the rescuers have to know where you are. You did not fill out a portfolio. No one made a signpost for you. Will you cooperate now?"

"What choice are you giving me?" he asked bitterly. "I'm surprised at you, Mother. I would have thought you would have filled everything out yourself."

"I admit, I did try to get everything sorted out ahead of time when it became clear you were going to stubbornly stick to your ridiculous attempt to opt out of a nonoptional event. However, it seems I don't know you as well as I perhaps thought I did."

Gerald snorted. "You've never known me, Mother."

"Perhaps that's true. After all, it turned out I didn't even know the most pertinent information to put on your signpost. Who do you want to be rescued by, Gerald? A prince or a princess?"

Gerald put his face in his hands. "I don't know," he said softly. "Neither."

"Either?" she said.

Gerald wasn't sure if she had actually misheard him or was deliberately changing his words, but he shrugged. *What does it matter? The one is just as unsuitable as the other.* "Either," he echoed.

"Well, that should speed things along, I imagine. I'll get everything circulating. And remember: this is for your own good. I really do want you to find a suitable match, Gerald. And this is the way it's done."

The window went white and then cleared again to show the desert beyond. There was no sign of Queen Danya or any indication a spell had been cast there.

Gerald flopped on the bed and sighed.

"I don't want to be married!" he shouted at the wall. "I don't want to fall in love! I don't want to sleep with anyone! Why is that such a *problem* for everyone?!"

There was no answer.

He hurled his pillow against the wall in frustration and then laughed at himself. "Honestly, Gerald," he said, mimicking Queen Danya. "Control yourself." He was not prone to tantrums. He'd always been overshadowed by his siblings, and as a result, he wasn't nearly as spoiled as other royals he could name. Throwing pillows and shouting at the wall wasn't really his style. Once he got a grip on his temper, he snatched up another piece of paper and began planning.

First... I need to get out of the tower.

Then... I need to get out of the desert.

Then... I need to get out of this culture.

He smirked. *I have the feeling the first two are going to be much easier than the last... But first things first. Getting out of the tower.*

He turned back to the window, bracing himself this time in case anyone was looking back at him. But the only face in the glass was his own: a reflection. He walked over and tried to open it, but it wouldn't budge. He ran his hands around the window frame, looking for catches or clasps, knowing there had to be a way for the rescuer to get into the tower—and get him out.

After a few fumbling moments, he found the latch, undid it, and pushed the window open. It was a large window and it swung wide, letting a wave of hot air rush in, so different from the cool autumn air he had gone to sleep with, and so dry it felt like it was sucking every last drop of moisture out of his skin. He swallowed reflexively, already feeling thirsty, and he leaned over the sill to get a better look at his prison.

The ground was a long, long way away, and a pile of boulders at the foot of the tower promised a painful landing if he tried to get out that way. He squinted at the boulders—*where did all those rocks come from in the middle of the desert?*—and then he blinked several times and squinted again. *Did they* move?

While he was trying to convince himself it was heat haze making it look like the boulders had shifted, they suddenly reared up—and up—and up—and he finally realized they weren't boulders at all.

They weren't even a *they*.

It was a dragon.

And it had decided to stand up.

Gerald stumbled back from the window just in time for the dragon's head to take his place.

"Good dragon," he said nervously. "Nice dragon."

The dragon snorted and Gerald jumped back, half expecting flames to come shooting out its nostrils with the air it had exhaled. But there were none, and he felt silly for reacting like he did. *It's supposed to guard me, not hurt me!*

He took a cautious step toward it and the dragon pulled its head away. With its bulk no longer blocking the light, Gerald could actually get a good look at it.

Its skin was pebbled and rough looking, mottled in dozens of shades of tan, beige, and rust. It seemed to be made of sand. It was the desert come alive, the desert personified.

And it looked... curious. It was studying Gerald with the same care with which Gerald was studying it.

The air sacs on its cheeks inflated and deflated as it let out a soft puff of air; the breeze it created rustled through Gerald's hair. Then it rested its chin on the windowsill and blinked at him slowly.

"I guess you're not going to roast me, then," Gerald said, and the dragon snorted again. It felt so much like a response to his words that he hurriedly added, "Sorry. I've, uh, never seen a dragon before. In person, I mean."

The dragon snorted again, as if to say, "Well, why would you have?"

Gerald hesitated and then said, "You—you do understand me, don't you?"

A long, slow, two-stage blink answered him, as the dragon closed and then opened both sets of eyelids.

"Is that a yes, then?"

Another blink.

"Well. Either way, I suppose I'd rather talk to you than myself. I'm Gerald, by the way." A sudden thought struck him. "You know, I didn't see—I didn't see any oases or anything, before. Do you have water down there? I suppose you're adapted to the heat, but even so... And food! Do you go hunting, even though you're supposed to be guarding me? Or does food appear for you the way it's supposed to pop into the kitchen for me?"

The dragon made no response for a long moment, perhaps waiting to see if Gerald was actually done talking. Then it snorted and its neck rippled in a manner oddly reminiscent of a shrug, if one could shrug without shoulders.

As it did, Gerald caught sight of something shiny around its throat. "What is that?" he asked, moving closer. "Is that a necklace or...a collar," he finished as it lifted its head. "Oh, dear."

The collar was only shiny in the center. It was tarnished all around the edges, where it had dug into the dragon's neck. The flesh around the metal ring was swollen and looked painful.

"It doesn't even fit! Does it hurt a lot?" he asked, and he knew the answer even before the dragon gave him one of its long, slow blinks.

"I'm sorry," Gerald murmured, reaching a hand out to gently touch the dragon's muzzle. "You're as trapped as I am, aren't you?"

The dragon leaned into his touch, acting like the castle cats. Despite the rough appearance of its scales, they were actually quite soft and smooth, almost slick—except around the collar, where they were cracked and dry. Gerald thought of Vani telling him about the new training methods, the ones that were meant to ensure the guardians didn't mortally wound any of the would-be rescuers. He hadn't realized the new methods involved collars and chains and pain.

"Poor old fellow," he said, not unkindly. "Let me see if I can find any salve for that." Gerald had a lot of experience tending injured animals— lame horses and ones that had thrown a shoe; cats with shredded ears or infected rat bites; hunting dogs that hadn't quite gotten the better of their prey. But he'd never dealt with a dragon before. He wasn't sure what would work on dragon skin. It was supposed to be impervious to quite a number of things. But because of that, he didn't think he could make it any worse.

He heaved the trapdoor open again—*I should leave it open*, he thought. *I think I can manage not to fall through it*—and trotted down the stairs to the kitchen to search out the cooking items he'd used medicinally in the past: garlic, honey, marshmallow root, and juniper berries.

There were a lot of long-lasting foodstuffs in the cupboard—journey bread, flour, oats—but not very much that looked likely to be useful. He started pulling out bags and bins and jars, trying to see if anything was hiding behind them. *Even some herbs might work if I can't find anything better.* But when the cupboard was bare, he still hadn't found anything he thought would be useful. With a sigh, he turned to pick up the nearest bag to put it back, when a clap of displaced air drew his attention back to the cupboard.

It had filled up again.

I guess that's what triggers the spell to send more food. I have to use what's here first.

Then a thought struck him. He opened up the barrel of water in the corner and began emptying it carefully into an empty basin. And when he scooped the last bit out of the barrel, it too filled back up with a clap of displaced air and then a gentle sloshing.

He hurriedly pulled everything else out of the rest of the cupboards and drawers, and again and again, they filled up after him. There was no apparent limit or oversight—the spell didn't realize he couldn't possibly have used all his supplies in so short a time. A grin split his face as Gerald grabbed the few items he thought might help the dragon—he had stumbled across garlic and juniper berries in the end—and charged back up the stairs.

"I have a fantastic idea," he told the dragon, who was still resting its chin on the windowsill. "If I can get that collar off you—if I can set you free—will you transport me out of the desert? I can stockpile as much food and water as you can carry if you'll bring me with you when you leave."

The dragon lifted its huge head and cocked it to the side, bringing one of its eyes around to focus on Gerald's face. He had a feeling if the dragon had eyebrows, it would be lifting them right now.

"The kitchen refills itself," Gerald said. "When I took things out of the cupboards, the cupboards filled up again. The same with the water barrel. But I wouldn't be able to carry enough water myself to get out of here, and I don't have a horse...or a camel. I don't have a map and I don't know if I could make it to an oasis. But with you...we could both get out of here."

The dragon did its long, slow blink again.

"You will?"

It blinked again and then nodded emphatically so there could be no mistaking its answer. Gerald had the sudden urge to throw his arms around the creature's neck—which reminded him of its predicament.

"All right, well, let's take a look at that collar, then. And I brought some stuff to make a poultice. It should help with the infection, although I don't think there's too much I can do unless I can get the collar off. *Until* I can get it off," he corrected himself. "It's too tight, it's going to keep rubbing your scales away."

The dragon obediently snaked its head through the window—it was a tight fit, but after a bit of wiggling it managed—so Gerald could get at the collar.

The wounds looked quite a bit worse up close and Gerald swallowed hard, torn between nausea and rage that someone had treated a living creature so badly. And done it because of Gerald, to control Gerald, to make him fall into line.

"Er...this is probably going to hurt," Gerald said hesitantly. "So don't, you know, bite me or anything. Please."

The dragon snorted, a noise Gerald was starting to realize meant it thought he was being ridiculous. "Right. Not that I really thought you would, but you know, it never hurts to make sure everyone's on the same page," he said under his breath.

Very gently, Gerald began to dab at the crust of blood and pus around the edges of the too-tight collar. The dragon rumbled deep in its throat, but it held still and made no move to snap at him. By the time the dragon's neck and collar were clean, the bowl of water Gerald had carried up from the kitchen was stained a muddy red and his hands were shaking with anger.

"I can't believe they did this to you," he kept saying. An awful thought struck him then. "That's not—do they do this to all of you? All the guardians?"

The dragon blinked an agreement and Gerald closed his eyes. "And they're still convinced this is such a perfect system. Forcing kids into a role they might not even want. Marrying us all off as soon as we're of age. Telling us suffering together will bring us closer, help us find True Love. And to do it they torture you as well. Dragons and manticores and sea serpents and all the other guardians."

The dragon nudged him gently, but the size disparity meant even a gentle nudge saw Gerald stumble back several feet.

"Right. You know, I think I've decided what to do next. After we get out of here, I mean. We should set the rest of the guardians free."

The dragon made it quite clear it was in agreement.

There was no obvious way to unlock the collar and Gerald's heart sank when he saw the rows of symbols carved along the edges. "It's bespelled. I should have guessed. Otherwise what good would a collar be without a chain?" He sighed. "I don't have magical talent. I'm not going to be able to just...improvise something." Once again, he wished he could get in touch with Erick. "But I'll work on it," he promised. "There must be something in the library I can read. And some of these symbols look familiar... If I can work out the spell structure, I might be able to work out how to unlock it."

He smiled in spite of himself and added, "It's not like I have a lot of other commitments right now."

The dragon snorted and pulled its head back out through the window. Its neck glistened with the juice from the juniper berries, and the crushed garlic cloves provided an interesting complement to the dragon's natural smoky odor. Gerald had smeared the mixture thickly over the wounds and the collar itself, hoping it would provide a little bit of lubrication to keep the metal from digging in so deeply.

The dragon looked around and, apparently seeing nothing amiss, settled back down at the base of the tower, wrapped around it and once again looked like little more than a pile of boulders from Gerald's perspective. He suspected the camouflage would work as well from ground level. Any would-be rescuer would get quite a shock when they climbed onto a pile of rocks that suddenly came to life.

I don't need anyone to rescue me, Gerald thought fiercely. *I'm going to rescue myself.*

Chapter Four

A WEEK LATER, Gerald was no longer quite so confident. He managed to dig up a few books that looked relevant among the handful that were in a language he could read, but the more he read, the more out of his depth he felt. *I wish Erick were here,* was a constant refrain as he stumbled over magical terminology he failed to learn, followed closely by the realization that, even if he understood the theory, there was likely to be little he could do with it without talent of his own.

On the bright side, the dragon's neck was beginning to look slightly better after a week of poultices, although the odor of garlic now clung to its scales day and night. The smell didn't seem to bother the dragon any, and Gerald felt it would tolerate a lot worse in exchange for a lessening of the pain it had suffered for who knows how long. The wounds were deep enough Gerald knew it had been collared long before Gerald had been spirited away to the tower. He suspected the collar fit when it was put on, but no one had bothered to adjust or replace it as the dragon grew. And like most long-lived creatures, dragons grew slowly.

The dragon had obviously worn the collar for many years.

Gerald stopped feeling sorry for himself. All of his emotions were tied up in the dragon, and he wanted to free the dragon much more than he wanted to free himself. He had a sinking feeling any escape he made would be temporary. Although Queen Danya's face hadn't appeared in the window again, he knew she wouldn't necessarily adhere to the prohibitions against checking in on him.

He looked up from the book he was working through—*A Royal's Guide to Rescue*—and rubbed his sore eyes. He snapped the book shut with a frustrated sigh, and the breeze it stirred up blew the scattered pieces of parchment across the desk. He picked up the loose papers and saw his note to Erick, which was still unanswered.

"I wish he had told me how his two-way spell worked," Gerald mused aloud. "If I could get in touch with him, I bet he would help me figure out the dragon's collar."

Aside from his mother's brief and unwelcome appearance in his window, no one had been in touch with him. There was *so much* parchment in the desk he was sure he was meant to be corresponding with someone—probably attempting to entice an appealing royal to come fetch him from the tower—but he couldn't figure out how he was meant to *post* any messages he might write.

"I can't figure *anything* out," he grumbled. He stalked across the room and threw the window open, even though it was nearly noon and the sun was brutal. As soon as the window was open, the seal on the room broke, and the climate-control spell failed and the blistering desert heat crawled inside.

"Can I come out?" he yelled down to the dragon, and after a moment it slowly unwound itself from the base of the tower and reared up to the upper window.

It gave him a look when it reached the open window, one Gerald had no trouble interpreting as it asking, "You *do* realize how *hot* it is out here, right?"

"I'm sick of looking at these books and the walls," Gerald sighed. "Let's look at the sand for a while."

The dragon maneuvered itself up against the windowsill and Gerald climbed out on to its neck, taking care to avoid the collar and the sores around it. The dragon waited until Gerald took a firm grip with knees and arms and said, "All secure!"

Then it slowly sank back to the ground.

It was even hotter at the base of the tower. The sand held all the heat from the sun, but once Gerald broke through the upper crust, the sand underneath was cool. He settled into the depression with a sigh and leaned back against the dragon's bulk.

They had reached quite an understanding over the course of the week, and the fact that they had no common language was not nearly the hindrance it could have been. The circumstances were enough of a common denominator to make speech all but unnecessary to understanding.

I guess Mum was right, Gerald thought, remembering Queen Mixte's attempt to convince him the system worked. *Going through this together really does form bonds. Of course, I don't think she expected me to bond with the guardian dragon... But at least they're not going to make me marry it!*

"It would be nice to talk to you, though," he said aloud to the dragon. It snorted and Gerald amended, "I mean, have a conversation. With both of us speaking a language we both understand."

The dragon lifted a foreleg and tapped a claw against its collar.

"Don't tell me it makes you mute, too!"

The dragon blinked and nodded, and Gerald groaned. "Who put that damn thing on you, anyway? And can I kill them?"

The dragon made a rumbling noise in its chest and Gerald was once again reminded of the castle cats. It sounded like the dragon was purring, and he relaxed back against its side. The thrumming of its chest was comforting, and he sighed. "If it weren't for the heat...and the being locked up part...I'd be quite happy to stay here with you."

The purring intensified and Gerald smiled. He understood that much. The dragon was in agreement.

"I *will* figure out how to get that collar off," he said with feeling. "I think I'm on the right track. I wish there were more books of magic in the library, but that's never been an approved topic for us royals. I suppose they don't want whoever's locked up here to get any ideas...although it seems like I'm the only one who has ever objected to the system in the first place."

Gerald and the dragon stayed like that, curled up in the meager shade at the base of the tower, enjoying each other's company, for close to an hour. Then the prince's stomach began to rumble, and the dragon peered at him critically and shifted so Gerald could climb back on to its neck for the trip up to the window.

"Sunburned again, am I?" Gerald asked with a sigh. "Well, there's aloe in the kitchen now." He smiled then and added, "You know, I always resented my looks—taking after my father, whoever he is, instead of the Queen, so I didn't look anything like her or her first child. But if I had her skin, I'd be burned to a crisp right now!"

WHEN GERALD CLIMBED back into his room, he was distracted from his sunburn and the search for aloe by the pile of papers on the desk. It caught his eye because it had not been there when he climbed out the window an hour ago—he distinctly remembered tucking the loose papers he had picked up into a drawer.

He scrambled across the room and started flipping through the pile. There was a thick packet and several thinner missives, all with "Prince Gerald" written on the envelopes in various hands, none of which looked familiar.

So there is some way to receive messages... That surely must mean there's a way to send them as well?

He opened the packet first and groaned. *The Who's Who of Rescue Quests,* he read with disgust. There were dozens of pages inside, each profiling a different royal, and there was also an interactive map. *Well, that at least might be useful,* he thought. He spread the map across the desk and dipped a quill to fill in the blank space labeled "YOUR LOCATION HERE." As soon as he had written "Yevin Desert", the surface of the map shimmered and cleared to reveal his tower and the surrounding area. There were five circles on the map as well, three blue and two red, and his brow furrowed as he considered what they could mean. One of them moved and Gerald hesitantly tapped it with the tip of his quill. A tiny drop of ink sunk into the fibers of the parchment and turned into a label: Prince Lukas.

He turned back to the *Who's Who* and hurriedly flipped through the pages—and sure enough, he found a page labeled with the same name.

So there are five would-be rescuers in the vicinity. He tapped each circle and waited for the names to form. The idle thought struck him that the map was much like Erick's two-way parchment, and he wondered if Erick had adapted his enchantment from the one on the maps. Then he wondered how the maps knew where the questers were. Erick's parchment only worked for the writers when the spell was keyed to them. How was the map keyed to the rescuers?

He pushed that thought aside—he had enough magical theory to think about with the dragon's collar—and instead he pulled the five matching pages out of the Who's Who guide to look at in detail.

Not, he reminded himself, that he wanted to be rescued by any of them. But it seemed important to know who was out there.

But before he read their profiles, he turned to the individual letters. He had a suspicion they were from the nearby rescuers.

He opened the first and immediately looked for the signature at the end. As he had thought, the name there matched one of the ones on his map.

Dear Prince Gerald,

I received your page in my Who's Who *guide a few days ago, and as I happened to be in the area, I thought I would strike up a correspondence and see if a rescue could be mutually beneficial to us. I encourage you to read my page and respond at your earliest convenience.*

Yours,

Prince Lukas

Gerald blinked at it. *Well, that's certainly romantic,* he thought. *It's a good thing I'm not sitting here waiting for a heartfelt offer of marriage. Mutually beneficial rescue, huh? I somehow don't think so.*

The next letter was much more the sort of thing he had been expecting.

My dear Prince Gerald,

I read your Who's Who *page with great interest as it seems we have a good deal in common. I too have a twinling and two older siblings, and my kingdom, Areia, is of a similar size and climate to yours. I also have a fondness for animals and my horse, Linny, is quite dear to me.*

I was also quite taken with your portrait. I hope you may find mine equally pleasing, and I wonder if our common experiences might serve as the basis for a good friendship and perhaps something more?

I would be most honored to be chosen as a potential rescuer for you. Please let me know if you have an interest in further correspondence.

With affection,

Princess Kinda

Although the other three letters were closer in tone to Kinda's than Lukas's, none of them particularly made him want to meet their writers, let alone marry them. But he endeavored to respond anyway, as the fact that they had all requested responses surely meant they expected to receive them, and if he could figure out how to reply to them, surely he could figure out how to get a message to Erick...

He quickly drafted a noncommittal, boilerplate response for the rescuers, thanking them for their letter and listing the difficulties of trying to rescue him in a way he hoped would discourage them without being too obvious about it—he didn't want to rouse any suspicions. Once the ink dried, he folded each piece of parchment in half and then began to address them. Prince Lukas, he wrote on the first one and then he dropped his quill in surprise as the paper vanished from his desk with a soft whooshing noise.

More magic, he noted. *Interesting how we're all discouraged from actually practicing it, but no one seems to mind using other people's spells so long as it's convenient...*

He hastily scribbled a note to Erick—

> *Seeing if the magic message system works for you too. Write me back as soon as you can, I need to talk to you. G.*

—and then folded it and addressed it exactly the same way. When it disappeared with the same soft whoosh Gerald jumped up and danced around the room in excitement. He was about to open the window and shout the news to the dragon when he decided he'd better wait and see if he would get a response. He didn't want to raise any false hopes.

In the meantime...he wanted to discourage the rest of the would-be rescuers. Not only did he not want to be forced to marry any of them, but he didn't want to leave the dragon behind.

One by one the letters vanished as he addressed them. His stomach was grumbling in earnest now and he realized he had spent more than an hour going through the mail.

He left the letters and profiles out to study more later, and then he made a beeline for the kitchen, taking the spiral stairs two at a time.

When he returned to his room with his stomach sated and a mug of tea in hand, he shuffled through the papers on his desk, looking hopefully for a reply from Erick. There wasn't one.

He sighed and began to read the profiles instead.

There were three princesses and two princes on his list. The dots on the map, he realized, were color-coded: blue for princesses and red for princes. He wondered idly if he should have told Queen Danya to put one or the other on his signpost. At least it would have cut down on the competition. *Too late now,* though, he thought. *I'll have to make the best of it.*

The profiles were all set up the same way and he laid all five across the desk to make it easier to compare: Prince Lukas and Prince Yerson; Princess Kinda, Princess Olivia, and Princess Meiji. He noted Lukas was the oldest, at twenty; he'd been out questing for two years and still had nothing to show for it. Gerald recalled his terse, business-like letter and wasn't much surprised. For most of his royal cohort, these marriage quests were fraught with Romance and Destiny and the hope of finding True Love. He doubted Lukas's idea of "mutually beneficial rescue" would appeal to most of those awaiting a prince or princess charming. The other four were closer to his own age, and Princess Olivia had only started her own rescue quest two weeks ago. That made Gerald a bit nervous: he might be the first rescuee she had come across, and she might be determined to make a good impression, perhaps even going so far as to fight the dragon.

He knew the collar would prevent the dragon from injuring the rescuers. But they had no such restrictions to keep them from hurting the dragon.

I might have to write a more strongly worded letter.

Aside from the portraits in the upper corner of each profile, there was little to distinguish them. They were, essentially, fact sheets. Name, age, kingdom, family, hobbies and interests. Even there they were all nearly the same. All five had written they enjoyed horseback riding and swordplay—no surprise, given their choice of going questing. Princess Kinda's did also indicate she was fond of animals, so she had told the truth in her letter, then, it wasn't a ploy to get Gerald to like her. Even so, that wasn't enough to get Gerald's interest. *She's been questing for eight months,* he noted. *She's surely come across at least two guardians. She says she likes animals, but she has no compunctions about the guardians being magically enslaved to their tasks? No. Even if I were interested in general...I wouldn't be interested in her.*

He set the profiles aside and turned back to the library books. Now there were actual potential rescuers on the horizon, he wanted to be completely sure he understood his rights regarding them.

If any of them do come this far, can I turn them away before they challenge the dragon? If they refuse to leave and challenge the dragon anyway, do I have to go with them if they win? These marriage agreements are supposed to be made mutually, aren't they? The rescuee is supposed to have a say in it, I'm almost certain. Or is it still like the old days, where whoever defeated the guardian automatically won the rescuee's hand?

Not for the first time, Gerald wished the library had more books in a language he could actually read. After picking through another chapter of *A Royal's Guide to Rescue*, he was no closer to finding an answer to his questions—it had clearly been written for a rescuer, rather than a rescuee—and he still hadn't received a reply from Erick.

He picked up the *Who's Who* packet again, thinking if he could find Erick's profile page maybe he could at least find out where his cousin was, and that's when he noticed a little booklet buried under the loose bundle of profiles.

He picked it up and laughed out loud when he saw it was exactly what he had been trying to find in the library.

Royal Rescues: Rules, Regulations, and Procedures was emblazoned across the front of the booklet in a large, bold hand.

Gerald hurriedly opened it to the contents and then turned to the section labeled *Rights and Responsibilities of the Rescuees* and began to read.

1) Rescuees have the RIGHT to select their Rescuers. While the approval of a Rescuee is not in and of itself sufficient—the Potential Rescuer must still defeat the Guardian and remove the Rescuee from their Tower—no Attempted Rescue may be undertaken without the express written or verbal consent of the Rescuee. Consent given under DURESS will not be recognized and an Appeal may be made to the Court of Arbitration in the event of a Rescue Under Duress.

2) Rescuees have the RESPONSIBILITY to clearly inform the Potential Rescuers of their approval or lack thereof for a Rescue Attempt and in the case of a refusal of the Potential Rescuer's petition, a Clear and Valid Reason for the refusal must be provided either verbally or in writing.

2a) When a Rescue Attempt is Approved, the Rescuee has the RESPONSIBILITY to accurately inform the Potential Rescuer of the Hazards of the Attempt, including any pertinent information on Climate, Tower Structure, Wild Animals, and the like; in addition, the Rescuee has the RESPONSIBILITY to provide all pertinent information about the Guardian, including Strengths, Weaknesses, and Manners of Potential Defeat.

The list of rules and responsibilities went on for several more pages, but Gerald had found all the information he needed. He closed the guide feeling rather smug about how well everything was starting to come together—if he could only get the collar off the dragon!

I'll keep looking through the library, and I'll wait for a reply from Erick. But in the meantime, I know I can keep those five away. I can't let anyone ruin this. It's not only about me not wanting to get married anymore. It's not fair to the guardians to treat them like that.

He looked at the interactive map again and saw all of the dots had stopped moving. It looked like everyone was making camp for the night. He picked up the Who's Who guide again and started listing every royal awaiting rescue and their location. *If we're going to free all the guardians, we have to know how many there are and where they are. And we may as well do it logically. It won't take long for word to get out. We'll have to take advantage of the element of surprise while we have it.*

Gerald kept taking notes and sketching plans until the room grew dark. He thought about lighting the lamps and continuing to work, but he was tired of squinting at line after line of text.

It's not going anywhere, he thought. *It will still be here in the morning. And until the collar comes off, I can't put any of these plans into action, so there's no rush.*

But still, as he climbed into bed, the memory of the vivid wound on the dragon's neck kept him from falling asleep immediately. It had gotten immeasurably better in the week since Gerald had arrived and begun applying poultices twice a day, but he knew it would never heal entirely with the metal band continually chafing at it. He knew there were dozens of other guardians enduring the same fate and with their wounds likely going untreated.

It made him want to jump up and return to the library immediately, but he knew he would be no help to any of them if he worked himself into exhaustion and a state of collapse. As callous as it felt even to think it, the fact that they had all survived so long with such mistreatment was a strong argument for their continued survival until Gerald was ready to act.

Eventually, he slept.

Chapter Five

THE NEXT MORNING was overcast. Gerald peered out his window at the clouds with great interest, as the previous seven days had all featured a cloudless sky and a blazing sun. It looked like the desert was about to receive one of its infrequent but brutal rainstorms.

"Hello!" he called to the dragon. "Are you awake?"

After a moment, the dragon lifted its head in response.

"It's going to storm!" Gerald called. "Is there somewhere you can take shelter?"

The dragon shook its head slowly and then gave Gerald one of its sinuous shrugs. It didn't seem too worried, but Gerald was annoyed on its behalf. "Bad enough you have to roast in the sun all day, for all that you're adapted to it," he grumbled. "I doubt you're adapted to thunderstorms."

The dragon rumbled with amusement and Gerald pulled his head back inside and shut the window. "It's a wonder they even bother to feed you, the way they treat you," he muttered to himself. That had worried him as soon as it became clear the dragon couldn't leave the immediate vicinity of the tower, not even to hunt. But there seemed to be a spell of some sort on the tower itself—*another spell to make their lives easier*—that attracted game, such as there was in a desert, and every few days a startled looking piece of livestock would materialize out of the air. Their shock never lasted more than a few breaths.

Gerald shook his head and climbed downstairs to the kitchen to scrounge up his own breakfast. He had never been so pleased to have taken those cooking lessons since coming to the tower. Back at the castle, Lila mocked him for it, since the royal family had the best chefs to serve them and she didn't think it a skill fit for a prince. *I bet she's not laughing at me now*, he thought. *She's probably stuck with journey bread. She doesn't even have a kitchen to cook in, not that she would know how to if she did.*

As he dug through the supplies—literally dug; his experiments on the first day had resulted in an excess of foodstuffs, which were now piled up haphazardly all over the small kitchen—the waxed canvas bags holding oats and grains caught his eye. They were waterproof... *There aren't enough to make a dragon-sized shelter, not unless I force the cupboards to give me a whole lot more. But then I'd be drowning in oats and I wouldn't be able to sew anything that large before the storm starts anyway. But I bet I can cobble together something to keep its head dry, at least.*

Gerald began shuffling supplies from container to container until he was able to empty a dozen of the waxed canvas bags. He used his pocket knife to pick apart the seams, drawing the thread out and spreading the deconstructed bags flat across what empty bits of floor he could find. *Definitely enough for a hat*, Gerald thought with satisfaction. He gathered up the threads he picked out and rummaged around in the miscellaneous storage drawers until he came up with an assortment of sewing supplies, a mix of tiny tools that had clearly been used for delicate embroideries and rougher ones that had likely been left behind from some rescuer's field repair kits. He was a deft hand with a needle, having had a lot of practice sewing up wounds in various castle animals, both domestic and wild, and he had his (hopefully) waterproof creation ready to go just as the first crack of thunder shook the air.

He ran back up to his room and threw open the window. "Hello down there!" he yelled. "Present for you!"

The dragon lifted its head up and Gerald waved his canvas construction. "It'll keep your head dry, at least!"

He folded it up and dropped it to the dragon, who used its front claws quite delicately to unfold and arrange it. It rumbled happily and Gerald smiled with pleasure.

"Now don't get struck by lightning!" he warned as the skies opened up.

He hurriedly pulled his head back inside and shut and latched the window. The wind was picking up and the glass was rattling in its frame. The sky had darkened considerably, and Gerald hurried around the room lighting the lamps before it got too dark to see them. The only light coming from outside was the product of the branching lightning bolts that split the sky every few minutes. The thunder that followed was loud enough to make it feel like the tower was shaking.

Gerald swallowed. He didn't usually mind storms, but this was a magnitude fiercer than any thunderstorm he'd ever been in.

He took a lamp and retreated into the tower, wanting both to get away from the windows and to get further away from the sky. The more stone he put between himself and the fury of the storm, the better.

He took refuge in the library and kept himself occupied searching the shelves once again for anything in a language he could read. He got caught up in it and when he finally raised his head, he realized he couldn't remember the last time he had heard a clap of thunder.

Gerald started climbing back to his room, and he could see out the windows that the rain had stopped. The storm had died down as quickly as it had come, its fury spent. The sun had already come out and he could see waves of steam rising from the sand as the desert heat baked away the gallons of rain soaked into it.

He opened the window to check on the dragon, who rumbled up at him. The length of its body was steaming like the surrounding sand as the heat of the sun evaporated the water, but Gerald was pleased to note its head was completely dry. He gave the dragon a wave and ducked back inside.

He sat to continue working on his translation project when he noticed a new letter had appeared on his desk. This one wasn't just folded but was tied with a piece of ribbon that had a yellow bead attached.

Gerald nearly tore the parchment in his hurry to get the ribbon off.

Dear Meathead,

It's a good thing you wrote me when you did. I was about to disable the tracking spell they've got on me. I'll wait until you get this to do so, though, just in case. You said you had some questions and it sounded urgent, so I thought I'd break out the two-way parchment for you.

Erick

P.S. I saw your page appear in my Who's Who guide. I guess your intention to sit this whole thing out didn't exactly go according to plan, huh? Need me to swing by and rescue you? I'm only about two weeks away.

Gerald smiled as he read the postscript and then he penned his reply underneath Erick's note.

I'm actually planning to rescue myself, but thank you for the offer. I do need your help to do it, though, because I'm taking my guardian dragon with me. If I copy over the symbols from its collar, can you tell me what spell(s) they're from? I thought if I knew all of what the spells were doing I could try to unravel them. But it's hard to apply theory when I don't know all the components of the spell.

He sat back and waited, but he didn't have to wait long before the paper chimed. He dripped ink on it and waited for Erick's words to climb out of the blotches.

Breaking the rules? I'm in! Show me the symbols and I'll see what I can do.

He carefully traced over the symbols he had sketched into his notes and as soon as he was done Erick replied.

Wow, those are some nasty spells. Deity. It binds the guardian to its location, within a pretty narrow radius, too; it takes away the guardian's voice, if it's a species that can speak to humans; it binds it to the inhabitant of the location, and prevents it from harming that person at all—it does so coercively, I mean, and the same with those who come on rescue attempts—although it can hurt them, it can't maim or kill them. It also contains a tracking spell.

What's the point of a tracking spell if it can't leave? Gerald wrote.

The collars go on before they get bound to a location. There are adjustable parameters surrounding that part of the spell. The tracking spell is to find them so the rest of the spells can be activated and the guardian bound to the chosen location.

I should have guessed. You should see the collar, Erick. It's about three sizes too small. It was clearly put on a long time ago and never adjusted as the dragon grew. The wounds from it were horrific, and they're not going to heal the whole way until I can get the collar off.

I think you can do that with a few modifications to the symbols. Do you have any metalworking tools?

I'm locked in a tower in the middle of a desert. Why wouldn't I have metalworking tools?

All right, all right. Cut the sarcasm. I'll send you some, and a diagram of which symbols you need to modify. The good thing about these spells being pre-set is they need to be adaptable, so they—the Council, I guess—can add in the location and whatnot. So that means it should be easy to at least take out the location, and then the dragon will be able to leave.

That won't do us much good if the tracking spell is still active, though. And I guess I have one too, don't I?

Yeah. Well, that part is easy, I've figured out how to disable mine. You should be able to do the same with yours.

Hey—are there any spells on the collar for its preservation? To make it hard to damage or anything?

Not in any of the symbols you sent me, no. But there must be if the collar's as old as you think. It would have rusted off by now, surely. Why?

Well, if you send me the right tools, maybe I can cut the collar off. And then it won't matter what spells are still on it, because it will stay here while we leave.

Yeah, that's a thought. It could work. I'll send you as many tools as I can, I'll send you my whole kit. You'll have to send it back when you're done though. Are you sure you don't want me to come over and help?

Let me try to do it myself first. If we get in trouble, then maybe. But you have better things to do, don't you? Have you made any progress in finding a spouse?

Don't get me started. And I know you don't care about that, Meathead.

I don't care about it for myself. You want to get married. I don't have a problem with anyone else getting married. If it makes you happy, then I'm happy.

Yeah, well. I'll send the tools over and some more parchment. I'm going to disable my tracking spell, so you won't be able to reach me the way you did yesterday. But I'll stay in touch. Good luck.

Thanks. You too.

Gerald smiled as he pushed away from the desk. He opened the window again and called, "Hey! Can I come down?"

Once he was on the ground with the dragon, he began excitedly babbling about everything he had learned and everything Erick had said, until he got himself completely tongue-tied from trying to talk too fast.

The dragon looked at him with that "I'd be raising my eyebrows right now if I had any" expression and Gerald smiled sheepishly before starting again from the top.

"I got in touch with my cousin Erick, and he thinks I should be able to get the collar off you. At the very least I can disable the spells that are keeping you here. And if we get out of here, we can definitely find some way to get it off if the tools he's sending don't work."

The dragon lowered its head and nudged Gerald gently. It still couldn't talk, but Gerald understood it loud and clear.

"And then we can free all the rest."

THE DRAGON LET him stay out there longer than usual, having arranged the canvas cover into a sunshade for him. But he still started to turn pink in the end, and the dragon lifted him back to the window.

There were more new letters on the desk, as well as a package wrapped in oilcloth.

"That must be from Erick! Stay up here, will you?"

Gerald unrolled the oilcloth and an array of hammers, chisels, and miscellaneous metal-working tools gleamed up at him. He picked up the letter emblazoned "READ ME FIRST" and he opened it to find step-by-step diagrams of which symbols to modify and how to modify them.

He turned back to the dragon and asked, "Do you want me to disable these spells first? Or should I go straight to trying to break open the collar?"

The dragon shook its head fiercely, but Gerald wasn't sure which question it was responding to.

"Sorry, the first option or the second?"

The dragon blinked once.

"The spells, then?"

Another blink.

"All right. Let's do this!"

The dragon snaked its head in through the window and rested its chin on Gerald's bed. The prince climbed over and around the dragon's neck as he carefully examined all the symbols again. He used a piece of white wax to mark out the symbols Erick wanted him to alter, and then he double-checked all of them.

When he was satisfied he knew exactly what he was doing—Erick had even organized the list by which symbols he needed to start with—he picked up the chisels and took a deep breath. "Here we go," he said, and he carefully scored a new line across the first outlined symbol. He worked slowly and carefully but was pleased to note the metal was fairly malleable. There was no great difficulty in carving in new lines, which made sense based on what Erick had said about the Council needing to be able to adapt the spells themselves. It also made Gerald think it wouldn't be too hard to break the collar open once the spells were disabled.

Finally, what felt like hours later, with his fingers cramping and a headache forming behind his eyes from squinting at the symbols, the chisels, and Erick's diagrams, Gerald scored the last line across the last symbol.

Before his eyes, the tarnished metal began to rust and flake. He reversed the chisel in his grip and gave the weakening collar a sharp rap. It split open and fell to the ground, where it continued to rust away.

Gerald dropped his tools and raised his hands to the wound on the dragon's neck. "It worked," he breathed.

"It did," the dragon repeated, in a hoarse voice cracked with disuse. "It worked. And I cannot thank you enough." The feeling in its voice came across clearly despite its roughness.

"It was Erick who figured it out," Gerald demurred.

"Because *you* asked him to," the dragon said. "You are not the first royal I've guarded, Gerald. But you are the first one who has ever taken the time to do anything for me."

"I couldn't just let you suffer!"

"And for that, I cannot thank you enough," the dragon repeated.

Gerald rubbed at his nose, embarrassed. "I didn't do it to be thanked."

"I know," it said.

"Now that you can talk," Gerald said, "can I ask what your name is? I don't want to keep calling you 'the dragon'."

"Why not?" it asked. "That's what I am."

"Well, it seems rude, you know. I mean, I wouldn't like it if you called me 'the human'. I have a name, I like people to use it."

"I have no objection to being called Dragon," it assured him. "It fits and it's not rude to me. Dragons are fairly solitary creatures; we don't have a great deal of need for names. And when we do use them, well, they're *very* draconic. You wouldn't be able to pronounce what other dragons call me."

"Well...all right, then," Gerald said. He was still somewhat hesitant, though, and wondered if he should suggest giving the dragon some name he *could* pronounce or if *that* would be rude in a way calling it "Dragon" apparently wasn't.

The dragon, sensing Gerald's continuing discomfort, changed the subject. "Now that beastly collar is off, we can make our plans in earnest. How soon can you be ready to leave?"

"Well...I need to disable my own tracking spell," Gerald said. "I don't want them to find you again because of me. There's plenty of food and water stored up, though, so as soon as that's packed, we'll be able to leave. Shall we say the day after tomorrow?"

"We shall. Now, if you don't mind, I would like to stretch my legs—and my wings...and hunt something that has not been brought stumbling to my feet." The dragon gave him a grin Gerald could only describe as "bloody minded" and he hastened to assure the dragon he didn't mind in the least.

"I'll be back by dawn," the dragon assured him, and then it snaked its head back out through the window. Gerald hurried over to watch as the dragon unfurled its wings with an audible *snap* and then launched itself into the air with a few powerful beats of those wings.

It was a sight to behold and Gerald watched it climb into the air, turning circles around the tower until it vanished from sight.

Only then did he turn away from the window. It was getting toward dusk and the air was starting to cool. It amazed him every night how suddenly and how sharply the temperature plummeted when the sun was no longer in the sky.

He sat back at the desk to write Erick and let him know he disabled the spells and got the collar off. But when he was only halfway through the note, his handwriting degenerating into a messy scrawl of enthusiasm, the interactive map caught his eye. Three of the dots on it had moved significantly closer to his tower.

Gerald turned to look at the pile of letters that had built up over the course of the day, which he had ignored in favor of his messaging with Erick and then in altering the collar. It was with a sense of foreboding that he now opened them.

> *My dear Prince Gerald,*
>
> *I would very much like to meet you in person. There is only so much that can be conveyed in a letter, even when one writes as beautifully as you do. It is hard to sense the true emotion behind the words. I am making my way to your tower and I should arrive upon the morrow.*
>
> *Yours truly,*
>
> *Princess Kinda*

Gerald groaned. The other two said much the same thing: they wanted to meet him face-to-face before they decided if he was worth spending the effort of a rescue on. Of course, that second part was all in the subtext. Not even Prince Lukas had gone quite so far as to actually spell it out.

I'll have to talk to the dragon and decide what to do. We can't let them come here and find an empty tower and no guardian. The news of our escape would spread like wildfire and we need to keep it secret for as long as we can!

But he didn't know how they could do that. Even if they turned away the three approaching royals—and Gerald was well within his rights to do that, it even said so in the manual—nothing would prevent more from coming, or even prevent those three from staying in the vicinity and trying again. And as soon as he left, he would vanish from the map, and then anyone looking at it would know something strange had happened, because there would be no amendment to his page indicating he'd been rescued.

Is there some way to leave the tracking spell active, but detach it from me? Gerald wondered. *Could I make it look like I'm still here? But if I do that, then there will really be a problem when someone turns up trying to rescue me and finds the tower empty.*

He crumpled the letters in disgust and turned back to his note to Erick. If anyone could find a solution for his problems—at least the magical ones—it would be his cousin.

But as he finished writing, he came up with a solution for the rest of it on his own: when the first would-be rescuer showed up in the morning, Gerald would be quite ill. The poultice he had been making for the dragon looked rather nasty when it dried and would definitely give him the appearance of suffering from some sort of pox. Add a bit of flour to give his skin a pasty, sickly appearance...and he was sure he could fool whoever showed up, especially since they would only be seeing him from a distance.

The words "highly contagious" would certainly deter his rescuers, especially since none of them seemed all that committed to him. And if any of them did turn out to be interested after a brief meeting with an "ill" and "feverish" Gerald, then they would be sure to spread around the story of his illness in order to keep away any potential competitors.

Gerald was quite pleased with the plan and he hummed to himself the whole way to the kitchen to stir up his "pox"—and some dinner.

WHEN HE RETURNED to his room, Erick's two-way parchment was chiming, and Gerald hurriedly dripped some ink on it.

The reply spooled out, and out, and out. Erick had apparently realized Gerald wasn't at his paper, and had decided to treat it like an actual letter rather than a written conversation.

By the time the ink stopped spreading itself into letters and words, nearly the entire page was filled. Gerald squinted at it—Erick's handwriting had started out neatly enough but had quickly degenerated into a scrawl to match Gerald's own enthusiastic chicken scratching. He lit an extra lamp and began to decipher the missive.

> *Dear Meathead,*
>
> *Good to hear the spells are off the collar! Although I don't know why you're so excited the spell alternations worked—I told you they would!*
>
> *Now, about your own spell...*

I disabled mine easily enough. Nothing finessed, though, just a bit of raw power. I admit it was rather a "blast first, examine later" approach. It was quite skillfully placed, too; I didn't even know it was there until I showed up in that damn Who's Who guide. Which is to say...I don't think I can relocate yours. I can tell you how to disable it, but I don't know how you can move the focus while keeping it active. I expect I can tamper with the Who's Who, though, to make it look like you're still there even after you've gotten your spell off.

To be honest, I'm not sure why you're concerned with that. If you and that dragon of yours start rampaging across the Thousand Kingdoms destroying collars, freeing guardians, and generally wreaking havoc on the system, I daresay someone is going to notice sooner rather than later. Unless you convince them to keep quiet, the royals waiting for rescue are going to spread the word as soon as you take off with their guardians. And if you've been getting fan mail, you've probably noticed most royals aren't as sensible as we are.

I may have to rethink your nickname. I can now easily list at least half a dozen people who are more meatheaded than you by far.

In fact, with all this planning and plotting and scheming, you're starting to look downright sensible.

Keep me in the loop.

Erick's thoughts about the tracking spell were a disappointment, but Gerald knew his cousin was right. The news would be hard to contain. The best he could hope for was to remain anonymous, so even while news spread of a rogue royal, no one would be able to say that royal was *Gerald*.

Gerald wanted to discuss it all with the dragon before replying to Erick, but when he got up to look out the window, stifling a yawn, the dragon had yet to return. He considered waiting up for it, but another yawn decided him. *I'll tell it everything in the morning...*he thought, and then he crawled into bed.

Despite all the thoughts buzzing through his head, with the excitement of moving ahead with their plans, the nervous anticipation of trying to fool the rescuers, the contented feeling that he was really doing something worth doing, rather than what his parents or tutors or sister told him he should be doing, exhaustion overcame him quickly and he was asleep within minutes.

Chapter Six

GERALD WOKE UP with the sun on his face and his first instinct was to pull his pillow over his head and go back to sleep. Then he remembered everything that had happened the previous day and he couldn't get out of bed fast enough. He threw the window open anxiously and he was relieved to see the dragon was still there, apparently asleep.

"Hello down there!" Gerald called and the dragon stirred and lifted itself up to his window. Gerald quickly filled it in on everything in Erick's letter and how he had decided to keep the would-be rescuers away. "Of course, that means we'll have to stay long enough to speak to one of them, but it sounded like they would be arriving today, and we weren't planning to go till tomorrow, so that should be okay."

The dragon nodded. "I see no problem with that." Then it cocked its head to the side, as if considering a new idea. "How much of a range does the spell to disable the tracking device have?"

"Um...I have no idea," Gerald said.

"Your cousin drew a diagram for you, correct? Of how to implement the spell?" When Gerald nodded, the dragon said, "May I see it? I am fairly handy with a spell, myself."

The dragon produced a pair of spectacles from midair and squinted through them at Erick's letter. "I have no idea why you humans insist on writing everything so small," it grumbled under its breath. Gerald covered a smile with his hand and waited for its verdict. "Hmm. Well. I should be able to amplify that easily."

"I'm afraid I'm not quite following you," Gerald said. "Why do you need to amplify it?"

"To cover our tracks," it said with a very toothy smile. "If the only ones who disappear from that map of yours are you and your cousin, it will be quite obvious who is involved. But if we disable the trackers on the three who are on their way to the tower...and on those we pass while traveling...and on those we see when we free their guardians...the trail will be a good deal muddier, don't you think?"

Gerald returned the dragon's smile. "Not to mention that would disrupt the whole rescue process and cause even more confusion. Oh, I *like* that plan."

THE FIRST WOULD-BE rescuer showed up at noon, when the sun was brutally bright overhead. Gerald had applied his "pox" right after breakfast, unsure of when they would come and wanting to be prepared. The dragon rumbled deep in its chest and Gerald heard a high, clear voice command, "Stand down! I am not here to fight." After a breath, she added, "Yet."

Gerald walked to the window and looked out. The young woman— Princess Kinda, he presumed—was mounted on a fine chestnut horse that had stopped a prudent distance from the dragon. The princess was not dressed for battle, as she had said, although Gerald could see bits of armor poking out from her saddlebags. She was dressed to impress him, he suspected, in a forest green riding dress that looked striking against her dark skin. Her hair, a deep brown shading toward black, was pulled back into a severe braid.

Physically, she looked nothing like Lila and yet she reminded Gerald strongly of his sister. Something about her bearing, as if she were used to getting her own way.

Not this time, Gerald thought grimly. He opened the window and leaned out. "Hello!" he shouted and then, covering his mouth, succumbed to a coughing fit.

"Prince Gerald!" she called back. "Are you well?"

He brought the coughing fit to a halt and took a breath. "I'm afraid I've come down with something. It seems to be dragon pox. Do you have it in your kingdom? You should be safe down there, but it is rather—" He interrupted himself with another bout of coughing. "Excuse me. As I was saying, it's rather contagious. I wouldn't want you to come any closer until it's run its course. It would be dreadfully awkward if I infected my rescuer with dragon pox, don't you think?"

Kinda had gotten visibly more flustered as Gerald spoke. "Oh, I, yes. Dreadfully awkward. Er...how contagious did you say it was?"

"Very," Gerald said. "It spreads like wildfire whenever there's an outbreak. Oh, it's nothing *serious,*" he hastened to add. "A cough, a bit of fever. But the pox are really quite itchy. It makes the whole thing rather a trial. I certainly wouldn't want to be responsible for inflicting such sores on your lovely skin." He bit his lip to keep from laughing. *I'm spreading this a bit thick, aren't I? But she seems to be falling for it.*

"Well...perhaps it would be better for me to come back at a later date?" Kinda suggested. "When you're feeling more yourself?"

"Oh, that would be most kind," Gerald said. "It generally runs its course within two weeks. I'm afraid there's really no point at all in *anyone* trying to rescue me before then. Anyone who tries is apt to come down with the pox themselves."

"Well...I do appreciate the warning, Prince Gerald."

"Why, of course," he said gallantly. "Oh—" he added, as if it were an afterthought. "If you see anyone else, would you pass the word along? I would hate to make anyone trek all the way out here in the desert heat only to have to turn around and trek back through it."

"Why, of course," she echoed, and Gerald could almost see the calculating glint in her eye. She was used to getting her own way, and even if—even *though*, in all likelihood—she hadn't decided *she* was interested in Gerald, she wouldn't want anyone else to have a chance to rescue him before she did.

"I wish you a speedy recovery," she said. "I shall return in two weeks. Although, if you recover sooner, please don't hesitate to write to me. I shall be here whenever you are feeling ready for visitors."

"That's most kind," Gerald said, before dissolving into another bout of coughing. He raised a hand weakly to wave as Princess Kinda remounted, tugged at the reins, and turned her horse away. As soon as her back was to the tower, the dragon raised an arm and quickly sketched a series of symbols into the air with a claw. There was no visible effect, but when Gerald ducked back inside to check the map, he saw *all* of the dots around his tower had vanished. Not only his own, or even his own and Kinda's, but all of them. He broke into a grin and stuck his head out the window to give the dragon a thumbs-up.

The dragon mimicked his gesture with a claw but didn't otherwise move until Kinda and her horse had vanished from sight. When he was sure she wasn't coming back, he wiped the "pox" off his face—the illness might be imaginary, but the itchiness was uncomfortably real. The dragon waited for him to clean up and then lifted him down to the sand. They settled into their usual places and Gerald patted its foreleg.

"That worked even better than we hoped," he said gleefully. "*Both* parts. We'll have no trouble leaving tomorrow."

With that said, he unrolled the map and laid out his notes on the other royals awaiting rescue and their locations. The dragon once again plucked its spectacles out of thin air and perched them on its nose, and together they began to plan their route.

"I think we should start with Princess Elinore in the Burning Swamp," Gerald said thoughtfully. "She's not quite the closest, but she's the one who's been locked up longest. I think we might be able to recruit her—not just free her guardian but get her to help free the others. I mean, she's been there for..." He consulted his notes. "*Three years!* And I suppose it's one thing to take that long when you're the one doing the rescuing, when you're traveling around and having adventures and enjoying yourself, but to spend three years trapped in a swamp? Surely that's enough to sour anyone on the system. Even taking into consideration that everyone else is a great deal more enthusiastic about it than I am," he finished bitterly.

The dragon cleared its throat softly, or at least as softly as it was possible to clear a throat that was longer than Gerald's entire body. "About that..." it began. "I will admit to some curiosity. I told you that you are not the first royal I've been set to guard, and all of them were quite excited to be courting. But you seem intent on chasing all your suitors away."

Gerald scowled at the sand. "I don't wish to be married," he growled. "And I don't wish to discuss it."

"I was only curious," the dragon said gently. "It is such a, hmm, uniquely *human* convention, you see. I don't believe I've ever met a married dragon; it's not something we do. But it seems quite important to you humans. I only wondered why it wasn't important to you."

Gerald pushed himself away from the dragon and scrambled to his feet. "I don't wish to discuss it!" he repeated, nearly shouting. He was flushed and had a strong desire to flee, but there was nowhere to go. As soon as he moved out of the dragon's shadow, the sunbaked sand began to burn the bare soles of his feet. *Forgot my boots*, he realized. He'd gotten used to going barefoot since arriving in the tower, since he hardly went outside and when he did, he didn't walk anywhere.

The sudden thought of how ridiculous he would look trying to rescue the guardians barefoot distracted him from the current conversation long enough for him to regain control of his emotions.

He ducked his head and apologized to the sand. "I'm sorry," he muttered. "It's a bit of a...sore point."

"You don't say," the dragon said drily.

Gerald shuffled back into the dragon's shade and they turned back to their maps and their plans with the topic of marriage set quite firmly aside.

No other would-be rescuers showed up for the rest of the day, which gave Gerald plenty of uninterrupted time to get their supplies packed. Inspired by his success with the waxed canvas rain cover, Gerald had sewn together virtually every bit of cloth he could get out of the kitchen to make a giant pouch and a harness to attach the supplies to the dragon.

Once that was done, Gerald spent the rest of the day repackaging all of the extras from the kitchen. The dragon had examined the supplies and said it could magic the water barrel so the lid would stay on and it wouldn't spill during transit, and it promised its spell wouldn't affect the refilling spell that was already on it, so Gerald acquiesced. It certainly seemed easier than decanting the barrel into dozens and dozens of jars and water pouches. He did insist on bringing a few water pouches along, though, so he would have access to water during their flights without the dragon having to land and dig out the barrel.

The dragon itself, Gerald had learned, had a rather camel-like ability to store its own water. It would not need to drink nearly as often as Gerald would. "I've often thought you humans were rather thoughtlessly designed," the dragon sniffed when Gerald marveled at its newly-revealed ability. But it gave him a wink so he would know it was teasing. Ever since Gerald's temper had exploded, it had been treating him rather delicately, seemingly intent on avoiding another outburst.

WHEN THE SUN dawned bright and hot, everything was packed and ready to go. After a quick breakfast for the both of them, the dragon lifted Gerald down to the sand—which was already hot enough for him to feel through the soles of his boots—and Gerald began to wrestle the harness onto the dragon. Gerald carried a small knapsack with a water pouch, a few snacks, the map, Erick's two-way parchment, and the *Who's Who* pages—which, he had noted, were not affected by the dissolution of the tracking spells, as there was still a page for Gerald, Erick, Kinda, Lukas, and all the rest. He had also fastened a compass around his wrist like a bracelet, even though the dragon swore it had an internal compass that never went awry.

Finally Gerald declared everything secured, and the dragon reared up on its haunches and gave a fearsome shake. When nothing fell out and no ties slipped, Gerald and the dragon exchanged triumphant smiles.

The dragon settled back down and said, "Well? Climb on, then. Let's go!"

Gerald needed no further urging to scramble up the dragon's side, using the harness ropes to haul himself up the slick scales. Gerald settled in between the dragon's shoulder blades, just ahead of its wings, and tied himself to the loop of the harness in front of him.

"All secure?" the dragon asked, craning its head around to take a look.

"All secure!" Gerald echoed.

"Then let's go!" the dragon cried, and it reared back on its haunches as it prepared to spring into the air. And then it stopped abruptly. "What's *that*?" it hissed.

That was a young man stumbling toward them across the burning sand. He was on foot, unlike Princess Kinda the day before, and Gerald briefly wondered how he had even made it so far into the desert without a horse or camel or other mount. But he didn't have time to consider it for long because the young man stumbled coming down a dune. He fell to his knees and collapsed prone into the sand, and he didn't get back up.

"Let me down!" Gerald called urgently to the dragon. "We have to help him."

"We have to get out of here," it countered.

"If we leave him there, he'll die!"

"That's not certain."

"If we leave him there, and he lives, he'll tell everyone about our escape," Gerald pointed out.

The dragon huffed out a resigned breath. "Fine, fine. But I won't let him delay us. We're not staying to tend to him. You can either bring him along or leave him where he lies."

"Bring him along," Gerald said immediately, and the dragon dropped back to all fours reluctantly.

"This is a mistake," it warned as Gerald untied himself and dropped to the ground. He ran to the young man and knelt next to him, wincing at the heat of the sand burning through his trousers.

The young man was flushed, but whether from the sun or a fever Gerald couldn't say. He had a small carry sack with him, but no water pouch was in evidence. Gerald uncorked his own and splashed water on the youth's face. He sputtered and opened his eyes, but only stared blankly at Gerald when he tried to ask what had happened to him.

"Can you stand?" Gerald asked, holding out a hand to pull him to his feet. The young man blinked several times and then clasped Gerald's hand in his. Gerald bit back an exclamation—his skin was burning, as hot as the sand—and levered him up.

"Come on." Gerald tugged the youth's arm across his shoulders and headed back toward the dragon, half carrying, half dragging the fevered young man.

The dragon lowered his head to peer at them when they returned. "Why, he has the look of the desert dwellers," it said in surprise. "How did he end up here, sun-fevered?"

"I haven't the faintest," Gerald said irritably. "But he's burning up. Lift me back into the tower, will you?"

"We're not delaying," the dragon warned.

"We're not letting him die, either," Gerald snapped. "It'll be less of a delay for me to get willow bark from the kitchen than to untie the netting and dig it out of the supplies. That fever has to come down."

The young man was still slumped against Gerald, and he lowered him gently to the ground in the shadiest spot he could find, before turning back to glare at the dragon. "Are you going to help or what?"

Without a word, it lifted Gerald up to the window and he returned in record time with an ample supply of willow bark, both fresh and dried, and a freshly-filled water pouch with shreds of bark steeping inside.

He dribbled some of the willow bark water down the semiconscious man's throat and then the dragon helped him haul the invalid up onto its back.

Gerald settled the young man in front of him and tied them both to the dragon's harness. He tied the waxed canvas sheet around them as a sunshade and then, once he was satisfied everything was in place, said, "All right, let's go," to the dragon.

It reared up and launched itself quickly, before another delay could manifest. Gerald yelped as they left the ground, and he clutched at the harness, fighting back the sensation he was about to fall off the dragon's back. He swallowed rapidly, trying to force his stomach back down his throat to its more customary spot, and he breathed out a sigh of relief when the dragon's near-vertical angle leveled out toward the horizontal as it reached a cruising altitude.

When his stomach and his nerves settled, Gerald cautiously peered out from under the sunshade and yelped again when he saw how high they were. The tower was already dwindling from view, turning into an ever-smaller and more distant blotch behind them.

He hastily ducked back under the canvas, having decided he was really happier not knowing quite how far away the ground was, thank you. The takeoff hadn't wakened their passenger at all; he was still slumped semiconscious against Gerald.

Gerald took the opportunity to examine him carefully, as he hadn't yet done in the rush to get water and willow bark into him and then get him on the dragon for their escape. He had, as the dragon had said, the look of the desert on him. His skin was nearly the same shade as Gerald's, but with different undertones, cool shadows instead of Gerald's own warmer, russet tones. His hair was dark and cropped short, but not short enough to hide its curl. He was wearing desert garb, loose, lightweight trousers and tunic, but he had no head covering, no hat or burnoose.

"No wonder you got sun fever," Gerald murmured. There was no response from the young man, whose eyes were closed, his face still flushed. Gerald wasn't sure how much of the pink tinting his cheeks was due to fever and how much to sunburn, but the youth's dazed state made it very clear he was still ailing.

Gerald drizzled more willow bark water into his mouth or tried to. The dragon was flying very smoothly now and hardly jostled the passengers at all, but even so at least half the water Gerald tried to get down the youth's throat ended up spilling onto his tunic.

Gerald slipped the water pouch back into his knapsack and wished for a cloth he could soak and lay across his patient's forehead. If he couldn't get the willow bark into him, he would have to treat the fever as best he could by external means.

Gerald considered wrestling the young man's tunic off and soaking it with water, but the garment was long and unwieldy, and the youth was about as much help as a dressmaker's dummy. He gave it up for a bad job and considered his other options.

Gerald glanced up at the canvas canopy above and around them and sighed. "Well, *I'm* not going to get sunburned, at least," he muttered to himself, and he pulled his shirt over his head. It was a simple short-sleeve shirt, without buttons or ties, and it was a matter of seconds to drench it in water from the pouch and lay it across the young man's forehead. He splashed what was left of the water over the young man's tunic. Even in the shade, and even with the dragon's flight creating a pleasant breeze, it was hot. It was a dry heat, though, dry enough for the water to evaporate quickly and cool the fever.

Or so Gerald hoped.

But after hours of flying, including a pair of stops for Gerald to empty his bladder and fill the water pouches, the youth remained feverish and unconscious. The water poured down his throat and over his head did nothing to revive him. *At least he's not getting any* worse, Gerald thought helplessly. "Do you think we should stop and find an apothecary?" he called to the dragon.

"If he doesn't wake up soon, I'll see what I can do with a spell," the dragon promised. "Healing isn't a specialty of mine, but I can probably manage something."

After another hour without the youth regaining proper consciousness, the dragon suggested it might be time for it to try a spell. Immediately, as if the suggestion had been a spell itself, the youth began to stir, moaning and turning his head.

"Come on, then," Gerald encouraged him. "Are you in there? Wake up, come on." He drizzled more willow bark water between his lips and was rewarded by a spluttering cough as the youth attempted to breathe the water rather than swallow it.

He kept coughing, hard enough that the dragon called, "Is everything all right back there?" but after Gerald pounded him on the back he gasped once and then began breathing normally.

"We're fine!" Gerald called back to the dragon.

He looked at the young man, and said, "Come on, you were almost awake. Come on, wake up. Wake up!"

And the young man opened his eyes. He blinked in confusion, turning his head to try to take in his surroundings. When he focused on Gerald, his eyes widened, and he began fighting to sit up and move away. When he couldn't, when he discovered the ropes and harnesses keeping him tied to the dragon, he began thrashing about even harder.

"Whoa, whoa, it's okay!" Gerald cried, reaching for his flailing limbs and trying to restrain the youth before he hurt himself or managed to pull out of the harness. "You've been sick, you're okay, relax, relax!"

"Are you sure everything's all right?" the dragon called again.

"Who said that?" the youth gasped. He continued turning his head from side to side, but he had stopped fighting against the harness and Gerald.

Nevertheless, Gerald was afraid he would panic again if he mentioned the dragon, so he responded with a question of his own: "Are you all right?"

"I... My head hurts. What happened?"

"You were stumbling through the desert with sun fever," Gerald said. "My, uh, companion and I were leaving when we saw you. We had to take you with us."

"You *abducted* me?"

"Er... Well, yes, I suppose, technically. But honestly! You would have died if we left you there. I would hardly call that an abduction."

"You bodily moved me from where I was and you've tied me up. I *would* call that an abduction."

Gerald held his hands up defensively. "You're tied up so you don't fall! You've been unconscious with fever all day and we're traveling. As soon as we land, you're free to go."

"As soon as we land?" the young man repeated. "You mean we're on a ship? How far did you take me from the desert?"

"We're over the desert now," Gerald said.

"We're *over* it?" he echoed. "You don't mean we're flying!"

"Er...yes, actually." And then, with a mental shrug—in for copper, in for gold—he added, "On a dragon. That's who was speaking earlier, actually."

The young man boggled at him. "I'm still feverish," he declared. "This is all some sort of fever dream." He paused thoughtfully and added, "That *would* explain why you're not wearing a shirt."

Gerald blushed furiously at that and snatched his still-damp shirt off the youth's head. "I'm not wearing a shirt because I was using it to lower your fever!" he snapped as he hastily pulled it back over his head. "Which seems to have worked. *Finally.* So no, you're not hallucinating. We're flying on dragonback."

"Not for much longer," the dragon called cheerfully. "I've spotted our camping site. It will just be a few more minutes now."

"I believe I'll close my eyes until then," the young man said weakly. "I suspect I will open them to find this has all been some sort of hallucination. Wake me when the world's gone back to normal, please." So saying, he shut his eyes and lay back against Gerald's shoulder.

Gerald rolled his own eyes but didn't otherwise protest. *He's had a shock. Or several. Would I be taking everything so well if I were in his shoes?*

The dragon landed gently enough the youth didn't even open his eyes. *I didn't ask his name*, Gerald realized belatedly as he unbuckled the harness, prodded the young man into a sitting position, and wiggled out from behind him.

"*Oye*, we've landed," Gerald said. "You can wake up again. Who are you, by the way?" he asked when the youth's eyes flickered open once more.

"Who are *you*?" he retorted. "You're the one who abducted me."

"I didn't abduct you—" Gerald started and then he cut himself off. "All right, let's not get into that right now. I'm Gerald."

"That's...not very informative."

"Prince Gerald of Andine," he elaborated.

"Oh. Of course you are," the youth muttered. "How did you abduct the dragon, then?"

"I didn't abduct the dragon!"

"It abducted you, then? I didn't think that kind of thing happened anymore, not since the reforms."

"No one abducted anyone!" Gerald exclaimed, throwing his hands up in frustration. "With the possible exception of you, and that's only if you want to get technical. The dragon and I escaped. Mutually."

"Right," he said disbelievingly.

"I'm not getting into this right now," Gerald warned. "Your fever might've broken, but you're still sick. We can argue about it when you're more recovered. But for now, I've told you who I am. So who are you?"

"Omar."

"A first name? That's it?" Gerald mimicked teasingly, although he thought he remembered seeing that name in the *Who's Who* pages.

"Prince Omar, if you must," he sighed. "Like you, a younger son."

"All right. Prince Omar of...Yevin?" he guessed.

"What gave me away?" Omar asked sourly, looking down at his tunic.

"How does a native of Yevin end up wandering the desert with sun fever?" Gerald asked curiously.

"The same way anyone else does, I imagine. I didn't drink enough water and I forgot to cover my head."

Gerald could practically hear the quotation marks around the word "forgot" and he frowned at Omar. "I doubt anyone else sets out to get sun fever deliberately," Gerald said lightly. Omar scowled and looked away, but he didn't deny it.

"I went to a lot of trouble to bring you out of it," Gerald said. "So kindly restrain yourself from setting off a relapse, all right? Now, I'm getting down to set up camp. Are you coming?"

"Please do," the dragon called. "I want to go hunting and I'd rather not have passengers—or cargo. It might get a little...messy."

"I'm coming," Omar said hurriedly. "Er...how does one get down from here?"

"Just slide down the side," Gerald said, "or use the harness to climb if you'd rather." He untied the canvas covering as he spoke and within moments they were squinting against the late afternoon sun. The dragon craned its head around to look at them, which helpfully had the effect of a sunshade.

"Oh," Omar said faintly as the shadow it cast allowed him to fully open his eyes and take in the full size of the dragon. It smiled at him, but as it did so by showing all of its very large, very pointed teeth, the gesture oddly enough did not seem to reassure the Yevish prince. "Oh," he repeated.

"Oh yourself," the dragon replied. "Move along now, please, I'm rather hungry. Not all of us slept all day, you know."

Omar hastily let himself down the side and backed away from the dragon's mouth, moving back until he bumped into a stand of date palms.

"That's good, get into the shade," the dragon said cheerfully. "Gerald can unburden me."

Gerald was already in the process of undoing the ties and straps that kept the harness and the supplies attached. "Almost done," he called. "All right, stand up so I can see if I got all of them."

The dragon reared up on its haunches and the net of supplies remained on the ground. "Excellent," it said, showing all its teeth again. "Move aside, will you, I'll set this under cover..."—and saying so, it gathered up the edges of the net and lifted the whole bundle into the shrubbery around the oasis. "There we go. And I'm off. Don't expect me before dark."

It launched itself into the air and soon disappeared from sight. Omar swallowed audibly. "Nothing that big should be able to move that fast," he breathed.

"Don't worry," Gerald said. "It's on our side."

"Yeah? What side is that, exactly?" Omar challenged.

"It's on my side, then," Gerald amended. "And its own. But neither of us mean you any harm."

"Yeah?" Omar repeated. "What are you planning to do with me, then?"

Gerald shrugged. "I'm not planning to do anything. You can stay here, you can come with us, we can give you a lift somewhere. Whatever you want."

"You'll just let me go?"

"I told you, I didn't *abduct* you. We were leaving and you showed up and I could hardly leave you there to die. But I don't have any ransom plans, if that's what you mean."

"But what other plans do you have?" Omar demanded, crossing his arms across his chest.

"None involving you," Gerald said. "I mean, unless you want to come along. But we weren't planning on that."

Omar shook his head in disgust. "Are you always this dense?" he wanted to know. "You're a *royal*."

"So are you," Gerald snapped. "I don't see what that has to do with anything."

"You were in a tower."

"Yeah, so?"

"So you're supposed to be there, waiting for a spouse!"

Gerald opened his mouth to make his usual retort and then it dawned on him what Omar was refusing to come out and say. "I didn't change roles, if that's what you're asking. I have no intention of marrying you, or anyone else. If you want to leave, I'm not going to stop you—well, so long as you agree to two conditions."

"What conditions?" Omar asked. His arms were still crossed in a defensive posture.

"First, that you wouldn't tell anyone anything about me or the dragon—that you saw us, where we landed, where we're going, anything."

"We're in the middle of a desert," Omar pointed out. "There's not exactly anyone *to* tell."

Gerald continued as if he hadn't spoken. "Second, that you wouldn't try to make yourself sick again, or do anything else to hurt yourself."

That got no response at all. Gerald waited a few moments, but when Omar looked away, he decided not to press it. Instead he said, "I'm going to start setting up," and walked over to the supplies, giving Omar some space.

Gerald stretched the canvas sheet over the ground to keep out the dampness in the spring-fed soil, and then he laid some bedding out on top of it. He and the dragon had calculated how much of everything they would reasonably expect to need and had then doubled most of it—the dragon could easily carry all of that and more, and neither of them had wanted to be caught short of something vital in the case of unforeseen circumstances. That meant he had enough blankets to keep one person warm in the midst of a blizzard, which meant there were certainly enough to make up two carefully separated pallets on either end of the canvas.

Even though it was still late afternoon, not nighttime, not even evening, Gerald eyed the bedding with no small degree of longing. Although most of the day had been spent sitting quietly on the dragon, he was deeply tired, an exhaustion borne of mental activity far more than physical activity. All the worry and exhilaration of planning and carrying out an escape, the fear and helplessness of tending to someone quite ill, even the conversation with Omar that had taken a serious turn, it all left him ready to lie down and relax, if not sleep.

But the idea of collapsing on to the clean blankets in the filthy state he was in gave him pause. He wanted to wash away the dirt and sand and sweat of the day.

Omar was still standing in the same spot Gerald had left him in, and he still had his arms crossed defensively across his chest, but he had turned to watch Gerald set things up.

"There's food in the knapsack if you're hungry," Gerald said. "You probably should eat something. Feed a fever, right? Or—I'm going to go for a swim. You might want to wash up as well."

Omar shook his head and Gerald shrugged. "Maybe later, then."

The oasis was a fairly small one—likely the reason it was not on any of the maps—but the pool in the center was still more than large enough for Gerald to splash around in, even if it was perhaps a bit too small for actual swimming. He took off his boots, stripped off his filthy shirt and socks, rolled up his pant legs and waded into the water.

It was pleasantly warm, although still much cooler than the surrounding air, and for a few moments, he let himself enjoy it. He ducked his head under and let the water block out the sounds of the desert. The water was clear and empty—no fish or algae like in the ponds back in Andine—and for a brief moment he was able to pretend he was completely alone. But he had to breathe and to do that he had to surface and then he saw Omar again—still standing in the same spot, still silently watching Gerald—and his brief feeling of peacefulness popped like a bubble and evaporated.

Why did he do it? Gerald wondered. *Why did he make himself sick? Does he know how sick he was? If we hadn't been there, he could have died. Did he* want *to die?*

Gerald didn't know how to ask him any of those questions. He hoped Omar would choose to stay with him and the dragon if only because that would mean he wouldn't *need* to ask those questions. If Omar didn't want to travel with them, Gerald would have to be sure it would be safe to leave the Yevish prince behind.

I guess I could tell him about what we're doing...about how the dragon was being treated, and how we're going to rescue the rest of the guardians. If I tell him something, maybe he'll tell me something. And maybe he'll want to help us.

Gerald scooped up a handful of sand from the bottom of the pool and scrubbed himself clean. After a few rinses, he waded over to the edge and climbed out, gathering up his discarded clothes. By the time he dug clean clothing out of the supplies, the dry desert air had sucked the moisture off his skin, and he could dress without getting his clean shirt wet. Even his pants were already nothing more than damp, so he didn't bother changing into a new pair.

Omar was still leaning against one of the date palms.

"I'm not going to bite," Gerald called. "You can come sit down, you know. You must be hungry, you haven't had anything to eat all day."

He shrugged.

"You're not trying to starve yourself, are you?" Gerald asked.

"No," Omar snapped.

"Then come sit and eat something."

Gerald pulled apples and journey bread out of his knapsack without waiting to see if Omar had listened. He started slicing up one of the apples with his pocketknife. He hid a smile when Omar sat across from him with a rustle of canvas. Gerald wordlessly handed him a slice and the two princes sat quietly for a quarter of an hour, sharing bread, apples, and water.

When they finished eating, it was Omar who broke the silence. "If I go with you...what will that mean, exactly?"

"A lot of traveling," Gerald said. "We're heading for the Burning Swamp right now, but that's only our first stop. I don't know how closely you looked at the dragon, but you might've noticed a scar around its neck? No? Well, there's a big scar all the way around its neck, from where it was collared. A too-small collar dug right through its scales into its skin and left an infected wound, and that left a scar that will never go away. The collar was also full of spells. Spells to keep the dragon from flying, from using its own magic, even from talking. Spells so it could be located and assigned to guard duty, spells to keep it shackled to that job."

Gerald, realizing he was starting to rant, stopped and took a breath. "Sorry. I guess you've gotten the picture. It was treated very badly, very cruelly, and that's the same way all the other guardians are treated. I don't think all this rescue nonsense is the best way to get us all married off in the first place, and the fact that it's being used to create a need for this kind of cruelty is flat-out wrong. My cousin was able to show me how to cancel out the spells so I could get the dragon's collar off, and he also figured out how to disable our tracking spells—the ones on him and me, I mean, the ones that make us show up on the interactive map. The dragon used its own magic to amplify the disabling spell, so everyone who was anywhere near the tower—including you, by the way—had theirs canceled as well.

"And now we're going to do the same for the rest of the guardians. And we'll cancel the spells on any of the rescuers we see and on the rescuees when we free their guardians. So if you came, I guess you'd be helping with all that."

"Sounds like a revolution," Omar commented. "That could be interesting. It will throw the whole system into chaos, you know."

"Like I said, I don't think it's a very good system in the first place," Gerald replied.

"What were you doing in that tower, then?"

"I wasn't there by choice. My parents forced me."

"Forced you how?" Omar wanted to know. "You could have said no."

"I *did*," Gerald said angrily. "Several times. I told them I wanted no part of it, in no uncertain terms. And then my eighteenth birthday came, and I woke up in that tower. They spelled me there while I was asleep."

Omar whistled. "All right. You win. That's pretty cold."

"They seemed sure it was for my own good," Gerald said, suddenly feeling the need to defend them. He wasn't sure where that feeling had come from and he wasn't sure he liked it. "But what about you?" he asked.

Omar looked away.

"You don't have to tell me," Gerald said hastily, but Omar shrugged.

"I guess you won't judge, considering your own circumstance. I didn't want to participate either. I don't know if my parents would have gone so far as yours—I don't think so, not really—but I didn't want to risk it, I guess. I said I'd go questing, but I didn't—don't—have any intention of rescuing anyone."

"You don't want to get married?"

"I don't want to be forced to get married," Omar corrected. "I don't mind the idea, you know, eventually. But not right now. I'm the youngest son; I'm not the heir. There's no reason for me to have to rush. I like the travel, seeing other kingdoms, all of that. I just don't like the reason for it. But with the *Who's Who* nonsense and the tracking spells, I have to at least make a token effort at it, so it's not obvious I'm avoiding all the eligible royalty. That's why I was near your tower."

"Oh," Gerald said. "That explains why I didn't get any letters from you. I got one from everyone else who was nearby." He tried to hide his disappointment that Omar was opposed to the rescue system but not to the idea of marriage. *Well, why would you think there was anyone else in the Thousand Kingdoms as strange as you?* he chided himself.

"Yeah. I only got in range of the map a day or so ago, anyway. I probably would have sent you a note to keep up appearances, but..." he trailed off, apparently not wanting to bring up the touchy topic of his self-induced sun fever. He cleared his throat and said, "So, you know, I guess I'm game for disrupting the system."

"You'll come along, then?" Gerald asked.

"Sure. It's not like I want to go back to 'trying' to rescue a spouse. And I'll get a lot more traveling done on dragonback. Plus we'll get to sow some chaos... So as long as the guardians aren't going to want to marry us when we rescue them, I'm sold."

Gerald smirked. "The dragon probably has more to worry about on that front than we do."

"Then I'm in."

Chapter Seven

GERALD CLUTCHED AT the harness as the dragon launched into the air with its usual enthusiasm. He squeezed his eyes shut and waited for the dizzying climb to stop and flatten out and allow his stomach to catch back up. Meanwhile, Omar let out a whoop of enthusiasm loud enough that Gerald cracked an eyelid to check on Omar. He was looking much recovered after a pair of meals and a swim, with the flush gone from his face. The food and a loan of clean clothes and the easy way Gerald and the dragon interacted had also seemed to reassure him of their intent; the standoffish wariness had gone.

At the moment he looked much more relaxed than Gerald, who was feeling a little green. Omar had thrown his head back into the wind and lifted his arms into the air, and the sight of him only tenuously attached to the dragon was enough for Gerald's stomach to do another flip.

"*Please* hold on!" Gerald implored and Omar smirked.

"I'm not going to fall! That's what all these ropes are for, right?" But he relented and took hold of the harness in front of them until the dragon leveled out.

"Nervous flier, huh?" Omar asked. "Interesting choice of transportation, considering."

"How was I supposed to know I was afraid of flying until I tried it?" Gerald asked rhetorically. "In any case, it wasn't like I had a lot of options. It was get a ride with the dragon or try to walk across the desert on foot..." *And we all know how well that works, don't we?* he thought but restrained himself from saying aloud. He knew he should ask what Omar had been thinking to inflict sun fever on himself and what he had been trying to accomplish, but he was unwilling to broach the topic while flying at a considerable altitude. *I don't want him to decide that his next drastic act will be to jump off the dragon.*

But Omar made a face, apparently guessing what he was thinking. "It's perfectly safe to walk across the desert so long as you're prepared. Like you said yesterday, most people don't set out to get sun fever."

"So why did you?" Gerald asked. "I mean, is that the sort of thing you normally do? Because if I need to watch out for you trying to throw yourself off the dragon or anything, I'd like some warning."

"I'm not suicidal," Omar said flatly. "And if I were, there are easier ways than sun fever." He pushed his sleeves up to show a pair of knives in wrist sheaths before revealing another pair at his ankles and a longer knife against his back. While Gerald gaped at the arsenal, Omar added, in a lighter tone, "Anyway, if I jumped off the dragon I'd miss out on this whole adventure. Plus I imagine the landing would hurt a bit."

"So why did you make yourself sick?" Gerald persisted. "You were in really bad shape, you know. The dragon nearly had to cast a healing spell."

Omar looked down at his hands. "I didn't mean to get *that* ill. I wanted to get sick enough that I could stop trying to rescue anyone for a while. You know, I was back in Yevin, I figured I could go home and relax for a few weeks. I wasn't trying to get deathly ill."

Gerald shook his head. "I can sympathize with not wanting to participate in this nonsense, but really? That's how you decided to get out of it?"

Omar shrugged self-consciously. "It seemed like a good idea at the time."

"You didn't think it would be at all suspicious for a native of Yevin, who surely would know better than anyone how to safely travel through the desert, to suddenly forget basic safety and get struck down by sun fever?"

"I didn't think it through, okay? It was an impulse, it went wrong, I learned my lesson and I won't do it again. So you can stop with the lecture," Omar snapped.

"You were in really bad shape," Gerald said quietly. "I was worried. That's all. I won't mention it again."

He looked away and his stomach dropped as he caught sight of all the empty air around him. At Omar's request, he had rigged the canvas above them in a simple canopy instead of around them like yesterday's cave, and the view was making him regret it. He took a deep breath and concentrated on the comfortingly solid feel of the dragon under him and the harness holding him safely in place. After a moment the view even began to impress him, as long as he kept his gaze focused on the horizon and resisted the urge to look straight down.

After a few moments of silence, Omar nudged him. "Hey. I'm sorry for snapping. Truce?"

"Truce," Gerald agreed readily.

By the time the dragon drifted down to land for a short break, they had relaxed into a comfortable comradery.

"I like this one," the dragon confided to Gerald in one of its loud whispers. "*And* I like your cousin. They're really turning out a better breed of royal these days, I think."

"Well, if that's true, it should make our quest a bit easier," Gerald said. "Hopefully everyone we come across will be as sympathetic."

"Speaking of," Omar said as he returned from behind a nearby dune, "I know where we're going but not who we're going to. Who's stuck in the swamp?"

"A Princess Elinore," Gerald replied. "And get this—*stuck* is right. She's been there for *three years*!"

"Three years in the Burning Swamp?" Omar asked incredulously. "Are you sure she hasn't gone mad?"

"Pretty sure. I mean, the towers are designed to be quite nice on the inside." *Except mine*, he added silently, *but that was supposed to be a punishment*. "And they're safe," he continued. "She won't have been bothered by anything living in the swamp."

"Regardless," the dragon broke in with a rumble. "We're there for the guardian, not for the princess. The princess agreed to be put in the swamp. The guardian did not."

"The princess *may* have agreed to be put in the swamp," Gerald said quietly. "*I* didn't agree to be put into my tower, remember."

"And you got yourself out of it in what, two weeks? She's been there for three years. She's clearly not too bothered by it."

"Or she didn't have access to a cousin who's half a magician, so she couldn't break her tracking spell or the spell on her guardian, so she couldn't get herself out," Gerald countered.

The dragon sniffed noisily but conceded the point by not continuing the argument. After a moment, it said, somewhat snarkily, "If you're quite finished playing devil's advocate, I would like to continue."

Gerald hid a smile and he and Omar climbed back up and buckled themselves in. Gerald squeezed his eyes shut in preparation for the dragon's launch, and this time he kept them firmly closed even when Omar started whooping with delight. *Don't look at him, don't look at him, you're holding on, you're both tied down, it doesn't matter what he's doing, he's not going to fall.*

When the dragon leveled out at cruising altitude, Gerald opened his eyes with a sigh of relief. "No snide remarks!" he said, seeing the grin on Omar's face. "Let's do some planning instead."

Gerald explained everything they had had to do to disable the spells on the dragon's collar, and finished by saying, "I don't know if the swamp guardian is going to let us do that. I mean, first of all, it has to trust we're really there to do what we say and not to add some more restrictions. How is it going to know what marks I'm adding and what they do?"

"Don't you think the dragon will help with all that?" Omar wanted to know. "I mean, the fact that we're flying around on the back of an uncollared dragon is kind of a big hint you're telling the truth."

"Oh. Right," Gerald said sheepishly. "Adventuring has never been my strong suit, you know. That was always Lila's domain."

"Lila?"

"My second mother's daughter," Gerald said.

"Your—oh, your twinling, you mean?"

"I don't like that word," Gerald explained. "We're *not* twins. We're no better than half-siblings, and probably less than that. Neither of us knows who our father was, of course, you know how all that works, complete secrecy to keep the father's family out of the line of succession. But the way we look, I wouldn't believe we have the same one. So she's not even a blood relation, and she's definitely not a twin. We're no more related than any two children born at the same time to different mothers."

"Yeah, okay, but by that logic your second mother—your mother's wife, right?—she isn't a blood relation, either. Why does she get the 'mother' designation, then?"

"Because she's always treated me like family," Gerald said quietly. "More so than my birth mother, frankly. While Lila's never exactly treated me like a brother."

"I'm sorry," Omar said.

Gerald shrugged. "It's fine. I'm used to it."

"I haven't always gotten along with my family, either," Omar said. "But none of them ever locked me in a tower."

"That's the worst thing they ever did," Gerald said. "It's not like I was abused or anything. But Mother simply didn't care and Mum was kind, but she always deferred to Mother... even though it was her kingdom, you know, originally. Mother married in. Mum was always the heir."

Gerald smirked then and Omar raised a questioning eyebrow. "Oh, I was thinking about how much it's always bothered me that I didn't look like Mother, not the way my older sister did. Lila and James are carbon copies of Mum, and Vani is a carbon copy of Mother, and then there I was, not looking like either side of the family. It always made me feel like an imposter. I thought maybe that was why I didn't fit, why I didn't seem to get along with any of them."

He shook his head. "Now I'm sounding whiny. But what I was smirking about is that Mother doesn't look like anyone else in the entire kingdom! I look a lot more like a native Andinian than she does, at least, even if I don't look much like my family. Mother's blonde and pale and has icy blue eyes," he explained. "Of course, it never bothered her that she doesn't fit in. I think she likes it, actually. It makes her seem more imposing, I think, to stand out so much. And me, well, I would rather blend into the background."

Omar gestured vaguely at himself. "Well, if we keep traveling together, you'll blend in well enough. We're not too dissimilar, and I look exactly like everyone else in Yevin, including both my parents. My father is Yevish, and my mother is from Grënick. Neighboring kingdoms, similar people. They look alike, and I and all my siblings look like them. But back to the point at hand. You're saying you have no adventuring experience, and yet you're determined to fly all over the Thousand Kingdoms on a dragon?" He shook his head with a mix of incredulity and admiration. "You'll get plenty of experience, don't you worry."

"What about you?" Gerald asked. "I mean, how much adventuring have you done?"

"Prior to this?" Omar asked, making a vague, sweeping gesture. "Not all that much. I mean, I've traveled. I crossed the desert a few times with caravans. But in terms of independent adventuring, going out to prove my worth or anything like that..." he shrugged. "This rescue quest stuff was pretty much the start of my own career in adventures."

"The blind leading the blind, then."

The dragon cleared its throat loudly at that.

"The dragon leading the blind leading the blind," Gerald amended with a smile.

"That's better," the dragon said. "We're about an hour away now. Can you see it yet? I forget how your distance vision compares to mine."

"Unfavorably, I'm sure," Gerald said, but he obediently squinted into the distance. "I can't see anything that looks like a swamp," he said after a moment. "I just see the desert is about to stop."

"It's grasslands for quite a while after that," Omar said. "Eventually the grassland turns into a marsh and then into a swamp. But I can't see it either. I just know it's there."

"Humans," the dragon muttered again. "I really don't understand how you were designed so poorly."

Omar shot Gerald a questioning look and Gerald smiled reassuringly. "It's joking," he mouthed at Omar. "Draconic humor."

"Yes, well, we can't all be dragons," Gerald said aloud. "It's a constant source of disappointment to us, never fear."

The dragon swiveled its head around to fix Gerald with a huge golden eye. "I do believe you're making fun of me," it said.

"Who, me?" Gerald asked innocently. "Never."

The dragon harrumphed but turned its head back toward the front. There was little danger of them crashing into anything at their height, even with the dragon's momentary distraction, but Gerald felt better when the dragon was "watching the road", as it were.

"Anyway," it called back over its shoulder, "we're getting close. So perhaps you should do some of that planning you mentioned before."

Omar and Gerald exchanged guilty glances and settled down to it.

"So," Gerald said, ticking points off on his fingers, "first we have to get through the swamp to Princess Elinore. Then, we have to disable the spells on the guardian's collar and then remove the collar. We also want to disable the tracking spell on Elinore, although the dragon can do that, and can even do so from a distance. What else?"

"Well, what are you planning to do with Elinore?" Omar asked. "Are you trying to be stealthy about all this, or do you want to recruit her? Are we leaving her in the tower, sans guardian, or are we bringing her with us, or at least giving her a lift to some intermediate point?"

Gerald hesitated. "That's the problem, isn't it? I don't suppose there's any real way we can free the guardian without her noticing, so I guess there's no need for secrecy. We can explain the whole situation and let her decide if she wants to participate or not. If not... as long as she's not hostile to the idea, we can leave her be."

"And if she is hostile to the idea?" Omar persisted.

"Dragon?" Gerald called.

"Yes?"

"How much of a magician are you, exactly? Can you devise your own spells, I mean, or only perform them?"

"I've never been too good at creating my own spells," the dragon admitted. "However, I've come across a great many in my time and I never forget an incantation. Your cousin is quite innovative, and that two-way writing spell of his is something I've never seen before. But I'm well versed in all of the classics. Why, what did you have in mind?"

"Well... It might be rather, um, unethical..." Gerald hemmed, fiddling nervously with the harness. "But I was thinking perhaps...maybe we could...if you don't think it's too problematic—"

"Oh, just spit it out already!" Omar exclaimed. "Come on, it's not like you're planning to murder her or anything. After all, we wouldn't need magic for that."

"Of course not!" Gerald snapped. "No, I was thinking more of silencing her. But not to the extreme your collar took it!" he hastily assured the dragon. "I don't want to render her entirely mute. Just...mute on this particular topic. So she couldn't tell anyone who we are or what we did."

"It would actually be much easier to render her entirely mute," the dragon said thoughtfully. "Not that I'm condoning that, mind. It was a singularly unpleasant experience."

"Is that a no, then?" Gerald asked.

"Well, the more nuance a spell has, the more difficult it is. However...I think I know something that might work. It's a secret-keeping spell that needs to be modified with the key words. It will block communication surrounding those key words. Of course, with enough creativity, it can be gotten around. But it should serve for the short term."

"Excellent," Gerald said with relief. "That sounds like exactly the thing."

"We're going about your list backward, though," Omar pointed out. "There's still getting through the swamp to consider. And I think I see it now."

Gerald leaned over to peer around the dragon's head, and in the distance, he could see the grassland turning to marsh and then swamp.

"I'll fly in as close as I can," the dragon said. "But there aren't going to be many suitable landing places. We may have to walk a good distance."

"And a 'good' distance in the Burning Swamp is really a *bad* distance," Omar said.

"Just get us as close as you can," Gerald said. "We can improvise once we're on the ground. The dragon's presence should keep most of the wildlife away, don't you think? So we'll just have to watch out for natural hazards."

"'Just'," Omar said gloomily.

"I'm sure we can manage between the three of us."

"There's no time like the present to find out," the dragon said cheerfully. Flying over the largely featureless desert had warped Gerald's perception of how quickly they were moving. Now that the terrain had more variety and more landmarks, the ground seemed to be moving past them at a rate of speed all out of proportion to the dragon's slow wingbeats. They were already over the marshier part of the grassland and shrubs and water-loving trees were beginning to emerge. The ground cover grew thicker and thicker and the atmosphere took on a decidedly ominous aura. Trickles of smoke rose up from trees and visibility steadily declined as they flew further over the swamp.

The dragon began to circle, losing altitude in a lazy spiral. As they got closer to the trees, Omar held his arm up in a futile attempt to protect his eyes from the smoke and Gerald started coughing.

"Hold on!" the dragon called, and then it plunged through the trees. The branches buffeted at Gerald and Omar, but the harness kept them firmly attached to the dragon's back.

Then, with a thoroughly unpleasant squelching sound, the dragon touched down into the mud.

"Ah," it sighed. "That's nice. Very warm."

"I hope your supplies are waterproof," Omar said to Gerald, looking at the morass the dragon had landed in. Their drop to ground level had at least brought them below the haze of smoke, and they could see and breath with a degree of normality.

"Oh," the dragon said, looking down at its belly. "Oops."

"Let's worry about that later," Gerald said. "Which way to the tower?"

"North by northeast," the dragon replied.

Gerald looked at the compass tied to his wrist. "Let's go, then."

"How?" Omar asked.

They took in the scenery. All they could see was water and mud, and thin, spindly trees stretching up the sky. The trees were thin and poorly leafed, but the smoke blocked out most of the afternoon light, leaving only dim, gloomy illumination. The only brightness was provided by periodic belches of sparks and flame that appeared at random from the muck and murk.

"Maybe we should stay on the dragon," Gerald suggested. "You can walk through this, can't you?" he asked it.

"For now. Not if the trees get much closer together. But I think it's too hot for you two to get down and wade here," it said, prodding at the mud with a foreleg. "You're right; you should stay on my back for now."

It angled itself north by northeast and began trudging through the swamp. The intermittent bursts of fire didn't bother it at all, nor did the temperature of the water, which was lightly steaming.

"How did they expect anyone to rescue her?" Omar asked quietly. "I mean, a desert is one thing. You take some water, buy a camel or a horse, no problem. All you have to worry about is the guardian. But this... I have the uncomfortable feeling the guardian is going to be the *easiest* part of this trip."

"Yeah," Gerald said. "I know what you mean." The hair on the back of his neck was standing up and he had the uncomfortable feeling they were being watched. "You're not going to take off suddenly, are you?" he asked the dragon, raising his voice only enough to get its attention.

"I couldn't even if I wanted to," the dragon replied calmly. "This is not good ground to launch from. Why?"

"I think Omar and I should undo our harnesses," Gerald said. "It feels like we might need to be able to move in a hurry."

He put his words into action even as he was saying them. Within minutes, he and Omar were able to move freely over the dragon's back. Its walking gait was not as smooth as its flight, though, so they largely stayed where they were. Neither one wanted to get bounced off into the steaming water and mud.

"I almost wish Lila were here," Gerald muttered. At Omar's raised eyebrow, he explained, "If nothing else, she's quite handy with a sword."

"So am I," Omar replied. "And other edged weapons." He showed his knives again; Gerald had nearly forgotten they were there and startled again at the reveal.

"What exactly *were* you planning to do to the guardian?" Omar asked curiously. "They're there to fight and be fought, you know."

The dragon rumbled grumpily at that and Omar patted its scales in apology. "Or at least that's what we're told," he said soothingly.

"I was on the other side of the equation, remember?" Gerald said. "I wasn't supposed to—or intending to—fight anyone. I have a chisel to change the spells carved into the collar. I don't have an *arsenal*."

"It's only a *small* arsenal," Omar said soothingly. "And I have a feeling you're going to be happy I have it before the day's done."

That remark sent Gerald's gaze back out into the gloom. He wracked his brain, trying to remember all the dangers of the swamp. Snakes and fearsome meat-eating lizards, giant boars and will-o'-the-wisps, although the dragon should keep most of those away...and Omar's knives wouldn't do much against those it wouldn't. A dagger wouldn't harm the malevolent fire spirits that drove travelers into the depths.

Gerald shuddered as he thought of them and then screamed as the water two feet to their left abruptly erupted into a boiling column with the strong impression of *teeth* behind it. Omar had his wrist knives released and in his hands before the hot water even landed on Gerald's skin, and the dragon whipped its head around in time to knock the snarling lizard back into the marsh. It roared at the lizard, a ferocious, echoing sound, and a few drops of fire burst from its lips. The lizard hastily turned tail and slipped away, and Gerald tried to remember how to breathe.

"All right back there?" the dragon asked. It still had drops of flames dripping from its snout.

"Y-ye-yes," Gerald stammered.

Omar patted his shoulder reassuringly but didn't resheath his knives. Gerald was torn between wanting to close his eyes and ignore everything else that might come their way and being completely unwilling to close his eyes even long enough to blink, for fear of what else might come out of the depths or the dark.

In the end, fear won. He kept his eyes peeled and scanned the water and the trees obsessively.

"I don't think another lizard is going to try that," Omar said softly. "The dragon is still dripping fire."

"Fire is not exactly an unknown threat here," Gerald muttered back. But he nevertheless found himself reassured almost in spite of himself.

"The water is getting shallower," the dragon reported.

"Makes sense," Omar said. "The trees are getting thicker. We're getting more ground."

"That means we're going to have to get down," Gerald pointed out. "If there's not enough room for the dragon to get through."

But the dragon said, "No. I don't believe this is the most hospitable environment for humans. If I cannot fit between the trees, I will clear a space."

Gerald thought of protesting the damage to the swamp's own environment and ecosystem, but it was a decidedly half-hearted thought. *If it can survive randomly bursting into flames, it can survive a few trees being knocked over*, he decided.

And so they forged ahead.

The sounds of splashing turned to squelching as the mud to water ratio steadily increased, but other than the noise caused by the dragon's passage, and the crackling of burning twigs and leaves, the swamp was eerily silent.

"Why is it so *quiet*?" Gerald hissed.

Omar gave him a look. "Do you really want me to answer that?" he asked.

"No," Gerald admitted. He knew what the silence meant: something was watching them. Something whose attention the rest of the wildlife didn't want to attract.

Gerald's heart rate ratcheted steadily upward until it felt like it was going to beat its way right out of his chest. It thumped hard enough that it was actually painful and he rubbed at it absently. He was sure he was going to have a heart attack or at least a panic attack if something didn't happen soon to break the tension.

But there was nothing to be seen in the gloom.

"Next time we're bringing lanterns," Gerald muttered.

As soon as the words were out of his mouth, lights flickered on all around them. Small balls of fire appeared all around them, in front, to both sides, above, and behind; they were on the ground and in the trees and Gerald stopped breathing when they appeared. Omar tightened his grip on his knives. The dragon slowed and then stopped altogether.

"Don't follow them," Gerald moaned, convinced they were will-o'-the-wisps there to lead them all to their doom.

But then the flames all rose up as one and they saw they were nothing more than ordinary—albeit small—torches, which were now being held high enough to illuminate their bearers instead of hiding them.

Gerald blinked and blinked again, but the scene didn't change. Standing all around them with their torches held aloft were...squirrels?

Chapter Eight

THEY WERE SURROUNDED by squirrels. Not the same fluffy, nonthreatening squirrels Gerald had so often seen in the forests in Andine, but fierce-looking squirrels wearing helmets and breastplates and assorted other bits of armor. Squirrels holding swords and daggers or bows with quivers of arrows slung over their shoulders. Squirrels that looked rather more intelligent—and quite a lot more dangerous—than usual. Gerald didn't know what to do other than stare at them. Next to him, Omar looked equally confused; his knives were in his hands, but he seemed unsure if he should try to use them.

It was the dragon who finally broke the silence. "Greetings," it said in a friendly rumble.

One of the squirrels, a pitch-black one wearing what appeared to be an eye patch, stepped forward with a torch in one hand and a sword in the other.

"Greetings," it returned, albeit in a decidedly less friendly tone. "I am Nadia, leader of the Swamp Squirrels. You are intruding in our domain."

"I beg your pardon," the dragon said politely. "We're simply passing through, you see. We were unaware this was occupied territory."

"Ignorance of the law is no excuse for breaking it," Nadia said severely.

Gerald fought back the urge to giggle somewhat hysterically. One squirrel, even one with a sword, is not terribly threatening. A hundred of them, on the other hand...

"How may we obtain permission to pass through?" the dragon asked, still politely. It did not seem to find their situation at all unusual or alarming. Gerald wondered how many talking squirrels it had run across in its lifetime that it took Nadia in stride. On the other hand, he figured it was probably quite difficult to intimidate a dragon.

Gerald didn't want to take his eyes off Nadia, but he examined Omar out of the corner of his eyes. Omar seemed to be more of a mind with

Gerald than with the dragon. His eyes darted from squirrel to squirrel like he couldn't decide which one was most likely to attack first. From the way he was still holding his knives, he seemed to think a fight was a foregone conclusion.

Gerald wished, possibly for the first time in his life, that he had a weapon of his own.

But negotiations had been ongoing while Gerald looked around and the dragon seemed to have gotten the upper hand. Several dozen squirrels were melting back into the swamp. The torches winked out one by one, either extinguished or simply carried out of sight.

Gerald and Omar watched them go. The dragon kept its eyes focused on Nadia.

"I know the place," she was saying. "It has been a blight on our domain for generations. You're telling me you can remove it?"

"After a fashion," the dragon clarified. "We will remove its guardian. If the resident doesn't wish to leave, we will not force her."

Nadia bared her teeth in a smile. "If the guardian is gone, we can handle the rest."

"You're not going to kill her, are you?" Gerald burst out. He gulped when Nadia turned her good eye toward him. "Sorry," he said.

"We're not murderers, boy," she snapped. "If the guardian leaves, the girl will follow. That is how it has always been."

"So we may pass?" the dragon interjected gently.

"You may pass," she sniffed. "Keep your passengers in hand, if you please."

"Of course."

The rest of the squirrels melted back into the swamp until Nadia was the only one left.

"We'll be watching you," she said. Then, with a flick of her tail, she extinguished her torch and vanished into the gloom.

None of them said anything for a long, long moment. Then Omar said conversationally, "You know, I think that was the smallest sword I've ever seen. By rights, it really should have been a knife. But it was definitely a *sword*. Isn't that interesting?"

"I bet it still would've hurt," Gerald said.

"Let's not find out," the dragon said. "Let's get to the dratted tower before something *else* decides to threaten us." It started wending its way through the trees as fast as the sticky mud would let it.

Gerald noticed it was now doing its level best to go *around* the trees rather than *through* them. *Doesn't want to upset the squirrels,* he thought. Every so often a torch would appear off to one side or another, always far enough away to not be an immediate threat, but close enough to clearly be a warning—a reminder they were allowed passage only conditionally, and they were being watched.

It made the rest of the journey to the tower incredibly tense, even though Gerald had a feeling the squirrels were keeping everything else away. He couldn't imagine the kind of creature that would want to mess with a hundred well-armed squirrels. Even the dragon hadn't wanted to fight them.

The trees eventually began to thin back out, and the smoky haze lessened enough to let some sunlight through. It had the welcome effect of lightening the gloom, and, from the dragon's perspective, the even more welcome effect of drying the perpetual mud into something that squished a bit less under its feet.

As they moved further into the lighter, drier part of the swamp, the trees thinned still more until they stopped altogether to reveal a clearing—and a tower.

"Here we are," the dragon announced cheerfully. "I believe it's safe for you two to get down now."

Omar and Gerald exchanged looks, but there was no sign of squirrels, toothy lizards, or anything else threatening. Omar shrugged, sheathed his knives, and slid down the dragon's side. Gerald followed him.

They approached the tower cautiously.

"What, uh, *kind* of guardian does Princess Elinore have?" Omar asked in a low voice.

"I don't know," Gerald said. To Omar's inarticulate noise of shock or dismay, he said, "That's the one thing they *don't* put in that stupid *Who's Who* book. They don't want the rescuers to know what to prepare for."

"It's just that I don't *see* one," Omar said, still speaking barely above a whisper. "I can't stab anything I can't see."

"We don't *want* to stab it, remember?"

"Right, right."

They were within half a dozen yards of the tower and there were still no signs of the guardian. "I know it's not supposed to attack us unless we attack *it*, or try to mount a rescue, but shouldn't it be, you know, visible?" Omar asked. He was fiddling with his knife sheaths again.

Gerald opened his mouth to reply but before he could a sharp voice interrupted from above.

"*Boys?*" it said disdainfully.

"Men?" Omar suggested.

Princess Elinore leaned out the window to get a better look at them. "No beards yet. You're boys. And boys *or* men, I'm not interested. Didn't you bother to read my signpost before walking through the swamp? If you weren't bright enough to check that first, I'm frankly astonished you haven't been killed by now."

"We were with a dragon," Gerald explained. "But we're not interested in you. Or," he added, with a sideways glance at Omar, "at least, we're not here to marry you."

Elinore snorted. "Good thing, too."

"We're here to free your guardian," Gerald persisted. "Er... Where is it, please?"

There was a moment of complete silence, and then the princess burst into laughter. She laughed for so long that Omar and Gerald exchanged nervous glances.

"I *said* she was probably mad," Omar said in an undertone. Gerald elbowed him sharply.

"Um... Princess?" Gerald called.

With a visible effort, Elinore pulled herself together. "Whew!" she said, wiping her eyes. "I can't remember the last time I laughed that hard. You're telling me you two dragged yourselves—*and a dragon*—through this miserable mud maze full of natural, supernatural, and *un*natural hazards to free my guardian, and you *don't even know what it is*?"

The princes exchanged looks again.

"Um. Yes. That's about the size of it," Gerald admitted. He quickly explained the rest of it in broad strokes, waiting to see if he was going to get a sympathetic reaction or an uncaring one. Waiting to see if Elinore would be coming with them, staying behind unspelled, or staying behind magically muted.

She waited for him to finish speaking, and then she started laughing again, although not nearly as hysterically as the first time. "Is that seriously the best story you could come up with?" she asked. "You really expect me to believe that nonsense? The guardians are barely sentient. They're *tools*. You can mistreat a horse. You can't mistreat its saddle."

Gerald sighed. "Dragon?" he called.

"I heard," it responded. There was a definite warning note of anger in its voice and Elinore's eyes widened. But before she could respond, her mouth snapped shut with an audible clacking of teeth that made Omar wince in sympathy.

"Not entirely mute!" Gerald hastily reminded the dragon.

"I will adjust it before we leave," it promised. "But for the moment...I've heard enough of her blather. And that laugh was getting on my last nerve."

"Mine too," Omar muttered.

"All right, all right," Gerald said. "We still haven't found the guardian, though."

Then the ground in front of them exploded.

Omar and Gerald stumbled backward; Gerald lost his footing and fell over entirely. Omar crouched in front of him protectively, his knives back in his hands, and waited for the air to clear.

When the dirt settled, Gerald wished it hadn't. There was a giant, angry-looking snake swaying back and forth over them, its mouth open to reveal glistening fangs.

A tarnished collar encircled its neck.

Neck? Do snakes have *necks?* Gerald wondered hysterically. *Or are they* all *neck?*

"Whoa!" Omar called, the same way one would halt a horse. He had seen the collar as well. "We're not mounting a rescue and we're not attacking you, so you can't attack us! Right? The collar won't let you!"

The snake hissed, but it didn't strike, and Gerald rather thought that answered that. He got shakily to his feet.

"Dragon?" he said. "A little help?"

"Let's see...my Reptilian is a little rusty," the dragon apologized. After a moment of thought, it hissed a reply at the snake. The two guardians carried out a long, sibilant conversation while Omar watched with interest, his knives sheathed once more, and Gerald wished for a convenient stump or bench or *something* to sit on. His knees didn't feel entirely solid yet.

After an indeterminate interval, the dragon, looking pleased, switched from Reptilian to Common to address the princes. "You can undo the spells now. Tska won't bite."

"You're quite sure?" Gerald asked and the dragon gave him a look. "Right. Okay then."

Tska had stopped swaying threateningly over them and now lowered the top half of its body back to the ground. Gerald stepped cautiously toward it and tried to ignore the way its tongue kept flicking out to taste the air.

I'm good with animals, he reminded himself. *I'm good with animals and the dragon says it's safe, and I'm helping it, and it's more than an animal, it's like the dragon, it's a guardian and it thinks and it* knows *I'm helping it, it's not like a cat that's going to bite when I try to bandage it because it hurts and it doesn't understand that I'm trying to help it.*

Even so, Gerald was nervous. There was no good reason to be more afraid of a snake than a dragon, but he was. Omar walked up next to him and asked, "Can I help?" and Gerald was immeasurably relieved to have someone there with him, next to the head and fangs of the giant venomous snake.

"You can help me mark where to carve," Gerald said, handing Omar a stick of wax from his knapsack. He spread out the diagram Erick had drawn and said, "I'll check it over before I start carving, so don't worry too much about making a mistake, but if you help with the wax marks it will go faster."

"Sure," Omar said. "I'll start on this side."

He knelt on the damp ground next to the snake—*serpent? "Snake" feels too ordinary for Tska*, Gerald thought—and found his place on the diagram. Within moments, he was carefully marking in the new lines Gerald would need to make to render the spell diagram inert.

Seeing Omar's complete lack of fear and commitment to the task, Gerald felt guilty about his own hesitation. He knelt to start on the other side and soon he was too distracted by the task to worry about the serpent he was kneeling next to. He didn't even flinch when he had to ask Tska to lift its head so he could get at the underside of the collar. He crouched calmly under the snake's head and got to work, distracted more by its hypnotic swaying than the fact that its fangs were mere inches from his head.

When all the marks were waxed and checked, Gerald got out his chisel. Erick had magically re-claimed most of his tools, but Gerald still had the one he needed most. He thought absently that he should pick one up from a blacksmith's shop the next time they went through a town so he could return this one to Erick, and then he thought of nothing but carving over the guiding lines and freeing the serpent from the spells.

By the time he finished, he was sweating and filthy from crawling all over the damp, muddy ground. The spells were disabled, the metal was tarnishing, and with a last sharp blow, the collar split and fell to the ground.

Tska shook itself all over like a dog, hissed, "Thankssssssss," in sibilant Common, and then dove back underground without another word.

Gerald blinked at its sudden disappearance. Omar looked similarly nonplussed. The dragon showed them its toothy grin and said, "Snakes have never been good conversationalists. Climb back up, now. I want to get out of here before dark."

A shoe came hurtling out of the window at the dragon's suggestion that they leave, and they all looked up to see a furious Princess Elinore leaning out the window with another shoe in her hand.

"I forgot about her," Gerald said ruefully. "Dragon, you had better modify that spell now, before we leave."

It let out a gusty, sulfur-scented sigh, but it gestured with its claws and muttered under its breath and the Princess got her voice back in midscreech.

"—believe you did such a thing, I don't know *what* you think you're playing at, but my parents are going to hear about this and then you'll be sorry!"

"Come on, now," the dragon said. "I want to get out of earshot."

The Princess continued to hurl insults and invective at them as Gerald and Omar scrambled back up the dragon's slick sides and tied themselves in.

"I think I can launch from here," the dragon said, looking around the clearing. "I'd rather not have to fight my way back through the swamp to where we came in."

"Do it then!" Gerald said, his eyes already squeezed shut in sick anticipation of the climb. "It's better to get it over with," he added to himself in an undertone.

Omar patted his shoulder reassuringly. "We haven't fallen off yet!" he said cheerfully.

Gerald made a seasick-sounding noise in return as the dragon reared up and launched itself skyward, the princess's words growing ever fainter behind them.

"It's girls like that who make me glad I like boys," Omar commented when she was finally out of earshot.

"There are boys like that too," Gerald pointed out.

"Yeah, but at least their voices aren't so shrill."

Gerald couldn't come up with a good response to that, so he said nothing. They flew in companionable silence until the dragon spotted a good place to camp for the night. They left the marsh behind and were flying back over grassland now. It was a great deal cooler than the desert and Gerald had a feeling the night was going to get downright cold.

The dragon landed gently next to a body of water—Gerald wasn't sure if it should be called a small river or a large stream—and took care, this time, to not dip the net of supplies into the water. "There's a bit of high ground over that way," it said, waving a claw. "It's far enough from the stream that the ground will stay dry, but close enough that I can have a bath." It looked at its scales with a fastidious expression. "I can't abide swamp muck."

"We'll unharness you, then," Gerald said. He and Omar unbuckled themselves and began to unburden the dragon. When they had undone the harness, detached the supplies, and taken down the canvas sunshade, the dragon gathered it all up and lifted it over to the hill it had mentioned.

"After you set up the camp," the dragon said, looking at them with the same fastidious expression, "I would suggest you bathe as well."

It didn't wait to hear their responses, but immediately turned and dove into the river, displacing a significant wave of water. The princes ducked instinctively, but they were out of the splash zone. The dragon started *frolicking* in the water, rolling around and splashing like a small child instead of a huge reptile.

It was quite a sight. Omar and Gerald exchanged looks and then broke into grins.

"I think I'll wait until it's done before I jump in," Gerald said. "It might drown us accidentally."

"Yeah," Omar agreed. He looked down at himself. He wasn't quite as filthy as Gerald was, but his shirt was a far cry from the color it had started out as that morning.

They had the camp set up and a small fire pit prepared by the time the dragon heaved itself out of the river and walked over, water cascading down its sides. It was completely clean and looked very pleased with itself.

"Your turn," it caroled. "I'll light the fire for you. I don't think you humans dry as efficiently as dragons do." The dragon's sides were already steaming as its internal heat caused the water to evaporate.

"Another one of our design flaws," Gerald agreed with a smile.

He and Omar left the dragon to it and headed to the river, carrying clean clothes and towels. Omar stripped and jumped in with no hesitation.

"Brr!" he said when his head popped up. "That's chilly. Not too bad once you get used to it, though." He ducked his head back under and scrubbed mud out of his curls.

Gerald was still standing on the bank when Omar emerged again. "Come on, it's not *that* cold," Omar said. "The sun's going to set soon, though, and then it's *really* going to get cold."

"I, uh, I'll wait till you're done," Gerald said. "I forgot the...thing...at the camp."

He headed back to camp at a pace just shy of a run while Omar watched with bewilderment.

"What's wrong?" the dragon asked when Gerald reappeared. "You're not clean yet."

"I'm waiting my turn," Gerald muttered.

The dragon cocked its head to the side and considered him. "It is a small river," it admitted, "but surely it's big enough for both of you."

Gerald ducked his head and didn't answer.

"I fit quite nicely," the dragon continued, "and I'm much bigger than the two of you put together."

"He's *naked*," Gerald hissed at it.

"Oh," the dragon said.

There was a long pause. Then, "Is that not how humans usually bathe?" the dragon asked cautiously.

"I don't like naked people," Gerald muttered. "I don't even like being naked by myself. I'm not getting undressed in front of him!"

"Oh," the dragon said again. Then, very, very cautiously, it asked, "Is this about you not wanting to marry?"

But instead of exploding again, Gerald covered his face with his hands.

"Gerald?" Omar asked from behind him. "Are you all right?"

"Fine!" he said brightly, but the illusion was somewhat ruined as his hands were still over his face.

"Did I offend you somehow?" Omar asked. "Because I really didn't mean to—"

"No, I think that was me," the dragon interjected. "I'm afraid I'm not always very good with your human nuances. But it was an unintentional offense."

It nudged Gerald gently. "Go on, get your bath," it said. "You'll feel better when you're clean."

Gerald didn't think so, but he didn't want to stay there with the dragon and Omar both giving him worried looks. He was still covering his face, but he could *feel* the worried looks. "I'm going," he said, and he did.

I am such an idiot, he thought as he undressed and ducked into the river. It *was* cold, initially, a shocking cold that made him gasp. But he adjusted to it quite quickly and by the time he had scrubbed away the last bit of sweat and swamp muck, he had to admit the dragon was right. He did feel a little better.

I'm still an idiot, though.

He dried off and got dressed quickly—the sun was setting and the air was starting to bite at his damp skin—but he didn't want to go back to camp. He didn't want to face the dragon and Omar and have to explain himself.

What is there to explain? I'm abnormal.

He stayed on the bank and watched the river flow until it grew too dark to see the rippling current, until he grew too cold to stay there and shiver. The fire on the hill looked warm and welcoming and he could hardly avoid Omar and the dragon forever.

He sighed and trudged up to the camp. His legs felt heavy and uncooperative. He dragged his feet rather than lifting them. It was a long, slow climb.

Neither the dragon nor Omar said anything when Gerald finally shuffled into the firelight. Gerald was relieved. If they had, he might have bolted.

They waited while he spread his damp clothes and towel out to dry. They waited while he sat down. He took his usual spot against the dragon's side and the heat of the fire and the heat of the dragon started to take away some of the evening chill.

Omar handed him a blanket, and after Gerald had wrapped it around his shoulders, a mug of soup. Gerald looked at it blankly.

"You're supposed to eat it," the dragon said.

Gerald could feel the rumble of its voice through its side. He was once again reminded of the castle cats and he wished they had one with him that would curl up in his lap and purr. It wasn't impossible to be sad with a purring cat in one's lap, but it was a lot harder.

"I'm not hungry," Gerald said. His stomach was tied in knots and he couldn't imagine spooning the soup down his throat. The idea of it was making him feel vaguely ill.

"I don't understand what's wrong," Omar said, finally breaking his own silence. "And don't say it's nothing, because clearly it's something. And if it's my fault—if I said something or did something, you have to let me know, because otherwise I'm probably going to say or do it again without realizing."

Gerald set his soup down and leaned his head back against the dragon's side, tilting his neck to look up at the sky. It was deeply black and speckled with stars. They looked cold and far away.

"It's not your fault," Gerald said. He kept his head tilted back and his eyes focused on the sky. These conversations never went well, had never gone well in all the times he'd attempted to have them, with his parents, with his siblings, even with Erick. He didn't want to have to see Omar's face as he attempted to have this conversation again. He was silent for a long moment after that, trying to decide how to start. *For all the times I've tried to say this, you would think I would be able to put it into words.*

"Well, good," Omar said after the silence had stretched out a little too long. "But can you tell us what happened?"

"I don't know how to start."

"Do you want me to ask you questions? Would that make it easier? I—we—just want to help. But you have to talk to us."

"It's not something you can help with," Gerald said. "I know that sounds melodramatic. Sorry. I don't mean to sound so ridiculous. It's just—it's me. There's something wrong with me. It just...spilled over."

The dragon nudged him gently and Gerald put his hand on its nose. The additional contact grounded him, and he tried to explain. "When we went to the river, I wasn't thinking. I only wanted to wash the muck off. It didn't occur to me we would be undressing. I mean, I knew we weren't going to bathe in our clothes, but I wasn't thinking about it, about what it meant. I don't like being naked and I don't like other people being naked around me. I panicked a little when you got undressed."

He was still looking up at the stars and he wished he could float away and join them. "This is going to sound vain or arrogant or something, but it's really not, it's part of my problem. You said you like guys, and... I don't want you to like me like that. And it's not that I think I'm all that great or extremely attractive or anything, it's not like that, it's that people have liked me like that in the past and I haven't known. They say things they mean one way and I don't understand it and I take them another way. I can't tell when people like me like that."

Gerald closed his eyes and got to the heart of the problem. "I can't tell because I don't like people like that. Not girls, not guys, not anyone. I don't understand the attraction. And *yes*, I know the mechanics of, of bedding and how it's supposed to feel but I *don't* feel that and really it all just makes me uncomfortable. And no one *listens* to me when I try to explain it, they tell me I'm a late bloomer, or I haven't met the right person yet, or they think I'm shy, and I *don't want to marry anyone,* and I'm going to have to and I will be miserable for the rest of my life and—"

"Gerald! Gerald, take a breath," Omar interrupted. "You're going to pass out."

But now that he had gotten going he was finding it difficult to stop. "And so it's not anything you did, and it's not your fault, or the dragon's fault, and neither of you offended me or did anything wrong, it's just me, it's me being different from everyone else and being strange and odd and freakish and *wrong* and being reminded about all of that and also today's rescue didn't really go as planned and I know the guardians need to be freed, they're really being treated abominably, but the other royals don't want that, they don't see anything wrong with any of this, they're happy to be meeting others and getting married and I'm never going to be happy with any of this—"

"Gerald!" Omar said. "Really, it's okay, you're okay, but you need to calm down. You're not a freak, I don't think anything's wrong with you and I'm sure the dragon doesn't think anything's wrong with you, so *please* take a breath!"

"Of course nothing's wrong with him," the dragon said indignantly. "He's making a lot more sense than most of you humans." It nudged Gerald again. "You probably should breathe, though. You humans need your oxygen. Those pesky design flaws again."

Gerald had run out of steam in any case. He closed his mouth and took a breath and was horribly ashamed to feel tears trickling down his face.

"Hey, hey, it's okay," Omar said softly. He sat next to Gerald, close enough to touch, but he didn't reach for Gerald, not wanting to spook him. "You've been waiting to get all that out, huh?"

Gerald swiped at his eyes, but there were more tears following the first ones. "No one ever listens."

"We're listening."

Gerald gave up trying to dry his face and let the tears fall. "I feel like an idiot."

"I feel like an idiot at least twice a day," Omar said cheerfully. "Don't worry about it."

Gerald tried a watery smile. "I'm starting to be glad we abducted you."

"Me too," Omar said. He put an arm around Gerald's shoulders, and Gerald let him. "We're friends, right? If I start to like you more than that, I'll let you know. Clearly, in plain Common. Okay? So you don't need to worry about misinterpreting something or not understanding anything."

"Thank you." Gerald used a corner of the blanket to dry his face. "I'm sorry about all this."

"Don't be. Is it okay if I ask you some questions, though? Just to be sure I understand everything. You can say no. And you can tell me to shut up at any time. I want to understand, but I don't want to upset you."

"No, go ahead," Gerald said. "No one's ever tried to understand before. But I don't really understand it myself, so..."

"You're the expert on you," Omar said. "But if you don't have an answer, say so. And if I ask something stupid or offensive, say so. Okay?"

"Okay."

"I guess my main question is... What exactly do you mean by 'liking people like that'?"

"Liking people in the way that makes you want to go to bed with them," Gerald said awkwardly. "I've never had a crush, I've never wanted anyone in my bed. I've never looked at anyone and wondered what they looked like naked. I've never wanted to...to see anyone or touch anyone."

Omar nodded like that made perfect sense. "So you mean you don't like people physically. You don't like people sexually."

"You say that like there are other ways to like people."

"Well, there are." He started ticking them off on his fingers. "There's liking friends, liking family, liking the way people look—in the same way you'd like a painting or tapestry or work of art, I mean. Aesthetics, not physical attraction."

"Oh."

"Yeah. So, now that's clarified. You said you don't want to get married. Do you not want a relationship at all, or just not a sexual one? Relax," he added. "If you want me to stop talking, just say so."

"No, it's okay," Gerald said. "I'm just... I'm not used to talking about this. I'm especially not used to people taking me seriously. I tried to tell my parents. I tried to tell my siblings. I even tried to tell my cousin Erick, and he always listens to me. He calls me a meathead, but he listens. But none of them understood this, and none of them listened to it. I—not that I'm not grateful—but, I don't know why *you're* listening. I mean, I've known you for all of two days and you're nodding like this is normal, and my family has known me all my life and acts like I'm a child, like I'm immature or somehow damaged." He stopped and blinked furiously. *I'm not going to start crying again.* "I *want* to talk about it," he said, once he had himself under control. "It's—it's just hard."

"I'm sorry no one's listened before," Omar said. "Why I am—well, why wouldn't I? If some people like men and some like women and some like everyone, well, why wouldn't some people not like anyone? It makes sense. You know, one of my aunties, she's never married or even spoken about it. She's not interested in it. So I guess it doesn't seem at all unbelievable to me."

"I think you really sound very draconic," the dragon broke in. Gerald startled. Despite leaning against the dragon's warm bulk, he had forgotten it was there, listening. "I told you before that dragons do not marry. We don't form partnerships the way humans do. We care for friends and for families, but not for lovers. That is really more of a business arrangement, finding someone to have a child with every fifty years or so."

"But you do have children," Gerald said. "That's the part I'm least interested in. That's what I'm afraid of, really. I wouldn't mind having a partner, a partner who was a really good friend, a best friend, someone I cared about more than anyone else, but I wouldn't—I *couldn't* sleep with them. And who would want a relationship like that? Dragons might not pair up to court and have families, but humans do. And humans center those partnered relationships around their beds."

"Traditionally," Omar said. "That doesn't mean they have to. No, really," he added in response to Gerald's *don't patronize me* expression. "I mean, traditionally, these marriage quests were all princes rescuing princesses. Then they evolved. Princesses started doing the rescuing, too. Princes rescued other princes, princesses rescued other princesses, and no one says any of those relationships are wrong. They're just different."

"But they all involve...sex," Gerald said. Even saying the word made him blush.

"Traditionally, yes," Omar admitted. "But traditions can change and they can adapt. Are you really against getting married, full stop, or are you against entering a relationship where you think you'll have to go to someone's bed?"

"I don't see the difference," Gerald started to say, but Omar gave him a look and he sighed. "All right, yes, it's the latter. But even if I find someone who would be open to that... I'm still a prince. I still need to produce an heir."

Omar waved a hand dismissively. "Cross that bridge when you come to it," he advised. "Maybe your partner would be willing to provide the, uh, physical piece without involving you in the process. Or you could always adopt a child or even simply name another relative as heir. There's no actual rule that the heir has to be a child of the body. There have been childless monarchs before, and I'm sure there will be more in the future."

"I know," Gerald said. "But they haven't been childless by *choice*. My parents—they're never going to accept this."

"That's their problem," Omar said firmly. "Don't make it yours."

"And if it *is* a problem for them," the dragon interjected, "I could probably change their minds." It showed its teeth in a decidedly unfriendly grin and Gerald couldn't resist giving it a quick, fierce hug.

"I hate that they put me in a tower," he murmured into its ear. "But I'm glad it was *your* tower."

"Me too," it rumbled softly.

Chapter Nine

HE WOKE TO Omar shaking his shoulder. "Gerald? Your knapsack is chiming."

"What? Oh! It's the incoming message alert." Gerald reluctantly dug himself out of the blankets—they were damp with dew and the air was chill and biting—and groped around in the dark until he found his knapsack.

Omar stirred the fire back into life as Gerald pulled the two-way parchment and a bottle of ink out of his knapsack. As soon as he dripped ink on it, the message started appearing.

"Whoa," Omar said, watching the words write themselves by the firelight. "That's amazing! That's the spell the dragon mentioned before? Your cousin's?"

"Yeah," Gerald agreed distractedly. He was used to the process and was more interested in what the message said than how it was appearing. "I wrote him yesterday."

Meathead,

It sounds like you're having a better time of it than I am. Also, I cannot believe you of all people kidnapped someone. I thought you didn't want to rescue anyone? Changed your mind already?

Sorry for the delayed response, by the way. I imagine by now you've completed your first mission. Princess Elinore has vanished from the map, so I know at the very least you made it there. How did she take it? How did the guardian?

I just arrived at the outskirts of the Enchanted Forest. Princess Nedi is somewhere inside, and there are at least half a dozen would-be rescuers camped outside the forest. I've disabled all of their tracking spells. Every time I look at the map there are fewer dots on it. It's good they're disappearing from multiple locations now, or I suspect it would have been pinned on me already. I suspect it still will be, mind. I can't imagine the Council is very pleased with this disruption, and I don't think many of our peers have magical talent... I'm trying to determine if there's a way I can plant the disabling spell on my fellow rescuers here, so they could carry it off with them when they disperse and disable the trackers on everyone they pass.

But right now I'm busy modifying it to be self-maintaining. My tracker came back on this morning and I had to zap it off again.

I'll keep doing what I can at my end. If I can make it to Princess Nedi without an entourage, I'll see about freeing her guardian. I hear she has a unicorn. I'll see if I can approach it without getting gored. You know what the legends say.

Keep me posted,

Erick

"Dragon?" Gerald called. "Have our tracking spells come back?"

"Hmm?" it asked. It raised its head from where it had been pillowed on its forelegs and sniffed the air. "Hmm. Yes. And no. Yours has. Omar's has not. That's most irritating." It waved a claw. "There you go. Hidden again."

"Does that mean the others are being tracked again as well?" Gerald asked. "Everyone back in the desert, and Elinore?"

The dragon frowned. "I can't say for sure. I doubt Elinore's would have been restored so quickly. The others...maybe." It twitched another claw in Omar's direction. "I don't want his spell coming back either. I don't care for this at all. Let's get moving sooner rather than later."

"The sun isn't up yet," Omar pointed out.

"No, but we all are. And I can see quite well in the dark. It's a long flight to Mount Vidrian and we may as well get underway."

They packed quickly and soon everything was in place. The first streaks of pink were beginning to appear on the horizon when the dragon launched into the air. Gerald almost thought he might be getting used to it. The heart-pounding terror was still there, but the nausea wasn't as evident.

He and Omar shared a cold breakfast of fruit, jerky, and journey bread as they flew.

"I hope this goes better than it did yesterday," Gerald said.

"It probably couldn't go much worse," Omar said with a grin.

"Thanks. That's really helpful."

"Any time," Omar said cheerfully.

Gerald gave him a dirty look but let the conversation die. It was too early and he was too tired, and there were more important things to think about. *At least Erick's letter gave me something to think about other than how much of an idiot I made of myself last night.*

"Hey, Dragon?" Gerald asked.

"Yes?" it asked.

"The tracking spell—can you tell if it was new? I mean, did Erick's disabling spell simply wear off, or was it an entirely recast spell?"

"I wasn't looking for that," the dragon admitted. "I can't say for sure. Although...it does seem more likely it simply wore off. For it to be recast, whoever cast it would need to know where you were."

"Which they wouldn't know without the tracking spell."

"Or they could have scryed," Omar pointed out.

"No," the dragon said confidently. "Even with scrying, unless there is something linking the subject and the spell caster, the caster has to know where to look, at least in a general sense. One could scry the Yevin Desert looking for my tower, for instance. But if one didn't know which desert the tower was in..." it trailed off and shrugged, and Gerald yelped and grabbed at the harness. It was a very disconcerting sensation to feel a shrug underneath you. "Oh, sorry," it said. "You two are so light, I forget you're there."

"Wait, does that mean the tracking spell is permanent?" Omar asked. "You can disable it, but not remove it?"

"It's trickier to remove spells you haven't cast yourself," the dragon explained. "But it's not impossible. I don't know how much time your cousin has to work on this, Gerald; I would suggest he first modify the disabler to ensure it won't wear off. That will likely be much easier than removing the spell entirely."

"That's what he's planning, I think," Gerald said, pulling out the parchment to check. "But I should reply anyway."

By the time he had scribbled a quick response to Erick—the wind and the uneven writing surface doing nothing to improve his handwriting—the sun was firmly above the horizon and the air was warming up.

Omar shed his outer cloak and sighed with contentment. "You know, even with the creepy spells, and the killer squirrels, and everything else... I'm actually enjoying myself."

"I'm glad one of us is," Gerald grumbled, but Omar shoved him playfully and a smile broke out over his face too. "All right, it is kind of exciting."

"I'm revising my opinion of humans increasingly upward," the dragon added. "When we free the last of the guardians I might even like you two enough to make you honorary dragons." It turned its head as it said that so they could see it wink.

"Are honorary dragons a real thing?" Omar asked with interest. "My father gives out honorary knighthoods sometimes."

The dragon started to shrug again, and Gerald's grip tightened reflexively on the harness before it caught itself. "It can be. We're not as regimented as you humans. If I want to declare someone an honorary dragon, no one is going to stop me."

"Hmm. All right. Does it come with any perks?"

"Well, it would keep you from getting eaten," the dragon said, deadpan.

Omar laughed. "That's a perk, all right. Gerald, we better do a good job with this. I like the sound of being an honorary dragon. And we've established you're pretty draconic already."

Gerald ducked his head, embarrassed to have last night's scene mentioned again, no matter how obliquely. Omar noticed and the smile slid off his face. "Sorry," he said quietly. "If you're done talking about it, I won't mention it again. I'm not making fun of you, though, you know that, right?"

"I know. It's okay. I guess I have a kind of knee-jerk reaction to certain things." He shrugged self-consciously. "I know I shouldn't be so sensitive about it, but..."

"But?" Omar prompted.

Gerald looked at his hands and occupied himself with wrapping them around the harness. "It's going to sound melodramatic again," he warned.

"You're not being melodramatic," Omar said. "And if I didn't want to know, I wouldn't have asked."

"It, well, it makes me feel less than human. I already told you how I felt—feel—like an outsider in my family, how I don't look like anyone else, and that makes me feel like I'm not really a part of it. But this... feeling like I do, or rather, *not* feeling like everyone else, it makes me feel like I'm not really a person. It makes me feel wrong and broken." His voice dropped as he spoke until he was whispering the last words. He could feel his eyes starting to sting and he gripped the harness harder to distract himself and make himself focus. *You are not going to start crying again!* he snapped at himself. *You're supposed to be an adult, so act like one!*

"And comparing you to a dragon makes it seem like I think you're less than human, too," Omar finished. "Gerald, I'm sorry. I didn't mean it like that at all. Of course you're human, you're completely human."

"I know. I mean, I'm not a changeling or anything, I don't think anything like that. But I don't have the same feelings other people do."

"You don't have *one* feeling *most* other people do," Omar corrected. "It's not like you don't have feelings at all! It's not even that you can't like or even love people. You just don't want to go to bed with them. Who cares about that?"

Gerald looked up at Omar and raised an eyebrow. "Are you serious? Everyone cares about that. Ever since I turned, oh, thirteen or so, that's all anyone has wanted to talk about. Do I like boys, do I like girls, isn't so-and-so cute, have I kissed anyone, have I slept with anyone, do I want to sleep with anyone? Every conversation has a double meaning, everyone laughs at jokes I don't understand, everyone is dying to find their True Love and have children, and I'm... I'm disconnected from all of that, from a huge part of society."

"But you can have relationships without sex," Omar reminded him. "All right, yes, society does give more weight to relationships with sex. That's why people talk about being 'just' friends, like being 'friends' is inferior. But you can have relationships that go deeper than friendship, that are partnerships, that are couples, without sex."

"Maybe you can," Gerald said. "Maybe it's possible. But a lot of things are possible. That doesn't mean it's ever going to happen. Other people want standard relationships, and those involve going to bed with your partner. I'm never going to want that, and that means I'm never going to have a relationship that goes beyond friendship. I'm never going to have a marriage that means anything to me."

"Not with that attitude, you're not," Omar said. "There are a lot of people in the world, Gerald. There are a lot of preferences. There have to be other people who feel like you. And even if there aren't, if someone loves you, if you love them, you know, compromises can be made."

"I'm not going to bed with anyone," Gerald said flatly. "That's not negotiable. That's not something I can compromise on."

"I'm not trying to make you!" Omar said. "I'm just saying, if you've already decided you're never going to be happy, you're not going to be looking for happiness. Keep an open mind, okay? The world might surprise you."

"I guess so." Gerald looked out at the horizon and couldn't contain a smile. "It's been doing a pretty good job of surprising me recently."

"And besides," the dragon added, mock sternness in its voice, "why on earth would you think being draconic means you're *less*? I happen to think dragons are *more*."

Gerald laughed and patted its shoulder affectionately. "I think I agree with you."

The air grew increasingly chill as they headed both further north and to a higher altitude. By the time they stopped for a quick lunch, Omar had replaced his cloak and, although Gerald had never taken his off, both princes were shivering. The dragon wasn't bothered by the cold any more than it had been by the desert's heat, but Gerald's fingers, nose, and ears had gone numb.

"I don't suppose you packed any winter gear?" Omar asked when they landed. "It would make a pretty poor impression if we showed up frostbitten."

"I think we'll be able to manage something," Gerald said, and he dug through the supplies until he found warmer, hooded cloaks, and some gloves.

"What type of guardian do you think is up there?" Omar asked as they ate. "It's going to be freezing on that mountain, isn't it? So something adapted to the cold...a snow drake?"

"It could be anything," Gerald said. "We're not going to fight it, so I don't know if we need to be speculating. Whatever it is, we're taking the collar off and leaving."

"I know. I just thought it might be nice to be prepared."

"As long as it doesn't burst out of the ground, I think I'm prepared for anything," Gerald said. "I'm more worried about the prince."

"Ah. Right. Who's this one?"

Gerald dug out his copy of *Who's Who*, the pages looking decidedly ragged around the edges after the treatment they'd received in his knapsack. "Uh... Prince Thierry of Makandia. Eldest son and heir. No siblings."

"Never been there," Omar said.

That was no surprise. "Me neither. He's a long way from home."

"I don't know much about Makandia. I'm not even sure I could name the current monarch, let alone local custom. Let's just hope, if nothing else, that he's not as shrill as Princess Elinore."

"You know, when someone's yelling at me, I tend to be more concerned with the fact that they're yelling and less concerned with the pitch of their voice as they do so."

Omar shrugged. "It's easier to ignore when it doesn't feel like your eardrums are going to rupture."

"Right, well, regardless. Do you think we should show up and free the guardian and not even try to explain ourselves? That would at least prevent being laughed at."

Omar shrugged again. "It's your quest. I'm following your lead."

Gerald sighed. "I wonder if the dragon knows any invisibility spells."

The dragon had shed the supplies along with the princes and then disappeared to rustle up its own midday meal. But Gerald had a feeling that if the dragon could enable them to slip in and out unnoticed, it would have suggested it beforehand. Particularly after the scene with Princess Elinore.

Omar laughed. "What fun would that be?"

Gerald stuck his tongue out to make Omar laugh again but didn't otherwise respond.

The dragon soon returned looking full and self-satisfied, and Omar and Gerald hurriedly finished their own lunches and packed everything away. It was only an hour's flight from there to the base of Mount Vidrian, and they were glad of the warmer clothes by the time they got there.

"Is that *snow*?" Omar asked in amazement.

"Hmm...white, cold, flakey...yes, I do believe it's snow," Gerald said.

Omar gave him a light shove. "Shut up. How much snow do you think we get in Yevin? The whole kingdom's hot, even outside of the desert."

"Think of snow as basically cold sand," Gerald suggested. "They're both made up of lots of individual pieces and are about as easy to walk on."

"I can think of it as snow, goose," Omar said. "I know what it *is*, I've just never seen it before. Hey, Dragon, can we land for a minute?"

"No!" Gerald said, knowing landing meant they would need to take off again. *I can't deal with an extra take off. Only as many as strictly necessary, please!* "Anyway, I'm sure there will be snow at the top of the mountain too. More of it, probably."

"I agree with Gerald," the dragon said. "It makes more sense to fly you two up to the tower directly. And he's quite right about the snow. Are you two warm enough?" it asked as an afterthought. "I've noticed humans seem to be comfortable only in a quite small range of temperatures."

"Another of our design flaws," Gerald agreed good-naturedly. "I'm all right, though. Sitting on your back is like sitting on a heater."

"I'm fine, too," Omar added. "I'm glad for the gloves, though."

"Onward and upward, then," the dragon said. "It'll only be a few more minutes now."

All thoughts of trying to get in and out without attracting Prince Thierry's notice went straight out of Gerald's mind when they came within sight of the tower. There was someone else on the ground outside of it—someone fighting the guardian.

Chapter Ten

"STOP! STOP!" GERALD called frantically as the dragon braked and dropped to the ground in a much tighter, faster spiral than usual. "Don't hurt it!"

The would-be rescuer's attention was drawn away from the fight by the sudden appearance of a dragon landing scant yards away. Gerald hurriedly undid his harness and dropped into the snow with Omar hard on his heels. The guardian's own attention had wavered when they landed and it now froze and watched them.

Not a snow drake, Gerald noted absently. It was, in fact, an amarok, a giant, white-furred wolf. Gerald saw with a stab of anger that its creamy fur was stained red in several places. Its lips were pulled back to reveal black gums and sharp teeth as it growled, but it made no move to attack its opponent despite that individual's distraction. *The damn collar again. It can only defend itself. And clearly, that's not working too well for it right now.*

The rescuer was clad in armor, with thick quilted padding underneath. The amarok hadn't been able to do nearly as much damage to the rescuer as they had done to the unprotected wolf, although how much of that was due to the rescuer's protection and how much to the collar's restrictions Gerald wasn't sure.

"Stop!" Gerald said again. "Leave it alone."

The rescuer backed away from the amarok, prudently opening up some space between them even knowing it wouldn't be able to attack until they chose to start the fight up again. Then they turned to face the interlopers, taking off their helm as they did so.

"Get out of here!" they snapped, their green eyes flashing angrily. "Thierry and I have an understanding. He's not available, do you hear? I'm rescuing him and I'm not letting you get in the way!"

Gerald held up his hands placatingly and gestured broadly to indicate his weaponless state. "We're not here for Prince Thierry, or to fight you. Go ahead and rescue him, I don't care. But don't hurt the guardian."

The rescuer goggled at him. "Are you daft? I have to beat the guardian to get to Thierry."

"Only because it's been enslaved," Gerald retorted. "I can undo the spells on its collar. You won't have to fight it. You can rescue your prince, and everyone can leave without any further bloodshed."

"That's not how it *works*," the rescuer snapped. "Who the hell are you, anyway? Where did you *come* from?"

"I'm Gerald," Gerald said. "This is Omar. And that's Dragon."

"Prince Gerald," Omar added. "Prince Omar."

"And Prince Dragon?" the rescuer asked sourly.

"Dragons don't hold with royalty," the dragon replied haughtily.

The rescuer's eyes widened when the dragon spoke. For the first time, they began to look a little unsure of the situation.

Gerald sighed and tried again. "The dragon was my guardian until I took the collar off. The collar is what keeps them mute and keeps them guarding us, and makes them fight us, too. Let us take the collar off the amarok and you can rescue Thierry without anyone interfering or getting hurt."

"Says you," the rescuer snapped. "Taking the collar off would count as defeating the guardian, wouldn't it? And you're *not* taking Thierry."

"I don't *want* to take Thierry!" Gerald snapped back. "Neither does Omar. Neither of us cares about Thierry or about you—who are you, anyway?" he asked.

"Princex Taylor," they replied.

"Princess?" Omar asked.

"Prin*cex*," they repeated, emphasizing the suffix.

"Right, okay," Gerald interrupted. "Princex Taylor, I can assure you neither Prince Omar nor I have any interest in interfering with your rescue of Prince Thierry. I swear on my blood as a royal. But look at the guardian! Just look. It's bleeding. It has infected wounds around the collar. Look, you can see where it's lost fur, where the collar has rubbed it away. Does that look *right* to you? Do you really want to hurt it *more*? There's no need for further violence."

Taylor looked at their sword when Gerald said the word *violence* and Gerald did not like the gleam that came into their eyes. "You will not interfere," they repeated, brandishing the sword at Gerald. He stepped back instinctively, flinching, and Taylor smiled with satisfaction.

They put their helm back on and turned to face the amarok again. The wolf had stayed still and silent throughout their conversation, but now it growled and raised its hackles.

"Don't!" Gerald cried. He took half a step forward, but didn't know what to do, didn't know how to disarm Taylor without a weapon of his own—and then Omar strode over, unsheathed one of his knives, reversed his grip, and brought the hilt of it down on the back of Taylor's helm.

The sound was astonishingly loud, the metal ringing like a bell, and then the princex swayed on their feet and began to crumple to the ground. Omar, clearly expecting that reaction, caught them easily and laid them gently on the packed snow.

"Omar!" Gerald said, caught between shock and admiration.

Omar grinned. "They're fine. I just knocked them out, is all."

"They're fine!" he added, louder, to the figure Gerald had only now noticed was hanging out the tower window with a horrified expression on his face. "It's okay!"

"I refuse this rescue attempt!" Prince Thierry yelled back.

"This *isn't* a rescue attempt!" Gerald shouted. "Not of you, anyway," he muttered under his breath, and then he threw his hands up in disgust as Thierry kept yelling down at them. "I'm not having this conversation again," he told Omar. "Talk to him if you want. I'm getting that collar off."

He approached the amarok confidently, diagram, wax stick, and chisel all in hand, but he stopped a sensible distance away to make his case. Just in case. As soon as he opened his mouth, however, the amarok rolled its amber eyes expressively and flopped on the ground, wagging its tail like a puppy.

"I guess *you* don't need any convincing!" Gerald said, smothering a laugh. "Excellent." He knelt next to the wolf and laid his knapsack down, spreading the diagram out on top of it in order to keep it out of the snow. It was well packed down around the tower, enough that they weren't floundering through drifts, but he didn't want to risk getting the parchment wet and having the ink run. He quickly got to work making the preliminary marks in wax, while keeping half an ear on Omar and Thierry's conversation. *Not that it can really get out of hand, with Thierry stuck in the tower.*

By the time Gerald had made and checked all the preliminary marks, Thierry had gone quiet, apparently convinced Gerald and Omar weren't attempting to keep him from Taylor. Gerald shot a guilty look at the princex and saw they were beginning to stir.

"Dragon?" Gerald said.

"Yes?" it asked cheerfully. It had been sitting back and watching Gerald and Omar with evident amusement ever since Omar had knocked out the princex.

"Keep them from stabbing me when they wake up, okay?" Gerald said, nodding toward Taylor. "I'm ready to start carving and I don't want to be distracted."

"No problem," the dragon said. It moved closer, reached out, and delicately draped a forearm across Taylor's armored chest, holding them down with no effort on the dragon's part. "They won't be getting up anytime soon," it promised with a toothy grin.

"As long as they can breathe, that's fine," Gerald murmured and then he turned back to the amarok. "It won't be long now," he promised, and then he raised his chisel and got to work.

Taylor woke up about halfway through and the mountain started ringing with shouts and echoes as Taylor, Thierry, and Omar all started yelling questions, threats, and reassurances at each other and at Gerald. Gerald forced himself to tune out the noise and focus on the task at hand. He had had to take his gloves off for the delicate work of altering the symbols, and his fingers were starting to turn white and numb. *They can yell as much as they want. They're not going to interrupt me. And I'm going to finish this before I get frostbite!*

Finally, finally, the noise levels dropped—or he got better at ignoring them—and the symbols changed one by one until he made the last change and the collar abruptly began to rust.

"There we go!" Gerald said triumphantly and with a sharp rap that reminded him of how Omar had dispatched Taylor, he shattered the now-fragile collar.

The amarok lunged at Gerald and the prince had barely enough time to register the movement and tense with sudden fear before the wolf bowled him over. Gerald waited to feel teeth or claws rip through his clothes and into his flesh, but all he felt was the rough sandpaper of the amarok's tongue as it frantically washed his face.

"All right, all right!" Gerald said, laughing. "Good wolf. You're all right now. Okay! Okay, that's enough, you're going to wash my skin right off."

The amarok eased off but kept its giant front paws on Gerald's shoulders, holding him down against the snow.

"Not so fun now, is it?" Taylor groused. "Call off your dragon, would you?"

"It's not *my* dragon," Gerald said. "But—I think you can let them up now, Dragon. And I'd like to get up, too," he added to the wolf. "The snow's a bit cold for me." The amarok let him up and he brushed the snow off his back, but it had already soaked through his cloak and the damp chill made him shiver.

The dragon sighed theatrically and muttered something about humans and manners, but it let the princex up in the end. They immediately ran to the tower and Gerald watched, bemused, as they produced a grappling hook. Thierry prudently disappeared from the window and Taylor sent the hook flying toward the sill. After three attempts, it caught, and the princex scrambled up the wall with all the agility one would expect from a squirrel.

"Impressive," Omar said with admiration. "Well, they seem to be all right up there. How's the wolf?"

Gerald had begun examining its wounds after it let him up. "It's all right. You'll be all right," he said directly to it. "I bet it hurts, though. I have some medical supplies. One or two of those wounds could probably do with stitches, if you'd like?"

But the amarok shook its head and began to yip.

"Getting the collar off is enough," the dragon interpreted. "It—she—says amaroks are hard to kill. She's going to go back to her pack, and they will tend to her there."

The wolf darted in to lick Gerald's face once more, and then she took off at a deceptively fast lope, disappearing into the snow within minutes.

Gerald watched her go with an odd feeling of disappointment. The serpent guardian had disappeared even more quickly and with even less thanks, but that hadn't bothered him at all. *I guess that was the sort of behavior I expected from a reptile. Mammals, though, you expect a little more from...and she reminded me of the castle dogs, I think that's the real problem.* Gerald wondered how all his four-legged friends were getting along back home without him.

Omar snapped him out of his reverie. "I guess we're all done here," he said, half a question in his voice.

"I guess so," Gerald agreed.

"Then can we go somewhere warmer now?" he asked plaintively.

"We better," Gerald said. He was shivering in his wet clothes and even after he put his gloves back on, his fingers remained stiff and numb.

Omar helped him gather up his supplies—he saw with relief that the spell diagram had remained safely out of the snow despite the amarok's enthusiastic response to getting her collar off—and then gave him a boost to get back up on the dragon.

"Oh—" Gerald said as the dragon prepared to take off. "Wait—we better warn them not to say anything about us."

Omar smirked. "Trust me, they're not thinking about anything other than each other right now. And Taylor isn't going to want to let any hint slip that they didn't defeat the guardian and rescue Thierry in typical heroic fashion. I think we're safe to go."

Gerald hesitated, but the dragon agreed with Omar. "Neither of them is going to talk," it said. "And if we linger in this cold, you are going to catch your death."

Gerald sighed and let himself be overruled. "Let's go, then," he said, closing his eyes and bracing for takeoff. It wasn't nearly as violent this time, though, as the dragon chose to simply take a running leap off the side of the mountain, snap its wings open, and glide away on an updraft, a procedure that kept them much more horizontal than usual.

But the modified takeoff didn't affect the wind whipped up by the dragon's flight. The cold air felt even colder as it rushed over Gerald's wet clothes and he was soon shivering violently.

"Take your cloak off," Omar said. "It's soaked, it's only making you colder—here, take mine, it's dry."

"Then you'll be cold," Gerald protested through chattering teeth. "Better only one of us is."

"Don't be an idiot," Omar said. "Better for both of us to be slightly chilly than for me to be warm and you to freeze and make yourself sick." He hesitated, then added, "After you lectured me about deliberately making myself ill, I wouldn't think you would be keen to do the same thing."

"It's not the same," Gerald said, but he started making an effort to get the wet cloak off. He still made a token noise of protest when Omar shed his own cloak and bundled it around Gerald, but he couldn't put any force into it; he was shivering too much and the dry cloak was more than welcome.

"Dragon?" Omar called. "How far are we flying?"

"Far enough to get out of the mountains," the dragon called back. "I hope. There's a storm coming."

"Of course there is," Omar muttered, but they could both see the dark clouds boiling up from the south.

"Th-there's a storm, you sh-should k-keep your cloak," Gerald said slowly, reluctantly, slurring the words through numb lips and chattering teeth.

"We'll share, all right? You're going to freeze." Omar didn't wait for a response but simply shifted closer to Gerald as he spoke and wrapped both of them up in his cloak. "*Ras*, but you're cold!" he cursed.

Gerald flinched a little at the contact, but Omar wrapped an arm around Gerald when he started to pull away. "You're going to freeze," he said again.

The clouds were getting blacker and closer and then they opened up and began to dump thick, wet flakes of snow on the trio. The flakes melted in little puffs of steam where they fell on the dragon's hide, but the ones that landed on the princes stuck.

Omar's cloak was beginning to give off the distinctive odor of wet wool, and he was beginning to shiver. Gerald hadn't ever stopped.

"This is no good," Omar said, rubbing his hands together to warm them. "Dragon, we might need to stop sooner rather than later! We need better shelter."

"I have to find some first," the dragon said. Between the snow and the darkness caused by the heavy clouds, there was no visibility to speak of. The dragon began breathing fire periodically, although Gerald wasn't sure if it was to provide light or to melt a path through the swirling snow.

"C-c-canvas," Gerald stuttered through his chattering teeth. "W-w-waterproof."

"I'll get it," Omar said. "Hold the cloak—hold it tight, don't let the wind take it! Dragon, I have to stand up, warn me if you're going to make any sudden moves." He loosened the harness and carefully rose into a crouch so he could start to detach the canvas sunshade from its wooden frame.

It felt like hours before Omar crouched back down next to him with the canvas rolled up and tucked under his arm. The cloak, which Gerald was still clinging to fiercely, was completely soaked through, the wool heavy and several shades darker.

It was a fight against the wind and their own numb fingers, but they somehow managed to get the canvas sheet wrapped over and around themselves until they were huddled together in a cocoon, completely surrounded and sheltered by the fabric.

The waterproofing not only kept the snow off but also stopped the wind. It was dark and damp in the cocoon, but the temperature in their canvas cave was already beginning to climb. The simple absence of the wind was such a blessing that Gerald sighed with relief, even though he was still shivering and numb.

"The desert's looking really good right around now," Omar muttered when he had thawed enough to talk, and Gerald laughed weakly.

"The Burning Swamp is looking really good right around now!" he replied.

They huddled together under the canvas, sharing body heat and slowly defrosting and even beginning to relax until the dragon abruptly said, "Uh-oh."

"What do you mean, '*uh-oh*'?" Omar yelled.

"I'm landing!" the dragon called back, and Gerald's stomach lurched up into his throat as they went plummeting to the ground. It was more of a controlled fall than the usual graceful descent, and the dragon landed hard enough that only the harnesses kept Gerald and Omar from bouncing right off.

"Ooph," Omar grunted as the landing jolted all the air out of his lungs.

"What happened?" Gerald called, blinking and squinting into the snow. The rough landing had yanked the canvas out of his grip, and they were once again exposed to the storm.

"The wind... I had to slow down too much because of the visibility and that meant I couldn't fight the wind. I nearly flew right into the cliff face. We're staying here until the storm passes."

"Where *is* here?" Omar asked, rubbing his sternum and wincing.

"Well, I don't know exactly," the dragon admitted. "But look, I found a cave," it added, sounding pleased with itself. "Get inside, out of the wind."

"Is there anything in there that's going to eat us?" Omar asked doubtfully, but even as he asked he was untying himself and Gerald and starting to climb down.

"Of course not," the dragon said indignantly, but it snaked its head into the gaping cavern to check nonetheless. Omar shook his head and helped Gerald slide down the dragon's side. The snow was piled up past their knees and still falling heavily.

"Oh, it doesn't matter," Omar said. "It's too cold out here. We have to go inside regardless."

The dragon pulled its head back and said, "It's empty, anyway. Go on in. I can't fit, but I can block up the entrance. I'll keep the heat in and the snow out. Go on, hurry up," it said, nudging them forward. "You humans were not designed for these conditions."

They stumbled through the snow and across the threshold, moving more easily once they got into the cave mouth. Some snow had blown in and formed drifts around the entrance, but after a few yards, it became rough stone.

As soon as they were out of the way, the dragon shifted its bulk into the opening, cramming as much of itself as it could into the cave mouth. That blocked the wind and snow quite nicely but also plunged the cave into complete darkness.

"Oh, sorry," the dragon said and then a glowing blue orb appeared between its claws.

"I didn't know you could do that!" Gerald said, watching the mage light bob up and down in the air.

"It's only light, though," the dragon said. "No heat, I mean. You two better unpack the supplies you need to get warm."

"A fire would be nice," Omar said. "I don't suppose you're carrying any firewood in that net of yours?"

"I can get some from outside," the dragon said. "There's a stand of evergreens out there. It will be wet, though."

"As long as it burns," Omar said with a shrug. "We'll deal with the smoke. We need the heat too much to be picky."

The princes untied the supply net and dragged the whole thing further into the cave. The dragon's mage light followed them and took up a spot over their heads, casting a circle of light around them as they unpacked blankets, dry clothes, and journey bread, jerky, and dried fruit for dinner.

Gerald produced a pair of lanterns as well as a pot to boil water in for tea. But when he opened the water barrel, he saw with shock that it had frozen solid.

"Another reason for a fire," Omar observed when he saw the barrel of ice. "We need to thaw that. And ourselves," he added. He was shivering again, and Gerald hadn't ever stopped, although he was huddled up in a blanket now. Omar tossed a shirt at Gerald. "Here. I'll turn around or even go outside if you want, but you need to put dry clothes on. Wrapping up in a blanket isn't going to help when you're wearing wet clothes underneath."

Gerald blushed, but he didn't argue. "Just turn around. I'll turn around too, you should take your own advice. Let me know when you're dressed again."

Gerald faced further into the cave and Omar faced out toward the storm, and they both quickly stripped out of their soaked clothes and put on dry. The dragon had gone outside to get firewood and the wind whistling through the cavern gave them ample reason to hurry, on top of Gerald's embarrassment.

"I'm decent," Omar said, and they both turned to watch the dragon bring in an entire tree, which it had uprooted while they were unpacking.

"Watch your eyes," it advised, and then it squeezed the tree into fragmented bits of kindling, stripping off the pine needles as it did so. "Look, it's dry on the inside," it said when the sawdust settled, looking quite pleased with itself. "Where do you want it?"

They soon had a cheerful fire going, with their clothes and boots laid out to dry and the water barrel dragged over to thaw. "It would be quicker to melt some snow," the dragon observed, and Gerald started to get up to get some.

"Sit down!" Omar said. "You're staying by the fire. And put another pair of socks on, will you? I'll get the snow." He grabbed the pot and squeezed by the dragon to fill it. The dragon's body heat had melted the drifts inside the cavern and Omar had to go out into the storm to fill the pot. He got back inside as quickly as he could, brushing snow out of his hair and off his shoulders.

"*Brr*, it's really nasty out there." He hugged himself and shivered violently. "I think your crash landing was a good idea."

"Hardly a *crash* landing," the dragon sniffed. "It was an unexpected but completely controlled stop."

"Either way." Omar shrugged playfully and grinned.

He put the pot on the fire and sat next to Gerald, pulling a blanket around his own shoulders and sighing with contentment as he slowly warmed up.

"I take back what I said earlier about wanting to see the snow," Omar said. "I think I've seen as much as I ever want to."

Gerald smirked but didn't disagree. "I can't believe how fast you fly," he said to the dragon. It had snaked its head in to join them by the fire. "How many kingdoms have we flown over? Five or six? If we were on the ground, even with horses...this would have taken weeks. Months."

The dragon preened and looked smug. "I do have my moments," it agreed.

Omar threw tea leaves into the pot of melted snow and then said, hesitantly, "If you don't mind my asking...how did you get caught and collared? As fast as you are, I mean. I would never be able to catch you if you didn't want to be caught."

The dragon sighed. "I was young, and they had magic." It shrugged. "It's easy enough to catch a youngling, no matter the species. And at first, it's like nothing really happened. They catch us, collar us, and release us. We can live normally, for the most part, until one of you needs guarding. Then the spells are activated, and that's that. We're cut off from our own magic and from the power of human speech if we have it, and we're transported to the tower we're supposed to guard and then we're stuck there."

Omar echoed the dragon's sigh. "I can't believe they would do that. Just to get us married? I mean, I know it's important for alliances and that kind of thing. We can't simply date and flirt like normal people, we have to prove we're worthy of kingdoms and alliances and all that nonsense. But...there has to be a better way to do it!"

"That's the point of all this," Gerald reminded him, waving vaguely around the cave. "We're freeing the guardians so a better way can be developed."

Omar opened his mouth and closed it again.

"What?" Gerald asked.

"It's just... Well... What we're doing feels a little, um, haphazard. I mean, back there? If we had been even an hour later, Thierry would've already been rescued. The wolf would've been badly hurt, maybe even killed. Or simply gone—what happens, Dragon, when the royal you're guarding gets rescued? Do you get transported back home?"

"No. The spells tying us there and limiting our own powers are disabled again, but we have to find our own way home. And we're often half a continent away or more."

"And where the royals are left behind, like Elinore, eventually someone is going to realize the guardian is gone. And then what? They'll capture another one or send another one there, and then what? We go back? We keep moving from tower to tower, in an endless loop of freeing individual guardians? We need to do something more...systematic."

Gerald hunched his shoulders under the blanket. "I know. We're just...we're disrupting. We're not dismantling. I know. But I don't know what else to do." *Because I never know what to do. People are so much more complicated than animals... They want so many things I don't, I don't have the same motivations, I don't know what they want.*

"Stop that!" Omar said.

"What?"

"That look on your face—I can tell what you're thinking. You're criticizing yourself, aren't you? Well, there's no reason for it. You've already done more than anyone else has bothered to. We just need to stop and plan a little bit more. And," he said, with a shrug and a nod toward the mouth of the cave, "it looks like we'll be stopped for a while."

"How did you know what I was thinking?" Gerald asked.

"I told you. The look on your face. You looked the way you did when...well, when you were saying you didn't feel human. Looking like you think everything is your fault. And it's *not*."

Gerald hunched over further. "I know," he said softly. "I know it's not, but it feels that way."

"Well, it shouldn't. Look at everything you've done already! And we'll take care of the rest of it. The three of us—and your magic cousin—can definitely come up with a plan. I think what we need first is a replacement system."

Omar poured tea for himself and Gerald and handed him a cup, punching him gently on the shoulder as he did so. "So drink up, cheer up, and let's plot."

Gerald took the tea, took a sip, and smiled. Behind them, the dragon was starting to rumble contentedly. The cave was warm, the fire was bright, the storm was blocked away outside. His self-critical inner voice was drowned out by the dragon's purr and the crackle of wood.

"Let's plot," he agreed.

Chapter Eleven

"SO," GERALD SAID. "A replacement system. What do you mean by that?"

"Well, royals are still going to need to marry, right? So they're— we're—still going to need to meet other royals, still going to need to prove ourselves worthy of kingdoms and alliances and all that. If we get rid of the guardian system, the rescues will be much easier. They won't be a test of skill or proof of worth. The entire rescuer/rescuee system will fall apart. So, what are we going to put in its place?"

"A contest?" Gerald suggested.

"Hmm...maybe," Omar said. "What kind of contest?"

"Oh...I don't know. Each kingdom could have its own, maybe? Whenever a royal comes of age, each kingdom could decide its own contest to win their hand."

"I don't know if they would want to take responsibility for that," Omar said doubtfully. "Also, who would the suitors be, then?"

"The other—oh. They would be involved with their own contests. Okay. Yeah. So that won't work."

"It sounds like an interesting idea," the dragon interjected. "It just needs some tweaking."

"One big contest, maybe?"

"Of what, though?" Omar repeated.

"Whatever people are good at," Gerald sighed. "Lila could enter a weapons contest. Erick could enter a magic contest. You could enter a..."

"Enduring extreme temperatures contest?" Omar finished with a grin.

"Seriously, though. You could do weapons for sure. What else do you like?"

"Arguing."

Gerald rolled his eyes. "Diplomacy, then. Or debate. We could have a contest for everything! Cooking. Horseback riding. Singing. Metalworking. Dancing. Practical skills and royal skills and whatever else we can come up with. We could have open signups. Anything that gets at least two entrants could become a contest."

"That would cover the meeting other royals and proving worth aspects, definitely." Omar nodded approvingly. "It also sounds like a tremendous amount of fun. But how will it turn into pairings? Couplings and engagements?"

"Well...maybe not exactly contests, then, not in the strictest sense of the word. More like...like showcases. People show off what they can do, people find others who like the same things as they do, or who have skills that complement theirs...people make connections. That's how it works, isn't it?" Gerald looked to Omar for confirmation. "That's how people fall in love? They share interests, they find common ground?"

"It certainly helps," Omar said. "Especially if you want a real relationship. A real partnership, and not just...well." He made a crude gesture.

"Yeah. And...if we bring everyone together...there might even be someone else like me there, don't you think? Someone else who maybe wants a partnership but not the rest of it."

Omar opened his mouth and then thought better of what he was going to say. "Why not?" he said instead.

"*I* like this plan," the dragon said. "It sounds like it will be a fantastic spectacle. You will allow observers, won't you?"

"If it's you? Definitely."

"We'll need your help *getting* everyone there," Omar pointed out. "Wherever *there* ends up being. We'll have to collect everyone."

"Maybe we should stop disabling the tracking spells, then," Gerald said. "We might need them if *we* want to find everyone..."

Omar nodded. "You'd better write to Erick again. We can work out more of the details in the morning."

Omar was already yawning as he spoke, and he eyed the fire pensively. "I suppose it's probably safe to leave that burning as long as we don't sleep too close to it. Don't you think?"

"I don't know. It's not like it's in a proper fire pit..."

The bare stone of the cave floor meant they hadn't had to worry about the fire spreading to any nearby grass or brush. And that, coupled with their hurry to get the fire going, meant it was essentially burning away in the middle of the floor.

"If a log rolls off while we're sleeping, it could be very bad," Gerald finished.

Omar rubbed his eyes. "You're right. It's going to get very cold in here if we douse it, though. All right. I'll find some rocks or something while you write to Erick. Tell him *not* to spread the disabling spell, but to keep working on making it stick. Once we start gathering people up, we *are* going to want to take their spells off."

"Gathering people up," Gerald repeated thoughtfully. "That's going to be easier said than done, I think."

"Oh, definitely. But, hey, we can always abduct them. You've had practice…"

Omar ducked as Gerald tossed a handful of kindling at his head. "Start writing!" he called over his shoulder as he started scouring the cave for loose rocks. The dragon's blue mage light bobbed after him, floating over his head like a friendly will-o'-the-wisp.

Gerald shook his head in amusement and took out parchment and ink to do as he was told.

GERALD SLEPT FITFULLY that night. He woke up repeatedly, because he was too cold, the ground was too hard, the dragon was snoring…and sometimes for no reason he could determine. The dragon was sound asleep each time Gerald awoke, and although Omar stirred once or twice when Gerald crept over to feed the fire, he never came awake completely.

It's only me who can't sleep.

Gerald sighed. He wasn't sure what time it was, but he had a feeling it was close enough to dawn that there was little point in trying to go back to sleep. *Especially because I'll undoubtedly wake up again in thirty minutes. I don't even know why I can't sleep. The ground's not that uncomfortable, and it's not bothering Omar. I'm not having nightmares. I'm not even that worried about anything. Okay, the rescues haven't been going exactly according to plan, but they've still worked. We rescued Tska and the amarok. And now we have an even better plan. So why can't I sleep?*

He didn't have an answer for himself, and no one else was going to wake up and offer one. With another sigh, he dragged a blanket and his knapsack over to the fire and started going through the *Who's Who* guide, his lists of sequestered royals, and the maps.

The new plan means we need to gather everyone up; put them in one place; set up all these contests or showcases or whatever we're calling them; and we still need to free all the guardians. We...we could keep doing what we're doing, I guess. Going to the towers, freeing the guardians...take the royals with us afterward.

So we need somewhere to put them—and some way to keep them there.

I wonder how many relatives the dragon has...

Gerald counted up the pages in the *Who's Who* guide and rubbed his face. There were a hundred and twenty-five of them. One hundred and twenty-five royals to track down. Forget even getting them all into the same place, it was going to be a task and a half to find them in the first place. Only fifty of them were in towers. The other seventy-five were the rescuers, and they could be anywhere in the Thousand Kingdoms.

No wonder they put tracking spells on us. Deity. We have to stop disabling them. We need them to find everyone.

There was no response from Erick yet, but Gerald wrote to him again anyway. It was a short note this time, little more than a reiteration of what had already been said and an admonishment to write back as soon as he could.

He's been traveling too. He's been on the ground. Maybe he'll have an idea of where to put everyone. There's no point tracking them down until we have a place for the showcase.

Gerald turned back to the maps, looking for some bit of unclaimed land, or even a disputed bit of it, some borderland no one could agree on the owner of. He had a feeling not a single one of the Thousand Kingdoms would be open to hosting their showcase, not when it meant undercutting the entire current system. Not until they proved it worked. Not until they could turn it into a recurring event, for everyone who had turned eighteen since the end of the previous showcase, and for everyone who wasn't yet paired off.

Which will be at least one person, this year, since there's an odd number of us. He pushed down the automatic thought that the lone leftover would be him. *There's probably going to be at least half a dozen people who don't find a pairing. I didn't even look at the ratios of princesses and princes and princexes, let alone look at anyone's preferences. I only counted people. And even if everyone except the odd one out*—this time he wasn't able to keep from assuming it would be him—*pairs up on paper...there are still personalities to deal with.* He thought of the ridiculously socially inept letters he had gotten from Lukas before he had escaped from the tower and tried to imagine the type of person Lukas would impress at a showcase. He couldn't.

Gerald shook his head. *Ratios and personalities and all of that isn't going to matter one bit if we can't find somewhere to host this!* He went back to the maps and decided he wasn't going to think about or worry about any other aspect of the entire plan until he found a place that was big enough for all of them, and was politically and environmentally viable, and was private enough they wouldn't end up with curious neighbors from nearby villages, towns, cities, or farms stopping by to see what was happening, but also was close enough to somewhere they could get food and supplies.

Of course with a dragon around, "close enough" becomes quite a relative term.

Gerald pored over the maps until his eyes began to cross and he had filled two pieces of parchment front and back with notes and lists of what they needed and what they needed to avoid.

I'll think better after I have some tea, he decided. The water in the barrel had thawed nicely over the course of the night and he was able to fill a pot without having to squeeze past the dragon—who was still asleep and snoring—to get some snow to melt.

When the water was boiling and the tea leaves were steeping, Omar started to stir, his nose twitching. "That smells good," he said through a yawn. "Pour me some?"

"Sure."

Gerald parceled out the tea while Omar dragged himself out of his nest of blankets. He moved stiffly over to the fire, rubbing absently at his hip. "I don't care what people say about firm surfaces being good for your back... I want a mattress tonight."

"I'll see what I can do," Gerald said, hiding a smile as he handed Omar a tin mug.

Omar looked at the mess of papers, inks, quills, and maps spread out on the cave floor and raised an eyebrow. "You've been busy this morning," he observed. "What have you been working on?"

Gerald filled him in while he prepared some porridge for their breakfast.

"Yeah, that's a puzzle," Omar agreed. "We really need to set everything up first, and then recruit everyone. But if we recruited people first, they could help set things up."

"I know," Gerald sighed. "We need to balance it."

"Well, Erick's already recruited, right?" Omar said. "What about your twi—uh, what about Lila?"

Gerald shook his head. "Even if she liked the idea—and I doubt she would, she's been wanting to go on this rescue quest for *years*—she would oppose it solely because it's *my* idea. What about you? Siblings, friends?"

It was Omar's turn to shake his head. "I don't know anyone in the current group. Not well, anyway." He took another bite of breakfast and then said, "This porridge is excellent, by the way. I don't think I've ever had *good* porridge."

Gerald smiled. "I just seasoned it, that's all. People always serve it plain and then wonder why it tastes like grout."

The dragon roused itself then. "What's this about food?" it asked.

"Do you eat porridge?" Gerald asked.

"I could."

"Have at it, then." Gerald pushed the leftovers toward the dragon, and it quickly cleaned out the pot and then licked its chops speculatively.

"Not bad, not bad," it said. "A nice nutty flavor. Rich. A bit of meat would make it better, of course."

"Of course," Gerald echoed, straight-faced.

"Is it still snowing?" Omar asked, and the dragon shifted to look outside.

"Yes, but only lightly. Although...the sky does not look promising. There are more black clouds coming."

"Do you think we should try to beat the storm?" Gerald asked. "Or should we stay here for another day?"

"We-e-ell," the dragon said slowly, "I overheard some of your conversation and it seems like we don't currently have a destination in mind. Is that right?"

Gerald scuffed his toe on the ground. "We-e-ell," he echoed, "That depends on what you think of all this. I mean, our first priority was freeing the other guardians. If we change things around like this...we'll still free them, of course, but it won't be right away."

The dragon let out a porridge-scented sigh. "We've survived this system for several hundred years. We can survive a bit more delay. Especially if it means we'll be the last ones enslaved by it. If we take the system down, these will be the last guardians who need to be freed."

"Then no. We don't currently have a destination in mind."

"I suggest we stay in, then," the dragon said. "I *could* probably beat the storm. If it were only me, I might risk it. But you two are so *fragile*."

"I vote for not freezing to death," Omar said. "Let's stay. We can get a good plan squared away and get out of here tomorrow without worrying about the snow."

"All right," Gerald said. "You won't get your mattress tonight, though."

Omar made a face but said, "I expect I'll live."

"I'm going to hunt up something more substantial, then," the dragon said, standing up as it spoke. "I won't go far," it said over its shoulder. "Yell if anything tries to eat you."

As soon as the dragon moved out of the cave mouth, the ambient temperature dropped by several degrees. A breath of wind blew in and sent Gerald scrambling after the loose papers that got caught up in the breeze.

One of which started chiming as soon as Gerald grabbed it.

"I'll get the rest," Omar said, setting his empty bowl aside. "See what Erick thinks of our new plan."

Gerald dripped ink on the parchment and waited for his cousin's response to appear while Omar scrambled around the cave after the rest of the loose papers. By the time he returned with them—and set his empty bowl on top of the pile as a paperweight—Erick's response was fully written out and waiting to be read.

> *Meathead,*
>
> *Good timing with the change of plan! I tweaked the disabling spell to make it "contagious" and I was going to test it out this morning. I guess I'll hold off on that for the moment. I haven't reached Princess Nedi yet, or her guardian. When they say "Enchanted" Forest, they aren't kidding. I can't imagine anyone without some skill in magic being able to find their way through. I expect I* will *be able to manage it, but it's going to take a bit more planning than I had thought.*

Speaking of, it sounds like you've been doing quite a lot of that yourself. I like your new idea. For one thing, it would mean I could stop eating my own cooking.

In all seriousness, though, it seems like quite a practical suggestion. I know you've had objections to the current set up, above and beyond your own desire not to participate in it, I mean, and I think your showcase system addresses most of them. I also don't see why the Council would object to it since it will accomplish the same aims... But I agree this should be a case of "do it first and get permission later". But for most of the kingdoms, I imagine as long as their precious child comes home betrothed, they won't much care where that betrothal occurred.

I don't much care myself! And as I said...I won't have to eat my own cooking. Or fight my way through an enchanted forest. Or past a unicorn.

So I guess the question is: How can I help?

Yours,

Erick

"There," Omar said with satisfaction. "I told you, you had a convert."

"Yeah, but what am I supposed to tell him? How *can* he help?"

Omar rubbed his chin and said, "Well...it seems to me he'd be quite handy getting things set up. It's not merely finding a place to hold the showcase. We'd need to house everyone and their horses; we'd need to feed them, and have somewhere to cook; we'd need a jousting run, and an archery ground; a stage for plays or concerts; booths for people to display handicrafts... A bit of magic would come in handy while we're trying to construct everything. The dragon can do magic too, of course, but we'll need the dragon for transport and heavy lifting, and I wouldn't want to tire it out."

"I'm getting tired just thinking about it," Gerald said with resignation. "All right. I think you're right. We should rendezvous with Erick—and anyone he's run across who he thinks will be helpful and discreet—and start construction. At least of the housing and spaces for food storage and preparation. As soon as we have somewhere to put people and a way to feed them, we can go find them and bring them back with the dragon. Erick can supervise the people we bring and get them to help finish construction while we collect the rest. Maybe some of the guardians we free can help with the transportation, too."

"That's settled, then," Omar said with a grin. "So...where are we going to build all this?"

Gerald sighed and handed him a map. "You tell me."

THEY HADN'T MADE any progress in finding a suitable location by the time the dragon came back and settled in the cave opening once more.

"Good hunting?" Gerald asked.

"Not bad," it replied, showing its teeth. "But the snow is coming down harder now and most of the prey has gone to ground."

"Don't say that word," Omar groaned.

"Prey?"

"*Ground.* Unless you know where we can find some to put this showcase."

The dragon cocked its head thoughtfully to the side. "I might. How do you feel about hosting it in dragon territory?"

They exchanged glances and Gerald shrugged. "If the dragons don't object, neither do I. We've gotten along just fine with you, after all."

"Oh, I don't think they'll object. After all, they want this system to end as much as we do. No one likes losing their hatchlings. We'll fly there in the morning and get it sorted out."

Omar folded the maps up with an expression of relief. "Thank goodness. That was really the last stumbling block—at least for the moment." He and Gerald filled the dragon in on the rest of their plans, and it nodded approval.

"I can fetch your cousin after we talk to my relatives," it said. "Quite a few of us dragons are magic-users, and we already have guest caves and the like where we can store and feed you royals. I think we can have things ready to go in just a few weeks."

"And then back to crisscrossing the Thousand Kingdoms in search of everyone," Gerald said with resignation.

"As long as we leave the tracking spells on until we find them, that won't be too hard," the dragon said gently. "Especially if some of my relatives decide to help with that as well."

"Not by themselves!" Gerald said hurriedly. "We don't need to start up any stories about bloodthirsty rampaging dragon."

"Of course not. But if I take you, and someone else takes Erick—"

"And Erick might be bringing some people with him, too," Omar broke in. "And you know how fast our dragon flies. If there's even one or two others helping us, we'll gather everyone up in no time."

"I suppose so," Gerald said.

"This is *your* idea," Omar reminded him. "You should be happier about it."

"I will be when we're actually *doing* something," Gerald said. "Until then, I'm going to be worrying about everything that can go wrong."

"That's the spirit," Omar said wryly.

Gerald made a face at him. "I'm not *choosing* to worry. I just...am. I can't help it."

"We'll have to distract you, then." Omar looked around the cave for something to do, but not much was on offer. With a sigh, he looked at the pile of supplies. "I don't suppose you have a deck of cards in there?"

"I'm not sure," Gerald admitted. "There might be. We put most of the contents of the tower in there, minus the furniture."

Omar got up and began riffling through the bags and boxes. "I'll find something to do, don't worry."

"I thought this was supposed to keep me from worrying," Gerald said with a smirk. "Not give me something else to worry about."

Omar rolled his eyes and then straightened up with a triumphant exclamation. He tossed a pack of cards at Gerald, who caught them, opened them, and started to shuffle.

Before long, they had a three-way poker tournament going—with the dragon using a small spell to move its cards around—and Gerald was too busy trying to keep from losing his stake to fret about their upcoming trip to the dragonlands.

Chapter Twelve

THEY WOKE THE next morning to frigid temperatures but clear blue skies. "Good weather for flying," the dragon said, sounding pleased.

"Good weather for freezing," Omar said darkly. Gerald elbowed him and he subsided.

After a quick breakfast, Gerald and Omar packed everything away, bundled up, and took their places on the dragon's back.

As soon as they were settled, Omar brushed the snow off his boots and Gerald couldn't help but laugh. "You look exactly like the castle cats," Gerald explained. "They can't stand to have snow on their paws either, and they shake it off with exactly that annoyed expression on their faces."

"They sound like very sensible creatures," Omar said. He surveyed the snow-covered mountains surrounding them and added, "It still *looks* very pretty. I'm happy to *look* at it. But I've had my fill of *experiencing* it."

"I can't say I blame you," Gerald said. Then, as the dragon prepared to take off, he asked, "How far away are the dragonlands? I didn't see them on my map."

"They aren't *on* the map," the dragon replied. "There are boundary spells that keep them hidden. Historically, we haven't had the best relations with humans. It's best to remain apart."

"Um...are you sure this is a good idea, then?"

"Oh, well, it won't hurt to try. It's not like anyone will try to eat you," it added, in a tone Gerald thought was probably meant to be reassuring. "Anyway, assuming the weather holds...and we weren't blown further off track than I think...it should be about a four-hour flight from here. East by southeast."

"Is it warm there?" Omar asked hopefully.

"We're fire-breathers. What do you think?" the dragon asked sardonically, and then it launched itself skyward without waiting for a response.

Gerald, unprepared, gasped in surprise but he privately had to admit he was adjusting to the dragon's vertical takeoffs. *Next time maybe I'll even open my eyes.*

"Hey," Gerald said when they leveled out. "If the borders are magically protected and the dragonlands are hidden, how do you get captured to serve as guardians?"

The dragon let out a puff of air and said, "We don't all stay inside the borders. I told you we don't tend to form partnerships or close relationships. We like our space, and when you get to be this size, you like a lot of space. That's part of the reason I think the others will let you use the land. If this scheme works, we'll all be able to leave without fearing someone will put a collar around our necks."

Gerald nodded, unable to find an appropriate response. His gaze landed once again on the band of discolored, misshapen scales that wrapped around the dragon's neck and throat. The removal of the collar had allowed the dragon to use its own magic to speed its healing, and the wounds left by the collar were completely closed now—but the scars would always be there.

They flew in silence for most of the morning.

They were over a forest when the dragon decided to stop for lunch. A river ran through the woods, carving a gap in the canopy, and the dragon flew down through it to land in the clearing by the bank. The snowy mountains were leagues behind them, and the temperature had increased enough that Omar and Gerald had shed their gloves and heavy cloaks.

"It's not much further now," the dragon said as the princes climbed down and stretched their legs. "But I thought you might want to put your best foot forward when we get there, rather than arriving hungry and dirty."

Gerald looked at himself self-consciously. Wrestling with a wolf, flying through a snowstorm, and spending two nights in a cave hadn't exactly left him in pristine condition, and Omar wasn't in a much better state.

"I suspect the same is true of you," Omar said to the dragon. "You wanted an excuse to stop and polish your scales, huh?"

The dragon sniffed haughtily. "There's nothing wrong with making a good impression. Now, if you'll be so good as to unharness me, I believe I will go for a swim."

Gerald glanced over at the river and quickly looked away, his face reddening with the memory of the scene he'd made at the last river they'd stopped by.

When the dragon had been unburdened and started splashing around, Omar turned to Gerald as the Andinian prince rummaged through their supplies for a suitable lunch.

"We do want to make a good impression," he said carefully.

"I know," Gerald said. "I'll bathe after you're done."

Omar nodded and let the subject drop. He stretched out on the ground in a patch of dappled sun and said, "This is close to perfect weather, I think. Warm, but not unpleasantly so. What's the weather like in Andine, anyway? You mentioned you get snow."

"In the winter," Gerald acknowledged. "It's not like in the mountains, where there's snow year-round. We've got very distinct seasons. We get, oh, three or four big snowstorms every winter, and it's cold enough that the ponds freeze over for skating. Then in the spring, it rains for three solid weeks, but afterward, everything turns brilliantly green. It's hot in the summer, not like in your desert, but hot enough you know about it. I probably spend half the summer fishing or swimming because it's so much cooler by the water."

Omar started to ask a question and then cut himself off, but Gerald had a pretty good idea of what Omar had been about to say. "Swimming is different," he explained. "We have swimming clothes in Andine. No one's naked."

"So you swim with other people?"

"Sometimes. If they're around." Gerald shrugged. "I don't avoid them, but unless Erick's visiting..." He shrugged again. "I don't have many friends."

"Well, you've got at least one more now."

"Two," the dragon interjected as it returned from its bath.

Gerald smiled and ducked his head. "Next summer you two can go swimming with me, then." He tilted his head at the dragon, considering. "I *think* you would fit in the pond."

The dragon harrumphed and Gerald grinned.

"I'm only joking, I'm sure you'll fit," he said conciliatorily. He picked up a towel and started drying off the dragon's scales, even though it was already steaming gently as the excess water evaporated. As Omar walked off with another towel and a change of clothes, Gerald gave up on his futile chore. He set the towel down and dropped to the ground, leaning against the dragon like they were back at the tower.

"How long has it been since you were last home?" he asked the dragon, tilting his head up to meet its eyes.

The dragon let out one of its gusty, sulfur-scented sighs. "Not all that long, by draconic reckoning. But long enough by yours."

"I'm sorry."

"It's not your fault."

Gerald nodded. "Not mine, personally. But my species'. They won't apologize, so I'll apologize for them."

"Staying away from home is different for dragons," it said gently. "It's not...not as harsh as it would be for you."

As it will *be, you mean,* Gerald thought, his stomach clenching with the realization that, when all was said and done, no matter how it turned out, he was unlikely to find a warm reception in Andine. He stopped himself from speaking the thought aloud, but the dragon sensed his suddenly somber mood.

"It will be good to see them," the dragon acknowledged. "But—what is that saying you humans have? When you're not there, you want to be there; when you get there, you want to be where you left. It will be good to see them, but it will be good to keep traveling with you as well."

Gerald let out a startled laugh. "Oh, Dragon. I wouldn't have been hurt—I won't be hurt—if you wanted to stay in your own home territory. I was just thinking about, well, my own homecoming. Whenever that ends up being."

The dragon nuzzled him gently. "Don't fret before the shell cracks," it said wisely.

Gerald blinked at him.

"We'll cross that bridge when we come to it, it means," Omar said. He was clean and dressed, with his towel draped over his shoulders to catch the water still dripping from his damp hair. "So don't worry about it now." He nodded toward the river and added, "Go on, then, go clean up. We won't look."

AN HOUR LATER, they were fast approaching the dragonlands, at least according to the dragon. Gerald couldn't distinguish any changes in the landscape as they approached the putative border: everything was hilly and rocky, with patches of bare earth intermingling with piles of boulders and sections of sere grasses. There was no sign of other dragons.

"Make sure you're touching my scales with some bit of bare skin," the dragon called over its shoulder. "Otherwise the spell won't let you through."

Gerald blanched at the thought of hitting a magical barrier—or *any* barrier—at the speed and height the dragon was currently flying at. He let go of the harness and slapped both palms against the dragon's back. Next to him, Omar hurriedly did the same.

The dragon murmured something under its breath in a sibilant-filled language, and then a tingling, buzzing sensation spread over Gerald from head to toe. All the hair rose up on the back of his neck, but as unsettling as the sensation was, it didn't hurt. And it passed quickly, there and gone almost before Gerald could even categorize it.

"What was *that*?" Omar asked, sounding as rattled as Gerald felt.

"The barrier spell," the dragon said. "It didn't hurt you, did it?"

"No-o," Omar said, but he drew the word out as if he wasn't quite sure of his answer.

"No," Gerald agreed. "But I'm not in a hurry to go through it again."

Before the dragon could respond, a gout of fire erupted out of the air right above their heads. The dragon immediately stooped into a dive while Gerald and Omar threw themselves flat against its back. Another burst of flame spouted out of thin air, once again aimed at the princes. Gerald screamed as it caught his leg and the dragon whirled around and began shouting in the same hissing language it had used to move through the barrier spell.

Three other dragons winked into visibility, all dripping flame from their jaws. All four dragons immediately began screaming in that same incomprehensible language. Gerald didn't know what they were saying and was in too much pain to care. His leg throbbed dreadfully and even though he had slapped the flames out, singing his hands in the process, it still felt like the fire was licking at his skin. Omar pushed his hands away from the wound and upended their water pouch over the cracked and bloody skin. The water steamed and Gerald drew his breath in with a pained hiss.

It *hurt* and he could think of nothing but the pain, which was getting steadily worse instead of better. He vaguely heard Omar talking, but he couldn't focus on the words or respond in any way. "It hurts," he tried to say, and then his eyes rolled back in his head as he fainted.

Chapter Thirteen

GERALD WOKE SLOWLY and with a great effort. It was a struggle to fight through the semi-conscious haze, to break through the barrier between sleep and consciousness. *Why fight it?* he wondered. It would have been easier to simply slip back under. But something felt wrong. It felt like he was drowning in his dreams and he fought to break free of them. The struggle seemed endless but then, in a last panicked burst, he fought his way back to full consciousness.

The pain hit him immediately, a sledgehammer against his raw nerves.

He gasped and instinctively tried to curl up in a protective ball but doing so jolted his leg and he screamed from the pain. It felt like all of his skin was being ripped away.

His scream woke Omar, who was there in an instant, leaning over him with wide, frightened eyes. "Gerald! It's okay, it'll be okay. What can I do?"

Gerald gritted his teeth until the pain faded enough to speak. "Make it stop hurting," he gasped. The waves started washing over him again, trying to pull him back under, but he fought to stay awake.

"I'll get help," Omar said but Gerald grabbed his arm as he turned to go.

"Don't leave me alone," he begged. Tears of pain were running down his face.

"But I don't know what to do!" Omar cried. "I can't—I can't make it stop hurting. I have to get help."

Gerald shut his eyes as another shock of pain radiated up from his leg. If he let Omar go, sleep would pull him under again and he would drown in it...but at least it hadn't hurt when he was asleep. It hadn't hurt, but he knew—somehow—it would kill him.

With an effort, he loosened his grip on Omar's arm. "Hurry," he gasped.

Omar took off running, shouting for the dragon. Gerald gritted his teeth and looked around, trying to figure out where he was. There was a mattress under him, a real one; the walls around him were stone, but he wasn't in an ordinary cave. He didn't know how he had gotten there. The last thing he remembered was a rush of fire. The memory sent another wave of pain jolting up his leg and he bit his tongue to keep from crying out. The coppery taste of blood filled his mouth.

Omar ran back in, gasping for breath. Gerald couldn't say how long he'd been gone. "Calin's coming," Omar panted, reaching out and taking Gerald's hand, giving it a reassuring squeeze. Gerald didn't know who Calin was, but he nodded anyway. He didn't trust himself to speak.

After another disjointed interval of time, another figure came running into the room. Disoriented, Gerald thought it was a statue, that he was hallucinating a statue come to life, but as it came closer, he realized it was a living being—gray hair, skin, eyes, and all.

"Calin!" Omar said in relief.

Calin leaned over Gerald and snapped, "You're fighting the healing spell! Why?"

Gerald blinked at her and tried to fight past the pain long enough to respond. After another timeless struggle, he managed to say, "I'm drowning." A bit of blood dripped out of the corner of his mouth as he spoke, and Omar widened his eyes in panic.

"We have to move him," Calin said. "He needs the healer and the dragons can't fit in here."

"I'll carry him," Omar said. "Lead the way."

Gerald cringed away when Omar started to slide an arm under his shoulders. "No!" he cried. "No, it hurts!"

"I know, I know," Omar said soothingly. "But they'll make it stop hurting. We have to get you there. I'll be careful."

And he was, doing his best not to jar Gerald's leg and not to touch any of the bandages wrapped around him, but Gerald still screamed when he lifted him off the bed, blanket and all.

"It's okay!" Omar said. "It's okay, I've got you." Then, to Calin, "Let's go!"

He hurried after her, murmuring reassurances to Gerald, who only moaned in response.

When they reached the dragons, who were crammed together in the reception area, Gerald was breathing in ragged gasps and was only semiconscious. Omar set him down as gently as he could, keeping the blanket between Gerald and the stone floor and then sitting behind him to hold him upright.

"He's fighting the spell," the unfamiliar dragon—the healer—said. "He shouldn't be awake, or in this much pain."

"Cast it again!" their dragon growled, mantling its wings in agitation.

"He said he was drowning," Calin said at the same time the healer shook its head.

"He's having a reaction to the spell," the healer said. "I have to take it off entirely. We have herbs for the pain. Calin?"

She was already rummaging through her basket of supplies. "This is already prepared," she said, drawing out a jar. "How much?"

The healer cocked its head in thought and then said, "Two—no, three drops."

"That much?"

"He'll need it when the spell comes off."

Calin pried Gerald's jaws open with hands as strong and cool as the stone they resembled and used a hollow reed to drip the milky white liquid down his throat, drop by careful drop.

After several long, agonizing minutes, Gerald's breathing calmed and some of the rigid tension left his muscles.

Then, with a gesture, the healer pulled the rest of its spell away and Gerald's eyes popped open. "Oh!" he said in surprise. "I can breathe...but...oh, it *hurts* again."

"I'm sorry," the healer said. "The herbs are slower to take effect. We cannot give you more so soon."

Gerald nodded and leaned back against Omar, who wrapped his arms around Gerald. Gerald could feel his hands shaking as the adrenaline began to wear off. "What went wrong with the healing spell?" Omar demanded.

"Nothing," the healer said, affronted. "The spell worked perfectly. But it did not...agree...with your friend." It turned its attention back to Gerald. "Have you had any major healing spells before?" it asked.

"No," Gerald said drowsily. "I've always been healthy. I've never even broken a bone."

"Not a built-up resistance, then," it said. "Perhaps it's the draconic, hmm, *accent* to the spell?"

"Another design flaw!" their dragon broke in. "Honestly, you *humans*!"

"Does he need a spell?" Omar asked, choosing to ignore the dragon's outburst. "Won't the herbs work?"

The healer exchanged a long look with Calin before responding. "Well. He won't die without a healing spell, if that's what you're asking. But it will be a very long, very slow, very painful recovery without magic. The pain potion has to be used cautiously. Too much of it will stop his heart. Not enough, and the burn will be agonizing. And the burn is quite severe. Without a spell...even with a spell, there will be lasting damage...not to mention the possibility of infection."

Omar's arms tightened around Gerald with each word the healer spoke. "Does your cousin Erick know any healing spells?" Omar asked Gerald. "If the problem is the draconic cast to the magic..."

"I don't know," Gerald said. His eyes were starting to close again. The medicine was chasing the worst of the pain away and exhaustion was replacing it. He forced his answer out slowly. "Probably. He seems to know...a little of...everything. But he's leagues...and leagues away."

"I'll go fetch him," the dragon offered, turning toward the exit even as it spoke.

"You'll scare him half to death if you do," the healer responded. "Humans don't like dragons dropping in unannounced."

"I'll take Omar. Humans don't mind other humans."

"I can't leave Gerald here by himself!" Omar protested.

"I'll take care of him," Calin said. "I've been trained for it." The unspoken corollary—*and you haven't*—echoed loudly in the air.

The healer nodded. "Calin has been my assistant for a long time and is more familiar with tending those without wings and scales."

"How long will it take?" he asked the dragon.

"If you can sleep on my back while I fly...we can get to the Enchanted Forest in a day and a half. It shouldn't take long to persuade his cousin. Then a day and a half back."

Three days, at least. Make it four. Omar hesitated. "There's no one closer?"

"There are no humans in the dragonlands. The other dragons can't help any more than I can, and the piedlings have no healing magic. We need a human, and the closest towns are a half day's flight. I cannot know if they have healers in them, let alone if they would agree to travel to the dragonlands...or if the other dragons would allow them in. We've agreed to allow the royals. This cousin is the only royal healer I know of."

But four days...anything could happen in four days. Omar didn't want to leave Gerald for that long, not when he was hurt and in pain. "The two-way parchment," he said suddenly. "What if I write to Erick, warn him you're coming? You won't be unannounced. And he already knows we're traveling with a dragon..."

The healer shook its head before their dragon could respond. "And what will his reaction be when he learns why a dragon has come seeking him? Because another dragon has grievously injured his cousin? We've seen already how the young jump to conclusions. Both of you go or neither of you does." It softened its tone to add, "He will sleep for most of the time you're gone. And when he is not asleep, he will be muddled by the pain and the herbs. If you were here, he would only rarely be aware of it. The sooner you go, the sooner you will be back."

"Go," Gerald echoed faintly. Omar jumped—he had thought Gerald was asleep. "I'll be okay."

"I'll take good care of him," Calin said again. "My sisters will help. We will make a bed for him out here, so the healer can supervise as closely as needed."

Omar looked from Gerald to Calin to the dragons and then back to Gerald. His eyes were still closed, and Omar thought he might have slipped into sleep for real this time. "All right," he conceded. "All right. I'll get the harness."

Chapter Fourteen

GERALD SPENT THE next three days drifting in and out of consciousness. Even when he was awake, the pain and the medicine badly muddled his awareness. The dragon healer checked in on him regularly, but the actual tending was done by its assistant, who took care of changing his bandages, dosing him with potions, and performing all the other tasks the dragon was too large to manage comfortably. Gerald thought Calin was remarkably efficient until he finally noticed there were several different gray beings tending to him. They all looked like Calin.

"Of course they look like me," she said, laughing. "They're my sisters."

Gerald thought of Lila and Vani. "My sisters don't look anything like me."

"It's different for us piedlings," she said. "'Sister' doesn't mean the same thing for us."

"I don't understand."

"Piedlings are female. All of us. We don't reproduce the way you humans do. We form sisters out of ourselves, by ourselves. My sisters are individuals, but they are me, too. It helps us work in harmony. Our group is in charge of this suite of caverns; our affinity with stone created them, and we tend them and those residing in them. The dragons share their land and their protection with us, so we help them in return by carving new caverns, tending the livestock, or gathering and drying herbs."

Gerald blinked at her. "Oh."

Calin smiled and patted him on the shoulder. "Don't worry about it. Just concentrate on getting better."

He slipped back into sleep before he could ask anything more.

THE NEXT TIME he woke up, there was a soft, shapeless stuffed toy in his hand. He squinted at it in confusion and the piedling sitting at his bedside smiled and said, "You kept reaching out for something in your sleep. You stopped once we gave you something to hold."

Gerald returned her smile and drifted off to sleep again.

WHAT WOKE HIM next was an urgent need to visit the bathroom. "I'll get a bedpan," Calin said after he mumbled an embarrassed request for help.

Gerald went white at the thought. "No, please, just help me to the bathroom."

"You can't walk!"

"Yes, I can," he said stubbornly. The pain was still there, but he was aware of it without really feeling it. He threw the blanket aside and started to sit up before looking at himself and stopping abruptly. "Where—where are my pants?"

"We had to take them off to bandage your leg. They were essentially burnt off anyway."

"I can't walk around without pants on!"

"You can't walk around at *all!*" Calin snapped, but she handed him a robe even as she said it.

Gerald pulled it on and then tried to swing his legs over the side of the bed. The pain hit him like a hammer when he tried to move his right leg, but he gritted his teeth and forced his feet to the floor.

"Stop it!" Calin scolded. "You're going to hurt yourself!"

"Then—help—me," Gerald said, forcing each word out painfully through his gritted teeth. He used the bed frame and the wall to lever himself to his feet and he stood there, swaying and sweating and glaring at the piedling. *I can't go any further than this*, he admitted to himself. He couldn't put any weight on his burned leg.

"Humans!" Calin threw her arms up in disgust and called for a sister. By leaning heavily on the two of them and hopping, Gerald was able to get across the cavern to the bathroom. The sisters waited impatiently outside the door and grumbled to each other about uncooperative patients until Gerald said they could come in to help him back.

But the thought of crossing the room again was a daunting one. Calin took one look at his face and threw her arms up again, apparently having come to the same conclusion.

"I should leave you in here," she scolded. "You could sleep in the bathtub."

"Calin!" her sister said, scandalized.

"What? You could do with a bath, you know," she added to Gerald. "You've been wearing those clothes for days while you've been sweating with a fever. And we're here anyway... Shall we help you into the tub?"

"I'll change my clothes if you bring me some clean ones, but I'm not getting undressed in front of you." The thought of bathing in front of them was possibly even more horrifying than the thought of using a bedpan had been. He squirmed internally, then, wondering what had been done about all that while he slept and drifted in and out of fever dreams. *I don't want to know*, he decided. *I'm awake now and I'm keeping all my clothes on!*

"But why not?" the sister asked, sounding honestly confused.

"It's because we're female," Calin said impatiently. "Humans have male and female, remember? He's male. Females and males aren't supposed to undress in front of each other."

"Oh," she said doubtfully. "That seems impractical." She seemed to be referring to the entire idea of different sexes and not simply the nudity taboo, and if he had been in a bit less pain, Gerald might have found it amusing.

Calin ignored her and studied Gerald. "This is the longest you've stayed awake yet, but I still doubt you could bathe yourself now without falling asleep and drowning. We'll have to make do with clean clothes. We'll change the bedsheets, too."

After Gerald was dressed in a fresh shirt and undergarments, with the robe pulled back on and tied around his waist, he felt a little more able to face the long hop back to his bed. His burned leg was starting to throb and lying down was sounding like a better and better idea with every passing moment.

"How long *have* I been asleep for?" Gerald asked as the piedlings helped him back across the caverns.

"Most of three days," Calin replied.

"So Omar and the dragon might be back today?" he asked, perking up at the idea. "That's what the dragon said, right? Three days? I don't really remember very well," he admitted. "I only remember it hurting, and them leaving..."

"Well, they're coming back," she said, "don't fuss. I don't know about today, though; more likely tomorrow. Now, please, lie down already! You've gone completely white. Take your medicine and go back to sleep. I don't know why I let you talk me into letting you up in the first place. Next time, it's the bedpan!"

Instead, there was a wheeled chair sitting next to his bed when he woke up again. Calin glared at him, daring him to comment, and Gerald wisely kept his mouth shut.

HE SLEPT AND woke and slept again and the piedlings changed his bandages twice before he heard the familiar sounds of the dragon in flight. He had barely enough time to prop himself up on his elbows before the dragon swept inside with three figures waving from its back.

Three?

Omar was sliding down the dragon's side almost even before it came to a complete halt, and Erick wasn't far behind him. The third person remained on its back and Gerald was too distracted by the others to give their identity much thought.

He hadn't realized how much he had missed Omar and the dragon until they were in front of him again. The dragon leaned over his bed anxiously and Gerald wrapped his arms as far around its head as he could reach to hug. It nudged him gently and, reassured Gerald wasn't at death's door, moved back far enough to be out of the way—but still close enough for Gerald to hear its reassuring, cat-like purr.

A pair of piedlings had brought extra chairs over to his bedside for the princes, but neither of them made a move to sit down. They both hovered nervously over Gerald exactly the way the dragon had done. Omar seemed to want to follow the dragon's example and move in for a hug, but after a hesitation, he simply clasped Gerald's arm.

"How are you?" he asked anxiously. "You're still pale. Does it hurt a lot?"

"It hurts enough," Gerald admitted. "The medicine helps."

"I can't believe *you're* the one who got burned by a dragon," Erick said, shaking his head. "I would've put money on it happening to Lila—I might have even *paid* money for it to happen to Lila—but you?" His tone was light, but there was worry in his normally mischievous green eyes.

"Tease me about it later, all right?" Gerald said. "Like after you cast a healing spell. *Can* you cast a healing spell?"

"Of course," Erick scoffed. "I mean, I never studied them, but the principle is fairly straightforward...in theory. I'll warn you, I can definitely deal with your pain and the fever, but as for the wound itself... Well, let's take a look, shall we?" he said, reaching for the blanket covering Gerald's legs.

"I *just* changed his bandages," Calin said severely. "You shouldn't need to take them off to cast your spell. Can't you feel the damage with your magic?"

"Yes, well, it's easier with a visual aid," Erick said. "I told you, I haven't studied this...but there's no reason why I can't do it the hard way," he added as the piedling continued to fix him with a fierce stare.

"You don't really want to see it anyway," Gerald said. "It's disgusting." He had watched the piedlings change the bandages in one of his more clearheaded periods and he had been regretting it ever since.

"Burns usually are," Erick said absently. "Now hush."

He closed his eyes in concentration and Omar, Gerald, and Calin all watched him intently.

For a long moment, nothing seemed to be happening. Then Gerald gasped and sat upright as the ever-present ache the medicine never quite reached vanished abruptly.

Erick opened his eyes and smiled with satisfaction before swaying unsteadily on his feet. Omar caught his arm and guided him into a chair while Calin scolded him about overreaching himself. "But he does look much better," she admitted grudgingly as she looked back at Gerald.

"I feel much better," he said, moving his leg experimentally. There was no sudden stab of pain and he grinned and reached over to clasp Erick's hand in thanks. His cousin murmured something incoherent in response and Calin frowned.

"The healer is going to want to talk to you, in great detail, about what type of spell you used," Calin warned Erick. "And you clearly put too much of yourself into it, whatever it was. You better rest now or you won't survive the interrogation."

She sent one of her sisters to fetch the healer, adding to the rest of them, "We better have someone here who's awake and familiar with healing spells in case Gerald has a bad reaction again."

The ever-efficient piedlings soon had Erick tucked into a cot nearby and he was asleep within minutes. Omar covered a yawn of his own. "We flew pretty much nonstop to get back here," he explained. "It's hard to sleep on dragonback. Even with the harnesses, you can't quite convince yourself you're not going to fall."

"It's even harder to sleep when you're the one flying," the dragon pointed out.

"You can sleep now," Gerald told it fondly. "You must be exhausted."

The dragon sniffed. "It was important to hurry. But yes, now that you mention it, I am a bit tired..." It trailed off and soon its familiar rumbling snores were echoing off the cavern walls.

By the time the healer arrived, the only ones still awake were Gerald and Calin. The cavern was huge from a human's perspective, but their dragon was taking up a good deal of space and the healer took up even more. It took some maneuvering for it to get settled without stepping on any of the people, piedlings, or furniture scattered around the suddenly crowded space.

It took in the scene and grumbled half-heartedly about the crowding and the fact that virtually everyone it wanted to talk to was asleep. "I suppose I shouldn't wake them," it sighed. "All that flying... Well. *You* do look better, at least," it added approvingly to Gerald. "Fever's gone?"

"It seems to be," Calin said. "I don't know if the spell specifically targeted the infection or if it was a general boost to the overall rate of healing, which in turn caused the infection to clear, but his temperature is much better now."

"Hmm... I can't quite tell what he did," the healer said thoughtfully. Gerald's skin tingled as it cast some sort of magical scrutiny toward Erick's spell and he rubbed at his arms reflexively. "It's an *odd* spell... Did your cousin say what he was doing?" it asked Gerald, who could only shake his head helplessly.

"You do feel that it's working, though?"

"Oh, yes. The pain vanished completely. The medicine had been dulling it, but it was still there, underneath. Now, it's like there's nothing wrong with my leg at all."

"Well, there is," Calin said severely. "So don't get any more ideas about getting up and walking around."

The healer cocked its head at him. "You tried to walk? *Why?*"

Gerald turned red. "I had to go to the bathroom," he muttered. "Anyway, I have a wheeled chair now, so there's no reason to worry about it," he added hastily. *Let's change the subject now!* "I promise I won't try to walk until I have permission."

"See that you don't," the healer said, as severely as Calin had. "Especially the way you've been reacting to healing spells, it's better to be cautious. I do wish he would wake up," it sighed, looking at Erick. "I'm most curious to compare methodologies."

"He only just fell asleep," Gerald said apologetically. "You might have to wait a while."

"I should have more patience than I do, considering my profession," the healer sighed. "No one ever gets sick or injured at a *convenient* time, of course, and then they often insist on taking an unreasonable amount of time to get better."

Gerald was left feeling like he should apologize for his own eventful recovery to date, but Calin caught his eye and gave him a wink. *Dragons have the* oddest *senses of humor*, he thought wryly.

"I suppose I could run some diagnostic spells in the meantime," it said, looking around the cavern as if hoping someone would wake up if it *looked* at them hard enough. "I say, who's this?" it added, craning its head to peer at the dragon.

"You mean Dragon?" Gerald asked, confused.

It shot him a look that clearly said *don't be an idiot.* "The human here in the harness," it clarified. "I remember your friend, who's asleep in the chair, and the magician in the cot is presumably your cousin, but who is this other one?"

"Oh—I *thought* there were three people!" Gerald said. "But no one said anything and I thought it was the fever or the medicine muddling me again. I have no idea. Or—maybe—are they female?"

The healer squinted. "I think so?"

"It's probably Princess Nedi, then," Gerald said. "She was the one in the forest where Erick was. Omar and Dragon must have rescued her when they went to get Erick. But why didn't anyone say anything? Why didn't she say anything?"

The healer shrugged, its scales rippling with the movement. "I've long since given up on trying to understand anything humans do or don't do," it said dryly.

Calin offered a more practical explanation. "The others were caught up in being worried about you," she pointed out. "They weren't thinking about performing introductions or giving explanations. And she probably didn't want to interrupt your reunion or your cousin's spellcasting. I'm sure if they weren't all so tired it would have been handled a bit more, hmm, smoothly."

Gerald nodded. "It's not like there's not enough room for her," he said wryly. "And we are planning on bringing another hundred or so here. No reason not to get started with the showcase just because I got a bit seared." Calin had told him the dragon had gotten them permission for it; he had the impression the dragon had been so furious he'd been burned that no one had much wanted to argue with it about anything else.

His skin started tingling again and he cast a sharp glance at the healer. "Does your magic have to *tickle* like that?" he asked it. "It feels like there are ants crawling all over me."

"You can feel the diagnostic?" it asked with surprise. "But you didn't before. Or did you? You didn't mention it, but I suppose you may have been a bit distracted at the time. Do you remember if you felt the same, ah, tickle when I cast my healing spell initially?"

Gerald cast his mind back with an effort. His memories of the past few days were very hazy. "I wasn't awake for it, was I?"

"No, that's right, you weren't," it said, sounding disappointed. "You were quite thoroughly unconscious. Hmm. I wonder if that sensitivity had anything to do with the way you reacted to the spell... Did you feel anything when your cousin cast his spell?"

"Nothing like this. Only the pain going away."

"I suppose that's a promising sign," it said, but it sounded doubtful. "We really must compare methods. How long do you think he'll sleep for?"

"Oh... I don't know," Gerald said. He was starting to get sleepy again himself. He hadn't been awake this long since getting burned, and the excitement of seeing Omar and Erick, followed by the effort of holding a prolonged conversation, was starting to weigh on him. His eyelids fluttered and he murmured, "It could be a few hours," before he drifted off.

The last thing he was aware of was the healer plaintively imploring Calin not to fall asleep too.

A MURMURED CONVERSATION between the healer and Erick was what woke Gerald a few hours later. Erick was still wearing the same clothes he had arrived in and was looking distinctly rumpled, but much more alert.

"It's a balance between pain management and tissue regeneration," Erick was explaining. "It's not purely one or the other."

"Very few healing spells are *purely* one or the other," the healer responded impatiently. "That does not explain the way this spell feels at all."

"Maybe it's the energy requirements?" Erick suggested. "The spell has to be continuous, self-sustaining, but it needs too much energy to be powered by either me or Gerald—"

"The energy signature is about the only normal thing about this spell!" the healer snapped. "I'm quite familiar with self-sustaining spells. I cast the same sort of energy-looping with mine."

"They've been going on like that for ages," Omar said conspiratorially. Gerald stopped turning his head back and forth between his cousin and the healer and looked at Omar instead. He looked just as rumpled as Erick—maybe more so, considering he had slept in a chair— but Gerald reflected that he almost certainly looked no better and likely much worse.

"It sounds like they're going to keep going on, too," Omar added. "They're starting to repeat themselves, but I'm not sure they've noticed."

"Well, whatever kind of spell it is, I like it," Gerald said. "I had forgotten how amazing it is to not be in pain all the time."

"You'll be running around rescuing guardians again in no time," Omar said with a smile.

"That reminds me," Gerald said, propping himself up higher to peer at the dragon, who was still snoring gently at the foot of the bed. "Speaking of rescues—you brought someone with you! Was anyone going to mention that?"

"Oh! Didn't we? I was so tired, once I saw you were all right, I wasn't even thinking about anything else. Yes. By the time we reached the Enchanted Forest, Erick had already gone in. We didn't catch up with him until the tower and then, since we were there..." Omar shrugged. "Nedi's quite taken with your idea, by the way. She's all ready to help get everything set up. She's from one of the smaller kingdoms, too, so she's helped in administration for years. She'll have everything organized in no time." He lowered his voice and leaned in close to say, "Whether you want her to or not."

"I want her to," Gerald said fervently. "I also want to hear about the Enchanted Forest. And I want breakfast. Or dinner. What time is it, anyway?"

"You were right the first time," Omar said, laughing. "It is hard to keep track in here, isn't it? I'll see about breakfast. Do you need anything else?"

"A bath," Calin interjected. Gerald jumped. He hadn't noticed the piedling appear. "You can probably be trusted not to fall asleep and drown now that there's a healing spell on you," she continued. "And you'll feel better if you're clean."

"I'll feel better when I eat something," Gerald said. "Although, actually, I feel fine in the first place." It was still a novel sensation and he smiled as he said it.

"You can eat first," Calin said grudgingly. "But then you're bathing. Or you can tell the healer why you're choosing not to."

Gerald looked at that impressive personage and gulped. "That's okay," he said faintly.

"That's what I thought," Calin said with satisfaction. "I'll go find some breakfast."

When she returned carrying a tray—followed by several sisters carrying additional trays and a table to put everything on—Erick and the healer broke off their ongoing argument. As Omar had said, they were repeating themselves. Erick broke off a frustrated response in midsyllable to say, "Please tell me those drinks have caffeine in them."

"It wouldn't be a very good breakfast drink without it," Calin responded, handing him a cup.

"Ah, that's good!" he said after the first sip. "I could drink this all day." He dragged a chair over to the table and began applying himself with equal gusto to the rest of the offerings.

The healer let out an amused snort. "I suppose that's my cue to get some breakfast of my own," it said. "We can resume this discussion after we've both eaten."

Erick waved a hand at it in distracted acknowledgment, and the healer nudged the still-snoring dragon into wakefulness, murmuring to it about a quick hunt to restore its strength. With an exaggerated groan, the dragon got up, reassured itself Gerald was still all right, and followed the healer out of the cavern.

Gerald made a move toward getting up and joining Erick at the table, but Calin immediately pounced on him. "You agreed not to get up without permission!" the piedling scolded.

"It's three feet away!" Gerald protested. "Are you really going to make me eat in bed with everyone else sitting at a table three feet away?"

Omar nudged him. "I think she wants you to ask for permission," he stage-whispered.

Gerald grumbled half-heartedly under his breath and then said, as politely as he could manage, "Calin, would it be all right if someone helped me over to the table?"

"Of course," she said, equally politely.

Omar gave him a hand up and helped him hop over to the table, making a show of gallantly pulling a chair out for him.

As Gerald started to serve himself, he realized there was still an empty place at the table. "Is Nedi still sleeping?" he asked. *And why do I keep forgetting she's here? I thought my fever was gone. I shouldn't be getting confused by things any longer.*

Erick looked up from his plate. "No, she's been up for ages. She wanted to look around. But she must be getting hungry by now, she'll probably be back soon."

"In fact, there she is now," Omar said, nodding toward the cavern entrance. "Nedi, come have breakfast!" he called, and she waved an acknowledgment.

Gerald observed her carefully as she came closer. Her clothes— simple, practical trousers and tunic in a bright, cheery shade of yellow that stood out against her dark skin—were as rumpled as the princes', but that didn't seem to bother her at all. In sharp contrast to her clothes, her hair was neatly arranged in dozens of braids that hung down her back. Not a single strand appeared to be out of place.

She was tall, he noted as she got closer. Her height and the way she moved, smoothly, with no wasted motion, made her look quietly dangerous. *I wouldn't be surprised if she's like Omar, with knives up her sleeves.*

That, in turn, made him wonder why she had chosen to be a rescuee and not a rescuer.

She smiled at Erick and Omar as she approached, but her gaze caught on Gerald and held there. He wondered self-consciously how he was faring under her scrutiny. *Probably not very well*, he thought wryly.

I should have taken Calin up on that bath. He knew nothing about her or her kingdom, but both Erick and Omar seemed to like her and that made him want to make a favorable impression.

Not that Erick's approval was all that hard to get—he liked nearly everyone, at least on a superficial level of casual friendliness, but Gerald had gotten the idea Omar was a bit more cautious with his approval; not that he was unfriendly, but more...wary. *Not that we met under the most normal of circumstances,* Gerald reminded himself.

Nedi stopped when she was a few scant yards away. With her eyes still locked on Gerald's, she gave him a formal bow, dipping precisely to the depth considered appropriate for one royal child to greet another.

Gerald bobbed a sketchy, seated bow in return, feeling even shabbier and grubbier as he did so. "Forgive me for not rising to greet you properly," he said, striving to make his tone and his words appropriately formal to make up for the implied insult of remaining seated. "I am pleased to make your acquaintance, Princess Nedi."

She surprised him then by dropping all pretense of formality to give him a wide grin. "Likewise, I'm sure," she said. "Oh, don't worry, I wasn't expecting you to get up—although you do look a lot better than you did last night, if you don't mind my saying so. I was just wondering how you would react to me. It's odd, but I've found you can tell a lot about a person by how they chose to follow—or not—the rules of these interactions. You would think we would reveal more about ourselves in circumstances of our own choosing, but it's often not the case. I've noticed having the freedom to choose how to present ourselves often makes us more guarded. In a formal situation, no one thinks about how they might be giving something away."

Gerald blinked at her. "Oh," he said. "Um. What did I, uh, give away?" he asked with an air of trepidation. Nedi's gaze had turned a bit *sharper* than he was strictly comfortable with.

"That," she said primly, "would be telling."

She pulled out the remaining chair and sat down, calmly reaching for some fruit while Gerald gaped at her. Omar hid a grin behind his hand, but Erick didn't bother to hide his.

"Close your mouth, the flies will get in," he said. "Meathead."

Gerald closed his mouth with a snap.

"Sorry," Omar said, still grinning. "But she did the same thing to us. Now I can see why she finds it so amusing... I might have to start doing something similar."

"I think you're confusing enough as it is," Gerald grumbled. "But if everyone's done laughing at my expense, why don't you explain what happened in the Enchanted Forest?"

Chapter Fifteen

AFTER EXCHANGING GLANCES with Erick and Nedi, Omar started the story. "Well, the dragon got us there even faster than it thought it could," he began. "It was closer to a day than a day and a half, and we got there around dawn. But we couldn't go flying straight in looking for Erick, because there was a group of royals camped out along the edge of the forest and the dragon didn't want to start a panic. Since it was still pretty dark, the dragon was able to find a secluded place to land and then I walked over to the tents to ask about Erick."

He smiled wryly. "Unfortunately, there aren't any towns or villages all that close to the Enchanted Forest—you can imagine why—and my showing up on foot at the crack of dawn was deemed rather suspicious. I had a terrible time convincing the other royals I wasn't some shapeshifter that came out of the forest to eat them or something. It didn't help that we disabled my tracking spell, so I wasn't showing up on their maps. And, even though they said Erick wasn't there, you never actually *described* him to me, so I didn't even know if they were telling the truth or not."

"They were," Erick interjected. "I was on my way to Nedi's tower by then."

Omar flapped a hand at him. "Yes, but I didn't know that *then*. I went back to the dragon and we decided to write to Erick with the two-way parchment. If he *were* one of the people I had just spoken to, that would probably convince him I was telling the truth. And if he wasn't, then he could tell me where he was."

"I really have to come up with a silent alert for that spell," Erick interrupted again. "I was trying *not* to draw attention to myself in the middle of a highly magical environment with dangerous plants and animals and *other things* everywhere. Needless to say, I had to look at it immediately, if only to get it to stop chiming. Also needless to say," he added with a glare at Gerald, "I was not thrilled by the content of the message."

"You *do* realize I didn't do this on purpose, right?" Gerald said, gesturing at his bandaged leg. "I mean, there is actually a small percentage of my life that is not solely dedicated to annoying you."

Erick rolled his eyes but otherwise ignored him as he kept talking. "By that point, I was closer to Nedi's tower than to the edge of the forest, and Omar mentioned he was with your dragon, so I decided to keep pressing on. The tower would be a good landmark where we could meet up and I figured it would be easy enough for them since the dragon could fly over the dangers of the forest."

"He didn't think about how many of the Enchanted Forest creatures can *also* fly," Omar said.

"Yes, well, you got there, didn't you? And you didn't seem any worse for wear. Or at least not *much* worse for wear."

"It was one of the more interesting wake-up calls I've had," Nedi broke in. "Erick wasn't much of a surprise—I did get potential rescuers dropping by semi-regularly, despite the environment. But the dragon—that was new."

"We almost landed *on* the tower, too," Omar said, laughing. "The clearing around it was a bit smaller than the dragon was anticipating, but we were in too much of a hurry for it to worry about a little thing like *having a place to land*."

"I got there right after they did," Erick said. "Omar wanted me to get on the dragon and go immediately—"

"Which was perfectly reasonable considering your cousin urgently needed a healing spell!"

"But I didn't know how serious the situation was," Erick continued with a glare at Omar, "and since we were already there it seemed reasonable to take the time to free Nedi's guardian and see if we could interest her in our plan."

"And I didn't know anything about you at all," Nedi added to Gerald, "and I wasn't going to let them leave without learning why a dragon had come to visit."

"She was so calm," Omar said with admiration. "She opened the window and leaned out and formally introduced herself like everything was completely normal—"

"And Erick acted like you did," Nedi said to Gerald, "he tried to be very gallant, even though Omar was trying to physically *drag* him over to the dragon and the dragon was making a huge fuss itself—"

"And of course all the hubbub made the guardian show up," Erick added, "and then it was all such a mess—"

They were all talking over each other now, and talking loudly, and laughing, and Gerald felt both that he had a very good idea of what, exactly, that first meeting had been like, and also that he had missed out on something he rather would have liked to have been a part of.

They all have this story now, and I'm not part of it, even though I'm the reason they have it in the first place, he thought. He felt oddly left out and the feeling only increased as Nedi and Erick started laughing at some shared memory.

The dragon came back in then, licking its chops and looking full and content. It perked up even further when it heard the gist of the conversation. "Have you gotten to my part yet?" it asked eagerly. "I'm the one who spoke to the guardian," it added for Gerald's benefit.

"You have perfect timing," Gerald said, finding a smile. "I believe that's exactly where we are in the story. *Was* the guardian a unicorn, by the way?"

"It was," the dragon confirmed. "Omar and I had wanted to grab Erick and get back here as quickly as possible, but by the time the unicorn made an appearance, it was too late to leave in good time. With both Erick and Omar there, the guardian didn't know who to focus on. It didn't help that neither of them was making an attempt to rescue Nedi—it made the situation even more confusing for the poor unicorn. The collar exerts a type of...compulsion, I suppose is the word for it, to make the guardians act the way they're supposed to. You remember the amarok?"

"Of course."

"You remember she didn't *want* to fight Taylor. But because of the collar, she couldn't simply stand aside and give them access to the tower; she had to fight. Well, the unicorn didn't want to fight anyone either, but no one was following the protocols and the spells on the collar were pulling it in different directions: fight Erick, fight Omar, fight *me*, guard the tower..."

"It started going crazy," Erick interjected. "Lunging at each of us, running back toward the tower, spinning around and snorting and stamping its hooves. And I mean, people say unicorns are basically horses with horns, right? Well, let me tell you, there's one big difference. And I mean that literally: unicorns are much bigger than horses."

"They're more camel-sized," Omar said. "At least that one was. And the horn was proportional—it was like a spear sticking out of its forehead. It was, frankly, terrifying."

"I had a good idea of what was happening," the dragon said, "due to my own unfortunate experiences with the collar and its spells. So I chose to simplify the situation by the simple expedient of removing the confounding variables."

"It picked us up and stuck us in a tree," Omar translated.

"You didn't!" Gerald said to the dragon.

"I did," it confirmed. "When there weren't any royals threatening to broach the tower, the collar went quiescent and I was able to explain the situation to the unicorn."

"I still don't understand why it happened, though," Omar said. "I mean, nothing like that happened at the Burning Swamp or in the mountain, and there were *three* royals then."

"The ambient magic in the Enchanted Forest undoubtedly interacted with the spells on the collar," the dragon said. "Anything under the forest's influence is likely to suffer some sort of side-effect."

"Is that why I keep forgetting you're here?" Gerald asked Nedi. As soon as the words were out of his mouth, he realized how it sounded and blushed and began to stammer an apology.

Nedi waved it away with a lazy flick of her wrist. "The short answer is yes. Don't worry, the more you see me, the more it will wear off."

"If I can get back to the story?" the dragon interrupted, sounding aggrieved. "Once Erick and Omar were removed from the situation, I was able to explain things to the unicorn. It was, of course, delighted at the prospect of getting that hateful collar off, but it was wary about the fact that it would need to be one of the royals who removed it."

"And I was worried the environment might affect the spell," Erick broke in. "So I insisted on being the one to work on the collar, even though Omar was the one with more practical experience with actually altering them."

"The unicorn let you approach it?" Gerald asked curiously. "You weren't sure it would, in your letter."

"Yes, well, it seems that's just a myth. Or perhaps the collar prevented it from acting on its instinct to avoid me. In any case, yes, I was able to approach it, after the dragon did some negotiating on my behalf—the fact that it had obviously had its own collar removed helped there—and as it turned out, the spell did need a few small alterations."

"Meanwhile," Nedi broke in, "Omar was still sitting in a tree, and he was close enough to the tower window that I could bully him into telling me exactly what was going on. It would have been much easier to get the information if Erick had been up there, I think, since he had been acting the gallant. Omar was much more interested in the progress on the ground than in talking to me."

"Because we were in a bit of a hurry!" Omar protested. "Or at least, we should have been. But once he started in with the wax stick, it was obvious I wasn't going to get him out of there until he was finished, so there was no reason not to talk to you."

"All right, that's true," Nedi conceded. "It took a while to get to that point, but you did tell me everything."

"And then she said she would tell everyone unless we took her with us!"

"Hadn't Erick said you were going to do that anyway?" Gerald asked.

"Yes, but *she* didn't know that."

Nedi dismissed Omar's comments with another lazy flick of her wrist. "In *any case*, I didn't even need to blackmail you, since, as you said, you were planning to bring me along anyway. The unicorn is free and so am I, Gerald got his leg healed, and I am going to be *invaluable* to organizing this scheme of yours, so I really don't see what the fuss is about."

Omar opened his mouth indignantly and then visibly thought better of what he was going to say. "No harm done, I suppose," he said instead. "But I don't think Gerald's healed quite yet, or Calin wouldn't be making such a fuss still."

"He's not," Erick said. "It's not even all that close to being healed. There's a lot of damage. It's going to take a while, even with magic." He shrugged. "It won't hurt anymore, though."

"That's the most important thing to me right now," Gerald assured him. "I have time to wait for it to heal. We need to get organized here before we go haring off and dragging dozens of royals back with us."

"Leave the organization to me," Nedi said. "I think I saw some maps sticking out of one of those bags—"

"There are notes, too," Gerald said. "A tally of who's out there and where they are, that sort of thing."

"Let me at them," Nedi said with a gleam in her eye. "I'll start strategizing."

Within minutes, everyone was scattered: Nedi and the dragon to the maps, Erick and the healer to resume their discussion, and the piedlings carrying away the remains of the meal.

Calin popped up then, her gray hands on her hips. "Bath! Now!" she told Gerald firmly. "And then we'll change your bandages. I'll fill the tub. You can push the chair," she added to Omar.

Calin bustled off without waiting for a response, expecting she would be obeyed without question. And she was. Omar brought the wheeled chair over and pushed Gerald into the bathroom. The tub was already full, the water was steaming gently, and Calin was setting out towels and clean clothes.

Gerald focused on Calin instead of looking at the water. "Is it okay to get the bandages wet?" he asked doubtfully.

"We're changing them anyway," she reminded him. "Unwind them and hop in the tub. A bit of water and soap should do you good. But no *scrubbing*. Not with the towel, either. Pat the burns dry. *Gently*."

Gerald dredged up a crooked smile. "You don't need to tell me that twice."

She sniffed but then broke into a grin. "No, I suppose not. Don't drown, now."

She turned and left without another word. Omar was still standing there, though, and Gerald tightened his grip on the armrests. "I'm not going to drown," he said. His voice was strained and Omar said, "Oh!" He shook his head as if to wake himself up and said, "Sorry," blushing slightly. He slipped out of the room and Gerald heard the door close behind him.

Still, he made no move to get out of the chair. *You're being ridiculous,* he chided himself. *No one's here and this will be a nice change from washing in cold rivers...*

He slowly shrugged out of the robe and removed his shirt. Then he stopped, contemplating the yards of bandage wrapped around his leg. He wasn't sure he wanted to see what was under them again, especially now, not with clear eyes, not without the comforting fog of fever. *Erick even said it's not healed. It's just numb.*

After a long moment, he sighed. *It's not going to get any more healed while I sit here.* With unwilling fascination, he unwound the bandages and contemplated the ruinous mess underneath them.

Gerald had seen a lot of injuries in his life, between the animals he tended and the usual run of castle illnesses and accidents. He had thought his squeamishness had long since been lost in that regard. But seeing huge chunks of his leg looking like a mangled roast was enough to make his gorge rise in his throat.

There are not enough healing spells in the world for this, he thought faintly. *This is never going to heal right.*

He moved his leg experimentally and gagged as he saw the muscles moving in several places where ghastly windows had been burned through his skin. Even with the pain gone, blessedly gone, he couldn't force his leg to move entirely correctly. As he shakily rose from the chair and took two stumbling steps to the tub, he saw his knee refused to straighten completely. He couldn't feel it, but he could see it.

He didn't want to see it.

Gerald closed his eyes as he removed his undergarments, not wanting to see the fabric move across the destroyed skin he couldn't feel. With his eyes still closed, he awkwardly levered himself into the tub.

His eyes popped open at the heat of the water and he was swamped by a sudden, bitter wave of panic before he clamped down on it hard. *It's not that hot, it's just warm, it's bathwater, it's water, it's not hurting you, it's not burning you, it's not* fire.

He sat heavily and barely managed to prevent it from being a fall as his unused muscles protested the effort of keeping him upright. He closed his eyes again and it was several long minutes before he reached for the soap and scrubbed away the dirt and sweat of days of pain and fever. But even with his eyes closed he couldn't bring himself to touch his right leg.

He didn't know how long he sat there with his eyes closed. Long enough for most of the warmth to leech out of the water. Long enough that there was a tentative knock on the door.

"Gerald? You didn't drown, right?" Omar called.

"No."

"The healer and Erick want to look at your leg."

Gerald fought down another wave of nausea. "Just a minute."

He slowly pushed himself upright and got out of the tub. It was even more awkward maneuvering out than it had been maneuvering in. His eyes traveled insistently to his leg, no matter how hard he tried to keep them away. He couldn't decide if the burns looked better or worse now.

They glistened disturbingly with the damp, but some of the caked blood and pus had soaked away.

He dried and dressed as quickly as he could, his legs shaking with the effort of standing after so many days in bed. It was a relief to lower his weight back into the chair. He draped the towel over his right leg, to hide it from himself as much as anything, and then called to Omar that he could come in.

Omar opened the door even before the echoes of Gerald's words had disappeared into the air. His eyes went immediately to Gerald's leg and to the towel covering it. Then he looked up and met Gerald's eyes.

Gerald looked away, not wanting to acknowledge or respond to the concern he saw there. "It's a mess," is all he said. "You don't want to look at it."

"But it doesn't hurt?"

Gerald shook his head.

"You, uh, you look like you're in pain," Omar said gently.

"Do I? It doesn't hurt. I'm just tired, I guess."

Omar made a noncommittal noise in response, but he didn't force the issue. He pushed Gerald back into the big common area, where the healer and Erick were waiting with identical expressions he could only describe as "scheming".

"I think we've worked out the cause of the oddities," the healer said. It started to launch into an explanation and Gerald could feel his eyes glazing over. He had thought he had a good grasp of magical theory, but everything the healer said was going over his head. *Or maybe I don't want to hear it.*

Erick, seeing Gerald's expression, interrupted the healer. "I'm not sure the nonmagicians have the, um, training to appreciate the details," he said, and Gerald smiled. *Ever the diplomat. He'll make a good king.*

"Hmm? Oh. I suppose that's true. It will make a simply splendid academic paper, however. I'll have to get my secretary to start on a draft... But that's beside the point." It cocked its head at Gerald. "We have some variations in mind. Shall we see what we're working with?"

Gerald's hands tightened on the towel.

Erick sighed. "Is this really the time to worry about your cursed modesty?" he asked.

Gerald flushed. "That's not it," he snapped. "It's disgusting. My leg is disgusting. I don't want to see it. I don't want anyone to see it."

The healer lowered its head so it could fix one of its massive eyes on Gerald. "Do you know how many wounds I've treated?" it asked, not unkindly. "I have seen much worse than your leg. And I've seen your leg already. What will it hurt to let me see it again?"

"*He* hasn't seen it," Gerald said stubbornly, nodding at Erick. "And...neither has Omar."

"I have, actually," Omar said. "You were unconscious at the time. But I'll leave if you want me to," he added quickly. "I don't mind staying, but if you want me to go..."

Gerald hesitated. "Just...don't look. Okay?"

"Okay."

"Well, *I* have to look," Erick said. "And even though I didn't see it properly yesterday, it is *my* spell on your leg, you know. I know what's wrong with it, even if I haven't actually seen it."

Still, Gerald hesitated.

"If they can make it heal faster, it will be worth it," Omar said gently. "Won't it?"

"It's not going to heal," Gerald said pessimistically. "Not properly."

"It certainly won't if you don't let us tend to it," the healer said, a touch of exasperation creeping into its voice. "Now, are you going to let us, or should I call Calin over?"

After spending days under Calin's strict supervision, Gerald had worked up a healthy respect for the piedling. He was, perhaps, even more intimidated by her than by the healer, despite its imposing size.

Gerald forced his hands to open, his fingers to unclench. "Don't look," he said again to Omar. And then he drew the towel aside.

Erick and the healer leaned in and quickly began discussing spell variations, their conversation peppered with phrases like, "subverting analgesic energies" and "balancing regrowth with repair". Neither of them had drawn back in disgust. There hadn't been the faintest flicker of revulsion on Erick's face, and while Gerald was not entirely sure what revulsion would look like on a dragon, he was sure the healer hadn't flinched either.

He leaned his head back and caught sight of Omar, who was still standing behind the chair. Omar had angled himself so he could still see Gerald, but not his leg.

"Is it really that bad?" Omar asked quietly. "I mean... I saw it when it had first happened. I helped Calin bandage it. Did you know that? And it wasn't, I mean, it wasn't anything nice. But, well, it's not like it drove me away."

Gerald shrugged. "I don't know. Maybe it seems worse because it's *my* leg. But I think it's worse than it was at first. When the healer had to take the spell off, the pain got worse during those days when you were gone. It wasn't simply that it wasn't healing. It hurt *more*."

"Burns do that," the healer said absentmindedly, flicking its attention away from Erick for a moment. "The heat of them gets trapped under the skin, and they keep burning deeper for a day or two."

"But it's stopped now," Omar said. "It's healing now."

"The spells are working," the healer confirmed.

"But my leg's not," Gerald said. "Working, I mean. I can't move it properly."

"The muscle is damaged. It has to be repaired. I'm afraid you're going to have to be patient."

With that, the healer returned to its debate with Erick. After what felt like a small eternity, they were both satisfied. "I'm going to add another layer of spells," Erick said. "The healer is going to lend me some strength so I won't fall over this time. What I did last night was mostly pain relief and addressing the infection. This is going to start a deeper healing process. It might sting a bit," he warned Gerald. "Just until it takes hold."

"Go ahead," he said. *After the last few days, I can handle a little stinging.*

For a brief moment, it felt like dozens of hornets were jabbing their venomous stingers into every inch of his leg. But the pain passed as quickly as it came before Gerald could do anything more than gasp.

"Sting a bit?" he started indignantly, but Erick interrupted.

"Sorry, sorry, it shouldn't have been that bad! But that should really speed things up now. All right. I'm done with my bit."

Calin materialized at his elbow, as if she had been waiting for those words. Two of her sisters hovered behind her, holding baskets of bandages, ointments, and herbs. In the blink of an eye, they had Gerald's leg treated and bandaged once more. He relaxed as soon as the last bit of burn was covered, and only then did he realize how tense he had been.

He slumped back in the chair with a sigh and found himself smothering a yawn.

"Go back to bed now," Calin instructed.

"It's not even noon," Gerald protested. "I shouldn't be this tired."

She gave him a black look. "Days of fever, a severe injury, the strain of being up and moving around, the drain on your energy of healing spells... Oh, no, you shouldn't be tired at all."

"All right, all right," Gerald said. "I get it."

Omar started to push him back toward his sickbed, but Gerald stopped him. "I can go back to the other room, can't I?" he asked Calin. "I was only out here so the healer could fit, in case something went wrong, and it needed to get to me in a hurry. That's not necessary now, right?"

The piedling shrugged. "I suppose not. One bed is as good as another, as far as I'm concerned, as long as you're asleep in one!"

Omar changed directions and took Gerald through into the more human-proportioned caverns.

"I'm tired of everyone watching me," Gerald admitted a little sheepishly as Omar helped him move from the chair to the bed. "And there are so many more people to watch me now."

"Everyone's been worried," Omar said. "You were in bad shape."

"I know. I don't mean to sound so ungrateful." Another yawn interrupted him. "Sorry! I really am tired. I'm not fit company in any case."

"Oh, you're not as bad as all that," Omar said with a grin. "But I'd better let you go to sleep or Calin is going to have something to say about it."

Gerald shuddered theatrically and closed his eyes. "We can't have that," he murmured. And he was asleep before Omar could respond.

Chapter Sixteen

WHEN HE WOKE, Omar was sitting on the bed across from him, sorting through papers Gerald recognized as pages from the *Who's Who* guide. He pushed away a stab of guilt that the others had been working—*on my scheme, no less*—while he had wasted the day by sleeping.

"Hello, sleepyhead," Omar said as Gerald sat up. "I was just thinking about waking you. Are you hungry?"

"Famished," Gerald said, and his stomach growled as if to underscore his declaration.

Nedi and Erick were already at the table when they entered the reception cavern. They, too, had piles of paperwork in front of them.

"I told you she was going to organize everything," Omar said quietly into Gerald's ear as he guided him over to the table.

"Good," Gerald said. "I'm not good at following up with my ideas. If she can organize this, I'm happy to let her."

Nedi began talking as soon as Omar and Gerald were seated. With no preamble, she said, "It seems like there are really two prongs to this plan: one is bringing all the royals here for a showcase; the second is freeing all the guardians. There are a few ways to accomplish those things. The logistics depend on a few key factors: how we will be traveling to them, how they will be traveling to us, how much secrecy we need to have with either or both projects, and how long the dragonlands can provide hospitality for how many people prior to the start of the showcase."

She paused there, and Gerald tried to decide if she had stopped to draw breath or if she was waiting for someone to start elaborating on her key factors. When she looked up from her papers and looked around the table, meeting each of their eyes in turn, Gerald figured it was probably the latter.

"Well, you'll have to ask the dragon about that last one, but I would guess the answer would be 'a lot of people for a long time'. I mean, compared to dragons, people—even a hundred-odd people—don't eat much food or require much space," he said slowly. "As for secrecy, quite a lot. You know about Erick's spell to cloak the tracking spell, right? We'll be using that to keep the Council from knowing everyone is coming here. They're going to want to stop us, you know. I mean, we're undermining the entire system."

"But that in itself is going to raise suspicions," Nedi said. "When everyone starts disappearing from the map, don't you think the Council is going to investigate?"

"That's why we'll have to move people quickly once the spell takes effect. To scry someone, you have to know where they are, that's what the dragon says. So if we move them away from their last known position fast enough, they won't be able to find them."

"Which brings us back to transportation," Nedi interrupted. "I saw for myself how fast your dragon can fly, but it's only one dragon." She gestured to a map of the Thousand Kingdoms she had unrolled on the floor and marked with the locations of the royals awaiting rescue. "You can see for yourself how widespread all the towers are. Not to mention all the rescuing royals who are traveling freely. Using one dragon to round them all up and ferry them back here individually will take longer than I think you care to spend."

"You have a suggestion, then?"

"Several," Nedi said, glancing at another bit of parchment. "Again, there are different possibilities. The first option would be to recruit some more dragons. We could split up, with one dragon carrying each of us, and divide the towers between us. Another option would be to get some of the other royals to help us. We could send letters to the rescuers asking them to make their way to a specific town, and then we could gather up several at once and bring them here directly. That would prevent them from getting too close to the dragonlands while their tracking spells were still active. We could also try to recruit rescued guardians as we went. That would, of course, depend partially on the species of the guardian. Other dragons would be a big help; merfolk, not so much."

She paused to let them take all that in and then continued. "I personally think a mix of strategies would work best. The royals in towers are the easiest part, really; we have to go to all the towers anyway to free the guardians, *and* we know exactly where they are. It's the roving royals who are more trouble. If we can get them to concentrate in a handful of towns, that would be the easiest way to get them back here. And so long as we won't be wearing our welcome thin, we should start collecting people right away."

Erick cleared his throat. "And what about those who don't *want* to be collected? I mean, I think this showcase sounds like tremendous fun. But we can't really force people to participate."

"Why not?" Gerald asked heatedly. "We've all been forced to participate in the current system."

"Yeah, and how much did you like that, not having a choice?"

"We have to free the guardians," Gerald said, quietly but forcefully. "If there are royals who don't want to take part in the showcase, well, we won't force them to *participate*. But they have to be here, out of the reach of the Council, until those who are willing have a chance to show this will really work."

"Fine," Erick said. "I suppose that's all right. We won't be keeping them here that long, anyway."

"Especially not if we split up," Nedi said. "I'll talk to your dragon about finding some others to help us. I can work on some better harnesses as well. The more people that can be carried at once, the better. We can leave as soon as we have the transport and the harnesses."

Omar, who had been quiet all through the discussion, finally spoke up. "Gerald can't travel yet. And shouldn't Erick stay here until Gerald's leg is better? Especially since the dragon healers can't use their magic on it."

"We're splitting up anyway," Nedi said. "We don't all have to leave simultaneously. There probably should be someone here—someone human, I mean—to help get the new ones settled, too. You and I can get started, and the cousins can stay here until Gerald's ready to travel."

Omar frowned but swallowed whatever he was going to say, and Nedi nodded briskly. "Since that's settled... Shall we eat?"

THE NEXT FEW days passed in a whirlwind of activity. Gerald still spent long stretches of the day sleeping and recovering his strength, but when he was awake, he helped the piedlings sew new harnesses and helped Nedi plan their routes. The dragon had recruited two more who were curious about the human world and were young enough that they were restless and wanting to stretch their wings. Erick tailored his tracker-removal spell to make it longer lasting, and he also added another layer to the spells on Gerald's leg each day. Slowly but surely, visible signs of healing were beginning to appear. Nedi copied maps and made checklists and began drafting letters to the rescuers to draw them toward major cities. The rescuers all visited the cities sometimes anyway, to stock up on supplies or spend a night in an inn instead of along the side of the road, and they thought they could get as many as five or six in a single city without it looking overly suspicious.

"After all, there were at least that many camped outside the Enchanted Forest," Erick had pointed out. "And all of them had traveled at least part way with other rescuers at some point. Little clumps are normal. It would be stranger if we picked them all up one by one."

Omar was the only one who hadn't gotten caught up in the flurry of work, planning, or preparation. More than that, he seemed to have lost some of his enthusiasm for the endeavor. When Gerald was awake, Omar was always nearby and would lend a hand with whatever Gerald was doing, but one morning while Erick was renewing the healing spell, he mentioned that when Gerald was asleep, Omar was nowhere to be found.

"Nedi and I only see him at meals," Erick said. "No one seems to know where he goes, either. He hasn't been talking to your dragon, or to the new dragons; he hasn't been packing; he hasn't been helping the piedlings. I don't know if he's hiding somewhere, or if he's wandering around the dragonlands, but either way, it feels like he doesn't want anything to do with us or with the showcase."

Gerald frowned. "That doesn't sound right," he objected. "Are you sure he's avoiding you and it's not just coincidence? I see him all the time, and he's been helping me sew harnesses and plot routes between the towers. He thought the showcase was a good idea when we first talked about it, and he hasn't said anything to make me think he's changed his mind about it."

"Well, maybe Nedi or I did something to upset him, then," Erick said. "Insulted him by accident or... I don't know, but I swear, it's like he's a ghost, he's never around unless you are! Oh—" A brief flicker passed across Erick's face then, an emotion he hurried to hide. "Anyway, maybe you should talk to him about it. If I did something, I'm happy to apologize for it."

"Sure," Gerald said. "It's probably just some misunderstanding."

He kept an eye out for Omar as he worked on the tasks of the day, but hours passed without him making an appearance. That was unusual and Gerald caught himself chewing at his lower lip as he wondered if Erick was right and something had gone wrong.

He shook his head to clear it and forced himself to concentrate on the task at hand. With the harnesses nearly done, he moved on to making copies of the instructions for removing the guardians' collars and packaging them in waterproof pouches with chisels and wax sticks. Erick thought it was possible some of the royals they rescued would want to take part in the guardian rescue before coming in for the showcase, so Gerald wanted to have plenty of materials on hand for Nedi and Omar to hand out.

But that thought made him scowl at his leg. *I don't want to be stuck here doing busy work while they're out there accomplishing things.* And no matter what Nedi said, welcoming the influx of royals, getting them settled, and getting them to assist with the setup felt like busywork to Gerald. *It's a combination of host and steward, and I've never been good at either of those roles. And it'll all be about me delegating work to other people, anyway. I still won't be doing anything real.*

His leg was healing, at least. Already the edges of the burns, where the damage was least serious, were scarring over, and slowly the worst areas were starting to shade from "horrific" to "severe". He could look at it unbandaged without gagging. But he still couldn't straighten his leg the whole way and Calin was still determined to keep him off his feet entirely, so the only times he tried to walk were when he was getting in or out of the bathtub, and he couldn't move even those few scant feet without a bad limp and a lot of effort.

As much as he wanted to protest that he could travel, he was no longer fevered or fragile, he knew he would be more of a burden than a help. *I can't even get into a bathtub and I want to fly all over the Thousand Kingdoms and climb around swamps and enchanted forests and run around mountain peaks?*

He scowled at his leg again. "With everything that magic can do, I don't see why this is taking so long to heal," he grumbled to himself.

"Just think how long it would take *without* magic," Omar said. Gerald jumped and left a smear of ink on the instructions he was copying.

"Where did you come from?" he asked as he hastily blotted the paper. "I haven't seen you all day. You startled me."

Omar shrugged. "Oh, I've been around," he said vaguely. "What are you working on? Need any help?"

Gerald looked around to see if Erick was also going to pop up out of nowhere. *See?* he wanted to tell his cousin. *He wants to help.* Aloud he said, "I'm almost done with this, actually. But that reminds me—I did want to ask you something."

"Oh?"

Gerald capped the inkwell and set his pen down. "It's just...well, something Erick said this morning. He thinks you've been avoiding him and Nedi, and that you're not interested in the showcase or helping with it." Seeing Omar's face redden, Gerald held up a hand to forestall his protest. "*I* know you do want to help, I mean, look," he said, gesturing at the papers. "You just offered to help with this. So I know that part's not true. But the rest of it? I've been asleep so much, I don't know. Erick said if he did something or said something, you know, to upset you, he'll apologize for it. I guess what I'm getting at is, well, did something happen?"

"No," Omar said after a brief hesitation. "Erick didn't do anything wrong or say anything. I like your cousin. I haven't been avoiding him, not on purpose at least. But it's true that I've been...exploring, I guess you could call it. I haven't been staying in here all day."

"I told him it was probably a misunderstanding," Gerald said with relief. "So nothing's wrong?"

Again there was a hesitation, as if Omar had to decide how to respond.

"You can tell me if there is," Gerald said.

Omar rubbed his nose and sighed. "It's not... It's nothing serious."

"Nothing serious isn't the same as nothing."

He hesitated and then said, "I don't want to leave, okay? Nedi just decided she and I would go off to those far-flung towers and get everything started there. Even as fast as the dragons fly, it'll be weeks before we're back here to drop off the first royals and check in. And Dragon, our dragon, won't be the one taking me, it won't leave while you're still here. And I don't want to leave either." He crossed his arms as if expecting Gerald to argue. When he didn't, Omar added, "I mean, I know it's not like before, I can leave without worrying you're going to die before I get back. But, all of this, it's *your* idea, it's your plan, you started it. It doesn't seem right for me to go off and leave you here. Not when it's not really time-sensitive."

"Well...why don't you stay, then? It's going to take weeks anyway, delaying a little more isn't going to make a difference. I don't know how long it'll be before I can travel, but if you want to stay until then, well, it's not like anyone can make you go."

"You want me to stay?"

"You're my friend," Gerald reminded him. "I wasn't crazy about the idea of you flying off and leaving me behind either."

"Nedi won't like it."

Gerald shrugged. "And you and I won't like it if you do go. So it's two to one in favor of you staying. And I bet Erick would side with us, if only because he'll be relieved you're not mad at him. He gets all upset when he can't charm people."

That made Omar smile. "He does like to be liked, doesn't he? All right, then. But I'm going to let you tell Nedi."

Gerald had hoped to be able to ease into that conversation, but as soon as they were all gathered for dinner, she announced, "We'll be leaving tomorrow."

Omar shot Gerald a look and he set his fork down. "About that..." Gerald started.

"Everything's ready," Nedi said. "And they're long flights. There's no reason to delay."

"Well, Omar and I were talking," Gerald said, "and since the two of us and Dragon started all this together, and Dragon is waiting for me to get better, Omar wants to wait too. So the three of us can...pick up from where we left off."

Erick smiled like a cat that had gotten into the cream, but Nedi looked scandalized. "But we've planned it for two of us to go at once! The more tracking spells we disable, the more obvious the gaps will be. If I go by myself, it will be easy for the Council to track my flight path by looking at where the spells are going dark. They won't need to scry to find me!"

"But it's going to take you at least a week to get to your first tower," Gerald pointed out.

"And it will take *him* a week to get to his first tower! There will still be time when I'm the only one disabling the trackers! And we can't count on the Council taking time to notice, not when you and Erick have already been playing with them. They might already be on high alert."

"You'll still be mounted on a dragon. Surely that gives you an advantage."

Nedi gave Gerald a withering glare. "We've already seen the Council can get the better of dragons. Isn't that why we're here in the first place? No. I don't care to take the risk of implementing this scheme by myself. And I don't care to delay here unnecessarily."

"It's *my* scheme," Gerald pointed out, taking a firm hold of his fraying temper. "It's because of me you're involved in it at all. Maybe that should count for something here."

"Now, now," Erick interjected. His smug look had faded as Nedi's voice had gotten louder. "Let's look at this calmly, shall we?"

Nedi glared at him as well and fingered the dagger sheathed at her hip in what Gerald hoped was an unconscious habit and not an implicit threat. "Fine," she said. "I'm calm. I'm calmly seeing all my planning go to waste. I'm calmly seeing all my schedules fall to pieces. I'm calmly seeing—"

"Oh, relax!" Omar interrupted. "This isn't the kind of thing you can schedule to the hour, or even the day. There's too much ground to cover, too many variables in terms of weather and royal temperaments and types of guardian and all the rest of it. If you don't want to go that far afield by yourself, why don't you go rescue someone closer and recruit them to help you?"

"Or," she said, "You could stop being selfish and do what we agreed on."

"I don't actually remember agreeing to anything," Omar snapped. "I remember you telling me what I was going to do."

"And? I've spent my whole life being told what I was going to do. My kingdom is more conservative than most. I'm the oldest, but only the oldest *son* inherits. I was raised to be given away to forge an alliance. I'm better than my brother at statecraft and weaponscraft, both, and yet I wasn't permitted to take an active role. I was told to go sit in a tower and wait. Well, I'm out of that tower now and I'm tired of being told to wait."

The venom in her voice silenced all of them.

Then someone cleared their throat delicately from the shadows and all four of them jumped. It was Calin. "I couldn't help overhearing," the piedling said wryly. "In fact, I suspect a good deal of the dragonlands overheard... But that's beside the point. Gerald's leg isn't mended, but it's mend*ing*. Even if the healing spells were to be removed, he would stay on the road to recovery. He won't be lapsing back into fever. It's my professional opinion that—while Gerald shouldn't be traveling just yet— there's no reason why Erick couldn't."

The princes exchanged looks. Erick raised an eyebrow at Omar, who shrugged and looked at Gerald. Gerald looked at Calin, at his leg, and then at Erick. "If she says it's all right, then it's all right. Assuming you want to go?"

"Why *wouldn't* I want to fly around on a dragon?" Erick retorted. "Even setting aside all the rescuing and fomenting rebellion... This is perfect for me, meathead."

"There," Omar said with relief. "Erick and I will switch and all your plans and schedules will remain intact. Everyone's happy. Everyone's happy, right?"

There was a murmured chorus of agreement and the rest of the meal passed in a much better temper.

THE NEXT MORNING, Omar woke Gerald early. "Nedi's chomping at the bit to get out of here," he said. "You'd better get up if you want to say good-bye."

"What *time* is it?" Gerald grumbled, but he was sitting up even as he asked.

"Time to leave, according to Nedi," Omar said. Then, when Gerald glared at him, he said, "I don't know, exactly. But I'd be surprised if it's much past dawn."

"Can't we get some windows in here?"

"I'm sure there's a spell for that," Omar said. "I'll suggest it. Do you need a hand?"

"No. Well, probably. But no." Gerald swung his legs over the side of the bed and stood up. He paused then, half expecting Calin to pop out of the shadows to scold him. When the piedling didn't make an appearance, he took a few limping, awkward steps and nearly fell.

"Whoa!" Omar reached over and steadied him. "Let me get your chair, okay?"

"I'm not going to get better at this if I don't try."

"You're not going to get better at it until your leg's better!"

"I don't want to wait here for weeks! If I can just get around a *little*... I can stay on the dragon's back most of the time. But I have to be able to get *on* its back. I have to be able to walk."

"There's no rush, remember?" Omar said softly.

Gerald waved his hands in an aimless, frustrated gesture. "Nedi's tired of being told to wait. I guess I'm tired of it, too."

Omar looked at the chair and then at Gerald. He sighed and shrugged and said, "Lean on me, then."

With Omar next to him to keep him from listing too far to the side, Gerald was able to make it as far as the reception area, which was once again crowded with dragons.

He swallowed nervously.

He wasn't afraid of their dragon, or the healer. He hadn't even realized until right then that he *was* afraid of other dragons...strange dragons.

They're not going to burn me.

"Gerald?" Omar murmured.

"I'm okay," he said, swallowing again.

"Uh-huh... You know, I think you've done enough walking," Omar said. Gerald didn't argue and let Omar half guide and half carry him to the nearest chair. He kept an eye on the new dragons in spite of himself and he relaxed when their dragon moved in between him and them.

"You're ambulatory," it observed.

Gerald breathed out a laugh. "In a manner of speaking. Where are Erick and Nedi?"

"Nedi is checking harnesses. Erick was here a moment ago..." The dragon trailed off as he looked around for the magician. "Hmm."

"I'm here," Erick said, panting slightly. "I had to get something. Where's—oh, there she is. Nedi!"

She hurried over. "Aren't you ready yet?"

"Yes. But here, take this. And you two, too," he said, distributing packets of parchment to each of them.

"Paper? I already have paper," Nedi said skeptically.

But Gerald was smiling. "It's enchanted," he told her. "Instant two-way communication."

"What?"

"Whatever you write on it will show up on the paired pages we have," Erick explained. "And if any of us write to you, it will chime to let you know you have a message. Just drip ink on it and it will appear."

"Oh!" she said. "That's what you were talking about before, when you said you would need to mute it in the Enchanted Forest..."

"That's right," Erick said. "And I even color-coded the paper so you'll know who you're writing to." He fanned his packet out to show them colored dots in the upper corners. "Orange for Omar, green for Gerald, purple for me, and black for Nedi."

"Purple for Erick and black for Nedi kind of messes with your mnemonic," Omar observed.

"Purple like eggplants and black like night," Erick responded, grinning. "Look, there aren't a lot of colors that start with *e* and *n*, all right? I think I did pretty well. And there's also a page that's not color-coded, that will send your message to everyone simultaneously. So we can stay in touch, coordinate our schedules"—he said that with a wink at Nedi—"and you know, just generally gossip."

"It does sound useful," Nedi admitted. "I'll be sure to test it out once we're underway." She put a not-so-subtle emphasis on those last three words and Erick grinned again.

"We better get going, then."

That was all the excuse Nedi needed to say hasty farewells and mount the waiting dragon. Erick followed at a slightly more decorous pace, and then Gerald and Omar were waving as the dragons launched out of the mouth of the cavern, out into the amphitheater, and then away into the open air.

"Now I just have to heal enough that we can follow them," Gerald said with a sigh.

Omar patted him on the shoulder. "Soon," he promised. Gerald looked at his leg and didn't reply.

Chapter Seventeen

THE NEXT FOUR weeks sped by and dragged on by turns. Under Calin's close supervision, Gerald worked to regain his mobility, a process that left him sore, tired, and frustrated, while Nedi and Erick swooped in and out with royals and progress reports. By the time he was able to get around the caverns independently—albeit with a pair of canes—they had both come and gone several times, and there were now close to thirty royals in the dragonlands.

Gerald tried to avoid them. They *stared*. He was tired of their stares, and he was also tired of Calin fussing at him to not overdo, not least because he knew she was right; although he had snapped at her that muscles atrophy without use, he knew as well as she did there were a right and a wrong way to rebuild his strength. The burns had healed as well as he could have hoped—quickly, cleanly, without infection, and without pain.

But Erick's spells couldn't rebuild the muscle that had been burnt away, and they couldn't remove the thick bands of scar tissue that pulled at his knee and kept him from straightening his leg. Calin gave him ointments to rub into the scars to help improve their flexibility, but he hated touching them; the nerves were dead and the scars were disturbingly numb under his fingers, although they itched ferociously along the edges where they met less-damaged skin. He hated seeing them, too; raised and knobby, purple and red, they were ugly and lumpy and the only reason he kept applying the ointment Calin gave him was he knew she would do it if he didn't and he couldn't stand any more poking and prodding.

When Calin let him start walking again, he seized the opportunity to reclaim some of his modesty as well; a robe was good enough when all he was doing was lying in bed, but getting back on his feet meant wearing real clothes again—and that had meant having to take off his pants whenever the bandages on his leg needed to be changed. So he had taken a pair of scissors and needle and thread and transformed the solid seam along his right pant leg into a long row of buttons. Calin had rolled her eyes when she saw what he was working on, but she had to admit the finished product didn't interfere with her tending the wounds or changing the bandages, and it made Gerald much more comfortable with that tending—even now that he was the one doing it.

He was tired of other people seeing his scars, and when Omar came into their room while Gerald was treating his leg, he jumped and yanked a blanket over it.

"You know you don't have to hide that from me," Omar said softly.

"I'm not *hiding* it," Gerald said defensively.

Omar looked pointedly at the blanket and raised an eyebrow.

"I'm—oh well, fine. I'm hiding it. So what?"

"I mean, if you want to cover it, that's one thing. But you're... You're staying up here instead of mingling with the other royals or helping get the amphitheater ready for the showcase. You're hiding from everyone. Not just hiding your scars, but flat-out *hiding*. I don't want you to feel like you have to hide from me."

"I'm not hiding from *you*," Gerald said.

Omar looked pointedly at the blanket again. "Gerald..." he said. "I don't care about your scars. Believe me, no one will ever take as much notice of them as you will. And scars fade. Mine aren't nearly so impressive, but I have scars too—and so does everyone who's ever wielded a weapon." He held his arms out to show Gerald the dozens of small scars that marked his hands and forearms, which Gerald had seen before without ever really noticing. "I'm not hiding them."

"If mine were on my arm, I wouldn't hide them either," Gerald said. "I mean, look at this," he said, gesturing to the buttons along the seam of his pants. "I did this with three different pairs of pants, just because I couldn't be comfortable exposing that much skin to anyone. To Calin! Who's not even human!"

"If that were all it was, you wouldn't be avoiding everyone as well as covering your leg," Omar said flatly. "No one can see the scars when you're dressed."

"Why do you care so much?"

"Because you're *brooding* about it! You're constantly chewing on your lip, you won't go into any of the common areas because you're ashamed of your limp, and the dragon said you're not even sure if you want to go on another rescue!"

"I'd only be in the way," Gerald mumbled, looking away. "I can walk now, but I'm slow, and I'll be useless setting up a camp or climbing a tower or anything like that."

"So you'd need a little help. So what? You needed help before, in the snowstorm or when that princex was threatening you, and you took it without being ashamed of it. What's the difference now? Look," he said, softer. "I *don't care* that you got hurt. I don't care if you limp or if you need a hand. I'll set up the damn tents, I'll climb the towers. But you're going to be there with me. So you better get comfortable with that. And with me."

"I am comfortable with you," Gerald protested.

"Then stop hiding your scars. You're giving them too much importance. You're making it a bigger deal than it is."

"They're ugly," Gerald said, feeling childish even as he said it.

"They'll fade," Omar said again. "You need to stop thinking about it. Stop feeling sorry for yourself."

Gerald opened his mouth to protest, but Omar kept talking. "Look...why don't you come swimming with me? You've barely left the caves here. There's a lake, not too far—close enough for you to walk—and the piedlings have swimming outfits, so you can't use that as an excuse."

Gerald bit his lip.

"I've seen your scars before," Omar reminded him. "What do you think is going to happen if I see them again?"

Unable to think of a good response, Gerald just scowled at him, but when Omar held out a hand, he let Omar pull him to his feet. "It better not be far," he grumbled as he limped after Omar.

It was easy enough to move around in the caverns, where the ground was smooth and level and kept clean and free of debris. It was another thing entirely to navigate the path to the lake. The grasses and rock-clinging shrubs had been beaten down by hundreds of piedling feet, but the exposed gravel slid out from under Gerald's feet and canes and Omar kept him from stumbling and falling a dozen times.

By the time they reached the promised lake Gerald was dusty and sweaty and irritated. *I was fine in the caves. He could've let me stay there.* He scowled at Omar's back as the oblivious prince shed his boots and shirt and waded into the lake in a pair of short pants the piedlings had provided. Gerald had to persuade himself to do the same. *No one else is here. He's seen the scars before. I like swimming, and no one's naked this time...* Even though Omar hadn't said anything about it, the memory of his panic at the river still made him flush with embarrassment.

Eventually he stripped down to his swim shorts, set his canes aside, and limped heavily into the water. Omar watched him, and if there had been any trace of disgust on his face, Gerald would have turned around and left. But his gaze was steady and calm. He didn't avoid looking at the scars, but he didn't stare either.

Gerald's self-consciousness melted away when he got into the water. It was instantly easier to move, with the water supporting him and holding him up, taking the weight off his bad leg. He *swam*, he moved freely and easily and without the pain of cramping muscles for the first time in weeks, and he couldn't help but smile at it. Omar gave him a smug grin in response.

"Oh, shut up," Gerald grumbled. "You're a desert prince, what do you know about swimming..."

Omar smirked and splashed him.

IT TURNED INTO a routine, that trek to the lake. Gerald relaxed in the water in a way he couldn't relax anywhere else in the dragonlands, and he even started to get used to having so much of his scars on display. He could forget about them for long stretches, because Omar never stared, and he also never deliberately *didn't* stare in that way that felt worse than staring did. Omar acted like they were there, but they didn't matter, and so Gerald was able to start to feel like maybe they didn't matter after all, although he still didn't like them. But it was better to be at the lake than anywhere else. The amphitheater floor was always a flurry of activity, with the royals and piedlings and the occasional dragon working hard to get ready for the showcase, and Gerald avoided it. Omar was more social, but he still spent most of his time with Gerald. It was easy to stay by the lake or in their living space and forget about everything happening outside of it, let alone outside of the dragonlands, until the two-way parchment chimed with an urgent message from Erick.

> *Are you and Omar ready to go yet? The Council is starting to get frantic—too many royals have disappeared off their maps. There are wards popping up around the towers and tracker spells everywhere. We have to step up our speed and get*

everyone back here as quickly as possible. I'm on my way back now. Nedi, too. We'll talk tonight. See if your dragon can recruit any more, too; we might need to recruit some of our rescuees.

P.S. I picked up Lila this trip. Just so you know.

Gerald read the message twice, flinching at the postscript, and then handed the paper wordlessly to Omar. He read it and looked back at Gerald. "Are you ready?"

Gerald rubbed at his knee. "I'm going to be useless. It's hard enough getting to the lake. I can't ... I can't just go back to this like nothing's happened."

"No one's asking you to act like nothing happened. But you'll be sitting on the dragon's back most of the time. And when we need to walk somewhere, I'll be there to help you. You know how the collar spells work, you've had practice taking them off, you won't be *useless*. And I won't go unless you go, and neither will the dragon, and they need us to go. What if the Council realizes it's not only the royals disappearing and they change the spells on the guardians? We have to get all the collars off before that happens."

"I know. And if Lila's coming here, that's all the more reason for me to leave."

AGAINST HIS BETTER instincts, Gerald let Omar persuade him to go down to the amphitheater floor to meet Erick—and Lila. "You're going to have to face her at some point," Omar pointed out.

"But does it have to be *now*?"

"Don't you want to get it out of the way?"

"I want to know why Erick had to pick her up," he grumbled. But he went. The dragon was out hunting, so Omar helped Gerald limp down the stairs. He leaned on his canes and waited for Erick's dragon to land. His cousin waved when he caught sight of them; Lila didn't. Her eyes widened when she caught sight of Gerald's canes; then her mouth twisted in a grimace of disgust and he wanted to drop the canes and belatedly hide the evidence of his injury.

"What happened to *you*?" she asked as she dismounted. There was no concern in her voice. "How hard is it to sit in a tower? Do you deliberately mess up everything you try to do or are you really that incompetent?"

"Nice to see you again, too," Gerald said tiredly. "I got burned. I'm fine, not that you care. Erick cast some spells on it."

"So he can do something practical. Who knew."

Erick rolled his eyes behind her. "She's been like this the whole time," he stage-whispered.

"You abducted me and are forcing me to participate in this ridiculous scheme. I don't think you have the right to expect me to be happy about it."

"That's no reason to be nasty to Gerald, though," Omar broke in.

She turned to face him, raising her eyebrows. "And who are you, then, that my family reunion is any of your concern?"

"I'm Gerald's friend."

"Friend." Lila smirked in Gerald's direction. "Did he rescue you, then? I didn't think you were going to give in about that. Did you finally give up your anti-marriage crusade?"

"I rescued myself," Gerald snapped. "And I'm not anti-marriage. I simply don't want to get married myself."

"You may be in luck now, then," she said. "I can't imagine anyone will want a gimpy prince."

Omar snarled at her and took a step forward with his knives suddenly in his hands. Lila put a hand on her sword hilt and smiled. "Don't bring a knife to a sword fight," she advised.

"Stop it!" Gerald said, thrusting out a cane to keep them apart. "Both of you. No one's going to fight anyone. Omar, ignore her. I'm used to it."

"You better get used to the idea of getting married, too," Lila said. "Do you really think Mother—or even Mum—will let you come home without a spouse?"

"Maybe I won't go home, then," Gerald said quietly.

Lila rolled her eyes. "Do you really think they'll let you do that, either? Grow up, Gerald."

She turned and walked away before he could respond. He let her go. Omar and Erick were both watching him carefully. Erick looked apologetic. Omar looked angry. He was still fingering his knives and Gerald nudged him. "Put those away. That's...that's just Lila. I wasn't expecting anything better." *And it could have been a lot worse.*

"Where's Nedi?" he asked Erick in an attempt to change the subject. "I thought you two were getting in about the same time."

"They had some bad weather this morning," he replied. "They'll still get here today, but they've been delayed."

It turned out to be quite a delay; Nedi got in with her latest batch of royals as the sun was starting to set. There were four of them, and they were all drenched and miserable. Even Nedi was disheveled—the first time Gerald had ever seen her looking less than completely put together and in control. "I know," she said with a grimace while the piedlings hurried the newcomers off to bathe and get settled. "The storm came out of nowhere. There were no clouds, there was nothing building in the air. If that storm was natural, I'll eat my crown... I might go ahead and eat it now, I'm that hungry. Our supplies got wrecked; I haven't eaten since breakfast."

That at least was easily remedied and they were shortly sitting around Gerald and Omar's table discussing Nedi's misadventures over dinner and hot tea.

"But how did the Council find you?" Gerald asked. "If the dragons have been taking off all the tracking spells..."

"I don't think they did, not exactly," Nedi said around a mouthful of stew. "It was a...a *broad* storm. It took us a long time to fly through, and that was at dragon speeds. It wasn't targeted. I bet it was centered on Shira's tower and then spread in all directions for as far as they could power it. Less of a direct attack and more of a trap."

"We may want to rethink splitting up, then," Erick said. "If the Council is starting to react by targeting us... You three shouldn't be traveling without someone who can use magic."

"The dragons use magic," Nedi replied. "And splitting up is exactly what we need to do. There are what, fifty occupied towers? And we've gotten to how many between us? Less than half, and that's counting Gerald's and mine. We don't have time for the four of us to make that many separate trips. Especially if those two still won't split up," she added, gesturing at Omar and Gerald.

"Even if we put every royal here on a dragon," Erick said, "we can't be everywhere at once. And we've only gotten ten more dragons to agree to carry us."

"Thirteen is a lot better than three," Nedi pointed out.

Gerald stopped listening and let them argue. He knew Nedi would win in the end, because she was right. They had to move quickly. Before long, Erick gave in, and the debate changed from *if* they would send the others out to *which* of them would go.

"Not Lila," Gerald said, mostly to himself. Erick and Nedi were throwing names back and forth and he had nothing else to contribute. "Not anyone who seems unsure about being here."

"Not anyone who can't protect themselves," Erick added. "And not anyone who doesn't want to go."

They came up with close to twenty candidates and wasted no time in running off to gauge their willingness and narrow the list to the ten they needed. Gerald watched them go and said, "Do we even have that many harnesses?"

"If we don't, I'm sure the piedlings will remedy that," Omar said.

A few minutes later, a golden orb materialized in the air between them and popped like a soap bubble. "Meet on the amphitheater floor in half an hour," Nedi's voice said.

There was no way to reply. Like Calin, she assumed her commands would be followed.

THE DRAGON BROUGHT Gerald and Omar down at the appointed time and then settled in to observe the planning session. Nedi and Erick were bracketed by ten royals, including a few Gerald recognized vaguely from events of state over the years.

Spread on the ground and weighed down with stones was a large-scale map of the Thousand Kingdoms, with the remaining occupied towers marked in gold. Gerald drew in a breath to see how *many* there still were, and how widespread they were. Erick and Nedi had visited most of the furthest-flung already, but there were still nearly a dozen that were a week's flight away.

"As you can see," Nedi said to the group, "we have a lot of ground to cover. On the bright side, the towers in the most inaccessible locations tend to be clustered together, to entice more rescuers to go out of their way." She gestured, indicating a few places on the maps where there were three or four or even, in one case, five towers within a day or so of each other—and a day on horseback was merely hours for a dragon.

"On the other hand, that means the towers that aren't quite so hard to get to, or quite so far out of the way, are often the only ones in the area." Another gesture, at the scattered singletons.

"The plan is simple. Erick, Omar, Gerald, and myself will take the farthest clusters. We're most experienced on dragonback and we have all used the guardian-release spells before. We're best prepared to travel that distance and visit several towers each. When we started this, we started with the farthest towers, planning to work our way back toward the dragonlands. That means all the closest towers are still occupied. We'll take volunteers or draw lots for doing these circuits—" She gestured on the map, drawing invisible flight lines in a rough loop around the dragonlands, each circuit taking in the closest three towers. "The rest of the singletons will be divided up between the rest of you. Those fliers will be responsible for only two towers each, but there will be a longer flight between them."

She looked up from the map and met the eyes of everyone around it. "Any questions?"

There were none. Gerald privately thought everyone was too intimidated by Nedi's calm preparedness to admit they were anything less than as ready as she clearly expected them to be.

"Good. These are the assignments..."

In a remarkably short amount of time, Nedi had sketched out all the flight plans and paired a royal with each one. "The dragons all picked the flights they wanted," she added as she handed out copies of the maps and the instructions to disable the guardians' collars. "Remember your flight number. Your dragon will have the same one. Pack any personal supplies you need. The piedlings are taking care of food and water, medical supplies, and the like."

A few people swallowed nervously at the mention of medical supplies. Every eye flicked toward Gerald and his canes and he reddened under the scrutiny. He wanted to tell them his injury had nothing to do with the Council, but he didn't think telling them it had involved a dragon would be much better.

"Purely precautionary," Nedi said crisply. "We're not aiming to fight the Council. If anything goes wrong, you retreat. We can always go back to a tower. The dragons can all cast spells, and an adult dragon is more than a match for any human magician. Now... We'll be leaving at dawn. Eat, if you haven't yet, and then get some sleep."

She turned her attention back to the map and Gerald thought it was a pity her country had decided the heir had to be male. *She will make an imposing queen.*

The royals all knew a dismissal when they heard one, and they quickly dispersed. It was only once they were nearly out of earshot that they began to chatter at each other with varying degrees of excitement and nervousness.

Omar pulled Gerald to his feet. "You heard the general," he said, his voice solemn but his eyes dancing with amusement. "Let's go."

The dragon had watched the whole meeting in thoughtful silence, and it was still pensive as Omar and Gerald climbed onto its back for a lift back up to their chambers. "Penny for your thoughts?" Omar asked, but it shook its head.

Gerald glanced back at Erick and Nedi, who still had their heads together over the map, and Erick looked up and winked.

Before Gerald could wonder what that was for, the dragon pushed off the amphitheater floor. Gerald shook his head. He had enough to worry about without trying to understand Erick.

"I'm going hunting," the dragon said when it deposited the princes in the reception chamber. "I'll see you in the morning."

It took off without waiting for a response, and Gerald found himself smothering a sudden yawn as he watched it go. "It's not that late, is it?" he asked.

"Late enough," Omar said. "And I'm going to spend as much time in bed as I can. We'll be in a tent tomorrow."

IT WAS STILL dark when Gerald woke up the next morning. That was no surprise, given the lack of windows in the bedchamber, but Gerald had a feeling dawn was still a ways away. Omar was sound asleep across the room and Gerald didn't hear anyone else moving around in the halls.

So why am I awake? He hadn't been sleeping badly; he didn't remember any dreams at all, let alone unsettling ones, and his bedding wasn't rumpled like he had been tossing or turning. He wasn't even particularly worried about this next stage of their mission. If anything, he was looking forward to being alone with Omar and the dragon again, far away from all of the staring royals and even the too-solicitous piedlings.

He rubbed his eyes and tried to decide if he should get up or if it was early enough that it was worth getting a bit more sleep. But across the room, Omar began to stir, and Gerald gave up on the idea of going back to sleep.

"You're up early," Omar said with a yawn.

"So are you."

"True... I don't want to give Nedi a reason to snap at me. It's too early for a lecture about disrupting her schedules."

Gerald hid a smile. "Let's get moving, then."

THEY HAD DEBATED staggering departure times, so those covering the most and least distances would each reach their first targets around the same time. But Nedi had set aside her prior arguments about the need to coordinate their rescues to confound the Council, noting that this time there would be a dozen rescuers and not only one.

"With so many of us in the air, it's almost guaranteed there will be several rescues happening within hours of each other. That will split the Council's focus. Besides, with the increased scrutiny, it's more important to get to the towers as quickly as we can. As soon as someone finishes their tower assignment, they can move on to picking up the wandering royals. The dragons have assured us not even the full Council can get through the wards around their land, so it's imperative to get as many of us behind those wards as quickly as we can."

That meant the amphitheater floor was crowded with dragons, piedlings, and royals as everyone attempted to get ready and leave at once, not to mention the other royals there to see off friends or siblings, or those who simply wanted to keep working on the staging for the showcase—and the supplies and projects in progress for *that* were taking up no small amount of space as well.

Gerald surveyed the chaos from above, thankful they could take off right from their balcony rather than having to fight through the mob on the ground. "You chose a good chamber to put us in," he told the dragon as Omar packed away the last bundle of supplies.

The dragon preened and then bared its teeth at Calin when the piedling pointed out it hadn't had much of a choice at the time.

Calin had insisted on checking Gerald's leg once more before they left despite his protests, and she lectured him sternly about not overdoing.

"I'll take care of myself," Gerald promised her, trying in vain to cut off the flow of instructions, warnings, and recriminations.

"And if he doesn't, we will," Omar called from his perch on the dragon's back. "Come on, now, or we're going to have to wait ages before we have an empty bit of sky to take off into."

Calin crossed her arms but let him go and he crossed the cave as quickly as he could while minimizing his limp. He scrambled up the dragon's side and Omar reached down to haul him up the last few feet. Within moments, he was strapped in and the dragon took flight, beating the first dragon off the amphitheater floor by a scant few wingbeats.

As if all the dragons were harnessed together the same way the royals were harnessed to them, the other twelve all launched themselves in rapid succession and the air was suddenly full of multicolored scales and wings. Gerald's hands tightened on the harness as he remembered what had happened the last time he had been in the center of multiple dragons in the air.

Omar reached over and pried Gerald's fingers open before slipping his own hand into Gerald's grip. "It's all right," he said gently.

"I know," Gerald said. "I know, but..." He trailed off, but Omar squeezed his hand like he knew what Gerald was thinking—what he was *feeling*. The dragon gained altitude with a few powerful beats of its wings and Gerald relaxed once they were above the crowd and then relaxed further as they all began to scatter in different directions. But he didn't let go of Omar's hand.

Chapter Eighteen

"THERE IT IS," the dragon announced with satisfaction.

Gerald peered vainly out toward the horizon. "I don't see it."

"You will soon," the dragon said. "Watch the cliffs."

"I don't even know what I'm watching *for*," Gerald protested. "Are the towers on the cliff?"

"They're *in* it."

"They're *what*?" Gerald said.

"Oh," Omar said. "That's why there are two so close together. Of course. I've heard of this—it's the labyrinth."

Gerald was still staring out and as the dragon rapidly closed the distance, he realized the massive rock formations they were approaching weren't cliffs so much as canyons. He whistled softly. "How did they *make* that? It can't be natural."

"The canyons are, I think," Omar said. "Or were. I mean, there were canyons here before. This wasn't always a desert; I don't know what happened, but when the water here dried up, it carved canyons and tunnels as it went. But it *was* magic that turned the natural canyons into a labyrinth."

"And now there are two towers in the center."

"More like, there are two centers, each with a tower," Omar said. "You never heard of the labyrinth?"

"No. I don't think so. I didn't pay attention to any of this stuff, the towers, the questing." He shrugged. "I didn't think I'd be participating. But we don't have to go through the labyrinth, right? I mean, the dragon can fly us over it to the towers."

"Well..." the dragon said. "Not exactly. The canyons get quite narrow. I won't fit."

It sounded a little sheepish about it.

"You mean we're actually going to have to solve the maze, then?"

"Well, not exactly," the dragon said. "I can direct you. It's not so narrow I can't see into it. But it is too narrow for me to get in. I'll have to land at the entrance to let you in, and then direct you from the air."

Gerald rubbed at his knee, frowning. "I don't know. Maybe I'd better stay with you," he said to the dragon. "I'll only slow Omar down."

"It might take us longer to get to the towers but freeing the guardians will go a lot faster with you there," Omar argued.

"The Council, though... We shouldn't be here for any longer than we have to be."

"I haven't felt any spells," the dragon assured them. "Their attention will be divided, anyway, with all of us out at once."

"Divided attention is still attention," Gerald said.

"All the more reason for you to come, then," Omar said. "We can split up and each take one tower. You might take longer to get to yours, but you'll free your guardian before I free mine, I bet. We'll each take about the same amount of time."

Gerald hesitated but then nodded. "All right. Fine."

The dragon banked and spiraled to the ground. A cloud of dust puffed up under its feet as it landed. Omar and Gerald kicked up smaller clouds of dust when they slid to the dry ground.

Omar tilted his head back and whistled in appreciation. "It looks even bigger from down here," he commented, staring at the striped sheets of rock surrounding them.

Gerald nodded, but he wasn't looking up at the height of the canyon walls. He was looking ahead, at the entrance to the labyrinth.

"Do you have the supplies you need?" the dragon asked, breaking into their reveries. "I don't sense any magic, but we should not delay too long in any case."

Gerald patted his knapsack. "I do. Omar? I know you have a spell diagram, but do you have a chisel?"

"Yeah. The piedlings gave everyone a kit."

The dragon nodded, satisfied. "Get going, then. I'll take off once you're clear."

Gerald adjusted his grip on his canes and made his way toward the entrance to the labyrinth. He felt painfully slow and awkward next to Omar, who had easily caught up with him and was now adjusting his pace to not leave Gerald behind. *Whichever tower I end up at, the royal is never going to believe I'm a rescuer.*

"You can just walk," Omar said, and Gerald looked over at him in confusion. "I mean... You go faster when you don't think about it. You're walking like you're trying to hide your limp, and yeah, maybe you are making it less noticeable, but you're also slowing down. I don't care if you limp."

"I didn't realize," Gerald said. "That I was doing that, I mean. I know you don't care about it." The words *But I do* were left unspoken, but they still managed to hang in the air.

"I almost wish we weren't picking the royals up," Omar said quietly as they approached the first intersection.

"What? Why? I mean, I was kind of thinking the same thing, but you're much more social than I am."

"Just that," Omar said. "You're going to go all shy and distant like you did in the dragonlands."

"There won't be so many strangers," Gerald said. "It'll be fine."

"Go left!" the dragon called from above, and Omar swallowed whatever he had been about to say. They stayed together for two more turns and then the dragon directed them into separate corridors.

"See you soon," Gerald said.

"Be careful."

"You too."

The dragon flitted back and forth in the air above them, carefully monitoring their progress. "How much farther is it?" Gerald called up. Even with no effort to disguise his limp—there was no one there to hide it *from*—he had been slowing down. Erick's spells had masked the pain of the burns while they healed, but they did nothing for the cramping soreness in his back and hip as a result of his uneven gait. His walking around in the dragonlands hadn't built up that much stamina; he had been planning to stay with the dragon on these rescues.

"Not too far," the dragon said. "Omar is at his tower already."

Gerald adjusted his grip on his canes and forged ahead, trying not to think about having to make the trip back to the start of the labyrinth. *One thing at a time.*

Despite the dragon's assurances, it felt like an awfully long time before Gerald turned a corner and caught sight of the tower. There was no guardian visible, but he had learned from Tska that meant nothing. Whether or not he could see it, something was there, and it was undoubtedly watching *him*.

Whatever it is, it can't hurt me while it has the collar on. He took a breath and started moving toward the tower. "Hello!" he called.

"Oh, a rescuer! It's been a while since the last one." A dark-haired girl was leaning out of the window and waving. *So I got the princess's tower...Natali.* "Did you send a letter?" she asked. "I don't recall getting a notice..."

"No," Gerald said. "Um. It's a long story. Is your guardian around?"

"Of course. But you can't fight the guardian unless I give you permission to try to rescue me, and I don't even know who you are."

"I'm Gerald. But I'm not going to fight it. I'm going to free it."

"Oh. I see. That makes more sense, I suppose."

Gerald looked up at the princess, puzzled at her calm acceptance. "It does?"

"Well... It's not like you *could* fight it."

Gerald flushed and turned his attention from the princess to the surrounding area. "Regardless...the guardian doesn't know if I'm here to fight or not. It should show itself."

As soon as the words were out of his mouth, he heard a soft growl behind him. Slowly, slowly, he turned around and found himself staring into the bared fangs of a mountain lion.

Gerald gulped. *It can't hurt me,* he reminded himself. "Hello," he said. "I'm not here to fight you... No need for the growling."

The cat flicked its tail back and forth but made no move to either pounce or back away. "You want that collar off, don't you?" Gerald pressed on. "I can take it off you. I've done it before. It won't take too long... If you lie down, I can take the collar off."

"Are you a magician?" Natali called down.

"No. You don't have to be, for this. You just have to alter the symbols on the collar the right way."

He took the diagram out of his knapsack and showed it to the mountain lion, which made the princess laugh. "It's an animal!" she said. "It can't *read.*"

"I've found the guardians have all been a lot smarter than the royals thought they were," Gerald replied.

The mountain lion sank to the ground with the boneless grace so typical of cats of any size, and Gerald resisted the urge to say, "So there!" to the princess. He lowered himself to the ground with much less grace and set his canes to the side. "I'm going to chisel some new symbols and change some of the ones that are already there," he told the guardian. "It might be a little loud, but it's not going to hurt or anything. That's okay, right?"

The mountain lion stretched its front paws out and rested its chin on them. It flicked its yellow eyes toward Gerald, as if to say, "The collar's right here. What are you waiting for?"

He pinned the diagram flat and started working. Natali was calling something else from the tower, but Gerald tuned her out to concentrate on the collar. True to his word, it wasn't long before he made the final alteration. The collar immediately began to rust and weaken, and Gerald gave it a final hard tap with the butt end of the chisel. The metal split and the collar fell to the ground in two pieces, where it crumbled into dust.

The mountain lion immediately began to groom the matted fur around its neck and Gerald backed away carefully, suddenly aware that without the collar's restrictions, there was no guarantee the big cat wouldn't decide he was the right size for a meal. He used his canes to lever himself back up to his feet and then looked up to see the mountain lion watching him with those big yellow eyes. Despite what Natali had said, there was clear evidence of intelligence in them. It slowly climbed to its feet and stretched languorously before it turned and disappeared into the canyons.

Gerald let out a breath he hadn't realized he was holding and turned his attention back to the tower.

"You can come down now," he told Natali.

"I don't want to be rescued by you," she retorted.

"Good, because I don't want to rescue you."

"Oh? Then why do you want me to come down?"

"I said it was a long story, didn't I? I'll explain it as we walk, all right? I'm not trying to rescue you or marry you or interfere with you finding a spouse or anything. But you do need to come with me. Omar's at the other tower, and the dragon is waiting for us—"

"The *dragon*?"

"Yes, it was my guardian. I freed it and now it's helping us free the others. Look, just come down, will you? Please. Omar's better at explaining than I am. And it's a long walk and—" *I'm already tired and I don't want to keep standing here.*

"All right! You don't need to get so worked up about it." But she hesitated. "Um. How do you want me to get down, exactly?"

"How do... Oh." Gerald blinked. The dragon had lifted him out of his tower. They had left Princess Elinore in her tower in the Burning Swamp and Princex Taylor had rescued Thierry. "I think I have some rope..."

"This was a very poorly planned rescue," she grumbled as she rappelled down the side of the tower. "The rescuer is supposed to come get me, not make me come to them."

"Yes, well, I told you this isn't a rescue. It's more of a...*relocation*. Come on."

"Don't you want your rope back?"

"Who's going to climb up and untie it? There's more rope in the supplies." *And this way it might look like you ran away.* "Let's go."

Despite her grumbles about the unorthodox nature of the not-rescue, Gerald had to admit she was taking everything more or less in stride. If she had balked at climbing down the rope, what would he have done? She was correct in pointing out he couldn't exactly come up after her. She had also taken his warning that it was a long walk to heart, and she had climbed down wearing sturdy shoes and a split skirt of the sort that noblewomen often wore for riding.

She was moving a lot easier than Gerald was. If it hadn't been for the fact that Gerald was the only one who knew where they were going, he had the feeling she would have left him behind without a second thought. As it was, she would stride ahead and leave him limping along behind, only stopping to wait for him at the intersections.

"Which way next?" she called over her shoulder.

"Uh, left, I think," Gerald said as he navigated around a bit of rockslide rubble.

"You *think*?"

"I'll look when I get there."

"You're awfully slow, you know."

Gerald resisted the urge to pick up a bit of rock and chuck it at her head. "I am aware, actually," he said icily. "Thank you."

"I'm just saying, if you could tell me the turns, I wouldn't have to wait for you."

"You'd still have to wait for me. The dragon's hardly going to take off without me. Besides, you've been waiting around in a tower for how long? I can't believe you're this impatient now."

She sighed and flopped down on a boulder to wait for him to catch up.

A few intersections later, Gerald was ready to send her on ahead, if only to give himself a break. He looked up at the sky again, but the dragon was still absent. *I hope Omar didn't run into trouble.*

"All right," Gerald said. "We're almost out now. Go straight here, then left twice, right, and straight again. Can you remember that?"

"Straight, left, left, right, straight," she repeated.

"Go on ahead, then. But don't go wandering off once you're out of the labyrinth."

She was up and darting ahead almost before Gerald had finished speaking. "I'm not *that* slow," he grumbled to himself. But the pain in his back and hip had been growing worse and he had to admit he had been slowing down more and more. *At least Calin isn't here to tell me I'm overdoing it*, he thought as he gritted his teeth and continued to push ahead.

Straight...left...left again and he had to stop. The exit was so close, but not close enough he could get there without resting.

"Gerald? Where's your royal?"

Gerald looked up to see Omar coming around the corner with a prince dressed head to toe in black trailing behind him. *He must be roasting*, Gerald thought absently. "Oh... She went on ahead. I was too slow for her."

"Are you okay? You're kind of pale."

Gerald grimaced. "My... It's more walking than I was anticipating. I'm okay. We're almost out."

He pushed himself back to his feet and let out a hiss of pain.

"Oh yeah, you're fine," Omar said.

"We're almost out," Gerald repeated stubbornly. "Let's just go."

"If you're sure," Omar said doubtfully.

Gerald forced himself to start walking. He made it about a dozen feet before his bad leg buckled and he stumbled to his knees.

"Completely fine," Omar muttered under his breath as he helped Gerald back to his feet. "Give me that cane. Lean on me instead." He draped Gerald's arm over his shoulders and Gerald couldn't stifle a sigh of relief as Omar took his weight. "Stubborn," he chided.

Gerald wisely didn't respond and didn't mention it wasn't the first time he'd fallen. His knee felt scraped and bruised.

With Omar's help, their pace improved, and it was only a few more minutes before they reached the entrance to the labyrinth. The dragon had landed and was trying to persuade Natali to go ahead and climb up to its back, but it cut itself off when it saw Omar and Gerald limping in with the black-clad prince trailing behind them.

"What's wrong? Are you hurt?" it asked anxiously, lowering its head to peer at them.

"I'm fine," Gerald said through gritted teeth. "Just...overdid it. Don't fuss. We need to get going."

"I haven't sensed anything," the dragon started to say, but it subsided when Omar mouthed something at it. "Nevertheless, probably best to leave before I *do* sense something, I suppose. And I *was* trying to get the princess ready to leave," it added.

"I wasn't expecting a talking dragon!" Natali protested.

"I *told* you about the dragon," Gerald said.

"You didn't say it *talked*."

"Just get up there, will you? I am not in the mood for this."

"You need to sit down," Omar said to him. "Come on. You get up there too." Even though the dragon lay as flat as it could, Omar still had to give Gerald a boost. He buckled himself in and tried in vain to get comfortable while Omar chivvied the chattering princess and silent prince up to join him.

"All set?" the dragon asked. "Yes? Here we go, then."

Gerald's stomach dropped as the dragon took off with a jolt that sent a spasm of pain shooting through his hip. "*Oxa*," he muttered. "No, I'm fine," he added as Omar opened his mouth. "It hurts but it's not going to kill me."

"Can I have my explanation now?" Natali asked. "Did he tell *you* what was going on?" she added to the black-clad prince. "The crippled one just said it was a long story and he'd tell me later."

"He's not crippled," Omar snapped. "And it is a long story. Luckily for you, we've now got plenty of time to tell it."

The long story got even longer as Natali repeatedly interrupted with questions and criticisms. When she finally let Omar finish, they had been flying for some time. The prince still hadn't said a word. Gerald didn't blame him. He didn't think anyone would have much luck getting a word in edgewise until Natali ran out of steam, and he wasn't interested in trying.

The dragon's flight was as smooth and even as ever, but there was no way for Gerald to get comfortable sitting on its back. His back and hip were cramping and throbbing, and he had the feeling they were going to keep doing so until he had a chance to lie down flat on a surface that wasn't moving.

"Do you want to make camp early?" Omar asked him. "You're still awfully pale."

"No...we should be at the next tower soon. We should stick with the plan. As soon as the Council realizes the labyrinth towers are empty, they'll suspect we'll be heading for this one next. No point giving them more time to realize and set a trap."

"All right," Omar said. "But I'll handle it. You stay on the dragon's back."

"Trust me, I have no interest in going anywhere."

"We're picking up Padma?" Natali asked with interest. "We've been corresponding for a while. Oh, this should be interesting."

"Why do you say that?" Omar asked warily.

"She's a bit more, hmm, conservative, shall we say? I don't know what you told *him*," she said, nodding at the silent prince, "but *he*"—nodding at Gerald—"was not all that convincing. And Padma is going to need a lot of convincing."

"Well, the dragon will be with us this time," Omar said. "If necessary, it can simply spell her."

"You can't enchant her!" Natali protested. "That's unethical."

"We don't have time to argue about it. And dragons don't have the same ethics as us, anyway. It's not going to *hurt* her."

Gerald closed his eyes as they continued to argue. He was almost ready to ask the dragon if it could put a spell on Natali as well when it announced, "We're here."

"If you're so worried about it, then you can come and try to convince her while I free the guardian," Omar said. "Let's go."

Gerald cracked an eye open long enough to see the dragon had landed on a rocky spire jutting abruptly out of the landscape. The tower was perched right at the top and it looked like a long climb from the ground to the peak. *This isn't a natural rock formation,* he thought, but then again, neither was the labyrinth. He trusted the dragon and Omar to take care of things, and he was too tired and sore to get involved even if he didn't. He watched Omar and Natali slide down the dragon's side and then he got as comfortable as he could, closed his eyes again, and prepared to wait.

WHEN HE OPENED them again, it was dark, and Omar was shaking him gently. "Gerald? We're making camp."

"What? Oh. Did you get...uh..."

"Padma," Omar supplied. "Yes. No trouble. Natali was exaggerating, or else Padma just felt amenable to the quest."

"The guardian?"

"It was another dragon. I can't believe you slept through that, actually! It was quite the reunion. It was a very young one, only about half the size of ours. It's gone straight back to the dragonlands, ours was quite insistent about it getting out of danger."

"Did the Council—"

"Oh, no, no," Omar said hurriedly. "Theoretical danger. We're all fine, everything's fine. But how are you? Can you get down?"

Gerald considered it. Sleeping slouched over against the dragon's neck hadn't done anything to ease his muscle cramps. If anything, they were worse now. He moved his bad leg experimentally and winced. "Not without some help, I think," he said.

It ended up being rather a *lot* of help, but after the dragon obligingly flattened itself as low to the ground as it could, Omar was able to get Gerald down. He promptly slid to a seated position and leaned back against the dragon with a groan.

"What did you *do* to yourself?" Omar asked.

"Tried to walk two miles with one leg that's two inches shorter than the other." He kneaded at his hip. "My legs, my hip, my back, everything is cramped and screaming at me. I wasn't thinking. It's not only my balance that's shot. My whole body's twisted up."

The dragon nudged him, and he groaned again. "And now I'm whining again on top of everything else. Sorry."

"You're in pain, you get a bit of a pass on the whining," Omar said. "But only a bit," he added with a wink. "Look, what would help? I've got the tent set up if you want to go lie down; or if you're hungry, I—well, someone—can get some dinner going."

"You should go for a swim," the dragon said. "The water will help. You don't even need to *swim*, really, just float in the water."

"I'll keep the others away," Omar said before Gerald could object.

"I don't want to move," Gerald said.

"It will help," the dragon repeated.

"I don't think I can walk."

"I'll help you."

"I'm leaving my clothes on."

"No one's asking you to take them off."

The dragon nudged Gerald again and he sighed. "All right, fine." He held out a hand and Omar pulled him to his feet. With a great deal of cursing on both their parts, they managed to reach the lake. After pausing just long enough to get their boots off, Omar waded right in, dragging Gerald into the water with him.

Gerald started to object but broke off in a sputter when Omar swept his feet out from under him. "The dragon said *float*," he said sternly. "Lie back. And of course I came in with you, you think I trust you not to drown right now?"

Any further objections died unspoken as the water took Gerald's weight away and his cramped muscles relaxed.

They stayed in the lake until Gerald began to shiver with cold. Omar towed him over to the shore and helped him regain his feet.

"Can you walk now?"

"Better than I could before," Gerald said. "I'm still sore, though. I hope I recover before we get back to the dragonlands, or else Calin is going to kill me."

Omar hid a smirk. "I'll cover for you."

Gerald leaned heavily on his canes and followed Omar to the tent, picking his way carefully over the uneven ground. "Is it safe to be camping out in the open like this?"

"The dragon set a ward. And it took off all the royals' tracking spells, of course, so the Council can't scry us. They don't know where we are."

Omar held the tent flap open and Gerald ducked through it with a wince. "Let me know when you're done changing," Omar said as he let the flap close between them. "I need to put on dry clothes, too."

The tent was illuminated with one of the dragon's mage lights and Gerald quickly located his pack. Still shivering, he laboriously began to struggle out of his wet clothes. He winced to see his bad leg when he finally managed to wrestle the clinging fabric off. The scars were puffed up and his knee and hip were both badly swollen, even after soaking in the lake. He rubbed some of Calin's salves into his abused muscles before wriggling into a dry pair of trousers.

But when he tried to pull his wet shirt over his head, a stab of pain forced him to halt. His back muscles were so tight and twisted, he couldn't physically get his shirt off. "Damn it all," he muttered. Then, taking a breath to brace himself, he raised his voice just enough to carry through the fabric of the tent. "Omar? I, uh, need a bit of help."

Omar immediately ducked into the tent. "What's wrong?"

Red-faced, Gerald gestured at his shirt. "My back's too sore... I can't get my shirt off."

"Oh. All right, that's not a problem. You don't have to look so embarrassed." Omar knelt next to him and helped Gerald feed his arms through the sleeves so he could draw the shirt over his head. Gerald shuddered when Omar touched his bare skin and Omar paused. "Gerald? You're not just embarrassed, are you—you're frightened! But what do you think I'm going to do?"

He sounded so hurt and bewildered that Gerald fought down his unease enough to answer. "It's not you. It's not. I don't know what it is, but it's not you. I can't be scared of you. I'm *not* scared of you. It's just, it's just..." he trailed off. With Omar's confused eyes still staring into his own, he tried again to put his tangled thoughts and emotions into words. "It feels vulnerable," he finally said. "I don't know. I've never been comfortable being undressed or being touched. It's not you."

That was all he could say, and he kept trembling until Omar helped him into a dry shirt and he was fully clothed once more.

"I'm sorry," Gerald offered awkwardly, but Omar shrugged the apology away. He turned away from Gerald and quickly changed his own clothes while Gerald stared at the tent wall and wondered, not for the first time, what exactly was wrong with him.

"All right," Omar said into the brittle silence. "Let's just...move on. Are you hungry? I'm sure one of our rescuees is a better cook than I am."

"Do you think we should cook?" Gerald said. "I mean. Even if they can't scry for us directly, they could still be looking. Wards or no, won't a fire make us obvious? We have cold provisions, and it's warm enough here that we won't need to make a fire to stay comfortable overnight."

Omar rubbed his nose. "I don't know how the wards work. I guess it won't hurt to be cautious. We'd better spread the word, then. I'll go talk to them. Why don't you write to Erick and Nedi? Let them know we're on schedule." He put a slight emphasis on the last two words and Gerald returned his wry smile.

"I'll bring you back something to eat," Omar added over his shoulder as he ducked back out of the tent. "You should probably rest, anyway."

Gerald flopped back into his bedroll and stared up at the ceiling, his eyes stinging.

Why am I like this?

Chapter Nineteen

A GASP WOKE Gerald up midway through the night. He bolted upright in a panic—*did they find us? Are they attacking?*—and then hissed with pain when his sore back protested the sudden movement.

"Gerald?" Omar said sleepily. "What's the matter?"

"I thought I heard something..."

Another gasp sounded, and then a moan, and another and Gerald's face burned as he realized no one was being attacked—quite the opposite.

"Oh!" Omar said, smothering a laugh. "Well, I guess that explains why we didn't have any trouble persuading Padma to come along. She and Natali had been *corresponding*, huh? I'm not sure that's how I would have phrased it..."

Gerald pulled his blanket over his head. "I can't hear you. I can't hear them. I hear nothing. I *heard* nothing. La-la-la-la."

He drifted back to sleep with Omar's laughter ringing in his ears.

THE DRAGON ROUSED the five of them as soon as the sun rose. Natali and Mikkel—who still, so far as Gerald knew, hadn't said a single word—made quick work of breaking down the camp while Omar harnessed up the dragon. Gerald waited by the supplies, felt useless, and tried not to make eye contact with either of the princesses. His efforts were in vain, however, as Padma came over to introduce herself.

"Hello, there!" she said cheerfully. "I hope you're feeling better this morning. Omar said you were somewhat ill."

"Oh, um, yes, something like that," Gerald said, looking everywhere but at Padma. The princess was short enough that actually wasn't all that difficult. She didn't take up very much space. "I'm better this morning."

"I'm delighted to hear it. I'm Padma, by the way," she said with a curtsy. She was wearing breeches and a tunic for traveling, but she still managed a surprisingly elegant curtsy despite the lack of skirts.

"Gerald." He bobbed his head in a sketchy imitation of a bow.

"Are you sure you're all right?" Padma asked. "You're awfully red. Do you have a fever?"

"No, no, I'm fine. Really." He ducked away as Padma reached out a hand to feel his forehead, causing him to lose his balance, trip over a pack, and land heavily on the ground.

"Oh! I'm so sorry. Are you all right? Do you need a hand?"

"No!" Gerald snapped when Padma tried to help him up. "I don't— don't touch me. Just...just leave me alone. I'm fine."

He levered himself up with his canes, bit back a gasp of pain as his back protested, ignored the surprised hurt on Padma's face, and moved away as quickly as he was able—*not very*, he noted bitterly—to the relative safety of the dragon. It lowered its head to nuzzle Gerald and even that gentle touch was enough to knock him off balance again. "I hate these damn canes," he said into the dragon's neck. "I hate my damn leg."

He cut himself off there before he let all his frustrations bubble to the surface and turn into a full-on rant.

"You humans," the dragon sighed, "are so *fragile*. You are so easy to break and so hard to put back together."

"He's not broken," Omar snapped. With his face pressed against the dragon's scales, Gerald hadn't seen or heard him approach. "You're not broken. And *you're* not helping," he told the dragon.

"I only meant—" the dragon started, sounding abashed.

Omar cut it off. "It doesn't matter." Then, looking equally abashed, he rubbed his nose and apologized. "Sorry. Something in the air this morning. Everyone's snappish. Let's just get going. Gerald? Do you need a hand up?"

He wanted to say *No*. Firmly. Like he had to Padma. No help, no hands, no human contact. But his back still hurt and Omar wasn't Padma and so he nodded wordlessly and let Omar boost him up the dragon's side.

Natali, Padma, and Mikkel climbed up much more easily. The princesses watched him struggle into place—Natali with an uncomfortable combination of disgust and fascination, Padma still looking hurt by his earlier outburst. The prince was staring vaguely off into the distance. He still hadn't spoken. Gerald was starting to wonder if he *could*.

"Did you hear back from Nedi or Erick?" Omar asked once they were airborne.

Gerald shook his head.

Omar frowned. "I hope everything's all right."

"I'm sure we would have heard if it wasn't. It was late when I wrote to them, and there was nothing urgent in my message. They'll write back when they have time." A sudden thought struck Gerald then and he smirked.

"What?"

"Just—aren't I supposed to be the worried one?"

Omar made a warding gesture. "Oh no! It's rubbing off on me." But he was grinning as he said it.

"I'm glad *someone's* in a good mood," Padma grumbled behind them.

Gerald reddened and turned around to face her, his back protesting the movement. "I'm sorry about before," he said. "I shouldn't have snapped at you."

She brightened. "Oh. Well, thank you. I was actually directing that comment at Natali, though."

Natali scowled at her and Gerald frowned and looked at Omar. "When you said earlier that something was in the air—do you think that was true? I mean...could the Council be doing something? Trying to get us to fight with each other?"

He shrugged helplessly. "I'm not a magician. That sounds like something you could do with a spell, all right, but...wouldn't they have to find us to cast one on us?"

"Dragon?"

"The spell would have to be targeted," it confirmed. "But it could have been targeted on the towers. Any would-be rescuer would activate it, or perhaps it would only be activated in certain conditions, a nontraditional rescue effort...or it could have been targeted on an item one of our royals brought with them."

"Can you sense any spells?"

"This is ridiculous," Natali broke in. "We've been flying all over the continent, we slept in tents, we had a cold dinner and a colder breakfast, why wouldn't we all be a little touchy?"

"I would think *you*, at least, would be in a good mood this morning," Omar said with a meaningful glance between the two princesses. "You sounded happy enough last night." Padma blushed and covered her face while Natali glared bloody murder at him.

"Omar!" Gerald snapped, his face nearly as red as Padma's.

"Sorry," he said sheepishly. "But look! I wouldn't usually say something like that! Dragon, *is* there a spell here?"

"Not one I can sense," it said. "The princess may have the right of it. In which case... I expect you all to correct your behavior."

No one was inclined to argue with the dragon, and they subsided into silence.

IT WAS MIDDAY by the time they reached the next tower, and the general mood had improved as the sun rose higher. Mikkel still hadn't spoken, but Omar quietly told Gerald he *could*; they had spoken at his tower the day before. "He's just shy, I think. We're a crowd, for him."

Gerald, used to not fitting in with a group, wanted to say something to reassure Mikkel, especially when Natali began making snide comments about his silence—comments that were hardly likely to get him to speak. But he was afraid of saying the wrong thing and the persistent ache in his back, hip, and knee made it hard to concentrate. *I can't even make myself comfortable, let alone Mikkel.*

He was relieved when the tower came into view and gave him something to think about other than his physical and Mikkel's mental discomfort.

"Let's do this the same way as at Padma's tower," Omar said as the dragon began to glide in for a landing. "Everyone stay in your harness, be ready for a quick takeoff. I'll get the guardian's collar off, the dragon will grab the royal, and we'll be underway."

"Surely we can get down for a minute," Padma said, raising her eyebrows significantly.

"It's really better to stay on the dragon's back," Omar said. "If the Council is watching the tower—"

"Just for a minute," Padma insisted.

"I really don't—"

"She needs to relieve herself, idiot!" Natali snapped, causing both Padma and Omar to turn red with embarrassment.

"Oh. Oh! Well. Yes. Fine. Just don't, um, dawdle."

The three of them spent the next few minutes very pointedly not looking at each other while the dragon spiraled down for a landing on another unnatural-looking rock formation. *At least these are easy to get to. Canyons and mountains and all that—we can fly right in. No forests, no swamps, no murderous squirrels... It hardly seems like a challenge at all.* Gerald smiled wryly to himself, well aware of how difficult it would be to get out to the middle of the rocky plain—let alone to the top of the spire of stone where the tower rose stark against the sky—on foot or horseback instead of via dragon.

The dragon touched down delicately and a head immediately popped out of the tower window. "Wow! A whole rescue committee?"

"More or less," Omar called up. He was already undoing his harness. "Whoever's getting down, get down, but get back on the dragon sooner rather than later," he instructed. He raised an eyebrow at Gerald—*are you getting down? Do you need a hand?*—and Gerald shook his head.

The girls joined Omar on the ground. Mikkel stayed with Gerald on the dragon's back. Gerald couldn't help but notice Mikkel relaxed as the others moved away. He gave the silent prince a friendly smile and then turned his attention outward.

The princesses had vanished from sight, and Omar was standing at the base of the tower, his head tilted upward as he conversed with the tower royal. There was no sign of the guardian—or of any Council interference.

"Dragon?" Gerald said quietly.

It turned its head to regard him.

"They can scry a fixed point, right? Would you be able to tell if they were watching us?"

"No," the dragon admitted. "Scrying is a very passive spell. I can only sense active casting."

"Is there a way—can you hide us from scrying?"

"Ye-e-es," the dragon said slowly. "To a degree. I can 'fog' us, so to speak. Anyone scrying the tower will only see gray. But that will also reveal our presence."

"It will reveal *a* presence," Gerald corrected. "It will hide our identities. And it will keep them from watching us undo the collar spells."

"But why—oh. If they discover the weak points, they can modify them. Yes. I see." It narrowed its eyes in concentration, made a complicated series of gestures with its foreclaws, and then hissed a sibilant word in the dragon tongue. "There," it said. "We are shrouded."

Just as it spoke, a shriek split the air.

"Padma!" Natali cried.

Omar dashed around the side of the tower, his knives materializing in his hands, and the dragon lunged after him, jolting Gerald and Mikkel.

Padma, her initial shriek of panic transmuted into shouts of anger, was dangling from the claws of a huge, glossy-feathered bird, while Natali lay on her side, half-obscured by the dust cloud stirred up by the bird's massive wings.

"Release her!" the dragon commanded. "She is not a rescuer, nor has she challenged you. You have no leeway to touch her."

The bird opened its beak and croaked a response.

The dragon blinked. "Its collar is damaged. The restrictions against harm do not hold."

Omar, his knives still bared, flicked his gaze toward the dragon from where he was crouched defensively over Natali. "Do something, then!"

"I don't think it *wants* to hurt her," the dragon said hurriedly. "But it can."

"Well, I don't *want* to hurt it, either, but I will!" Omar snapped. "If it hurts Padma, I'm not taking its collar off."

The roc cocked its head and fixed Omar with one of its glittering eyes. It croaked again and the dragon hissed in response, and then it opened its claws and dropped Padma to the ground. She stumbled and fell to her knees but got up quickly and ran for the relative safety of Omar's knives. The roc dropped to the ground after her and folded its wings.

"It wants the collar off," the dragon supplied.

"Yes, well, how do I know it's not going to take my head off when I try?" Omar muttered. "Padma, are you all right?"

"Bruised. But I'll live. Natali?" She reached out a hand and helped the other princess to her feet.

The roc croaked again.

"It has chicks," the dragon said.

At that, Omar started shaking his head. "No. No. So I take its collar off, and it's going to take me to feed its chicks. This is too dangerous."

"I'm not going to let it take you anywhere," the dragon said. "And it didn't have all the facts before. It doesn't want to hurt you. Besides, rocs don't really eat people, that's all a myth. It wouldn't feed you to its chicks. You're entirely wrong for them, nutritionally speaking."

"That...probably shouldn't be as reassuring as it is," Omar said. He shifted his grip on his knives and then sighed and sheathed them. "Fine. You two, get back on the dragon. Just in case."

Padma and Natali didn't need to be told twice. They were clambering up the dragon's side in moments, and although they were both dusty, Gerald noted neither one looked to have any injuries beyond a few scrapes and bruises. Mikkel pulled his hood over his head and looked away as he hunched his shoulders again. Gerald once again was torn between wanting to say something to him and not knowing what to say. He turned away and watched anxiously as Omar approached the roc.

Omar was moving very cautiously, but he could only be cautious for so long. He had to get right up next to the roc to work on its collar, well within the range of its sharp claws and serrated beak.

"You're *sure* it's not going to hurt me?" he asked, not taking his eyes off the roc.

"Completely," the dragon replied. "Go ahead."

With a last moment of hesitation, Omar stepped within its reach. The roc didn't move as he took another step, and then another, and then he took out the chisel and went to work. The roc stayed as still as if it were carved out of rock, but the atmosphere was tense. The dragon had settled into a relaxed posture and was watching the proceedings with an air of extreme unconcern, but Gerald was focused intently on the roc, waiting for something to go wrong.

When Omar carved the final symbol into the collar, he backed away without shattering it. It wasn't until he was closer to the dragon than to the roc that he looked at it and said, "You can break it off now. The spells are dead."

The bird exploded into motion, moving far faster than anything of its bulk had any right to, and within seconds it was in the sky, the collar a pile of rusted scraps on the ground. Omar let out a shaky breath and sagged against the dragon.

"Just one more," he said, half to himself.

"Omar? You're all right?" Gerald asked hesitantly.

He looked up and found a smile. "I'm all right. Let's get the royal and get going."

He climbed up the dragon's side and clipped himself back into the harness. It took him two tries; his hands were shaking. Gerald took one of his hands in his own and gave it a reassuring squeeze. Omar smiled at him and squeezed back.

The dragon carried them all around the tower, where the royal—Robin, Gerald remembered—was still hanging out the window. "What *happened*?" they yelled. "I heard a scream and I couldn't see *anything*!"

"Your roc tried to snatch me," Padma said.

"Now *we're* snatching *you*," Natali added.

"That's really not how I would phrase it—" Gerald said hastily, but he was cut off when the dragon reared up and plucked the royal out of the tower. "Oh, well. It's like this..."

Chapter Twenty

GERALD'S TWO-WAY parchment finally chimed as they approached their final assigned tower. The cliffs and canyons had flattened out some way back and the landscape had slowly transformed into a desert like the one Gerald had been stashed in. They had put up the canvas covers to shade them from the sun, and the dragon's flight generated a constant breeze, but even so, the heat frayed at some tempers. The dragon had snapped at Natali twice to *just be quiet, please!* while Mikkel hunched further and further into his hood every time the acerbic princess spoke.

Gerald welcomed the distraction of the incoming message and he hurriedly shuffled through his pack to find a bottle of ink. Padma and Robin looked up when the chiming started, but the oppressive heat dampened their interest and Mikkel and Natali didn't react at all. Gerald dripped ink on the parchment and Omar peered over his shoulder to read the words as they appeared.

> *Get to your towers as quickly as you can and get back here as quickly as you can. The Council is starting to act. Nedi got tagged with a tracker at her last tower. They know where we're gathering. They're setting up on the outskirts. They haven't done anything yet, and they can't pass the borders. But they can stop the rest of us from passing, too. Get here FAST and SAFE.*
>
> *Erick*

Gerald swallowed. "You know it's serious when he's not calling me Meathead," he said to Omar. Then he read the message aloud for the dragon, who flicked its tail in irritation.

"They're not keeping me out of my own home," it said. "I can handle the Council."

"We have to get back there first."

The dragon scoffed and kept flying.

"EVERYONE STAY ON the dragon this time, please," Omar said as it began to circle the final tower. "At least until the guardian is gone."

But for once everything went smoothly. The guardian—a lovely chestnut Pegasus—was docile and easily divested of its collar. The royal, a bespectacled prince named Dion, was fascinated by the dragon and *asked* if he could join them before even hearing who they were or where they were traveling. "This will make a wonderful study," he kept repeating.

Less than an hour after landing, they were back in the air. The dragon flew past dusk and into full dark, and likely would have kept flying long into the night if its passengers hadn't begun to object. By the time it landed, Gerald's hip was aching fiercely, and his bad leg would barely take his weight, no matter how heavily he leaned on his canes. There was no lake to soak in, either.

"I think this is the first time you haven't landed by water," Gerald commented to the dragon while the others set up tents.

"There is enough water in the supplies," it said. "I'm going hunting."

It took off without waiting for a response and Gerald stared after it in surprise. *I guess Erick's message has it more worried than it let on.*

Mikkel had vanished into his tent as soon as it was standing, and no one else was acting particularly sociable either. The tents went up one by one and the royals quickly disappeared into them. Robin into one, Dion into another, and the princesses together into a third—all three set somewhat away from Mikkel's.

Gerald stayed where he was, leaning against the supplies until Omar came over and sat next to him.

"How's your leg?"

"Better than yesterday, but still not great," he admitted. The soreness and cramping had eased up, but the scrapes and bruises from his falls ached and his knee was swollen.

"Good enough to make dinner?"

Omar accompanied the question with such a pleading look that Gerald laughed. "I can make dinner. That might drag everyone out of their tents, too."

Omar widened his eyes in surprise. "You *want* them out of their tents?"

"Well... I mean, it's one thing for me to not really be all that social. I'd be happy to go into our tent and stay there, away from everyone. But when no one is being social, I don't know, it's different for all of us to be hiding than for there to be a group of people that I'm hiding from." He shrugged self-consciously. "I don't know, it makes more sense in my head."

"No, it's okay. I kind of get what you mean."

"It doesn't really matter anyway. Can you get a fire started? I'll find something to cook."

Omar tilted his head to scrutinize him, but then said, "Okay," and walked away. Gerald watched him go. He wished he knew what the right things to say were. *I couldn't talk to Mikkel. Now I can't talk to Omar. I don't even know what I want to say, but I know I want to say* something.

He shook his head and started looking through the supplies.

THE SMELL OF roasting vegetables and steeping tea slowly but surely drew the royals out of their tents, all but Mikkel. Gerald had to admit he hadn't been expecting the black-clad prince to join them. He put a tray together and Omar carried it over to Mikkel's tent without needing to be asked. *That's the one problem with tents*, Gerald thought as Omar set the tray on the ground outside it. *There's no way to knock.*

But the next time he glanced over at the lone tent, the tray was gone. He smiled.

The hot food and drinks had the others smiling as well. By the time the dragon returned from its hunt—and settled down to fastidiously clean its claws and teeth—the tension had broken and there was laughter and chatter flying around the fire. *This is the type of scene I don't mind leaving*, Gerald thought, and as if Omar were reading his mind, he caught Gerald's eye at that exact moment and glanced toward the tent, then back at Gerald, as he raised an eyebrow. Gerald nodded and raised an eyebrow in return, and Omar nodded back and held up a finger. *Just a minute—* he had to extricate himself from a conversation with Robin. No one was talking to Gerald; he levered himself up and started making his way toward the tent Omar had set up earlier. Natali watched him get up and limp away and he tensed, half expecting another comment. But none came and before too long he was far enough away that none would. It had grown dark enough that no one could see him once he left the circle of light cast by the fire.

The dragon had sent a mage light after him as he passed by, and under its light, he dashed off a quick note to Erick: *we're on our way back with everyone, has the Council done anything, keep us posted.* He was just finishing when Omar ducked into the tent.

"I think I understand what you meant before," he said as he sat and started taking off his boots. "It's normal for you to stay in the tent, but it's not normal for them to do it. That out there, that's their normal. You didn't feel right leaving them in their tents because that's not right for them."

Gerald nodded. "Yeah. That's exactly what I was trying to say." Something about the way Omar had phrased it made him think, though. It *was* his normal to avoid groups and gatherings, but he wasn't sure he liked other people pointing it out to him. He picked up his note to Erick as a way to change the subject and Omar smirked when he saw how little Gerald had written.

"How much do you want to bet we wake up with a ten-page missive from Nedi about every detail of the Council operation and a minute-by-minute plan to sneak us back over the border?"

"I don't take bets I'm going to lose," Gerald replied. "But I think I'll let the dragon handle getting us over the border. It's what we do after that we'll need Nedi to plan out."

Omar gave him a questioning look. "It's not like they're going to sit there quietly and let us get on with things," Gerald said. "They don't even know what we're doing! But I'm not going to worry about it now. Out loud, anyway," he added when Omar started to open his mouth. "We're still a few days away unless we start flying through the night, and I'm too tired to think about it."

Omar smothered a yawn. "*You're* tired? I'm the one who was running around dealing with guardians all day," he teased. "You just sat there on the dragon and relaxed."

"Pretty sure I was forbidden to get off the dragon," Gerald retorted. "By *you.*"

Omar closed his eyes and pretended not to hear.

PANTING AND MOANING from the neighboring tent woke Gerald up again and he buried his head in the blankets, wishing he slept a little more deeply.

He could still hear them, even with the blankets pressed against his ears. Now he was aware of the noise, it was all he could hear. He turned over and muttered a curse under his breath.

"Gerald?" Omar whispered. "Are you awake?"

"Unfortunately."

"Can I... Do you mind if I ask a question?"

"Go ahead."

"Does it bother you? What they're doing?"

Gerald hesitated. "Not exactly. I mean, I wish I didn't have to listen to them. It... It embarrasses me, I suppose. It's such a private thing, and I can hear them, and it's like I'm invading their privacy. But bedding itself... People like it, and I know that, and I don't care that they like it. It doesn't bother me what other people do, just as long as it doesn't involve me."

"You don't care that other people have sex?"

"Why do you sound so surprised? It's not that I object to the, the *act*. Not in and of itself. I don't think it's *wrong*. It's just, it's not something I want to do or am interested in doing. But, you know, I'm not interested in, oh, in sailing. I don't think about sailing, I don't particularly want to ever go sailing, but I don't care that other people sail. They can do all the sailing they want, so long as they don't try to get me on board."

"You sound so, I don't know, *nonchalant* about it now," Omar said carefully. "But the last time we talked about it, you were, well, you were very upset."

"I guess I don't feel like you're judging me for it," Gerald said quietly. "You listened, last time. And you're asking questions now, not to upset me or tell me I'm wrong, but because you want to understand. Right?"

It was also easier to talk in the dark. He could see Omar's outline, he could see Omar nodding as he spoke, but he couldn't see his expression; if he couldn't see surprise or shock, disgust or disbelief, it meant he could assume it wasn't there. With none of those emotions present in Omar's voice, either, Gerald was comfortable enough to press on. "If you look at my sailing metaphor—to me, it's all the same. Not being interested in one thing or another thing, to me, it's the same. It's just how I am. The difference is that the world doesn't care that I'm not interested in sailing. But it does care—a *lot*—that I'm not interested in bedding. The world acts like I'm saying I'm not interested in, in *breathing*. Like I'm not human, like it's a problem that needs to be fixed. And it's...it's just how I am."

"And there's nothing wrong with how you are," Omar said fiercely. "You're right. I don't think it's that hard to understand. I mean, it's unusual, definitely. But you know, there's so much variation. Some people like men, some people like women, some like thirds...some people like more than one, or even everyone. Why shouldn't some people like no one?"

"But I still have to marry someone," Gerald sighed. "And, you know, it's not only going to be me who's miserable in that marriage, not unless I can find someone else like me. And that hasn't happened yet."

"*Yet* being the key word there, I think," Omar said. After a brief hesitation, he asked, "And... Do you really need to find someone *like* you or just someone who understands you?"

"I don't know. Honestly, I don't even know how a relationship would work for me. I mean, without bedding...what would make it a marriage?"

"Well...your feelings. You can love someone without taking them to bed."

"But how do you know? How do you know if it's love?"

Omar shrugged helplessly. "You just know. You like being around the person, you think about them when they're not there, you miss them. You think about what you want to say to them when you see them again. You want to be around them all the time. You want to talk to them, to tell them everything, to listen to them, to hear everything they have to say. You want to share yourself with them, to share a life with them."

"I don't think I've ever felt that."

"Well, love, it's rare. You have to look for it."

"Like Natali and Padma are?" Gerald asked sardonically.

"Ah, well, that's sex. That's easy to find. Love is harder."

Chapter Twenty-One

GERALD WAS STILL thinking about their conversation the next morning. It had happened so late at night he could almost imagine it hadn't happened at all, that it had only been a dream. *My parents never understood or tried to understand. Neither did Lila, neither did Erick, neither did any of my family. Why should Omar be any different? Did he really say any of that?* But the way Omar looked at him over breakfast made it clear he was thinking about that conversation as well. But it wasn't something to be brought up in front of the others.

The others, who were barely out of bed and already starting to grumble. It *was* early—the dragon was prodding them all to hurry up and eat, wanting to get underway as soon as possible. Despite grumbles about the hour, there wasn't much real argument about it; with the Council lurking outside the border, they all wanted to get back to the dragonlands as quickly as possible.

Mikkel stayed in his tent until the last possible moment and then stayed huddled under his cloak and hood. Gerald once again desperately wanted to say something, knowing how miserable the silent prince had to be. *And if he's this overwhelmed with six strangers, what is he going to do in the dragonlands with more than a hundred of them?*

After some hesitation—he still didn't know what to say—Gerald approached Mikkel. He moved cautiously, not wanting to startle him, but he wasn't exactly subtle with his limp and his canes; Mikkel heard him coming and looked up warily, crossing his arms protectively in front of his chest.

"I—" Gerald started. "Um. Are you doing okay? I know this isn't so easy, especially when the others are in bad moods...and what Natali's been saying. I'm sorry about that."

A series of emotions flickered across Mikkel's face—surprise, relief, confusion, suspicion—before he schooled his features back into blankness. He shrugged or made a movement that might have been a shrug, a minute twitch of his shoulders.

"Right," Gerald said awkwardly. "I guess saying I'm sorry doesn't really help, does it? But I wanted to say something. Just so you'd know...I don't know. I would've liked that, I think, if in the past someone had told me the way I had been treated wasn't right. Even if they didn't fix it."

Getting no response, he gave Mikkel a friendly nod and then turned to pick his way back over to the dragon. It was early enough that a chill was in the air, and his leg was stiff with it. He hadn't gone more than a few yards before a presence at his side made him look up. Mikkel wordlessly offered his arm and Gerald took it.

"HOW FAR IS it to the dragonlands?" Robin asked after they had been in the air for a while. "The ground is going by so quickly... We must be days away from my tower by horse already."

The dragon snorted. "Horses are slow," it said disdainfully. "But even at this speed, we are still several days away. The situation is not so urgent yet that I need to fly through the night, so...hmm...we will camp tonight and tomorrow night and reach the dragonlands on the third day, I would think. Weather permitting," it added, turning its head to survey the encroaching clouds.

"*Don't* tell me we're going to fly through the rain!" Natali said.

"All right, I won't," the dragon said, showing its teeth.

Gerald sighed. *This is going to be a long day.*

Despite waterproof cloaks and canvas coverings, they all got thoroughly drenched by the rain. There was simply no way to shelter from it while flying through the clouds; it came in from every angle. Before long, everyone was soaked, chilled, and utterly miserable. *At least everyone is too miserable to complain,* Gerald reflected. A sullen, sodden silence had settled over them some time ago.

But that was the one and only positive effect of the rain, and as time wore on Gerald stopped thinking the tradeoff was worth it. The cold rain was playing havoc with his bad leg, and he shifted so often trying to ease the cramps in his thigh and back that he nearly worked himself right out of the harness, and still he couldn't find any relief. The discomfort ratcheted up into outright pain and the pain got steadily worse, no matter how he moved or kneaded at the tight muscles.

Finally, gritting his teeth, he said, "Dragon? Is there anywhere we can stop for a minute?"

"Anywhere *dry*?" Dion added hopefully. The bespectacled prince looked half-drowned and was blinking owlishly behind rain-spattered lenses.

"I'll look for a sheltered spot," the dragon said. "I suppose it's about lunchtime anyway."

There, Gerald thought. *We'll stop. I just need to hold on until then.*

It wasn't long before the dragon spotted a cave and spiraled down to land, but it felt like an eternity. The others sighed with relief as soon as the dragon ducked inside out of the rain.

"I hope the supplies stayed dryer than we did," Padma said. "I want to change clothes."

"I'll start a fire," Robin offered. "Er, that is, if there's any dry wood..." They looked back out into the storm and trailed off.

"Get some wood and I'll make it burn," the dragon said.

"Oh!" Robin blinked, gulped, and hurried away.

Gerald was still slumped over the dragon's neck, kneading at his thigh. He was only vaguely aware the rain had stopped falling on them. He was so thoroughly soaked it didn't make much of a difference.

"Gerald?" Omar said softly. "Come on, we all need to put dry clothes on."

Gerald raised his head and Omar let out a low whistle. "*Ras*, you look awful!"

"Leg's all cramped," Gerald managed.

"All right, let's get you down." Omar quickly undid the harnesses and helped Gerald to the ground. His leg buckled as soon as it touched the ground and then he was lying on the cold stone. "Straighten your leg, you have to stretch the cramps out," Omar instructed. Gerald wanted to curl into a ball, but Omar grabbed his foot and forced his leg to unbend as far as it would go while Gerald sucked in a ragged breath

"What's wrong?" the dragon was asking anxiously. Gerald closed his eyes and let Omar reassure it.

Finally the cramps began to ease and he was able to open his eyes and sit up. Omar and the dragon were both leaning over him and he resisted the urge to close his eyes again. Instead he looked back at them and said, "I can't do this. Not in this weather. I *can't*." His voice cracked. "I know we need to get back as soon as we can, but it hurts so much."

He hated the way he sounded: weak, pleading. But he knew it was the truth. He *couldn't* do it. Not *wouldn't* but couldn't. He simply wasn't capable of getting back on the dragon and going back out into the rain. He dropped his gaze to the ground, not wanting to see the looks of disgust on their faces. "I'm sorry," he added softly.

"No, I'm sorry," Omar said. "I was too busy feeling soggy and sorry for myself to notice you were in pain. We should have stopped sooner."

"Your injury is still recent," the dragon reminded him. "Even with your cousin's spells. We have been pushing you too hard. You are not recovered and I will not make it worse. The rain slows me down anyway. We will not lose that much time by waiting it out."

Gerald closed his eyes again, but this time with relief. *I don't deserve friends like these*, he thought, but he was too grateful for them to even think about saying so.

Omar reached out a hand and helped Gerald to his feet and dug through the supplies for a pack of clothing. "Go put on dry clothes. Here's Robin with the wood. We'll get a fire going. You'll feel better when you're warm."

He limped deeper into the cave until he was far enough from the entrance that it was dark and shadowed and he was sure no one could see him. He quickly stripped, dried off, and dressed, wincing as he ran his hand over the still-twitching muscles of his bad leg but thankful at least that his back wasn't sore enough that he needed help with his shirt.

The others were all huddled around the fire when he rejoined them, even Mikkel, although there was a sizable gap between the silent prince and the others. Gerald knew as soon as he warmed up, Mikkel would withdraw from the group again. From the way Natali was glaring at him, Gerald couldn't help but think that would probably be better for him. *Why does she dislike him so much?* he wondered. *I'd think she would simply ignore him...it's not like he's picking fights.*

The dragon's announcement that they would stop until the rain did was met with widespread relief. Dion even let out a small cheer.

Gerald was torn between wanting to cheer too and feeling desperately guilty at the delay, no matter what the dragon had said about not losing much time. They were still losing *some*.

He limped over to Mikkel, but the black-clad prince looked up from under his hood and shook his head. When Gerald didn't move away, Mikkel did. Without a backward glance, he slunk away from the fire into the shadows of the cave. Gerald knew what it was like to want to be left alone, so he bit back the instinct to call Mikkel back over to the warmth of the fire. He let him go and then lowered himself to the ground, setting his canes next to him and kneading at the sore muscles in his thigh.

I pushed too hard at the labyrinth and sleeping on the ground and flying in the rain isn't helping.

"How's your leg?" Omar asked, watching him knead at it.

Gerald shrugged. He didn't really want to talk about it in front of the others, but even without an answer, Omar's question sparked their curiosity.

"What's wrong with it, anyway?" Dion asked.

"I got hurt," Gerald said shortly.

Rather than quash Dion's interest, that vague answer seemed to increase it. "How? Were you a rescuer? Did a guardian do it when you were rescuing him?" he asked, nodding at Omar.

Gerald blinked. "I didn't rescue Omar. I wasn't a rescuer."

"Oh, he rescued you, then? But how did a guardian hurt you if you weren't fighting it?"

"He didn't rescue me. No one rescued me."

"But...if you didn't rescue him, and he didn't rescue you...how did you end up together? You're both princes, right?"

Gerald blinked at Dion and looked across the fire at Omar. Omar wouldn't meet his eyes. "Yes, but what does that have to do with—wait, do you mean 'together' like 'how did we end up traveling together?' Or do you mean 'together' like..."

"A couple," Dion finished. "Yeah."

"We're... We're not a couple. And I wasn't hurt by a guardian," Gerald added, hoping to change the topic, even if it meant talking about his leg.

"What do you mean, you're not a couple?" Dion sounded honestly bewildered. "You like each other, don't you? And you share a tent..."

Gerald could feel his face turning red. "We're *friends*. I can't set up my own tent with my leg like this, and it's stupid to make Omar set up two when we can share. But we don't—we're not—we're only sleeping. *Separately.*"

"Oh. Sorry. I just thought..."

Robin shushed Dion. "It's too late to stop while you're ahead," they stage-whispered, "but maybe you should stop before you get any further behind."

Gerald's face felt hot enough to rival the fire and he could have hugged Robin for their intervention. The princex caught Gerald's eye and winked and Gerald gave them a grateful smile. Omar was still avoiding his eye.

"Well," Dion said a moment later, sounding a little more subdued, "How about this weather, huh?"

THE RAIN PERSISTED throughout the day and the cave grew cold and clammy outside of the radius warmed by the fire and the dragon's body heat. They all stayed close to the fire as a result, even though the tension Dion had inadvertently caused had never really died down. Omar still wouldn't look at Gerald, who was beginning to envy Mikkel's decision to grab his tent and some blankets from the supplies and ensconce himself away from the rest of them.

But I can't set up a tent and I can hardly ask Omar to do it now. He rubbed at his face, annoyed and frustrated. *I need to talk to him, don't I? Stupid leg. Stupid rain.*

Tired of Omar ignoring him and tired of the others' banal conversation as they tiptoed around the tension, Gerald levered himself to his feet and limped away from the fire to join the dragon. It was at the cave mouth, staring out into the rain. Gerald squinted into the growing darkness, but he didn't see anything that could have caught the dragon's attention.

"I'm sorry we're stuck here," Gerald said quietly. "I want to get back there too."

He sat and leaned back against the dragon's warm side. It nudged him affectionately. "You have to be in shape to face the Council when we get there," it said. "And if we showed up with you looking the way you did earlier, Calin would skin me."

Gerald shuddered to think of what the fierce piedling would do to *him* for disobeying her orders. "She's probably going to take my canes and confine me to bed again regardless." He sighed. "Maybe she'd be right to do it, too. I *am* slowing us down, no matter what you said before."

"The Council can't get past the border," the dragon reminded him. "Our rush is self-imposed. And if they do somehow manage to get past it, they'll very quickly wish they hadn't."

Gerald flinched at its predatory grin and unconsciously started to rub his leg. The dragon noticed. "Is it still paining you?"

"What? Oh." He folded his arms self-consciously. "Not like before, but...yes. It aches. All my muscles ache."

"You shouldn't be sitting on the ground. The cold stone isn't going to help with that."

Gerald shrugged. "There aren't a lot of options here."

"At least sit on a blanket." The dragon lowered its voice, as much as it could. "You don't need to make yourself uncomfortable on top of being upset."

"Who says I'm upset?" he asked, but he sounded petulant even to himself. "Sorry. You're right. But I don't want to talk about it."

"That's fine; I'm not the one you need to talk to."

"I know." He rubbed his face again. *I told* him *I don't, I* can't *feel that way. He acted like it was okay... I told him! I don't want to talk about it again.* "I wish I were a dragon. I bet dragons don't have these problems. Maybe I should just stay in the dragonlands, assuming we ever get back there. Forget Andine. Forget being a prince. Forget people."

"Dragons have problems of our own. The neighbor's gold always glitters brighter."

"Yeah, well, it would have to. I think all my gold is tarnished."

GERALD STAYED AT the dragon's side, bundled in blankets, until it grew fully dark and the only light was coming from the fire. He had been semisuccessfully imagining he was alone, that it was only him and the dragon, that they were back in the desert, back before he had come up with this plan, before he had met Omar or any of them, before he had flown all over the continent and gotten his leg burned to a crisp. He could ignore the murmured voices and the incidental sounds of people moving in the background. But he couldn't ignore Omar sitting next to him with a mug of tea.

Omar offered it to him, and Gerald was tempted to ignore his outstretched hand the way Omar had been ignoring him. But the steam smelled good and his hands were cold, so he reached over and took it. He held it up to his face and caught a glimpse of his reflection in the dark liquid. He looked away before he could catch his own eye.

They sat silently for a long moment, long enough that Gerald thought Omar was going to walk away again without ever saying anything.

"There are enough tents," Omar said finally. "If you want your own. I don't mind setting up two."

"Should you have to?"

"What...what do you mean?"

Gerald turned his head to look at Omar. He was staring straight ahead, out into the rain. "I mean, is there a reason why I should want my own tent?"

He wanted Omar to tell the truth. But instead, he scowled and snapped, "Why are you doing this?"

"Doing what?" Gerald asked. "I don't know what the situation is. You know I don't like you like that. You know I have trouble telling when people like me. I *told* you that. And you said you would tell me if you started liking me like that. You said you would *tell* me, in *plain Common*. And you haven't. You haven't told me you like me, so, from my perspective, you don't. I didn't think anything of sharing a tent. I didn't even think there was anything to think about. And I didn't think you did either."

He took a breath. Omar was still looking out into the rain. He wouldn't meet Gerald's eye. The dragon was silent behind them. Even its breathing was quiet, as if it were trying very hard not to disturb them. "We're friends, aren't we? No matter what else is happening. And, all right, maybe I've been oblivious, maybe it would have been obvious to anyone else, but I'm not a complete idiot. Or maybe I am, because if Dion hadn't said anything, I never would have known. But he did say something and the way you reacted was obvious enough even for me to notice. I don't understand why you didn't tell me. You *said* you would tell me."

He hated how childish that sounded, but he couldn't stop it. He was hurt Omar hadn't told the truth. Had let him talk about personal things and had kept his own silence. Had pulled away when the truth came out, had ignored him, and even now was refusing to simply come out and say it, or even deny it. Until it was acknowledged, one way or the other, Gerald didn't know what to do with it. Didn't know what it meant, didn't know where they stood.

Didn't know where he *wanted* them to stand.

"I'm sorry," Omar said. "I didn't want to say anything. I knew you hadn't realized; I knew you weren't going to realize. And I wasn't planning to *do* anything, so I thought...well, I thought why did you need to know? I didn't want to mess things up. I didn't want to make you uncomfortable." He shrugged helplessly.

"You don't need to *protect* me," Gerald said. "You're my friend, not my, my *nursemaid*. You don't get to decide what I need to know! You don't get to decide what's going to make me uncomfortable, and you don't get to decide I can't handle being told the truth!"

Omar flushed. "I don't—I didn't—I wasn't thinking about it like that. I told myself it was for you, for your benefit. But really I didn't want to take the risk. I told you I didn't want to mess things up. I didn't want to risk losing you. I was being selfish. I'm... I'm sorry."

He sounded sincere, and contrite enough that Gerald didn't want to drag it out any longer. "Thank you," he said.

Omar exhaled loudly. "You shouldn't have to thank me for apologizing. I shouldn't have let it get to the point where I needed to apologize."

Gerald nodded. "You shouldn't have."

"I really am sorry, though. I didn't want to mess things up, and that's exactly what I did. I made it even worse."

"When Dion brought it up..." Gerald said. "You could've come clean. You could even have denied it—I obviously wasn't going to figure it out on my own! But you didn't do *anything*. You didn't admit it, you didn't deny it, and you wouldn't even *look at me*."

"Because I messed up!" Omar said. "Because I was afraid of how you would react. If I didn't see your expression, if I didn't hear what you had to say about it, I could pretend it hadn't happened, that I hadn't ruined things."

"We're still friends, I said. At least, I still want to be friends. But I don't know what you want now."

Omar shook his head in frustration. "It's not *now*. I mean, you just learned about it. But my feelings aren't new. They've been there."

"For how long?"

"A while," he admitted. "I don't know exactly. But when you got hurt...when we had to leave you there to get help and I didn't even know for sure you would be alive when we got back...that's when I knew for sure you were...you *are*...important to me."

Gerald leaned back against the comforting bulk of the dragon. "That's why you didn't want to leave by yourself when I was still healing. Why you fought with Nedi about it. Because you *liked* me."

"Yeah."

"You must think I'm an idiot for not noticing. *Erick* knew," he realized. "He said some things... I didn't understand it at the time. Everyone knew but me, didn't they?"

"I don't know. Maybe. I don't know how well I hid it. But no, Gerald, I didn't think you were an idiot. I was...all right, I was maybe a little surprised at first. I mean, I know what you told me, but part of me thought, you know, it can be hard to pick up on subtle cues, maybe all you'd ever gotten was subtle cues. But then I saw you really didn't notice. And you know, it was kind of a relief. I mean, it's not like I could flirt *wrong* if you didn't even know I was flirting. And like I said, I wasn't planning to *do* anything. So it was... I don't know, it was safe. I could like you without being rejected, without being hurt."

Gerald shook his head in confusion. "But... I mean, I was rejecting you, wasn't I? Maybe not directly, not *you* specifically, but I'm rejecting, you know, romancing."

"I don't know," Omar said again. He finally turned to look at Gerald and they made eye contact for the first time since Dion had made his comments. "I don't know how relationships work for you. How you want them to work, I mean. It didn't feel like rejection. It felt like... it felt safe. I don't know how to explain it."

"I don't know how relationships work for me either," Gerald said. "I don't know how I want them to work. I don't even know *if* I want them to work. I like... I like the *idea* of it, I think. Not of romance, not of bedding, but of a partnership. But I don't know what that means in reality."

"Well... If I haven't ruined it...if I haven't messed things up by not talking to you like I said I would...we could maybe try to figure it out? Together?"

He was all but vibrating with tension and nerves and his expression was painful for Gerald to see, it was such a mix of fear and hope. He wanted to say the right thing and he wasn't sure what that was. "I know I like you as a friend," Gerald said finally, haltingly. "I don't like that you kept this secret, not when it involved me, not when other people knew about it. I've been on the wrong end of that before, you know? Being outside of things. I'm hurt, okay. I trusted you with all this stuff, with things about me that have made other people reject me. Things I don't like to talk about. And you wouldn't trust me with something that was *about* me."

"I'm sorry," Omar said earnestly. "I really am."

"I believe you. And I...it's not like I hate you for it. I don't even know if I'm *angry*, really. But I just... I don't know where to go from here. Can we start by going back to how it was? Being friends. *Talking*. Sharing a tent without it being strange or awkward. Can we get back to normal and then think about if there's somewhere else to go from there?"

"I...yes. Yes. I can do that. We can do that. Friends?"

"Friends."

They both let out a breath and then exchanged a smile, a smile of relief and then of simple happiness.

Behind them, the dragon rumbled with contentment. "I knew you were a sensible pair. We'll make you honorary dragons in the end."

IT WAS EASIER said than done to go back to acting normally. They were still awkward around each other and when they rejoined the others around the fire, Dion watched them with open curiosity and Natali smirked. "Did you kiss and make up?" she asked.

Omar made a rude gesture and she laughed. "I'll take that as a yes."

Padma swatted her shoulder and she subsided, but Gerald could still feel himself blushing. He couldn't decide if he was more embarrassed by the idea of kissing Omar or by the fact that they all thought he had done it. He knew his blush would only confirm their suspicions. *Why do I care if they think I kissed him? I didn't, I know I didn't, he knows I didn't, and also—no one besides me thinks kissing is a big deal.*

"You know, my leg is still bothering me," Gerald said. "I think I'll turn in early. The dragon will probably want to get moving as soon as the rain stops."

It made for a convenient excuse, but it also happened to be true. When he was safely hidden away in the shadowy comforting darkness of the tent—the same single tent he and Omar had been sharing, which prompted another laughing comment from Natali that Gerald was relieved he hadn't quite heard—he dug out the supplies Calin had sent along and started massaging the piedling's creams and ointments into his aching muscles and swollen scars.

Omar pushed the tent flap aside and ducked inside with a mage light. Gerald flinched at the light more than anything, at the light that showed exactly how bad his leg looked with the scars puffy and purple and glistening under the ointments, but Omar stammered out an apology that made it clear he thought Gerald was flinching because of *him*.

"I can go back outside—"

"No, it's okay. We're going back to how it was, right? This is how it was. You've seen me do this before, I mean. If it were yesterday, you would've stayed. So...stay. But...you don't have to look."

Omar stayed. He set the light down and turned his back and got dressed for bed, exactly like he had done the previous night and the night before that, as if nothing had changed. But there was a new self-consciousness about his movements, and Gerald couldn't help the knot of anxiety that was growing in the pit of his stomach.

Forget what I said about not knowing what this means for me. I don't even know what this means for him. *I told the truth when I said I didn't think anything of sharing a tent. Even not wanting him to see my leg, not wanting help with my clothes when my back hurt so badly, I wasn't thinking about any of it like that. But was he? He can't find these scars attractive. But what does he think when he sees them? What did he think when he helped me take off my shirt?*

Gerald shook his head, three rapid, jerky movements, as if he could shake the thoughts right out. He didn't like the questions and was afraid he would like the answers even less. He didn't want to think about it.

"Are you sure you're okay with this?" Omar asked hesitantly. He still had his back turned, but he glanced over his shoulder to look at Gerald as he asked.

"No," Gerald admitted. "I'm not sure of anything. But... objectively...what reason is there for this not to be okay? I don't want to kiss you or bed you or any of that. And whether or not you want to, you're not going to, because I don't want to and you're not going to force me."

"I would never—!"

"I *know*. I know. That's what I mean. You're not going to do anything, I know you're not going to do anything, and so, objectively, there's no reason for me to be uncomfortable."

"But you are."

Gerald shrugged and tried a smile. "I'm always uncomfortable about something. I'm used to it. I'll get used to this."

"I don't want you to get used to being uncomfortable with me. I don't want you to be uncomfortable at all! Look, I'll put up another tent, it's okay." He moved toward the tent flap but stopped when Gerald shook his head.

"If you do that, it'll make it worse. It'll mean there *was* a reason for me to be uncomfortable. Just leave it, Omar. I'm tired and my leg hurts, and I don't want to think about it or talk about it anymore tonight. Go to sleep. It'll be better in the morning."

Omar hesitated but gave in. "Well, all right. I'll take your lead. Good night, then."

He extinguished the mage light and Gerald lay back in the darkness and stared at the shadowed canvas walls. He stayed like that for a long time, his eyes open, until Omar's breathing slowed and quieted into the sounds and rhythms of sleep. It was only then he closed his own eyes and waited for morning.

Chapter Twenty-Two

THE RAIN HAD stopped sometime in the night. The sky was still gray and cloudy and the air was heavy with moisture, but it wasn't actually raining. The sun hadn't yet broken through to burn away the chill dampness and Gerald woke up in pain, his bad leg protesting the cold and the damp and the hard stone underneath the blankets.

"*Oxa, oxa, oxa,*" he cursed under his breath as he sat up and tried to massage the stiffness and aches out of his muscles and joints and scars. It didn't do much and he bit back a louder curse of frustration. Omar was still asleep, and he didn't want to wake him, especially not now. He dug himself out of his cocoon of blankets, found his canes, and crawled out of the tent. The fire had long since gone out, no one wanting to let it burn unattended and no one wanting to stay up to tend it, but the dragon was still there, and Gerald was drawn to it for its body heat as well as its overall comforting presence.

Its eyes were closed, but it wasn't snoring, and he suspected it was only feigning sleep. "Dragon?" he said softly, and its eyes flicked open.

It took in his hunched posture, his white-knuckled grip on his canes, and his pale face. "You shouldn't be walking around," it scolded. "You look like you're about to drop."

Gerald grimaced. "We can't stay here until I'm better. We don't have that kind of time. I know healing isn't your specialty, but can you do something? Just for the pain?"

The dragon frowned. "You had such a poor reaction to draconic healing spells before," it reminded him. "I don't want to take the risk you would react poorly to mine. Not when we're so far from other help."

Gerald nodded, resigned. "The more reason to go, then. It will hurt whether I sit here or sit on your back, and at least the pain will have a purpose that way: we'll be traveling toward people who can help."

The dragon crooked its foreleg to make a seat and Gerald took it, relieved to get his weight off his leg, relieved to feel the warmth of the dragon's skin chasing some of the painful cold from his bones.

"What of the rest of it?" the dragon asked gently. "You spoke more with Omar." It wasn't a question.

Gerald closed his eyes. "I don't know. It's easy to say let's go back to how it was. It's harder to actually do it. I don't know what I want, I don't know what *he* wants, and I don't know what to do about it."

As if mentioning his name had summoned him, Omar stuck his head out of the tent and looked around. "Gerald?" he called softly.

"Over here."

"Ah." He held up a piece of parchment. "There's a message from Erick. Or Nedi. I didn't read it," he said, rather unnecessarily since the new-message alert was still chiming audibly.

"You could've read it," Gerald said. "It's not like there's anything personal in it."

"That you know of. Anyway," he added, "there's no ink in the tent."

He found some in the supplies and handed it to Gerald. He dripped it on the page and the gentle chiming faded away to be replaced by Erick's message scrawling its way across the page.

> *How far away are you now? More and more Council members started showing up yesterday; we might have the full thousand camped outside by now. They spent most of the day circling around, mapping out the borders and looking for weak spots. The dragons have been doing their own circling, following the Council members around. The border spell makes it so they can't see in, from their perspective the landscape just keeps going, but we can see out, so we know what they're doing even though they don't know what we're doing. I don't even know if they know what's behind the borders. I can't imagine they would be so calm and methodical about it if they knew there were dozens of dragons only a few feet away, watching them like hawks and leaking smoke from their nostrils.*

> *Nothing has happened yet, but it feels like something is going to. It looks like they're settling in for the long haul. Meanwhile, the dragons are up in arms. Some of them want to go out there and start breathing fire, strike first before the Council can do anything. That is obviously a terrifically bad idea, not least because it would guarantee the Council would attack. Right now they're only observing. But it's getting very tense. Nedi wants to parlay. She says for all the Council knows there's a nefarious*

plot and all the questing royals have been kidnapped for ransom or something more sinister. She thinks if we explain it all they'll have no choice but to go away and leave us to it.

She can make a forceful argument, but I'm not sure the Council would sit there and let her.

There's also nothing to stop them from casting a spell on whoever crosses the border. There are enough of them out there that even the dragons are wary of facing them—the dragons who aren't chomping at the bit to go start a war, at least.

Nedi's drafting a message to send to them to invite a parlay. But all of this was your idea. You should be here to meet with them, assuming they agree. So how far away are you now?

GERALD SWALLOWED AND then read the letter again, out loud this time.

"We lost half a day to the rain," the dragon said. "But we can make that up if we don't stop for lunch and wait a little longer to make camp. We can still get there by late tomorrow if we push."

Gerald rubbed at his leg and grimaced, knowing the kind of shape he would be in at the end of it, but all he said was, "We should get the others up, then."

"It's still not at a critical point," Omar started, but Gerald interrupted him.

"It sounds like it's getting there. I don't want to responsible for a *war*, Omar. Erick's right. It was my idea and it's my fault it's gotten to this point. I have to be there to face the fallout."

"It's *their* fault," Omar protested. "Their system, their corruption, their enslavement of the guardians."

"And I'll be sure to tell them that," Gerald said. "But I have to be there to do it."

He turned away and started writing a reply before Omar could say anything else. After a long moment, Omar muttered something under his breath, turned on his heel, and started rousing the others from their tents.

We can get there in two days, but late. The dragon's confident it can get us across the border, Council or no Council, although it hasn't said how. That should be soon enough. It'll take the Council time to discuss if they should agree to the parlay in the first place and then more time to negotiate terms. Especially if all of them are there, they're not going to agree with each other on anything. Nedi should be able to stall them for two days.

He hesitated and then wrote.

And three would be better. I'm not in very good shape. Calin's going to kill me when she sees my leg. You might, too.

AFTER A FULL day on dragonback, from dawn to long past dusk, Gerald started thinking he might just go ahead and kill himself and save Calin and Erick the trouble. For hours all he had been aware of was pain, which was so all-encompassing he had even stopped wondering when they would land and when it would end. It no longer seemed possible the pain would ever end.

"Gerald? Are you awake? We've landed. Let's get you down, okay?"

He was out of it enough that he wasn't sure he had responded, he wasn't even sure he was expected to, but he didn't resist when Omar started unharnessing him.

"There's a river here. Do you want to get in the water? Will that help? Gerald, are you listening? Gerald?"

Omar was starting to sound a little panicked and Gerald forced himself to respond. "It can't...hurt," he managed.

There was no suggestion of Gerald using his canes or getting himself to the river under his own power. He could barely manage to help keep his descent from the dragon a *controlled* fall, rather than a headlong tumble. His bad leg buckled underneath him when he touched the ground and he sat down heavily, leaning against the dragon's warm side.

"Can I do anything?" someone else asked. "Can I help?"

There was conversation in the background, but it floated over Gerald's head. He opened his eyes and saw Robin leaning over him, and then they helped Omar lift Gerald back to his feet. The two of them helped him to the river, half carrying him, one on either side holding him up so he could hop along without putting any weight on his mangled leg.

They stopped on the bank just long enough for Omar to take off his boots and wrestle Gerald out of his, and then he hauled Gerald into the water while Robin made their way back toward the camp.

The water was cool enough to startle a gasp out of Gerald and he thrashed a little, instinctively wanting to get out before the cold sent his muscles into further cramps, but then a comforting numbness began to spread and the support of the water, the weightlessness it provided, allowed his tense muscles to relax.

Gerald closed his eyes again and let himself float, trusting Omar to keep his head above water and keep the gentle current from tugging him away.

"I think you have a fever, too," Omar said. His tone was conversational, but Gerald realized he had been talking for some time and had stopped expecting a response. Omar rested a cool hand on his forehead. "Maybe the river's cooled you off. Or maybe it's just my hands that are cold. I wish Calin were here."

"You're...doing a...good job," Gerald murmured. "Feel better."

"Yeah? Better enough to eat some dinner? You didn't eat at lunch."

"If...you're...not cooking."

Omar let out a startled laugh. "You must be feeling better if you're joking. All right. Robin said they'd put our tent up, let's get into dry clothes. Can you walk at all now?"

"Don't know."

Omar towed him over to the bank and pulled him out. Gerald stood awkwardly balanced on his left leg, feeling the mud squelch up between his toes as he shivered in the cool of the night air. Omar pulled Gerald's arm over his shoulder and helped him take a halting step. "Are you okay? Or should I get your other human crutch?"

"No, 's okay."

They took another step and another and Gerald was concentrating so hard on remaining upright and in motion he didn't even realize they had reached the tent until Omar stopped walking.

The dragon, who usually remained slightly distant from the tents out of deference to its size and the fragility of the canvas, was right there, curled around the tent the way it had tended to curl around the tower back in the desert. It was watching Gerald with evident distress, and he reached out a hand to pat its scales.

"I'm okay," he told it. Its side was hot and he pulled his hand away quickly before it could start to burn.

"No, you're not," the dragon said frankly. "But this is not the time to argue about it. You're going to catch a chill on top of everything else if you keep standing here in wet clothes."

Omar helped Gerald into the tent and they both heard the dragon's muttered commentary about human fragility and design flaws as Gerald sat down heavily and straightened his leg with a grimace.

Omar closed the tent flap behind them and then looked everywhere but at Gerald. "What do you want me to do?" he asked.

Gerald squinted up at him. He still felt disoriented and muddled and like he had missed something. "What?"

"I mean... Well, can you get changed or do you need help?"

"Oh." He thought about it or tried to think about it. His thoughts were slippery and as he tried to chase them down and reach a conclusion, he lost track of what he was trying to decide.

"Gerald?"

"What? Oh." The idea of getting undressed and dressed again was overwhelming. It seemed like far too much effort. He was already tired. He closed his eyes.

"Gerald."

"I think...I...need help." Once the words were out, he noticed a vague sense of unease, a little knot of nerves in his stomach. There was a reason for it, he was sure, but he didn't know what it was, and he was too tired to try to pin it down.

"Okay. And you want me to help you, right?"

Gerald opened his eyes and blinked in confusion. "You're here."

"Right. I know. Okay. *Ras*, you really are fevered, aren't you?"

Gerald wasn't sure if that really needed a response. Omar didn't seem to be expecting one. He'd turned away and was rummaging through their packs and Gerald closed his eyes again. He opened them when Omar started to tug at his wet shirt. Gerald sat there passively and let Omar maneuver the clinging fabric over his head. Once it was off, Gerald started to shiver harder and he reached for a blanket to drape across his shoulders, but Omar handed him a dry shirt instead. Gerald held it and watched as Omar used the wet one to wipe the mud off his bare feet. Omar was still looking everywhere except at Gerald and once he noticed Gerald wasn't going to put the new shirt on himself, his lack of eye contact resulted in awkward fumbling with the shirt since Gerald couldn't seem to get his arms into the sleeves by himself.

His vague feeling of unease was increasing, fueled by Omar's own apparent discomfort. In his feverish state, Gerald still couldn't put his finger on the *why* behind it, but it seemed important. "What's...the matter?" he asked after a moment.

Omar sat back on his heels and finally looked at Gerald. "This feels wrong," he said bluntly. "You're sick, you're not thinking straight, and it feels like I'm taking advantage of you. You never wanted to undress in front of me. When I had to help you a few days ago, you *hated* it, you were so upset, and if you weren't feverish, you'd be even more upset by this than before, because of...because of me liking you."

Gerald blinked at him. "Oh. 'S true. But...too tired...to care...now."

Omar let out a breath that was half sigh, half laugh. "All right. I guess you'd hate it even more if it was one of the others. But here—" he grabbed a blanket and draped it over Gerald's waist before going back to helping him undress. "You'll appreciate this when your fever breaks."

He appreciated it *now*, albeit fuzzily. His unease faded with the blanket draped over him and Omar seemed more relaxed as well. At least until he got Gerald's pants off.

He hissed in dismay when Gerald's right leg came to light. "Oh... This looks a lot worse. No wonder it hurts." He dug through their packs again until he came up with the ointments Calin had sent and he started applying them to the swollen scars and scrapes. He did it gently, careful not to cause Gerald any more pain. Gerald held his breath and held still. The scars were so swollen that they were tender—he could actually feel Omar touching them. As disconcerting as the prior numbness had been, Gerald decided he would rather have numbness than this returned sensitivity. What was the good of having feeling in the scar tissue if the only thing it felt was pain?

"There. Is that any better?"

Gerald made a noncommittal noise, more an acknowledgment of the question than an actual response.

"Calin will fix you up tomorrow," Omar said. "Just one more day, one more flight."

Gerald didn't want to think about that. Dried off and dressed, his leg treated, he wanted to lie down and sleep and not think about anything: the pain, the flight, the awkwardness with Omar, the Council awaiting them...

He closed his eyes while Omar put his own dry clothes on, but Omar didn't let him slip into sleep. "You said you'd eat," he said sternly. "You need to eat something."

"Don't want...to move. And...no boots."

"Damn, I left them by the river. Mine too. All right, you can stay put. But if I bring you something, you have to eat it. Deal?"

"Deal."

GERALD'S HEAD WASN'T much clearer when he woke up. His skull felt like it had been hollowed out and then filled with wool; his leg still ached, and his scars and his knee throbbed in time with his heartbeats. He was tempted to close his eyes again and not face the world until he had to, but his bladder told him that time had come.

It was getting on toward dawn; the tent was still shadowy, but there was enough illumination he could find his boots and his canes. Moving enough to get his boots on was a chore—his bad knee was so stiff and swollen he could neither straighten nor bend his leg, it was stuck in one position—and he wasn't entirely sure how he managed to get himself out of the tent and then to a convenient bush.

The dragon had been snoring when he crept out of the tent, but it had roused in his absence.

"How are you feeling?" it asked when Gerald limped back over.

"Not great."

"Are you hungry? I can start a fire."

"No. Just tired."

He sat next to the dragon and rubbed at his swollen knee. "I want to be there already," he said quietly. "I want Erick to cast another spell and Calin to use her bandages and potions and I want my leg to be *fixed*."

"Some injuries can only be fixed so much," the dragon said, touching a foreclaw gently to the scars that ringed its own neck. "No matter how much we want it to be otherwise."

Gerald wanted to snap at it, tell it that its scars were only cosmetic, they didn't pain the dragon or keep it from doing anything. But he bit the words back unsaid and felt ashamed of himself for even thinking them. The dragon's scars were the result of years, decades, of slavery and ensorcellment. Even if the scars themselves didn't hurt—and he didn't even know if that was the case—he had seen the wounds that caused them, and he knew how painful those had been. The dragon had suffered that pain for years. It had been less than two months since Gerald was burned. How could he compare their pain? Why did he need to? It wasn't a contest.

"I know," Gerald said, his voice low. "How many of the guardians are like this, do you think? Like us. Is it enough to take the collar away and say, all right, go back to your life? Can any of us go back to how we were?"

"We can try. And we can make new lives, better ones, with those who understand what we've gone through."

Gerald leaned back against the dragon and closed his eyes. There was an idea there, somewhere, buried under the wool in his head. Something the dragon had said had caused a spark, but he was too tired to find it and fan it into life. "Remind me of that when I feel better," Gerald murmured. "I think it's important."

Chapter Twenty-Three

GERALD SQUIRMED AND twisted in the grips of a feverish nightmare, a childhood memory gone twisted, of when he and Lila were first taught to spar. In the nightmare, Lila's practice blade had morphed into sharpened steel, while Gerald's remained blunted wood. He stumbled and dropped his shield and it vanished as if he had never had one; Lila lunged and when he tried to block her strike his wooden blade was shorn right off at the hilt. Her sword continued on and drove deep into his knee.

He sat up with a gasp and then yelled in horror at the knife sticking out of his leg.

"Gerald! It's okay, it's okay, lie down." Omar's hands were on his shoulders, pressing him back down to the bed.

Gerald let himself be pushed back, his horror muted by confusion and shock and the realization that he didn't feel any pain, not from the knife and not from his aching hip or throbbing scars.

"There you go," Omar said soothingly.

"What's happening? Who stabbed me?" Gerald asked.

"No one *stabbed* you," Omar said. "Not technically... You have a bad infection. Calin is, um, draining the pus. No, sit down! You don't really want to see it. There's, uh, there's a lot of it."

"Oh." Gerald took stock. His memory was very fuzzy, and his head ached. "Calin... We're in the dragonlands?"

"Yes. We got here an hour or so ago. You've been very feverish, you slept almost the whole way here. Calin and Erick have been taking care of you. Just relax. Erick said you shouldn't be in any pain now, is that right? He's lying down, he was tired from the spellcasting, but he said to wake him up if you needed..."

"No," Gerald said slowly. "No, my leg doesn't hurt. I'm thirsty, though. And tired..." He started to close his eyes and then jerked them open again and sat up abruptly. "The parlay! When's the parlay?"

"Relax, relax," Omar said again. "They're still negotiating. The Council agreed to one, but they and Nedi haven't agreed on terms. Don't worry."

"Hold still," Calin said severely.

"Here, here's some water," Omar said. He held the cup for Gerald, who discovered he was weak and shaky, drained from the fever, when he tried to grasp it himself. After he gulped half of it, he felt better and didn't resist when Omar steered him back against the pillow. "Relax. Go back to sleep. You need the rest. I'll be right here."

Gerald closed his eyes and slipped back into uneasy dreams.

HE DRIFTED IN and out of sleep and fever dreams, never staying awake long enough to even know how much time had passed. Whenever he opened his eyes someone was there looking back at him—Omar, Erick, Calin or her sisters—and he would close his eyes and drift away again.

Slowly, the fever broke. Calin's herbs and ointments drew the infection out of his leg and Erick's spells took away the pain and worked to heal the damage. The next time he opened his eyes, he felt clearheaded for the first time since falling ill, and he was able to sit up and look around.

"What time is it?" he asked, after looking around for the windows that still weren't there.

"Around ten, I think," Omar replied. "In the morning. We got here the day before yesterday. You've slept almost the entire time."

"Oh. The parlay?"

"Tomorrow. Nedi was starting to fret about you not waking up on schedule. But how are you feeling?"

Gerald took stock. He wasn't muzzy or dizzy; his back and hip weren't sore; his leg ached a little when he moved it, but it was a far cry from the stabbing pain he had gotten accustomed to. "Not bad," he said. "A little sore. A little stiff. But overall...not bad at all."

Calin bustled in just in time to hear that and she put her hands on her hips to glare at him. "And that's no small miracle, after the way you mistreated yourself! I should never have agreed to let you leave. And now they want to drag you out to a parlay. Humans!"

"Oh," Gerald said slowly. "How *am* I going to get to the parlay?" He didn't want to limp out with his canes, even assuming Calin would let him. Putting his injury on display would hardly be a rousing endorsement of their decision to hold the showcase in the dragonlands.

"You'll be sitting on the dragon's back," Omar said reassuringly. "Don't worry, Nedi's got it all worked out. As soon as she hears you're awake, she's going to be in here filling you in on everything."

"So before she hears," Calin said, "you are going to take a bath, let me change your bandages, and have something to eat. She is not to overtire you. Nor is anyone else," she added with a significant look at Omar, who held his hands up placatingly.

Gerald looked around the bedchamber and was unsurprised to see his canes were nowhere to be found, but a familiar-looking wheeled chair was waiting in the corner. He didn't protest it.

AN HOUR LATER, he was clean and bandaged and sitting at the dining table in the bigger reception chamber, where the dragon could join them and reassure itself Gerald was all right.

"Calin might never let me out of her sight again," Gerald said ruefully while the dragon examined him carefully from every angle, "but I'm really okay."

"You probably *shouldn't* be allowed out unsupervised," Erick said. Gerald turned to see his cousin and Nedi coming in, trailed by piedlings bringing breakfast. "You had us worried for a while, Meathead."

"Yes, well, let's worry about the Council instead. I'm fine. As you know—it's your healing spell."

"Yes," Nedi broke in. "Let's discuss the Council. And I'm glad you're doing better, Gerald," she added as an afterthought.

"Thanks. So, what did you tell them?" Gerald asked. "When you asked for the parlay."

Nedi grimaced. "As little as possible. I didn't want them to know exactly what's on this side of the border spells, or who put them up."

"Don't you think they'll figure that out when we come out on dragon back tomorrow?" Gerald asked.

"It's one thing for them to know once they've agreed to the parlay," Nedi said. "But I didn't want to give away any information beforehand."

"All right. So what *do* they know?"

"I kept it all very vague," Nedi repeated, "but I told them all of the missing royals are here and none of them have been harmed or will be harmed. The Council isn't looking at all this as someone trying to change the system. They're viewing it more as...well, an act of war. Only they don't know who's to blame. The kingdoms have been unified for so long, there's no one obvious to point the finger at. There aren't any real enemies on this continent, no one's quibbling over borders or trade rights or any of that, and there haven't been any signs of an invasion from overseas—and that's not really the kind of thing you can miss.

"On the other hand, all of the marriages, and royal families joining with each other to create deeper bonds between specific kingdoms, has a lot to do with why there's peace here and why, as a whole, everything runs fairly smoothly. So...an attack on that marriage system is an attack on the backbone of the Thousand Kingdoms."

Gerald opened his mouth, but Erick kicked his good leg lightly under the table. "You don't need to argue with *us* about it," Erick reminded him. "But tomorrow, I'd go very heavy on the 'mistreatment of the guardians' angle and very light on the 'I don't want to marry' angle. You're not going to get very far if they can dismiss you as a spoiled prince having a tantrum."

Nedi nodded. "We want to hit them with three main points: enslaving the guardians is wrong; the questing system is outdated, and we've already put together an alternative system that accomplishes all of the same things and has the same benefits without any of the drawbacks."

"They're not going to agree right away, of course," Erick said. "But we have to convince them, at the very least, that we're not trying to destroy the Thousand Kingdoms—and that we won't inadvertently destroy them by doing this. The showcase is all ready to go. We've gotten a pretty enthusiastic response to it, too, from the royals, even the ones who had to be, um, *persuaded* to come along. And we've already got at least a dozen budding romances merely from having everyone in the same place for weeks. Besides, the dragons don't think the Council can break through the border...but if they try to, that would be just the excuse some of the dragons need to start attacking *them*."

"So," Omar broke in, "that means if we can't convince them we're in the right, we could go ahead and carry out the showcase and ignore the Council entirely. If they can't get in, they can't stop us. And I don't think I mind that much if the dragons chase them off."

"Except we want this to become a permanent thing," Erick reminded him. "We could go rogue for this year, sure, but what about the future? It would be back to the quests and the collars. We have to prove the benefits and that, at the very least, this method is worth a trial period.

Besides...we only rescued the guardians who were currently assigned to towers. How many more are still out there in reserve with their collars still on? And what's to keep the Council from enslaving more?"

That was a sobering thought. Gerald's eyes were drawn automatically to the scars circling the dragon's neck. *They can't do that again.*

"All right. So we'll parlay," Gerald said. "I'm guessing you've already got safeguards planned to keep them from spelling us once we leave the border?"

"We signed a binding parchment guaranteeing the parlay would be completely free of violence or coercion, both physical and magical. The worst they can do is not listen to us, and then we'll simply have to keep talking until they do."

She frowned at Gerald. "So you better eat up and rest up. You're not looking very imposing right now."

"I'll try to get sick on a more convenient schedule in the future," Gerald said sourly. "And I think the dragon will be imposing enough for all of us."

Chapter Twenty-Four

BUT THE NEXT morning he was no longer so sure of that. It wasn't that the dragon looked any less imposing than usual; it in fact looked quite intimidating. It had taken great care with its grooming and all of its scales were spotless, its claws were polished, and its harness was clean and the piedlings had even traded out the brass rings and linkages for gold ones. It looked much more like royalty than Gerald did. The piedlings had taken liberties with his wardrobe as well, but the formal clothes didn't suit him. He always felt awkward in them, and as a result, no matter how well they were tailored, they never seemed to sit right on his frame. His silver circlet weighed heavily on his head after so many weeks of not wearing it or even thinking about it, and he was horribly conscious of his leg. Calin had flatly forbidden him to even consider walking on it. He had yet to see his canes and he had a feeling he wasn't going to see them for quite some time.

Omar, Erick, and Nedi were likewise primped and polished and outfitted formally. The piedlings had even found or made decorative sheaths for Omar's knives, which Nedi ruled made them ornamental and therefore permitted, although Omar was strictly forbidden from drawing them, "and it would be better if you try not to even touch them."

Nedi was completely in her element and Erick couldn't stop smirking, pleased that all of his magical trickery was about to be recognized by the very people his spells had been causing so many problems for. Gerald thought they would present a much better picture if he stayed behind. Once again he felt like he was back in Andine, the odd one out, the gawky prince ruining the dignified royal tableau.

Omar nudged him. "It's going to be fine," he said quietly. "You're going to be fine."

"What are we going to do when we get there and they want us to dismount? I can't imagine they're going to want to parlay while we're looming above them on dragon back. You three can stand there and talk to them. I can't."

"There will be a table," Nedi broke in impatiently. "People don't just stand around and negotiate!"

"Well, how am I going to get to the table?" Gerald persisted. "Calin won't give me my canes, and I thought we were trying to hide my injury anyway. If they knew how I got it, that would be all they would need to say our plan is too dangerous to be sanctioned."

"I will put you where you need to be," the dragon said. "Do not worry about the details. The Council will be too busy looking at me to look at you too closely."

"Now let's go," Nedi said impatiently. "It won't do at all to be late."

Gerald let Omar boost him up the dragon's side, with Calin watching with a frown. He almost hoped the piedling would speak up and say he shouldn't go, that it would tax him too much so soon after his fever. But she stayed quiet and then the dragon was launching off the ledge and taking them to the parlay with steady wingbeats.

They crossed the border some ways away from the Council encampment, too far for Gerald to see any detail, but the *size* of the camp was crystal clear even from a distance. He whistled softly and Omar glanced at him, and then followed his gaze toward the tents and people blanketing the ground.

"That's right," Omar said thoughtfully. "You didn't see it when we flew in."

"How many of them are going to be at the parlay?"

He thought he had kept his tone admirably steady, but Nedi seemed to find the question ridiculous nevertheless. "Four," she said. "The same as us."

"Four Council members," Erick corrected. "They wanted to bring a secretary or aide-de-camp or some such thing as well. We said all right, so long as they weren't a magician."

At least we won't be outnumbered. He almost smiled then, realizing if something went terribly wrong and the supposedly binding agreement against harm was broken, *they* were the ones with the advantage in a fight. Several thousand pounds of fire-breathing advantage. But then he glanced once again at the scars on the dragon's neck and his budding smile died before it touched his lips. This wasn't the time for humor.

The parlay site came into view almost immediately. For the Council members, it would be a half-hour horseback ride; for the dragon, it was mere minutes away. The site was already prepared, with a large, rectangular wooden table surrounded by sturdy matching chairs sitting clearly visible on a flat outcropping. Gerald noted there was plenty of space for the dragon to land and the outcropping had an unobstructed view of the surrounding area in every direction. *There's nowhere to set an ambush, no way for anyone to sneak up on us.* He pushed aside the thought that of course there was a way—magic.

There was no sign of the Council delegation at the site or approaching it. The dragon circled the table, reducing its altitude but not yet dropping down to land.

"Where are they?" Gerald asked.

"They'll want to make a show of their entrance, too," Nedi said calmly. Then, to the dragon, "Go ahead and land. Let's force their hand."

The dragon flew two more slow circuits before folding its wings in and landing as instructed. As soon as it touched the ground, a blinding pulse of white light erupted in front of them.

Gerald squeezed his eyes shut against the painful brightness and bit his tongue to keep from yelping in surprise. *It's just light, it's just light, it's not hurting us.* He reflexively tightened his grip on the dragon's harness nevertheless. Next to him, he heard the sound of Omar drawing a knife, and behind him, he heard Nedi say, "Erick—" in a too-controlled tone of voice.

Then everything was drowned out by the dragon's roar. It was like thunder, if thunder were sentient and furious and right next to his head.

And the light faded away, leaving blotches in Gerald's vision when he cautiously opened his eyes. The Council representatives were there now and he realized the light must have been a byproduct of a teleportation spell. *Of course they wouldn't want to show up dusty or tired from walking or riding. And Nedi did say they would want to make an entrance.* The spell must have been preset, triggered by their party reaching the parlay site.

Gerald noted with satisfaction they didn't look nearly as calm or as dignified as they had no doubt hoped. The dragon's roar had left them somewhat disheveled, as if they had just walked through a windstorm.

"I thought we said there would be no magic," Nedi said stiffly while the Council tried to regain their equilibrium.

There were three men and a woman, all middle-aged, and a younger man clutching a sheaf of papers and looking at the dragon with saucer-sized eyes. The four Council members were dressed identically, in gray trousers, navy blue tunics, and tall black boots, with their cloaks of office—woven from magician's wool, which was all colors and no color at once, a shimmery light show—fastened with silver cloak-pins. The pins were the one thing that set their outfits apart—each one was a personal symbol, like a royal crest, and would, if one were familiar with the symbolism, identify each individual by their country of origin, school of magic, and rank within the Council. To Gerald, they were merely ornamentation.

"No *harmful* magic," the woman corrected. She had lost a handful of hairpins to the dragon's roar and several of her braids had come undone. "We did no harm. It was a simple transportation spell."

"With a rather nasty—and completely unnecessary—light show built in," Erick said sourly. "You could easily have transported here without the bells and whistles."

"Says the young man sitting on a *dragon*," one of the men snapped. His blue eyes were icy. "I daresay you can hardly accuse us of showmanship when you pull a stunt like that."

"I am not a stunt," the dragon said, a growl in its voice. The secretary gulped and clutched his papers closer to his chest.

Nedi cleared her throat loudly. "How we got here is not the issue. *Why* we are here is. Shall we stop with the posturing and take our seats?"

The Councilwoman gave Nedi a small, approving smile. "Quite right." She turned and strode toward the table, and her daring in turning her back to the dragon galvanized her companions into action. The secretary sidled after them sideways, like a crab.

"Now," Omar said quietly in Gerald's ear. "None of them are looking."

The dragon folded its forelegs and sank into a crouch, and Omar helped Gerald down and to the table. It was only a few yards away, and Erick likewise took Nedi's arm, so it didn't stand out that Gerald was leaning on Omar's arm. If they walked a bit slowly so Gerald could disguise his limp, no one seemed inclined to comment.

Once they were all seated and the secretary had taken out pen and ink, the Councilwoman nodded briskly. "Well," she said. "I suppose we should start with introductions. I daresay you are not quite what we were expecting."

"What *were* you expecting?" Gerald asked curiously. Nedi had been right to say there was no clear enemy, either within the Thousand

Kingdoms or abroad, to lay the blame on if the Council thought the royals had been kidnapped; he wondered what explanation the Council had come up with among themselves.

But the Councilwoman simply smiled and proceeded to introduce herself and her colleagues as if Gerald hadn't spoken. "I'm Arika, Speaker of the Council of Ten; this is Ivan, also of the Ten"—indicating the blue-eyed man to her right, who inclined his head gravely—"Pejman, of the Hundred"—the man to Arika's left, darker than Ivan, with a neatly-trimmed beard, who smiled at them— "and Sosha, of the Ten," she concluded with a nod at the one sitting to Pejman's left, who bowed, his long black hair gathered into a neat tail hanging down his back.

The secretary, who still looked ill at ease, got no introduction.

"I'm Princess Nedi of Eria; this is Prince Gerald of Andine; Prince Omar of Yevin; and Prince Erick of Anadac."

"Four of the missing royals," Pejman observed, his eyes dancing in amusement.

"I assure you, we know exactly where we are," Nedi replied. "And where the others are. None of us are *missing*. We are simply no longer being tracked."

"To what purpose?" Ivan asked sourly. "I suppose your presence here leading the parlay means we can take it as writ that you were not taken and are not being held against your will. So I am quite interested to hear your explanation for willfully disrupting the system that keeps the peace in the Thousand Kingdoms."

Nedi cast a meaningful look at Gerald and he cleared his throat. "The system is out of date and built on the very violence you claim it is meant to avoid," he said carefully. "What good is peace when its foundations are soaked in blood?"

Ivan scoffed. "Such melodrama, young man."

"The system depends on the guardians," Gerald persisted. "Guardians that are enslaved by spells. Guardians that are treated abominably, that are mistreated, that are injured out of both negligence and malice."

"Animals," Ivan said, waving a hand dismissively.

"Oh?" Gerald said, his voice tight with anger. "Is that how you justify it? The dragon speaks, quite eloquently; it is intelligent; it does magic; it has thoughts and feelings and a life of its own. And yet it was captured and collared and used as a tool; silenced, bound, and separated from its own kind. The collar was not even replaced as it grew. It was left to dig into its scales, to fester and rot, leaving the dragon in constant pain and leaving it with a permanent scar." The dragon leaned over and rested its chin on the table, forcing the Council to look at the discolored, knobby ring of deformed scales that circled its neck.

"You're saying all of that is all right because it is an animal? I would not treat the scrawniest stewing chicken the way the Council has treated the dragon."

"I did not deserve this," the dragon said, not angrily, but flatly, a simple statement of fact. Gerald thought that cold tone was more intimidating than its anger would have been.

"It's not only the dragon, either," Gerald said. All four Council members were staring at the dragon's scars and Pejman's tawny cheeks had gone pale. Even Ivan didn't seem inclined to interject again. "Every guardian we saw—and that was every single one currently bound to a tower—was mistreated. Those with voices were silenced. Those with magic had it bound out of their reach. Those with partners or offspring were separated from them. Most had similar wounds from ill-fitting collars. Even the ones not harmed by neglect were there for the express purpose of being harmed by the rescuers—and they could barely even defend themselves with all of the restrictions imposed on them," he said, remembering the amarok, the great white wolf, its fur stained with blood.

"We can't have the rescuers harmed," Ivan said, finding his voice.

"But we can have the guardians harmed?" Gerald retorted. "Look, you said it yourself, the Thousand Kingdoms are at peace. Do we really need to train our royals as warriors? Do these quests really need to be stained with blood?" Ivan opened his mouth, but Gerald pressed on, speaking over him. "The point of these quests is to pair up the royals, isn't that right? To form marriages and alliances."

"Correct," Arika allowed.

"There are better ways to do so. And we have found one. That's what we're doing here, that's what all of the royals are doing here. Finding a better way."

There was a moment of silence after Gerald's proclamation and he laced his fingers together under the table to keep his hands from shaking. The dragon withdrew its head—the wood of the table creaking and groaning as it was freed from its weight—and the Council and the royals were once again facing each other with their view unimpeded.

"This system has been in place for decades. Centuries," Sosha said, speaking for the first time. "It has worked for all that time."

"Traditional does not mean right," Nedi said with a frown, and Gerald knew she was thinking of her own kingdom's traditions.

Arika held up a hand and Sosha deferred to her, closing his mouth around whatever reply he had been about to make. She leaned forward across the table and met Nedi's eyes, then Gerald's. "I will admit the dragon's condition is troubling. So often spells are cast without proper regard for the consequences. As my colleague said, this system has been in place for centuries; we—the current Council—did not create it, but our predecessors did; and we do enforce it. Perhaps we have not done our duty in evaluating that enforcement appropriately. But the treatment of the guardians can be evaluated without disrupting the entire system. It does work well; it accomplishes its purpose."

Gerald shook his head. "It works after a fashion," he said. "It is assumed to work well because this is how it has been for us, for our parents, our grandparents, our great-grandparents. It is assumed that because it has lasted, it is not only the best way but the only way. Please, tell me—what does this system accomplish? What are all of its benefits?" he asked. "Tell us that, and then we will list not only the drawbacks of your system, but also how our proposal not only maintains the same benefits but also adds new ones."

"You haven't even said what your proposal *is*," Ivan pointed out.

"We'll get to that," Gerald assured him.

"Very well," Arika said. "But we will critique your proposal in turn."

"Of course."

After exchanging glances among themselves, the Council members began to speak, going around the table from one to the next and then back to the first to begin again.

"Well, marriage, obviously. Love."

"Travel—visiting other kingdoms."

"Friendship, alliances."

"Practical experience in planning and carrying out tasks."

"The bond of a shared experience."

"Independence."

"Self-reliance."

"It broadens the royals' horizons."

"Strengthening alliances."

"Maintaining peace in the Kingdoms."

They started to trail off then and exchanged more glances with one another. Pejman shrugged. Arika sighed. "I trust we can add to the list if something more occurs to us?"

At Gerald's nod, Ivan broke in. "So what's *your* proposal, then? And how it is better than this?"

"Well," Gerald said, "The reasoning behind the quest system is, essentially, to have the royals prove their worth, right? It can't be too easy to find a spouse; each royal has to prove to their partner's parents that they're a good match, worthy of becoming part of the kingdom's ruling family."

"Exactly," Arika said. "Other classes, the merchants, craftspeople, farmers, and servants, even the magicians of the Council, they may marry with no consideration for the worth of their spouse, but royals must be able to show their strengths and the benefits they will bring to their new kingdom."

"Our proposal," Gerald said, "is a showcase. Contests and demonstrations of skills. Any skill—every skill. Diplomacy, dancing, etiquette; singing or playing an instrument; needlepoint, embroidery, cooking, metalworking; horseback riding, archery, wrestling, swordplay. Royal skills, practical skills, and whatever else anyone can do well and is proud of. Everyone can show off what they can do. They can find a partner who likes the same things they do, or who has skills that would complement their own. Surely that is a better demonstration of what a royal will bring to their new kingdom, a better way to prove their worth. Especially because with the current system, only the rescuers actually show anything. The rescuees demonstrate, what? That they can sit quietly in a tower? They don't get to prove themselves at all."

Pejman was smiling again and Sosha had quirked an eyebrow. Arika steepled her fingers together and leaned over the table. "That is true," she said meditatively. "The kingdom must trust the rescuer's judgment as to the suitability of the rescuee."

"For as much as you say this system is traditional," Nedi broke in, "its traditions have still changed over time. It used to be that all princesses were sent to the towers and all princes were sent to rescue them. It was thought the women didn't need to prove their worth because they had none. All that mattered was that the men were strong and smart enough to find the tower and defeat the guardian. But military skill is no longer in such demand. We have been at peace for so long. There are other skills that are more valuable for today's royalty."

"Not to mention that every benefit you listed for the current system is also present—to a much greater degree—in our new one," Gerald said. He ticked each point off one by one on his fingers as he spoke. "Travel—the rescuees don't travel at all. They're transported to their tower, and they stay there until they're rescued. They only travel when they return with the rescuer to their kingdom. Even the rescuers don't see much of the Thousand Kingdoms. They may cross three or four borders, but how many visit more kingdoms than that? With this system, every single royal would travel to the showcase. Every single royal would *plan and carry out* a journey; they would be *responsible* for transporting themselves and their supplies; they would need to read maps, be adequate riders, and be *independent* and *self-sufficient*." He paused to make eye contact with each Council member. Pejman was stroking his beard thoughtfully and Arika was nodding along. Even Ivan seemed to be listening, although his eyes were narrowed as if he were listening for flaws.

Satisfied he had their attention, Gerald continued. "Then, if the trip itself wasn't sufficient to *broaden their horizons*, being exposed to dozens of fellow royals, from dozens of Kingdoms, with a wide variety of different interests, skills, home languages, customs, and modes of dress, would certainly be horizon-broadening.

"Not to mention that what better way is there to find a compatible spouse than to be exposed to every possible candidate? In the current system, how many rescuers visit any given tower? No more than half a dozen, on average. How many towers does each rescuer visit? It can't be much more than that. How many royals settle for the first adequate option because it's too time-consuming and difficult to examine all of them? What better way to *forge friendships and alliances* than by interacting with one's entire cohort? It takes all of the randomness out of the current system, where the rescuees are limited by who comes to their towers, and the rescuers are limited by which towers they manage to reach.

"Not to mention," he said again, thinking of Padma and Natali, "that the rescuer/rescuee system automatically takes half of one's potential partners out of consideration. If you're a rescuer, you can't marry another rescuer, and the same for the rescuees. What's to say one's perfect partner will be on the right side of the equation? Really, it's kind of amazing anyone ends up married at all in the current system."

Erick coughed when he said that, a strangled-sounding cough that was desperately trying to disguise laughter. Gerald had to bite his lip to keep from laughing himself when he realized what he had just said. *Of all the people to be advocating for getting us married off!*

But the Council didn't appear to find any of it amusing. Indeed, they were taking it all very seriously. "He has a point," Pejman said. "Several, actually."

"He does," Arika allowed. "On paper, at least." She leaned forward. "How exactly do you plan to implement this showcase of yours? This is no small undertaking, to feed and shelter a hundred-odd royals, to tend to their baggage and laundry and mounts, to provide all the supplies for the showcase... And if everyone is demonstrating a skill, who will they be demonstrating *to*?"

Nedi produced a sheaf of papers from her saddlebag. "I thought you'd never ask," she said with a grin. "In this instance, there are no mounts to worry about, since the dragons helped with transport. But there is plenty of space for stabling in the future, when the royals will be expected to make their own way here—"

"Excuse me," Ivan interrupted, frowning. "Did you say dragon*s*? That is, plural?"

"Oh, yes. That's right, you don't know," she said innocently, as if she hadn't been deliberately hiding the fact from them. "The showcase is in the dragonlands. It's their spell on the borders, by the way, and they're quite confident no human magic will be able to break the spell or breach the border. This parlay is really a bit of a formality, you know; we're all already here, and you can't actually stop this showcase from happening."

That got a stir out of the Council, but Nedi continued to speak over their murmurs. "However, as we said, we're concerned with the future royal cohorts, and with the guardians. We'd quite like to convince you all that this is the way forward. So, where was I? Oh, yes. There is plenty of fodder and grazing and there are also ample supplies for humans. The dragonlands are also inhabited by a race of humanoids called piedlings, who are very skilled in all manner of domestic issues. They've been more than happy to help with cooking and cleaning and generally welcome us to the dragonlands.

"As you can imagine," she added, gesturing to the dragon behind them, "space is not an issue for those our size. Now," she said, sliding a pair of papers across the table, "these are the diagrams of the showcase set-up. As you can see, we've roughly divided the floor into sections based on the category of skill being displayed. All the weapons in one place, all the crafts in another, all the musical or spoken displays in a third. The royals have been divided as well," Nedi continued, holding up another sheet of parchment covered in columns of names. "Everyone has been assigned to a group, and the groups will rotate through the showcase: one day as a performer, one day as an observer, and so forth. Even within groups, further divisions can be made—performing in the morning versus the afternoon, for example—to ensure every royal has the opportunity to both see and be seen by every other royal. There is also mingling over meals and in guided tours of the dragonlands. If by the end of the showcase someone has failed to meet and speak to every single other royal, it will have been solely due to a deliberate effort on their part. This should lead to much better matches among the royals than the current random nature of the quests."

"You've certainly taken great pains with this," Arika said, examining Nedi's charts and diagrams, "and my colleague is right that you've made many good points. At the very least, we must evaluate the way the guardians are treated. You're quite right that the current system has grown to be unnecessarily cruel to them. But the four of us here cannot simply say, yes, go ahead, change everything. This needs to be taken to the Ten, and then to the Hundred, and perhaps even to the full Thousand. We cannot give you an answer today."

"We expected as much," Nedi said graciously. "How much time do you need? We can return to this site at your convenience. But in the meantime...the showcase is ready to go. Is there a reason why we cannot run it while you are debating? If nothing else, it will provide more data for the Council to base its decision on."

Arika exchanged glances with the others and then smiled. "As you pointed out, I don't believe we have a way to stop you," she said lightly. "Although... I would be very interested in observing your showcase in action. You've set it up as a multi-day affair; perhaps we will have reached an agreement before the end of it."

"I am sure arrangements could be made for a small Council audience," Nedi allowed.

"Then we will be in touch. This has been a very...educational morning." As one, the Council members pushed their chairs back and stood, the secretary joining them a beat later, his papers hastily gathered up. Arika raised her hands and the five of them vanished smoothly and silently—and without the painful light their arrival had brought.

Nedi looked altogether smug as she gestured to the others to get back on the dragon. Erick opened his mouth to say something, but Nedi shushed him. She tapped her ear as if to show the Council might be listening in. "Talk at the caves," she mouthed. "Let's go!"

Omar helped Gerald up and Gerald winced when he tried to put his weight on his right leg. Sitting for so long had made his knee lock up, but he smiled reassuringly at Omar when he frowned with concern.

But by the time they got back to the amphitheater, as short a flight as it was, Gerald was ready to lie down again—which was just as well, since Calin, who had been pacing around the reception area, was determined to cart him back to bed as soon as the dragon landed.

"I won't be held responsible for you backsliding into another fever," she said, even though Gerald hadn't said a word in protest. "If you three want to keep talking to him, you can do so in his room."

Omar followed Gerald and Calin, but Nedi said, "I have to make sure the most recent arrivals are on the list. We have permission now, we might as well go ahead and get the showcase underway tomorrow!"

Chapter Twenty-Five

IT WASN'T UNTIL they all sat down to dinner that night to go over the final details that Nedi said, "Gerald, you haven't signed up for anything."

Gerald looked down at his plate. "I know."

"Well? What would you like?"

"I, um, wasn't planning on signing up."

She gaped at him. "It's your idea! How can you not participate?"

"There's no point," Gerald said. "I'm not... I can't get married. There's no point in doing the showcase."

"It's not going to look good if you don't," Nedi persisted. "And what do you mean, you *can't* get married? Of course you can. You *have* to, as a matter of fact."

Gerald wished he could get up and walk away from the conversation, but his leg kept him trapped at the table. "Well, I've actually been thinking about that," Gerald said slowly, "and I can always abdicate. Lila's the heir, anyway. Andine doesn't need me. And if I'm not a royal prince anymore, no one can make me marry."

Nedi looked like Gerald had announced his intention to learn how to fly. "You can't be serious. You would *abdicate* just because you don't want to get married?"

Erick sighed. "You can't simply abdicate, Meathead. The Queens would have to accept your petition, and frankly, I can't see them doing that. Look, you were the one saying all of that stuff this morning about meeting all the other royals and finding a match. How many of the royals have you actually spoken to? A dozen? Why so convinced you're not going to find one to marry?"

Gerald rubbed his face. "Because I don't feel that way about people."

"You don't feel that way *yet*," Erick corrected.

"No," Gerald said firmly. "I don't feel that way. I never have and I never will."

"You can't know that until you try it."

Gerald throttled the urge to throw his plate at his cousin. *No one ever listens.* His hands were shaking. He was so tired of having to defend himself, but it didn't seem like he had any other choice. "You like girls," Gerald said. "*Only* girls. Right?"

"Yeah."

"Well, how do you know you just don't like boys *yet*? Have you tried it?"

"No, but that's different..."

"*Why*? Why is it different? It's exactly the same. You know who you like. You know who you don't like. Well, so do I! And I don't like anyone!"

"Everyone likes *someone*," Erick said impatiently.

"No! They don't! I don't! And I'm *tired* of no one believing me!" Gerald could feel his face heating up and he blinked furiously, trying to keep the tears welling up in his eyes from spilling down his face.

"I believe you," Omar reminded him softly. "Erick, you're way out of line."

Erick shook his head in disbelief. "You, of all people—you're the one with a crush on him! Don't you want him to like you back?"

"It doesn't matter what I want. I can't force Gerald to feel something he doesn't feel, and neither can you. Neither can his parents, or anyone. Leave him alone, Erick. Nedi, if you're so worried about how it'll look, put down that he's medically unable to participate. I'm sure Calin will gladly forbid him to participate if you ask her. All right? Does that make everyone happy?" He glared around the table, challenging them to say it didn't.

Erick rolled his eyes but kept his mouth closed. Nedi nodded cautiously. She seemed unsure of how to respond to the rest of it. Gerald wondered whose side she was on. *Not mine.*

"That's a good compromise," she said. "I can do that. Um. I hope you'll come as an observer, though, Gerald. It *was* your idea. You should see how it's come to life."

Gerald made a noncommittal noise.

After a tense moment with the four of them looking at each other, waiting to see if someone was going to start the argument up again, Erick turned back to his dinner. With a quiet exhale that wasn't quite a sigh of relief, Nedi picked up her fork as well. But when Gerald looked back at his own plate, his stomach twisted. "I'm not hungry anymore," he said. "I'm going back to my room."

He pushed back from the table and tried to turn the wheeled chair toward the hall, but it was stuck on the table leg. That was almost enough to push him over the edge into furious, frustrated tears. *I am not going to cry in front of them!*

Omar hastily got up and untangled Gerald's chair. "I'm not hungry either. I'll take you back."

The chair moved smoothly with Omar guiding it and Gerald tried to relax. His hands were still shaking, and he clasped them in his lap in an effort to hide it. His eyes stung with tears he refused to shed, and he berated himself for even wanting to cry. *It's not like it's going to help anything. You'll just look like a child. That's not going to make anyone think you're worth listening to.*

"Do you want to talk about it?" Omar asked hesitantly when they were safely back in the bedroom. Gerald settled on the rush mattress and leaned back against the wall. He fingered the blanket folded at the end of the bed and considered pulling it over his head and hiding from everything until he felt less miserable. *Because that wouldn't be childish at all.*

He settled for wrapping the blanket around his shoulders, and only then did he look at Omar and shake his head. "If I start talking, I'm going to start crying. You saw that before. I'm not good at talking about this."

"That's okay. I don't care if you cry."

"Well, I do!" Gerald said. But the tears were already starting to spill over. He swiped at his eyes impatiently. "It's just...there's no way out. Erick's right. They would never let me abdicate. They're exactly like he is. They think I'll grow out of this, and I *won't.*"

"You don't have to convince *me,*" Omar said gently. "I believe you."

"So what are you doing here, then?" Gerald asked. Then he made a face. "That sounded meaner than I meant it to. But...if you believe me. If you don't think I'm going to change my mind. Why do you want to...I mean, what are you expecting from me?"

"I like you. A lot. I care about you. I want to be around you. I'm not expecting you to do anything with me, anything physical. I'm not here with an ulterior motive! You're my friend, you're upset. Why wouldn't I be here?"

Gerald just shook his head. He swiped at his eyes again and tried to change the subject. "What are you doing for the showcase?"

Omar gave him a crooked smile. "There's not much point in me doing the showcase either. I don't want to impress any of the other royals."

"I don't understand why not. Even if you like me... I can't like you back. Don't you want to find someone who can be in a normal relationship with you?"

"I want to be with you."

"I can't!" Gerald was crying in earnest now, the tears running down his face too quickly to be swiped away. "I can't be with anyone, and it's not fair to you to make you settle for the little I can give you. It's not fair to you. It won't be enough."

"Hey, hey, hey." Omar sat on the bed next to him and cautiously put an arm around his shoulders. Gerald tensed but then relaxed and leaned against him. He couldn't remember the last time anyone else had cared enough to try to comfort him, and Omar's shoulder was more comfortable than the rock wall. "Shh, shh," Omar was saying soothingly. "It's all right. Just listen for a minute, okay? Here's what I don't understand. I believe everything you're saying. I trust you to know yourself, to know what you feel or don't, what you want or don't. Why can't you trust me the same way? If I say you're enough, why can't you trust me to mean it?"

Gerald turned his head to look at him. He didn't have an answer. *I hate when people act like I'm going to change my mind. Why am I doing the same thing to Omar?* "I... I... I guess I wasn't thinking about it like that," he stammered.

"Well...if you *do* think about it like that, does that change things for you?" Omar asked. "I mean, are you afraid I'm going to change my mind and try to make you do something you don't want? Or do you really not want to be in even a platonic relationship with me?" He rubbed his nose. "Look, I know you don't know what you're doing. I don't know what I'm doing either. This is kind of uncharted territory for me too. But I'm... I want to try. But not if you're against it. Not just worried about what might happen in the future, but really against it." He trailed off and looked at Gerald, waiting for him to make eye contact, waiting for him to respond.

It took Gerald a minute to gather his thoughts. He was thinking half a dozen things at once, his mind a whirl of confusion. Finally he said, "I think... I think I can do platonic. I *can't* do anything more. But, Omar, I don't know what that *means*. If we're in a platonic relationship, what makes us more than just friends? What makes this acceptable to our parents?"

"Well, that's something we'll have to figure out, what it means for us. My parents won't care, Gerald, honestly. And yours, well, from what you've said...it seems like they might not want to ask too many questions. It seems like they want you to follow the rules...if you do what you're 'supposed to', I don't know that they'd quibble about the details."

Gerald snorted. "That's true. Sometimes I think they'd be happier if I didn't have a mind at all, if I were just a construct. And they can hardly be *more* disappointed with me than they already are. They're not going to like *this*, though," he said, gesturing to his leg. "Maybe they will let me abdicate after all, if they see I can barely walk anymore."

"Do you really want to abdicate?" Omar asked curiously.

Gerald sighed. "I don't know. Honestly, I've never been much good as a prince. I've always been better with animals than with people. But Lila's the heir; I don't really have to do much as a prince, I mean, diplomacy or foreign affairs or any of that. I'm not sure they really want me representing Andine, frankly.

"I tried to convince them I could do something else when I was trying to convince them I didn't want to marry, and they essentially said I could do whatever I wanted *after* I got married. So whether or not I abdicate won't really affect my life...except if I abdicate, I won't have to marry."

"Well, you've made it very clear you don't want to marry," Omar said. "So if that's the only difference—if they let you abdicate, would you?"

"Yes," Gerald said, without the hesitation this time. "But Erick's right. You don't know my parents. Mum might come around, eventually, but Mother never would. They *drugged* me, *enchanted* me, and put me in a tower... They're not going to turn around and say, 'All right, never mind, you don't have to get married, we'll let you abdicate'."

"Well," Omar said, picking his words carefully, "if you don't really have a choice, then...if you have to marry someone...wouldn't it make sense to marry someone without any, um..."

"Expectations?" Gerald suggested.

"I was going to say 'misconceptions'," Omar said. "But in all seriousness. I understand it's going to be platonic, but honestly that's a lot better than some marriages I could name."

"That's true," Gerald admitted. "But that's...that's still not what I want. I don't want a marriage at all, even if it's a marriage in name only.

It wouldn't be honest, and it would still carry...a weight, I guess. The word itself means something... People would think they knew something about me, and they wouldn't, they'd be wrong, but they'd still think it. And my parents, they would look at it and think they were right all along. That it was a phase, or I simply needed to find the right person."

"You're right," Omar said. "It wouldn't really solve anything for you, would it?"

"No. And—" Gerald went dead white as the thought occurred to him. "If I got married, even if it wasn't real, they'd think it was—and they would—they'd want heirs."

Omar shook his head. "Don't even start worrying about that! You're not getting married, you're sticking to that, and so it's not relevant. You are going to have to convince them to let you abdicate, though. And... I mean, just to clarify, are you still okay with me—with us—trying...to be something? Not as cover for your parents, not as an excuse for anything, but just as us, for us?"

"I still don't know what that means. But..." He shrugged. "I guess there's no reason not to try. As long as it's completely clear it's never going to be anything other than platonic. And you should still do the showcase, if only to keep Nedi from having a fit." *And so you can be sure you won't meet someone else. Someone who will marry you. Someone you can have a normal relationship with.*

Omar shuddered theatrically. "All right, if only for that reason. And Gerald...it's clear. Trust me. It's clear and I'm not going to try to change that. And...and don't worry about not knowing what it means, okay? I don't know either. We can figure everything out as slowly as we want. We can figure out what works for us."

Gerald swiped at his eyes one last time. "Well, one thing's for sure," he said wryly. "I'd like it to involve less crying. All this crying is *not* working for me."

Omar dug a handkerchief out of his pocket and dried the last of Gerald's tears with it. "I don't mind. I mean, I'd rather you weren't sad, of course, but it's okay to cry."

"You shouldn't encourage me," Gerald said. "I feel like all I've done since I've met you has been cry about relationships and whine about my leg."

"And yet you still managed to find time to 'disrupt the backbone of peace in the Thousand Kingdoms'," Omar said with a grin. "If you're going to cause a revolution whenever you're upset, at least I won't ever be bored."

"You're going to be bored in a minute," Gerald warned him. "I think I'm about to fall asleep."

"Do you want me to get up?"

"Well...no, not really," Gerald said cautiously. "I like sitting here with you. Will you stay until I fall asleep?"

"Of course."

Gerald closed his eyes and fell asleep feeling the steady rhythm of Omar's heartbeat against his back. *This isn't bad*, he thought as he drifted off. *This is nice. Warm and safe...*

He dreamt of the purring of the palace cats.

GERALD WOKE UP alone and confused by it until he realized he had just dreamed of the cats. They had been the one good thing about waking up in the castle, coming back to consciousness with warm bundles of fur curled up against his lower back or perched on his side or sharing his pillow. *The cats never cared that I never took another person to my bed. In fact, they probably preferred it!*

That thought reminded him of how he had fallen asleep, and what had prompted the dream. He sat up quickly to look for Omar and saw him right across the room, in his own bed, still asleep. His blanket was pulled right up to his chin and all Gerald could see was his curly hair, tangled and sleep-mussed. There was something comforting about simply seeing him there. Gerald had half expected him to be gone, to have decided Gerald's idiosyncrasies were too much to deal with, no matter what he had said last night. *I'm too used to people changing their minds.*

He sat there, rubbing absently at his stiff knee, and watched Omar sleep. *Could I really be in a relationship with him?* His stomach tightened at the idea, not of being in a relationship with *Omar*, but of being in one at all. He still couldn't quite believe they could stay friends—just friends—if they took that step. *Omar's not like me. He would bed me if I wanted to. He said to trust him, and I do, and I want to believe him, but how can I ever be enough for him?*

But under all the doubt was hope, a tiny seed of hope he was nurturing almost against his will, and certainly against his better judgment. But he remembered everything Omar had said, ever since

Gerald had first confessed his feelings—or lack thereof—in a flood of tears and self-loathing. *"I don't think anything's wrong with you...there are different ways to like someone...you can love someone without going to bed with them...traditions change...do you need someone like you or just someone who understands you?"*

They hadn't been empty words, either, Gerald had to admit, at least to himself. Omar had never done anything to try to make Gerald doubt his convictions. He hadn't tried to act on his own feelings, either; he had even hidden them, out of fear of disrupting their friendship. He hadn't so much as hinted Gerald could or should do anything he didn't want to, had in fact been quite adamant it was all Gerald's choice.

Maybe we can make this work.

Or maybe he'll meet someone normal in the showcase...

Gerald could have sat there all morning, going around in circles in his head, and he may very well have if Calin hadn't come bustling in without so much as a knock.

"Good, you're awake," she said briskly.

Gerald shushed her or tried to. "Omar's not," he whispered.

"Omar's not my patient. How's your leg this morning?"

"Stiff. As usual."

"No pain, though?"

"No. But that's only because of Erick's spells. When they wear off again..." he trailed off. "I can't spend the rest of my life having him cast spells on my leg."

"No, you can't," Calin agreed. "Not least because the more you use healing spells, the more resistant you become to them. Once the infection is cleared up, the spells will go."

"And the pain will come back."

"You weren't in pain before until you overdid it," Calin reminded him. "Go slowly this time. Rebuild your strength."

Gerald shook his head in frustration and threw aside the blanket. "It's not about that. Look. I can't straighten my leg. That's why it hurts to walk, because I have to twist my back and my hips to get my foot flat on the ground. It doesn't matter how much I rebuild my strength if my leg is always going to be two inches shorter than the other."

"A cobbler can make you special shoes," Calin said. "Or you can use crutches instead of canes. Or you can use your canes *sensibly* and for short distances. And you can work on restoring flexibility to your knee. Now, let's take a look."

Gerald didn't bother to argue. There was no point, with Calin, and he knew she didn't care at all about anything other than the injury. He was still internally reluctant, but he unbuttoned his pant leg without objection. Calin unwound the bandage around his knee and examined both the cloth and the joint.

"There's much less discharge," she noted. "The swelling is improved as well." She probed his knee carefully with her small gray hands; they felt cool against his skin. "Not as much heat, either," she said with satisfaction. "The infection is clearing up nicely."

She briskly cleaned the cuts she herself had inflicted to lance the swelling and coated them with yet another sharp-smelling ointment. She deftly wrapped his knee up again and Gerald couldn't help but ask, "How am I supposed to work on flexibility when you wrap it up so I can't move?"

"It's not *that* tight," she said firmly. "You can still flex your knee. Now, look here," she said, tracing a finger against one of the worst scars on his thigh. "Look how the scar tissue is pulling at your knee. That's part of the trouble." She produced another jar of ointment from one of her many pockets and handed it to Gerald. "Massage a grape-sized dollop of that into the scars twice a day, until there's no residue left on your skin, and work on bending and straightening your leg when you do."

"But not right now," she added as she turned to leave. "Right now, I'd advise you wake your prince and get to breakfast before Nedi comes charging in here carrying on about her showcase schedules."

Gerald couldn't help but grin at that—he thought Calin was just as imperious as Nedi was, if not more so—but he did as he was told as the piedling swept out of the room to her next self-assigned task. He didn't even quibble with her about the possessive she had assigned, although to himself he thought, *He's not* my *prince.*

NEDI AND ERICK were waiting at the breakfast table when Omar and Gerald came in, Omar pushing Gerald's chair. The dragon was there as well, and it raised its head away from its own meal to scrutinize Gerald. "I'm okay," he mouthed at it, but the truth was his stomach had knotted when he saw his cousin. The piedlings had already piled the table with food and drinks, but Gerald wasn't sure he could stomach any of it. Nedi caught his eye and smiled brightly before looking at Erick expectantly. When he turned away to stare at his plate, she elbowed him in the ribs.

That prompted him to actually look at Gerald, and he flushed. "Hey. I'm sorry about last night. About what I said. Omar was right. I was out of line. I don't... I don't understand how anyone can—" Nedi elbowed him again, harder, and he cut himself off with a wince. "I *don't* understand," he said to her, before turning back to Gerald. "But, you know, I don't have to. I shouldn't have argued with you. It's your life."

Is it? Gerald wanted to ask. *Is it really mine when all I'm doing is what other people want me to and tell me to?* But he didn't want to start another fight, so all he said was, "Thanks."

He still only picked at his breakfast.

Nedi hardly touched her food, either, too excited or nervous about the showcase to get anything down. She was talking nonstop about all of it, about which royals were performing today and which skills she was most interested in seeing. When she paused for breath, Gerald asked the question he had been wondering about.

"How are they going to pair up? I mean, with the rescue system, there was that whole booklet of rules about what the rescuers had to do and what the rescuees had to do and how they both had to agree and all that. Are there rules here, or is it just...I don't know...talking to people?" He shrugged self-consciously when Erick raised an eyebrow at him. *I don't know how this works,* he wanted to remind his cousin. *Not just here. At all.*

"It's less structured than the rescue system, certainly," Nedi said. "It's more, hmm, I don't want to say *casual*, but more...natural, maybe? We want to take the artificiality out of it, and really let people find someone they're truly compatible with. The only hard rule is no formal declarations can be made until each group has had a chance to perform. We don't want anyone making a commitment on the first day and then meeting someone they fit better with on the second. And of course, both parties have to be agreeable." She reached into a pocket and came up with half a dozen little wooden discs, like unfinished buttons. "We'll be handing these out. Erick enchanted them; if you hold one between thumb and forefinger, pinch it, and say your name, it will engrave itself on the disc. Every booth and station will have a jar with the performing royal's name; when you see someone you want to talk to more, you can drop one of your discs in their jar. That indicates your interest, which can be returned or...not."

"Clever," Gerald said, but he shook his head when Nedi offered him a disc.

She didn't press the issue, simply nodded and offered it to Omar instead. He glanced at Gerald, who nodded slightly, before taking it.

"You will come and watch, though?" Nedi asked.

"I don't know," Gerald said, rubbing at his knee. "It's going to be crowded. I'll be in the way."

"Nonsense," she said briskly. "Even with all of us down there, there's plenty of space."

"Maybe this afternoon," he said noncommittally. "I can watch from up here this morning." He had another thought, then. "Is Mikkel participating today?"

"Who?" Erick asked.

"One of the princes we brought in with the last group. He's...shy," Gerald explained.

Nedi sighed. "That's one way of putting it. He's pretty well terrified by all this. He's going to participate, but...separately. People will come to him, rather than the other way around. He was too apprehensive about going into a crowd. We'll set him up on one of the ledges."

"Is he performing today?" Gerald persisted.

Nedi consulted her lists. "No, it looks like he's in Group 3. Why?"

Gerald shrugged. "Just, if neither of us is going to be down there, maybe he could watch from here with me. Then none of you will feel like you need to babysit me instead of participating yourselves."

"None of us are on the roster for today," Nedi started, but she subsided when Erick caught her eye. "If that's what you want..." she said instead.

Gerald shrugged again. He found himself not wanting to take a hard position one way or the other. "Let's see how the day goes," he said. "Is any of the Council coming?"

"Not today. I doubt they've even gotten that far in their discussions, and even if they did want to come... I don't want them here on the first day. If anything's going to go spectacularly wrong, it'll happen today, and we don't need them here to see it."

"Nothing's going to go wrong," Erick said soothingly.

"Something *always* goes wrong," she retorted.

They started bickering amicably and Gerald tuned them out. He still wasn't hungry, but he poked at his breakfast to have something to do. *I wonder if I could talk Calin into letting me do some cooking... Maybe I'd want to eat if I made it.*

Omar nudged him and Gerald pulled his gaze away from the pattern he was making with his fruit. "Do you really want to stay by yourself up here? Or, not by yourself, but you want the three of us to leave you alone."

Gerald couldn't meet his eyes. "There's been too much happening, and I don't know what I think about all of it. It might be nice to spend time with someone who's not invested in what I do, someone who doesn't have an opinion about how I should behave."

Gerald winced a little as he said it, picturing Omar's hurt expression even though he refused to look at Omar to see his reaction. He was torn between wanting to apologize and wanting to say something worse. *I don't want to justify myself to anyone. I don't know what I want, and I want that to be okay! Even Omar wants me to try something that maybe I can't do. If we're going to still be platonic, why can't we just stay the way we are?*

"That's fair," Omar said, and he sounded like he meant it. "You need some space. We can give it to you." He put his words into action immediately, standing up to leave the table; Erick and Nedi had already started making their way to the amphitheater. "But...do eat something, okay? You didn't have much dinner last night, you can't skip breakfast too. Not when you're just getting over that fever."

"Yes, Calin," Gerald said and Omar smiled.

"I'll come back up at lunch if that's okay."

"Of course."

Then Gerald was alone—other than the dragon—and he let out a breath he hadn't realized he'd been holding. He still didn't have much appetite, but he ate a few pieces of fruit so he wouldn't have to lie to Omar. The dragon watched him pick at his breakfast with concern.

"Aren't you feeling better yet?" it asked.

"Physically, yes," Gerald said.

"Ah," the dragon said, "I see."

It didn't press any further and the echoing sound of a gong drew Gerald's attention toward the amphitheater floor. He pushed his chair away from the table and wheeled over to the edge so he could see. The scene below impressed him in spite of himself; it was so much more than he had imagined when he first thought of the showcase idea all those weeks ago in that frozen cave.

There were more than a hundred royals down there, dressed in all manner of clothing, with the majority of them wearing crowns and circlets and tiaras that shone and reflected the light. Half the amphitheater was divided up into fighting rings, jousting lanes, and archery fields, while the other half was organized into stages and stalls. Everything was new, but the wooden structures weren't raw; every inch was polished and stained and vibrant. Banners and signs hung over everything, depicting royal insignia and crests, and they brought the stone walls into brilliant life with every color of the rainbow draped over nearly every surface.

The upper levels of the amphitheater were filled as well, with dozens of dragons and even more piedlings settling in on seats and ledges to take in a morning's entertainment.

And there was Nedi in the center of it all, her voice easily carrying throughout the vast space—the result, no doubt, of a small spell of Erick's—as she introduced the day's performers and triumphantly opened the "first—and hopefully the first *annual*—Royal Showcase!"

The scene devolved briefly into chaos as the day's performers hastened to their places and the day's audience milled around and tried to decide where to look first.

Gerald, despite having a bird's-eye—or dragon's-eye—view, was likewise unsure of where to turn his focus.

"There are so many of them," he said quietly to the dragon. "I knew that; I made the lists, but it's one thing to look at a piece of paper and say we've got to get a hundred and twenty-five people here, and it's another thing entirely to see all of them actually here in the same place."

"It's not so many," the dragon said reassuringly. "Look how little room they take up!"

"Compared to you, maybe! They look like they're taking up a lot of space to me. It's probably a good thing I stayed up here. I wouldn't fit down there."

He meant it literally—his chair was awkward and it would be hard to steer it through a crowd—but he also meant simply that he would be entirely out of his element down there on the floor, with so many people actively seeking out something he couldn't muster an interest in, no matter how much he tried.

The dragon, sensing the way his mood was going, gave him a gentle nudge. "I'm happy to have company to watch with," it said. "If *you* wouldn't fit down there, *I* certainly wouldn't, and this is the most exciting thing to happen in the dragonlands in decades. It's giving me some ideas, too. I wonder if we could adapt this for us? Not for a purpose like marriage, of course, but just for fun. It might give the youngsters something to do besides getting into mischief."

Gerald couldn't help but laugh at that. "I guarantee that outside the borders, the Council is grumbling about this as an *example* of youngsters getting into mischief."

"They seemed quite reasonable at the parlay," the dragon said mildly.

"For the most part," Gerald agreed. "But that was a tiny sample. They might not have to bring the full Council around, but this is a big enough change the Ten won't be enough; they'll have to convince the Hundred. And getting a hundred people from across the Kingdoms to agree on anything is easier said than done."

The dragon looked at the showcase again. "I don't know about that. It looks like *you've* done it quite nicely."

Gerald colored and was saved from having to answer by the appearance of Mikkel, who climbed up into view somewhat hesitantly. He stopped a few feet away and looked at Gerald questioningly from under his hood.

He must not be sure if I really invited him or if Nedi was just meddling. "Hey," Gerald said. "Welcome. There are chairs at the table there if you want to bring one over."

Mikkel shook his head and sank to the ground at the dragon's feet, where he silently made himself comfortable.

"Well," Gerald said after a moment, "I'm glad you came to watch with us."

That got a look of polite disbelief.

"No, really. It's nice to have uncomplicated company. I don't care if you don't talk. I haven't felt much like talking this morning either."

Mikkel nodded and leaned back against the dragon and they all settled in to watch the showcase in companionable silence.

It didn't take Gerald long to realize their ledge was great for taking in the overall atmosphere of the showcase, but poor for watching anything individual. The dragon, with its superior eyesight, had no difficulty and provided periodic commentary on events throughout the amphitheater, but all Gerald could really see with clarity were the weapons events, partly because they were closest and partly because the spectators were kept at some distance from the participants, unlike in the other areas where they crowded right up to stages and booths.

He recognized Lila when she stepped into one of the sword fighting rings, even in armor. He recognized the armor; he'd seen it enough times. It was well-tended, lovingly cared for, but it was not immaculate. Her armor was clean, polished, and free of even the smallest speck of rust, but it had small dents and scratches she wouldn't deign to buff out. She was proud of them; they proved the armor was not just for show.

He swallowed. She was wearing her full armor, not simply quilted padding. That meant...yes, he could see her scabbard when she turned. She was using her real sword, live steel, instead of a wooden practice blade.

It's a competition, yes, but it's a friendly one!

He didn't realize he had made any audible noise, but he must have because the dragon swung its head around and asked, "What's wrong?"

Gerald gestured toward the ring. "I didn't realize they were using live weapons. It's Lila," he added.

The dragon cocked its head. "You're worried for her?" it asked curiously.

Gerald let out a strangled laugh. "Oh, no, no no," he said. "I'm worried for her opponent."

He remembered his fever dream of Lila stabbing him in the leg. The nightmare hadn't been too far removed from some of his real unpleasant memories of facing Lila in the training ring, although the two young royals had never been permitted to use edged weapons with each other. *I got quite enough cuts and lumps with the wooden ones.*

Mikkel raised an eyebrow again and Gerald realized he probably had no idea who Lila was.

"My...twinling," he said, allowing his desire for brevity to overcome his dislike of the term. "We don't get along."

Her opponent was similarly armored and armed, all identifying features hidden. They looked about the same height and build as Lila; perhaps it wouldn't be too lopsided of a fight.

They know what they're doing. They chose weaponry as their showcase skill. It's not going to be like when Lila fought me. Still... "I don't want to watch this," Gerald said abruptly, wrestling with his wheels as he fought to turn the chair around.

Mikkel stood up to help him, but Gerald waved him away. "Don't let me spoil the spectacle for you. I'll come back when her turn is over."

He got his chair straightened out and wheeled himself deeper into the cave. The noise of the showcase followed him, but at least the shouts and cheers and chatter were divorced from the visual. He could pretend they meant whatever he wanted them to. He didn't have to see what was really prompting the reactions.

He pushed himself over to the table, folded his arms on top of the wood, and rested his head on them.

This is what I wanted. Why is it making me want to be anywhere but here?

He wasn't sure how long he stayed there like that before a hesitant hand on his shoulder made him jump. Mikkel took a hasty step back, holding his hands up in front of him.

"Sorry, you startled me," Gerald said, trying to will his heart to stop racing. "You walk so damn quietly. Is it over, then?"

Mikkel nodded. Gerald briefly toyed with the idea of asking who won, but Mikkel wouldn't answer and he wasn't sure he really wanted to know.

He wasn't sure he really wanted to go watch any more of it, either.

It's not all about me, he scolded himself. *It's rude to ignore Mikkel. Especially because he gets enough of that already.*

Gerald pasted a smile on his face and followed Mikkel back over to the dragon. He pinched his fingers with one of the wheels and he bit back a frustrated curse as he shook his hand out. He glared futilely at the chair and at his leg. He was tempted to get up and limp the last few yards and join Mikkel on the floor, leaning against the dragon, but he had the feeling Calin would materialize just in time to catch him at it and give him a scolding he was in no mood to hear.

With Mikkel once again settled at its feet, the dragon turned its head to see what was taking Gerald so long. It saw him sitting several yards away, glaring at his chair in frustration and without a word, it reached out and snagged his chair with a foreclaw, towing it the last few feet as Gerald hastily let go of the wheels and grabbed at the armrests to keep from tumbling right out of it.

"When do you think you'll get your canes back?" it asked once Gerald was parked next to them.

"I don't know," he said flatly.

The dragon tilted its head. "Do you *want* them back?"

"I don't know," he said again. "It doesn't matter."

"It doesn't matter?" the dragon repeated. "You were in such a hurry to start walking again before..."

"So what?" Gerald snapped. "It doesn't matter what I want. It's not like I get to make my own decisions about anything anyway."

Mikkel flinched at the anger in Gerald's voice and he immediately regretted his tone. "Sorry," he said, fighting to found calmer. "I'm sorry. I'm just... I'm not very good company today. I'm sorry."

Mikkel stood up and indicated he was going to go, which only made Gerald feel worse. "It's not you," he said hastily. "I've been in a rotten mood all morning, long before you came over."

Mikkel shrugged, and Gerald wasn't sure if he meant he didn't think that was true or if he didn't think it mattered. "I'm sorry," Gerald said again, but Mikkel had already pulled his hood back up and turned away.

He descended into the amphitheater and Gerald could only watch him go, unable to navigate the stairs even if he had wanted to go after him.

He looked up to see the dragon watching him reproachfully.

"I *said* I was sorry," Gerald muttered, but it was half-hearted. *Am I really sorry? There's no reason for me to stay out here now. I can go back to bed and back to feeling sorry for myself.*

As if reading his mind, the dragon said, "But what is it you're sorry about?"

Gerald rubbed his face. "So many things. Most of them the wrong ones, I'm sure." He bit his tongue to keep from saying something else he shouldn't.

"How can I help?"

"You can't," Gerald said. "Not unless you can make me normal, or make my parents let me abdicate. And honestly I'm not sure which of those is more impossible."

"There's nothing abnormal about you," the dragon said sternly. "And I can be *quite* persuasive," it added, showing its teeth.

That got a smile from Gerald, albeit a wan one. "I feel like everything is out of my control. My whole life is being managed by other people. And I just can't handle it any longer."

"You can always stay here," the dragon said. "Your parents can't force you to do anything if they can't reach you. And if our borders can keep the entire Council out, I daresay they can keep your parents out as well."

"That's a thought," Gerald said, brightening slightly. "But hiding from my problems has never worked that well for me in the past."

The dragon shrugged. "Just something to keep in mind."

It turned its attention back to the showcase and they lapsed into silence once more.

Chapter Twenty-Six

LOST IN THOUGHT, Gerald hadn't noticed when Nedi struck the gong to announce an hour-long break for lunch before the morning and afternoon performers rotated and, as a result, was caught by surprise when Omar climbed up into view.

"Hey!" Omar said warmly. "This is pretty cool, isn't it? Even Nedi's stopped worrying something's going to go wrong. You should see her, she's walking around *beaming*, like everything is right with the world."

"Yeah," Gerald said. "It's...impressive."

Omar sat next to the dragon and craned his head to look up at Gerald in his chair. "You don't sound very impressed."

Gerald rubbed his knee and didn't answer.

"Gerald is having a difficult morning," the dragon said diplomatically.

"Is it your leg? Should I get Calin?"

"No, no, I'm fine. I'm just... I don't know, I'm just in a bad mood." Omar opened his mouth to say something and Gerald cut him off. "I'm not good company today. You sound like you're enjoying yourself. I don't want to ruin that. You should probably go back to the others."

Omar frowned. "If you don't want me here, you can say that. You don't need to act like you want me to leave for my own sake. Why are you in a bad mood?"

Gerald shrugged. There were too many reasons to put into words, and worse, they all sounded like stupid, hollow justifications even to his own ears.

Omar's frown deepened. "Is this about last night?"

"No!...well, maybe. Yes." He tilted his head back to look at the ceiling instead of Omar. "I *have* to make my parents understand this is not a phase, this is who I am. If they can't understand that, if they insist I have to get married to stay a prince, I'll abdicate. Even if they won't make it official, I'll say the words and I'll stay here in the dragonlands and they can say whatever they want about it. They may make it official after all, just to avoid the scandal. Or maybe I can get the Council to rule I should be stripped of my title for doing all this," he added, waving a hand at the amphitheater floor. "Inciting rebellion and all that. Then I could go wherever I wanted."

"And where's that?" Omar asked.

"Somewhere I can be useful," Gerald said. "Not for being a prince, but for myself. For what I can do."

"The guardians," the dragon said thoughtfully. "The *former* guardians. Not all of them have lives to go back to, now. And many of them, many of *us*, are injured. Physically or...otherwise."

"They need a refuge," Omar said, immediately understanding. "A sanctuary. And someone there to oversee it. To treat their wounds or purchase supplies or negotiate with humans on their behalf."

Gerald's breath caught in his chest. He looked at his friends, at Omar and the dragon, and saw them looking back at him with care and concern. "You think...you think I could do that?"

"I think it would be *perfect* for you," Omar said. "Don't you? You're good with animals, and more, you're good with the guardians. You're good at helping them—you treated the dragon's wounds! It would be somewhere where *you*, you specifically, would be incredibly useful, because of your skills and because of who you are. Don't you think the guardians know who's responsible for freeing them? They'll trust you."

Gerald could almost picture it. A little house somewhere, with Wisp and the cats and the more magical animals as well, somewhere where he wouldn't be the disappointing youngest prince of Andine. The only catch was... *How can I take care of anyone if I can't walk? The chair's all right here, where the ground is flat and smooth. I couldn't cross a field in it.*

"I'd have to get out of this chair..." he said hesitantly.

"You will," Omar said confidently. "You were walking before, remember. And you'll have help, too, if you'll take it."

Gerald looked at him harder. "You'd come with me? Even knowing I won't ever marry you? And what about your own crown?"

"I want to be with you. I've told you. As friends, as platonic partners, as whatever you want to call us. My parents are more open-minded than yours. I'm not the heir; they'll let me go where I want and keep my title at the same time. I don't even think they'll mind if I don't marry, to be honest. If they get worried about it, I can always tell them it's a long engagement. Like, *long*."

"And I'll come too, of course," the dragon said. "You'll need transportation and a translator."

"There," Omar said with satisfaction. "I guess it's settled."

Gerald was smiling too broadly to reply.

WITH A SOLID goal in mind for after the end of the showcase, something worthwhile Gerald could really see himself doing, something he wanted and not something he was being forced to do, most of his bad mood melted away. He no longer looked down at the showcase with resentment, annoyed despite himself that the other royals were finding something he didn't even want. He even let Omar persuade him to come down and join the crowd on the third day—the day Omar was performing.

"Nedi wouldn't let me out of it," he said, smiling. "She said even if the two of us have reached some sort of arrangement, it's against the rules for us to say so officially until the end of today, after all the groups have gone."

Nedi was particularly insistent they follow the rules or, at least, appear to because she had agreed to let the Council of Ten come to observe for the day. "Everything's gone surprisingly smoothly so far," she told them. "We've had a few minor incidents, but only minor ones. Certainly nothing worse than what happens out on the quests. I think we're ready to let them see how well we've arranged everything. And if some of the couples make their engagements official tonight while the Council is here, so much the better. They'll see this isn't simply a bit of fun, it's really serving its purpose."

"And if they see me?" Gerald broke in. "*When* they see me, I should say. What do I tell them about this?" he asked, waving at his chair.

"Tell them it's none of their business," Erick advised bluntly. "I've learned not to pry into your affairs. They can too."

"Yes, well, we're trying to be diplomatic," Nedi reminded him. "Gerald, you're going to be staying near Omar anyway, I assume?" At his nod, she said, "Well then, you can just sit in the audience then, in one of the standard chairs, and they won't be any the wiser."

"You can always tell them the truth," Omar suggested. "Not *all* of it, I mean, it's probably better not to mention the dragons. But you can simply say you were in an accident, you're healing, and you don't want to talk about it. They're trying to be diplomatic too. They're not going to pry. Just be polite about it."

"It's not only the Council," Gerald said. "I don't want *anyone* staring at me. I'll go, but not in the chair. I'll sit in the audience like the others."

"We better get going now, then."

The dragon obligingly lowered Gerald to the amphitheater floor and Omar and Erick helped him limp over to Omar's station. Even knowing it was too soon for Calin's latest round of ointments to have an effect, Gerald was still disheartened by the stiffness in his leg. *I can't run a sanctuary if I can't walk,* he reminded himself.

"Stop it," Omar murmured in his ear, quietly enough that Erick wouldn't hear.

"Stop what?" Gerald asked, equally softly. Omar raised his eyebrows, as if to say, *Really?* and tapped his lip, a reminder he knew Gerald's tells, the lip-chewing that gave away his anxieties. Omar might not know exactly what Gerald was worrying about, but he knew he was worrying about *something*.

"Here we go," Erick said cheerfully. "You'll want a spot in the front, I assume. Is this good?" He hardly waited for a response before getting Gerald seated and then turning to go. "I've got my own performance... Maybe you'll come watch mine later, huh?"

"Try not to make anything explode," Gerald advised as Erick hurried off.

"Hey, my show's probably safer than this one!" Erick called over his shoulder. "Try not to impale anyone, Omar!"

Omar rolled his eyes. "I only impale people when I intend to," he said. "If I impale anyone, it'll be deliberate. And if I don't, that'll be deliberate too."

It wasn't long before the other royals started flooding the amphitheater. Gerald was struck by how loud it was; it was one thing to hear it all from above, and quite another to be down in the middle of it. Everywhere he looked there were pairs and trios chattering away, although he couldn't imagine how they could hear a single word of the conversation. The noise was oppressive.

It's no worse than a big banquet back home, Gerald told himself impatiently. *People talking over each other, music, clatter, it's all the same. It only seems so much worse because it's been so long since I've had to deal with it. I'm not acclimated.*

He tried to ignore the crowd and the noise and the colors and focus on Omar. He looked calm and confident on his stage, bouncing lightly on the balls of his feet and waiting to attract an audience. He was wearing the traditional long tunic and burnoose of the Yevin desert, and the loose, flowing fabric hid the knives Gerald knew were secreted all over in hidden sheaths. Even knowing where to look for some of them—Omar's wrists, ankles, and the small of his back—he couldn't find any evidence of them. If it weren't for the targets scattered around, there would be no indication at all his performance would be weapons-based.

Gerald was heartily relieved Omar would be fighting targets and not another royal. Even knowing Omar's temperament was much different from Lila's, he hadn't been sure he would be up to watching actual combat, even in an exhibition. He had spent years avoiding the practice courts in Andine, not only as a participant but as an observer. His habit of disappearing whenever the court hosted a tournament had been one of the many reasons why his relationship with his mothers had frayed. Gerald was told over and over he was tarnishing Andine's reputation by neither participating nor joining the audience, that he was being disrespectful to the visiting combatants. But he simply couldn't bear to be anywhere near it.

It was different with Omar. He'd seen Omar draw his knives before, and it had never been to show off or to bully or intimidate. It had been as protection, as assurance, as safety. *This is only a show*, Gerald reminded himself. *It's only targets. It's like archery.* The bow, the only truly solitary weapon, was the only one Gerald had any real ability with. It was also the only one he'd never had to face Lila with; they shot at targets, not at each other, unlike when they had been taught swords, staffs, and hand-to-hand combat.

A small crowd had accumulated while Gerald was lost in thought, and when there were half a dozen other bodies in the seats, Omar bowed to them and began his performance.

There was no fanfare, no introductory speech; Omar came up out of his bow with a knife in his hand and he launched into a pattern dance, swiping, slashing, and stabbing at invisible opponents as he moved nimbly across the stage, all lethal grace. Gerald caught his breath and watched entranced as Omar moved through a series of increasingly complex pattern dances, incorporating kicks and punches, blocks and dodges, and a varying number of knives. Only after he had traversed the small stage several times and thoroughly captured the attention of the audience did he move into the second stage of his performance.

The blur of motion slowed and stopped, and Omar held up his hands, empty once more. His chest was rising and falling rapidly as he caught his breath, but he otherwise seemed as fresh as when he had begun: he wasn't red-faced and there was only a slight sheen of sweat across his forehead. One or two of the observers began to clap, thinking the show was done, but their applause stopped abruptly when Omar spun and threw a knife—plucked out of a hidden sheath with no one the wiser—at a target the size of a playing card across the stage.

It struck dead center.

Again and again, Omar combined sleight of hand with impressive accuracy as he made knives of all shapes and sizes appear apparently from thin air before sending them soaring and spiraling into targets in all directions. At the end of it, there were an even dozen knives sticking out of various surfaces and even Gerald was left wondering where, exactly, all of them had come from.

There was a moment of hesitation after the last knife struck home and stayed there, quivering. Then, when it was clear Omar really was done that time, the audience—which had swelled noticeably from the original half-dozen—broke into enthusiastic applause.

"Amazing," Gerald heard one prince say to another. "I wouldn't want to come across him in a dark alley."

"Oh, I might," the other responded archly, his tone of voice causing the first to burst into laughter.

At least half of the audience dropped a token into Omar's jar before moving on to another show. Gerald watched them leave their names with a mixture of jealousy and anxiety that surprised him, torn as he was between thinking, *Omar won't even look in the jar* and *What if he does?* and *I'm the one who insisted he had to be sure I'd be enough* and *What if I'm* not?

*Oh damn...*Gerald realized. *I might not want to marry him, but I don't want anyone else to, either!*

Omar hadn't watched to see who dropped a token in his jar. He smiled and bowed to the audience when he finished, but then he turned away, unconcerned by their reactions, focusing instead on retrieving and re-concealing his knives. With that done, he hopped off the stage and slipped into the empty chair next to Gerald.

"What did you think?" he asked.

"That was *amazing*," Gerald said. "And you know it. You're fishing for compliments."

"I think a deserve a few," Omar said, grinning. Gerald rolled his eyes but smiled back.

"That really was great," Gerald admitted. "You made it look so...elegant. I mean, knives, weapons in general, you don't think of them as being *pretty*. You think of them as being brutal. Deadly. And you looked deadly, but not brutal. Dangerous, but controlled, you looked completely in control of yourself, of your body..." He trailed off, embarrassed by his enthusiasm.

Omar was beaming. "Thank you," he said, simply, sincerely. "I know how you feel about weapons, so that means a lot."

"I'm not the only one you impressed," Gerald said, nodding at the jar of tokens.

"Yeah, but you're the only one I wanted to."

Gerald ducked his head, blushing.

BY THE TIME the lunch break rolled around, Gerald had watched Omar's performance four more times, and he hadn't lost any of his fascination with it. The last show was as impressive as the first one, even though the signs of exhaustion were starting to show around the edges when Omar wasn't in motion.

"Thank goodness I don't have to do that again this afternoon," Omar said. "I would hate to have to face Erick if I got tired enough to really hit someone in the audience. You ready for lunch?"

"Yeah," Gerald said, unable to keep the slight hesitation out of his voice.

"What?"

"Just..." He gestured at his leg.

"Oh, Gerald, no one's looking. No one will care, anyway. You can lean on me."

He hesitated, but Omar was right. Everyone was concerned with finding their own lunch. *And so what if they stare. They'll be gone in a few more days. So will I,* he realized. He quickly shut down that train of thought—thinking about the upcoming confrontation with his parents would be a surefire way to lose his appetite—and focused instead on

Omar, who was still glowing with happiness and pride even under the sweat and tiredness. He held out a hand and let Omar pull him to his feet. Leaning against him, he limped across the amphitheater to a nearby ground-level cavern where a horde of piedlings was serving food and drinks.

One of them caught sight of Gerald and glared. She dropped her ladle to stride over and snap, "Sit down this instant!"

"Hi, Calin," Gerald said meekly. Omar hurried him to the closest table, and he sank into a chair. "It was a very short walk," he tried.

Calin sniffed. "I suppose you're going to spend the afternoon walking around the showcase."

"Erm, well, I hadn't really thought about it..."

"You have to see more than just me," Omar said. "There's a lot of talent here. I can get your chair," he added, half to Gerald and half to Calin.

"No, I need to start walking again," Gerald said. "You're the one who told me to build up my strength," he reminded Calin.

"I'll get your canes," she sighed. "But don't overdo it! Omar, you watch him."

"Yes, ma'am."

But when she returned with the canes at the end of their meal, Gerald had to beat back an almost overwhelming sense of self-consciousness in order to take them. *I have to start practicing again. I have to be able to move around if this sanctuary idea is going to turn into anything real. And I have to get over my embarrassment about it or I'm never going to be able to face my parents.* The idea of limping up to them with a pair of canes was an awful one, but the idea of rolling up to them in a chair was so much worse. *They're already so disappointed in me. None of this is going to help.*

"Gerald? Penny for your thoughts."

Gerald brushed it off. "They're not worth that much."

Omar cocked his head. "What are you worrying about now?"

He said it lightly, good-naturedly, but the question still made Gerald flinch, the "now" echoing in his head, emphasizing he was always worrying about *something*. The worry never changed, only the subject of it. *It's a wonder he's not sick of me yet,* Gerald thought bitterly.

"Nothing," he said. "Just...nothing."

"All right," Omar said, not believing him but willing to let the topic drop. "Let's get going, then. What do you want to see?"

"Whatever you want to show me."

That turned out to be quite a lot. Gerald lost track of all of it: concerts, singing, juggling, pottery, painting, calligraphy, acrobatics and tumbling, a debate...

He was almost relieved his leg and his canes gave him a built-in excuse not to participate. *I can't do anything like this. Everyone else is so talented. I'm...not.*

On the other hand, he could have done without the stares. Royalty, as a rule, was healthy. They all had the best nutrition, the best medical care, and if there was ever an injury, illness, or weakness that couldn't be cured by mundane or magical means, it was carefully disguised and hidden behind a façade of royal perfection. Gerald was throwing a wrench into that façade by being out there with his canes prominently displayed. People who hadn't given him a second glance that morning, when he was seated and therefore in stealth mode, were now openly watching him limp along the aisles. If it hadn't been for Omar's reassuring presence at his side, Gerald would have made a hasty retreat some time ago.

As it was, with Omar jokingly offering to stab anyone who bothered him, he stuck it out for several hours. But by the end of the afternoon, Gerald was exhausted. Omar had been solicitous, making sure he sat down frequently and didn't walk too far or too fast—not that anyone was moving quickly in the crowds—but it was still a lot for his first day back on his feet. He hadn't said anything about the growing ache in his knee and hip, not wanting to ruin the day and unwilling to once again complain about something, even though he knew he was making things worse by ignoring it.

"You're going to get me in trouble with Calin," Omar said conversationally when they stopped to watch a glassblowing princess. Her booth was covered in finished pieces, polished bowls and globes and intricate little statuettes. A little rearing horse caught Gerald's eye and he leaned over to look at it, careful to keep his balance—the idea of falling into the stall and breaking all the beautiful glass was enough to keep him at a distance—and he had to drag his attention away from it when Omar spoke.

"Hmm? What?"

"You're limping more and pretending you're not. Let's go back. We've seen nearly everything but the weapons stuff now, and it must be about closing time anyway."

Almost as soon as the words were out of his mouth, the big gong that opened and closed each day's showcase rang out, echoing throughout the amphitheater. Nedi's magically amplified voice followed it.

"The first rotation of the showcase is complete! The next two days are set aside for meeting and mingling; if you haven't handed out your tokens yet, now's the time!"

Gerald thought again of Omar's jar, of how many tokens had been dropped into it that morning, and he swallowed hard against the uncomfortable mix of jealousy and anxiety that was once again bubbling up in his chest.

But Omar didn't seem to be thinking of the tokens at all. "I wonder what the Council thought about today," he said. "I don't think I saw any of them. Did you?"

"No," Gerald admitted, looking around even as he answered. "That's odd. I didn't think about it, but you'd think they would've stood out. Even the oldest of us aren't more than twenty-two or so, and I would be very surprised if any of the councilors are under thirty."

"Oh, they're here," Erick said, and Gerald jumped and nearly lost his balance as his cousin materialized in front of him. Omar grabbed his arm to keep him steady and Erick grimaced a quick apology as Gerald took another limping step away from the glassworks booth. The princess, who had finished the globe she'd been working on, was watching Gerald out of the corner of her eye as she began to pack up her things.

"They wanted to observe," Erick continued. "Only observe; they didn't want to be involved, or inadvertently affect what we would do or how we'd behave. So they've been hidden."

"Invisibility spells?" Omar asked.

"Nah, those aren't as easy—or as effective—as everyone thinks. They're visible, you just don't want to look at them."

"Eh?"

"It's like a repulsion," Erick said. "You know, like if you try to put the wrong ends of magnets together, they kind of...slide off each other? You look at the Council and your eyes just...slide off them. Now, if *I* did that spell, you'd notice the sliding, you might wonder why you couldn't focus on a certain spot. But they're much better than I am. You wouldn't notice—you *haven't* noticed—the slide. I can sense the spells, that's the only reason I know for sure."

"That seems...potentially awkward," Omar said carefully. He seemed unsure of how much to say, now that he knew there could be a Council member anywhere.

"Oh, don't worry about it," Erick said nonchalantly. "The dragons are keeping a close eye on them. *Their* eyes focus past the spells just fine."

Gerald's self-consciousness about his canes returned in force with the knowledge that people he hadn't even noticed could have been—could still be—openly staring at him, wondering what was wrong with him. "I think I'm ready to go back now," he said, and Omar immediately apologized for keeping him standing there.

The dragon was leaning over the ledge watching for them, and it lifted the three of them up to save them the climb. Gerald needed the lift. His leg was starting to ache in earnest and he absently rubbed at his knee.

The dragon crooked its forearm and offered it to Gerald as a seat, but he shook his head. "I think I'm going to go lie down," he said. "I'm fine," he added when Omar turned to scrutinize him. "Just tired."

Omar looked like he was going to say something or perhaps follow Gerald to their room, but Nedi appeared then, bubbling over with enthusiasm, and he lost his opportunity. Gerald hastily limped away before he could get trapped there by Nedi's excitement. *If I don't sit down soon, I'm going to fall down. And I don't want another lecture from Calin.*

Chapter Twenty-Seven

WHEN OMAR CAME to fetch him for dinner, he stopped in the doorway and raised an eyebrow at the mess. "What's all this?" he asked, looking at the crumpled papers spilling off the bed to pile up on the floor. Without looking up, Gerald crumpled up the paper he was writing on and threw it angrily into the pile. He looked like he was considering tossing the inkwell after it and Omar gently took it out of his hand and set it on the table.

It was only then Gerald registered his presence. He looked up and blinked, still holding his quill in one hand. "Oh. Sorry. I'm trying to work out what to say to my parents about this...about me. It might help to write them first, you know, kind of ease them into the idea. It might cut down on the yelling."

"It doesn't look like it's going that well," Omar observed, not unkindly. He sat next to Gerald and picked up one of the balled-up drafts.

"No, don't read it!" Gerald said. "I threw it out for a reason."

Omar opened his hand and let the paper drop to the floor, and then he put his arm around Gerald. "Hey. There's no rush. We won't be leaving for at least a few days, and even with the dragon flying us it's going to take, what, a week to get to Andine? We can stretch that out, too. Don't worry about your parents right now. Tomorrow's supposed to be a day for talking, right? So tomorrow we'll talk, really talk, about the details of this. Of us. And we can write to your parents together."

"What about yours?"

"My parents?" Omar shrugged. "I told you, I don't think they'll mind us going nontraditional. I think they'll like you, too. Maybe we should stop there first, do you think? It'll give you more time to prepare for your family, and that might help, too, if we can tell them the King and Queen of Yevin are in agreement."

"*If* they're in agreement," Gerald sighed.

Omar pulled Gerald into a half-hug. "They will be. Stop worrying and come to dinner. How's your leg? Do you want your canes or your chair?"

Gerald made a face. "'Want' is a very strong word," he grumbled. At Omar's look, he sighed and admitted, "I should probably use the chair."

GERALD JERKED AWAKE out of a dream that was already fading from his mind. He had no idea what it had been about, but the deep feeling of unease it had created didn't fade when the memory of the dream did. He squinted into the darkness and tried to determine if there were any lights on in the hall, if it was still early enough he should try to go back to sleep or if he were better off just getting up. *I have to talk to Erick about magicking a window in here.*

He decided it didn't matter what time it was; the knot in his chest wasn't fading and he didn't want to stay there in the dark and the silence. The only sound was Omar's quiet breathing and once again Gerald wished for the palace cats. Their purring never failed to settle his nerves after a nightmare.

The dragon's snoring is probably the next best thing, he thought wryly. He slipped out of bed as quietly as he could, not wanting to disturb Omar. He winced as his leg and back let him know he had, in fact, overdone it the day before, but he still took up his canes and made his way stiffly toward the reception chamber.

The dragon's snores guided him through the dark and Gerald lowered himself to the ground next to its comforting bulk, wishing absently that he had thought to bring a blanket with him. He leaned against the dragon's side and closed his eyes, letting the thrum and hum of its breathing loosen the knot of unformed anxiety in his chest.

When he opened his eyes again, the sun was up and the snoring had stopped.

"Good morning," the dragon said when Gerald sat up.

"Good morning," Gerald repeated. He rubbed his nose sheepishly. "Sorry. I didn't mean to fall asleep here."

"I don't mind. It feels like I haven't seen much of you lately, between the showcase and the Council negotiations."

The mention of the Council sparked his anxiety back to life. "They are gone, aren't they?"

"Oh, yes. We escorted them out after the closing gong, and you know they can't cross back in without our help. Why the concern?"

"Oh, I don't know, really." He craned his neck to look up at the dragon. It was regarding him patiently, waiting for him to elaborate, but he couldn't. "I don't know," he said again. "Nedi was so pleased at dinner last night. She's convinced they're going to approve this, all of it; not only the pairs that are forming now, but the process. For the future, I mean. I suppose I just...don't trust it."

"You do seem to have difficulties with that," the dragon observed, not unkindly. "Trusting, I mean."

"Yes, well, you remember how I ended up in your tower," Gerald said sourly. "I haven't exactly had the best experiences with trusting people in authority."

"Of the two of us, I'm the one who should be most inclined to distrust the Council," the dragon replied mildly. "But nevertheless, I find myself agreeing with Nedi that it will all work out."

For everyone else, maybe, Gerald wanted to say. *For everyone who can do this properly. Not for me. Nothing has ever worked out for me.* It sounded like whining even to himself and he kept his mouth shut.

The dragon snorted softly, as if it knew what he was thinking. "I can understand why you are unable to trust your parents. I can understand why you are worried about the Council. But surely you can trust Omar, and Erick, and Nedi, and me. No matter what happens with the Council. No matter what happens with your parents. *I* do not need their permission for anything. I can take you and Omar away, and who will stop me?"

Gerald's mouth quirked but didn't quite make it as far as a smile. "I'd rather not have to be rescued at all."

GERALD SLIPPED AWAY from the others after breakfast. The amphitheater had undergone another transformation, with dozens of small tables set up for the royals to meet and talk one-on-one. Several couples had already posted their engagements. It was all making Gerald's stomach knot with anxiety. No matter what the dragon said about trust, the thought of sitting down like that with Omar, of talking about what their lives could be like so far outside the conventional mold, made him feel like he was going to pass out.

So he hid.

It never helped, hiding. It merely postponed the inevitable, and it added another layer of anxiety because he never knew when he would be found and be forced to face whatever it was he was dreading. But the habit was ingrained. Never mind that he didn't know the caverns very well. Never mind that he was sore and limping heavily. Never mind that he knew the dragon was right.

He hid.

And Omar found him. Tucked away in a dead-end storage tunnel that smelled strongly of herbs.

"Hey."

"Hey."

Omar sat next to him, close enough to touch, but he didn't bridge that small gap between them.

They sat in silence for a few minutes as Gerald's anxiety ratcheted steadily upward. A nervous glance at Omar out of the corner of his eye showed he was calm, although not quite relaxed; there was tension in the set of his shoulders. But he didn't seem angry at Gerald's disappearing act.

"Sorry," Gerald said finally. He didn't speak loudly, but the word seemed harsh against the silence. He cleared his throat and tried again. "I panicked a little. As usual."

"What are you afraid of?" Omar asked. "What made you need to hide from me?"

Gerald shook his head. "Not from *you*. I wasn't hiding *from*, I was just...hiding."

"Why?" Omar persisted. "We have to talk to each other, Gerald. We're making our own way. We don't have a, a framework. We don't know what the expectations are, what our roles are. So we have to talk. We have to say what we want and what we need and what we're going to do."

"I know," Gerald said, and he did. "It's, well, talking about important things, it's not something I do well."

"You'll have to practice. It'll get easier. But do you want me to go first?"

That simple question sent a spike of nerves straight through Gerald's gut. He unconsciously pressed his palm against his stomach, as if he had been stabbed and needed to staunch the blood. He was afraid of what Omar would say. *What if he wants more than I can give? What if he wants me to be someone I can't?* But he was also afraid of letting his imagination get the better of him, of letting his nerves create dozens of what-if scenarios that would only fuel his panic. And he was even more afraid of having to speak himself. So after what felt like an endless frozen moment of terror he straightened up, set his shoulders, and nodded. "Please."

"Well, broadly, I want to be happy." Omar smiled a little sheepishly as he said that. "Who doesn't, right? I want to be happy and I want you to be happy, and I want us to be happy together. I want to live with you and spend time with you. I want to help with the sanctuary, and I want to do my own things, too. I've always wanted a garden. There's not a lot of call for that in a desert kingdom, but I've done a bit around the oases. I want to grow *everything*. Flowers and ornamental plants, but also food and herbs. And then I want you to cook with them! I don't want to eat my own cooking. I want to enjoy your company and I want you to enjoy mine. I want to know what your boundaries are because I don't want to overstep them."

Each word Omar spoke dissolved another thread in the knot of anxiety in Gerald's stomach. He was so earnest, so sure of what he was saying, and everything he said sounded wonderful to Gerald. He was so happy to hear it he didn't respond, but simply sat there and enjoyed the idea that the dragon was right, it really was going to work out.

"Gerald?" Omar prompted after a moment.

"That sounds nice. More than nice. I want that too. Working on the sanctuary, working with the guardians and the animals, cooking, spending time with you. Being happy."

"And the boundaries?"

"Boundaries?"

"Well, I mean, I know you don't want to make it formal. You don't want to get married. And you don't want to have sex. But what about other forms of affection? Can I hug you? Kiss you? Hold your hand? Do you want to sleep in the same bed? What do you want, and what's off limits?"

Gerald blushed but forced the words out anyway. "I... I liked the other night. When I fell asleep with you there. At home, the castle cats always came in to spend the night with me. You don't purr, but it was nice in the same way. Having another body there...not being alone." He flicked his gaze over to look at Omar, who was watching him patiently, nodding along as he spoke. "But that's all it could be. Only sleeping. Maybe, I don't know, cuddling a little. Hugging is nice. But, you know, with clothes. It's not just no s-sex. I can't be naked in front of you. I don't want you to be naked in front of me, either." He waved a hand vaguely at his belt, his face burning. "Nothing below the waist. Seeing or... touching."

Omar kept nodding, his face calm. He was unsurprised and unfazed, and it made Gerald feel guilty.

"Does your leg hurt?" Omar asked.

"What? Oh. No." Gerald moved his hand away from his knee, where he had been worrying the scars. "Just... I feel bad. You're letting me decide everything. I can say what I want or don't, and you're just going along with it. But I'm saying you can't do things you want. What about when you, you know, get aroused?"

To his surprise, Omar laughed, a low, rich chuckle. "Oh, Gerald. I can take care of that myself. I'm quite happy to take care of that myself. I've had enough practice! I can do it out of sight and out of earshot and that should work for both of us. As for no sex, well, it's not like I've had that much of it. I enjoyed it, sure, but it's not like I've gotten so used to it I can't live without it." He shrugged. "That's the difference, I think. Why you get to decide, I mean. I'm more...flexible, I guess the word is. I can do what you want without it bothering me. It's no big deal for me. But the other way, it would be a big deal for you. It's not something you can compromise on, and it's something I can, so I am. All right?"

"All right," Gerald repeated.

"You don't have to worry so much," Omar said gently. "If anything changes, we can talk about it. But don't worry about things that haven't happened and might never happen."

"My parents—"

"It's not their life, Gerald." Omar regarded Gerald seriously. "What's the worst thing that can happen? The absolute worst thing they can do to you?"

"I don't know. Lock me in the dungeon? Refuse to let me leave with you?"

"But they can't keep you there. Even if they put you in the dungeon, the dragon can break you out. They can't do anything to you, Gerald. They can say nasty things, they can disagree with you, but they can't keep you there, they can't keep you away from me, and they can't force you to do anything you don't want to do. We'll be in and out. That's it."

"Okay. You're right. In and out. They accept it or they don't. That's it."

"And then we'll go to the sanctuary."

"Which will be where, exactly?"

"Wherever we want. Even if your parents disown you, I'll still have money. We can buy land anywhere we want, in any kingdom we want. Since we're going to have at least one dragon with us, we'll probably want to be somewhere a little out of the way. But not completely isolated, either. We'll need some towns nearby to trade with."

"Nearby is a relative term, with a dragon," Gerald pointed out wryly.

"Near enough we don't need the dragon to get there," Omar said. "It doesn't have to be within walking distance, but somewhere we can easily get on horseback. I don't want to be too isolated." He shrugged. "That desert upbringing, I guess. If you were alone, you were in danger. I don't need a *lot* of people nearby, but I need some. Trust me, no matter how much you like someone, if they're the only company you have, you start to get on each other's nerves."

"We should ask the dragon," Gerald said. "It's traveled more than either of us. And it will know what kind of climate would be best for what we want to do."

"We will. And we'll keep an eye out when we're in the air. I want to find a good spot for us. Somewhere that's *ours*."

Gerald leaned against him. "I want that, too."

Chapter Twenty-Eight

A WEEK LATER, they were ready to leave the dragonlands. Nedi had been right about the Council. The showcase had resulted in nearly fifty engagements—Gerald had been pleased to see Mikkel had apparently found someone who didn't scare him, because his name was on the list of engagements; Lila's was, as well, next to that of a prince Gerald didn't know; and also present was Erick's, next to (to no one's surprise) Nedi's—and even the two-dozen-odd royals who were still single remained enthusiastic about the idea and were already planning ahead for the next round when the newest crop of royals came of age.

The Council had approved it all, including the complete dismantling of the guardian program, effective immediately. They were busy drafting an announcement of the new format, and a revised and updated *Rules, Regulations, and Procedures* handbook was in the works, with Nedi consulting. Gerald was happy to step back and let her handle all of that. The Council still made him nervous. He kept waiting for them to say "never mind" and go back to the old way.

It was quieter in and around the dragonlands now. Most of the Council had left; only the Ten were still in semipermanent attendance, although a number of other individuals were teleporting in and out to take part in different votes and discussions. The amphitheater was empty once more as well, with the newly engaged couples returning to their home kingdoms to spread the word of the new system as they went. And Gerald and Omar were preparing to head to Andine to face down the Queens.

Gerald had written and thrown out and rewritten at least a dozen drafts of his letter to his parents before he had something he thought might prepare them for his in-person arguments. He had no illusions about the letter itself convincing them of anything, but he still wanted it to be as perfect as possible. He had shown draft after draft to Omar, to Erick, to Nedi, to the dragon, and even to Calin, who had even less of a concept of romance and marriage than Gerald did. Finally, Erick had gotten fed up with the endless drafts and said he was going to send the next letter Gerald gave him—and he did.

So now the Queens of Andine were advised that their youngest son's rebellion was still in full force; he was sticking to his conviction he would not marry; and he was on his way to the capital—with a dragon and a nonromantic partner—to discuss a possible abdication. Their bags were packed and Gerald was torn between a feeling of imminent doom and the knowledge it would be over soon, one way or another. He also had to admit, regardless of what was waiting on the other end of the journey, the idea of being alone with Omar and the dragon again was an appealing one.

Calin hovering over them and checking they had all of the medical supplies she thought they might possibly ever have even the slightest chance of someday needing only added to Gerald's growing excitement at being *alone* for the first time in too long.

Erick had furnished them with a fresh supply of two-way parchment and he and Nedi were there to see them off. It was Nedi who reassured Calin that "the boys will be fine", a sentiment that caused the piedling to snort dismissively but she did then back away and give the dragon enough space to take off.

Omar waved enthusiastically while Gerald shut his eyes and took a firm hold of the harness.

I'm never going to get used to these takeoffs.

THE DRAGON FLEW neither slowly nor speedily; with nothing to rush toward or away from, it flew at a leisurely, but steady, pace. Of course, a leisurely pace from the dragon's perspective still saw the ground disappear beneath them at a rapid clip from Gerald's.

"You're biting your lip again," Omar chided him gently. "It's a beautiful day. Nothing is going wrong, nothing is *going* to go wrong, there are no crises, no unpleasant passengers. Let yourself relax."

Gerald wished he could turn his worries on and off as easily as all that. But Omar was right: there was really nothing his anxiety could cling to up there in the cloudless blue sky. He leaned against Omar, who draped his arm over Gerald's shoulder. Over the last week, they'd discovered Gerald liked that sort of companionable touch, as long as he was expecting it.

"I'm trying."

BEING ALONE WITH Omar and the dragon soothed nerves he hadn't realized had been so badly frazzled by the intensity of the showcase and the crowds it had entailed. Being alone with his two closest friends, who understood him better than anyone else in his life ever had, also helped wear at the barriers he was still unconsciously putting up between them.

When he craved touch but was also still too easily overwhelmed by it, there was no judgment. Omar didn't push anything; he sat back and followed Gerald's lead and that emboldened Gerald to take it. There was no one to comment when Gerald pushed their separate pallets together into one on the second night and there was no one to smirk when all they did on it was sleep.

ON THE MAP, Andine looked a long way from the dragonlands. But even with the dragon flying at a leisurely pace, the distance collapsed at a rapid rate and they flew over the border into Andine much sooner than Gerald wanted them to.

Not that it even matters, Gerald thought. *It wouldn't matter if it took us a month to get here instead of a week, or if it took six months, or a year. It wouldn't make a difference; I'm never going to feel ready for this.*

Omar squeezed his hand. "You're going to give yourself an ulcer," he said gently. "You're too young to have a bleeding stomach. I'm not going to tell you to relax, but trust us, all right? You're walking out of that castle with us no matter what they say."

"I know. But you don't know my parents. It's going to be very unpleasant before we walk out." *On the other hand, the sooner we get there, the sooner it will be over.*

"But we *will* walk out. Keep reminding yourself of that. It will only be unpleasant for so long, and then we'll leave. We'll leave and we'll find some land and start the sanctuary."

Gerald nodded and squeezed Omar's hand back.

In no time at all, they were flying over the capital and approaching the castle. The dragon had refused to stop a discreet distance away, saying, "If you are in need of rescue, I will be on hand, not hiding miles away to avoid upsetting anyone." Now Gerald was wishing there was a way to bring the dragon directly into the audience chamber with them.

As the dragon back-winged down into the abruptly abandoned central courtyard, Gerald hoped the queens had thought to warn the castle residents and staff he was returning with a dragon. There was no swarm of guards, at least, which he took as a positive sign.

Aside from the echoing emptiness, the courtyard—and the castle—looked exactly the way Gerald remembered it. The tall stone walls looked as imposing and as oppressive as ever. He felt small and young and out of place. The mismatched prince, once again set to disturb the royal tableau.

The urge to flee to the stable, to saddle Wisp and ride away, rose up in him and he cast a longing glance toward that building. But they had dressed up for this visit and it would rather ruin the impression he hoped to make if he arrived with straw on his clothes and horse slobber in his hair. *After*, he promised himself.

Omar followed his gaze and asked, "What's over there?"

"My horse. I wonder if I can get permission to bring her, too..." Even as he said it, he had the feeling Queen Danya would refuse to let him have Wisp just to spite him. "On the other hand, maybe it's better not to ask."

"Easier to get forgiveness than permission, eh?"

"I don't think it'll be easy to get either," Gerald said morosely.

"That's the spirit," Omar joked. "Are you ready?"

"As ready as I'll ever be," Gerald sighed. He undid the harness and slid down the dragon's side, with Omar close behind.

The dragon scrutinized them as they gave each other a last once-over, straightening collars and brushing out wrinkles. Omar was wearing his royal circlet, the silver shining out from within his dark curls, but Gerald had flatly refused to wear his. "I'm here to *abdicate*. I want to look like I already have, like this is just a formality." In his heart, he doubted the gesture would make much of a difference, but it made him feel better.

Omar wore traditional Yevish formal clothing, as well as the circlet and a small but noticeable collection of jewelry—a ruby drop in one ear, several rings, and a necklace—while Gerald was dressed nicely but plainly in a well-tailored, well-made shirt and trousers and a pair of polished boots. Omar had successfully talked him into a pair of ornamented canes—"If they're going to stare, give them something worth staring *at*"—but standing there in the courtyard Gerald was having second thoughts about them.

"You both look very handsome," the dragon pronounced. "I do wish I could fit in there...but I'm sure you will impress them in your own right."

"You'll be watching us, though, right?" Gerald asked nervously.

"The seeing spell is already cast," the dragon assured him. "Go on, now. They surely know you're here. It won't do to delay too long."

Gerald took a deep breath, adjusted his grip on his canes, and took the first step toward the castle.

To his relief, he found the first step was the hardest. Once he started moving, momentum took over. It felt like mere moments before they had crossed the length of the courtyard and a slightly pale steward in immaculate livery was opening the gate for them with an apprehensive glance at the dragon. She quickly remembered herself and tore her gaze away from it, bowing deeply to Omar and Gerald.

"Welcome back, Prince Gerald," she said warmly. "And welcome, Prince..."

"Omar. Of Yevin."

She bowed again and stepped aside for them. "Their Majesties are in the Great Receiving Room. You are expected."

"Thank you," Gerald said automatically. He headed for the stairs as quickly as possible, partly due to an unwillingness to lose his momentum and partly to get away from the prying eyes of the castle residents.

The courtyard had been deserted due to the dragon, but that meant the halls were more crowded than usual, filled with all the people who had been chased inside.

His limp had lessened somewhat after judicious use of Calin's ointments to loosen the scar tissue, but he still needed the canes and he was still self-conscious of them. The steward hadn't reacted to them at all, either because she was distracted by the dragon or because she was too well-trained to show it, but they clicked noisily on the polished floors and the sound echoed throughout the entryway, making him feel awkward and exposed.

"Breathe," Omar murmured in his ear.

"I am," Gerald said under his breath. It was about all he was doing: breathing and walking. His nerves were giving him tunnel vision and wreaking havoc on his ability to perceive time or distance. They could have been walking through the castle for seconds or minutes or hours. The halls were lined with familiar faces, but he didn't see or recognize any of them. He barely recognized the halls, but his body knew the way and suddenly the doors to the Great Receiving Room were looming large in front of them.

Gerald stared at them for a moment. Those oak planks were the only things between him and his parents and the familiar crushing weight of their disapproval. *There's still time to run,* a small voice whispered, but even as he had the thought it was no longer true. The steward posted there seized the initiative and opened the doors to announce them. The courtyard doorkeeper had apparently managed to pass the word about Omar's name and title because there was no hesitation in his voice as he said, "Prince Gerald of Andine! Prince Omar of Yevin!" and bowed them into the room.

Omar gave Gerald a sharp nudge to get him moving and he limped inside with Omar right behind him. As soon as the two of them had cleared the doorway, the steward returned to the hall, pulling the door shut behind him.

They were alone with the queens.

No audience, he thought. The queens had chosen the Great Receiving Room solely for the size and intimidation factor, then, not to bully Gerald in front of the court. They were sitting on the dais at the far end of the room, dressed in full formal court wear: elaborately tailored gowns in green and gold, the Andinian colors; full crowns, not the more informal circlets; and jewels—necklaces, earrings, and rings. It was not the tableau one would expect when ostensibly welcoming home a child from a quest; it was nothing like the reception Lila would receive when she returned with her betrothed prince.

And there's one bit of comfort, Gerald thought as he limped across the seemingly endless room. *There's no way Lila could have made it back here yet. It's only Mum and Mother...and that's frankly more than enough.*

They sat still and silent on the dais; Queen Danya, as ever, looked like she had been carved out of ice; Queen Mixte, normally more expressive than her wife, was likewise statuesque. Gerald thought she at least would have reacted to his canes, but he didn't see so much as a twitch or a raised eyebrow.

Bit by bit the distance between them shrank until Gerald and Omar stopped a few yards away. Omar bowed precisely as deeply as protocol demanded and waited for the Queens' acknowledgment before straightening up gracefully. Gerald made a passable attempt at a modified bow, helped by the fact that as a royal child of the blood, rather than a foreign prince, his bow was allowed to be much shallower. He straightened and stood silently, waiting for his parents to guide the conversation.

"We received your letter," Queen Mixte said after a long moment.

Gerald nodded acknowledgment and continued to wait. Mixte's tone had been blandly conversational, with no hint of her feelings toward the letter or its contents.

Queen Danya was not so circumspect. "We were...most displeased," she said coldly. "I would have thought you had learned the consequences of shirking your responsibilities."

Gerald flushed but kept his own tone level with an effort. "I have no responsibilities. No true responsibilities. Lila is heir; she is engaged; she will continue the line of succession. Andine is prosperous; the Thousand Kingdoms are at peace; we have favorable trade agreements with our neighbors. I am an ornamental prince, nothing more. An ornament Andine can do without."

"You are a *child*," Danya spit. "What do you know of responsibilities?"

"I'm an adult in the eyes of the law," Gerald said quietly. "I'm old enough to guide my own life. If Andine needed me, that would be one thing; I'm not interested in shirking. But Andine does not need me, and I can do something useful, something needful, elsewhere."

"To be perfectly frank," Danya said coldly, "you do not look capable of doing *anything* useful at the moment."

Gerald bit his tongue to keep from rising to the bait. After a breath, he said, still managing somehow to keep his tone even, "If I were truly as useless as all that, what reason would you have to keep me here? If I am not capable of doing anything useful, what could I possibly do for Andine?"

Mixte laid a restraining hand on Danya's arm. "Now, Gerald, I'm sure that was not how she meant that to sound. But you can see why we— as your parents—are concerned about you wandering the Thousand Kingdoms. Your adventuring to date has clearly not agreed with you."

"Perhaps you should have considered that before *enchanting me against my will*," Gerald snapped, his grip on his temper fraying, "and locking me in a tower in the middle of a desert. My injuries can be laid squarely at your feet, Mother. You are the one who had me magicked away—illegal as it is, I might add, to work magic on an unaware and unwilling person—and put me in position to be hurt. But I am healing, and I can set that aside. I don't feel the need to point fingers."

Danya waved a hand dismissively. "I am hardly to blame for encouraging you to take up your responsibilities, to participate in the Royal Rescue. If you were not as prepared as you might have been, well, whose fault was that? How many of your *willing* cohort were injured?"

Omar cleared his throat. "With all due respect, Your Majesty... I don't see the point of laying blame with anyone. The past cannot be changed. We're here about the future."

Danya gave him a withering glare, but Omar only smiled blandly in response.

"He's right," Gerald said. "Let's talk about the future. My future isn't here. Surely you can see that. I've never been the prince you've wanted, the son you've wanted. What do you gain by keeping me here, other than my bitterness? A feuding royal family hardly serves Andine's interests."

"You don't know what you're talking about," Danya said. She waved Gerald's letter at him. "The things you've written show so clearly you're a child still, even if not in the eyes of the law. You need time to mature. This is not the time to make rash decisions."

"What, exactly, have I done or said that's been childish?" Gerald asked. "I stood up for the oppressed. I changed an outdated, slavery-fueled system. I negotiated with the Council. I planned, and researched, and persevered. How is any of that a sign I am immature?"

"You know very well your intentions were not nearly as noble as you're making them out to be. You were clinging to your childish declaration you would never marry, and like a child, you acted out to ensure you would get your way. You threw a tantrum, Gerald, and you dragged your entire cohort and the Council into it. That is hardly something to be proud of."

"I think the guardians would disagree."

Omar cleared his throat again. "With all due respect... Don't you think the fact that Gerald was willing to go to such lengths—to plan and carry out a *revolution*—to avoid marriage shows how serious he is about this? If it were merely some childish tantrum, do you really think he would have pursued it so far? Do you really think he would be willing to give up the safety and security of his life here, to *abdicate* and leave the country, simply out of a childish need to get his way?"

"He does make a point, darling," Mixte said to Danya in an undertone, but she waved her spouse's words away.

"And you," Danya said to Omar, as if she were only now truly registering his presence, "How are you involved in this? Why are you indulging him? The two of you are in a relationship, Gerald wrote. Why, then, this refusal to make it official? Why this continued rebellion? Gerald, you swore you wouldn't find a partner, and here you have one. Why should we believe you won't change your mind about marriage as well?"

"I don't believe I said I wouldn't find a partner," Gerald said. "I said I wouldn't marry. I said I wouldn't fall in love. I have done neither of those things and I will not do either of those things."

"We're not in a romantic relationship," Omar added. "Gerald doesn't feel that way about me. About anyone. It's not *indulging* him to acknowledge that!"

"As I've told you," Gerald said, "I've never felt that way. I've never even felt a hint of it. A marriage would give entirely the wrong impression of our situation. It would cause people to make assumptions. It would be a lie. I don't want to marry Omar. I don't want to go to bed with him. And I don't want to have to justify myself for the rest of my life. You don't believe me; you've never believed me. You've always said to wait until I'm older. Well, how old do I have to be before you'll agree I simply don't have those feelings?"

When he got no response, he said, "I don't want to wait for your approval. I've accepted I'm never going to get it. To be honest, at this point, I don't know if I even *want* it. Would I prefer you believed me, you treated me like an adult, you trusted me to know my own mind? Of course. But right now, I will happily take your permission to abdicate, no matter how grudgingly given, and I will withdraw from your lives."

Mixte laid her hand on Danya's arm before she could say anything in the heat of anger. "Gerald, this is a lot to take in. Surely you can concede that much."

"I'm not saying anything I haven't said before," Gerald pointed out. "Not to mention I sent a letter ahead."

"Reading it is a lot different than having you standing here telling us face-to-face," she said gently. "Let us speak privately, please. This doesn't only affect you. It's your life, but when you're a prince, your life is not entirely your own."

"One of the reasons I wish to abdicate. And, Mum, you should *let* me. If you don't trust me enough to even know my own feelings, how could you possibly trust me with a kingdom?"

Now it was Omar's turn to put his hand on Gerald's arm. "Let them talk," he said softly.

Gerald turned back to his parents. "How long do you need?"

They exchanged glances. "We'll send a page when we're ready for you," Mixte said. "Go. Give Prince Omar a tour."

Omar bowed, acknowledging the dismissal, and tugged at Gerald's sleeve until he bobbed his head and turned away.

It took just as long to cross the room in reverse, even without the weight of nervous anticipation dilating the distance, and when they finally reached the hall with the doors closed firmly behind them, Gerald had to stop and lean against the wall.

"I need to sit down," he said. "It doesn't *hurt*," he added quickly, seeing Omar's expression. "I'm just...tired. Not tired enough to sit on the floor, but I'm getting there. Come on. My room's not too far."

He pushed himself away from the wall with a bit of effort and started down the hall.

"I'm sure we could get someone to bring a chair," Omar said, but Gerald stubbornly pressed on down the hall. "If you collapse, I'm not picking you up," Omar warned him, but he followed Gerald nevertheless.

It was something of a near thing, but they did reach Gerald's room without any major incidents. "Damn," Gerald said, staring at the largely empty space. "I forgot about the bed. I guess they left it in the tower..."

"Well, there's no reason I can't stay standing," Omar said. "But you— sit down before you fall down!" He pulled the desk chair out and all but shoved Gerald into it, and he was too relieved to get his weight off his leg to say anything about it.

"So?" Gerald asked as he kneaded at his thigh and knee. "What do you think they're going to say?"

"They have to give in," Omar said. "There's no real reason not to let you abdicate. And surely they have to see how miserable *everyone* will be if they refuse. Not to mention the dragon waiting in their courtyard for just that eventuality... But Queen Mixte seemed reasonable. I think they'll approve it, in the end."

"They still don't believe me, though," Gerald said. He wondered why that still hurt. *I knew they weren't going to. I knew it. And yet, I still hoped they would listen. But no, they still think I'm lying, or mistaken, that one day I'll just wake up and fall in love! I suppose that's better than them thinking something's plain old wrong with me. But still... I wish they could understand.*

"I believe you," Omar reminded him. "And they'll come around eventually. Maybe not anytime soon," he added when Gerald made a face. "But what you said, when you asked how old you would have to be before they would believe you—there was something on their faces, then. A flicker. At some point, they *will* have to admit you're not...that you just don't have, you know, romantic feelings."

"Better late than never, I suppose," Gerald said. But his expression said it still hurt.

Omar leaned over the back of the chair and wrapped Gerald up in a hug. "It'll be okay," he said. "If they can't see how wonderful you are, that's their problem. The dragon and I will appreciate you more than they ever could."

"This was such a stupid idea," Gerald said, shaking his head. "I shouldn't have even come back. I should've sent the letter and left it at that."

"It wasn't stupid. It was the right thing to do. Running from your problems doesn't solve them. At least this way, it'll all be over. There won't be anything hanging over your head."

Gerald leaned back into Omar's arms and didn't answer.

When a knock on the door came to announce the queens were once again ready to receive them, that thought—it would soon be over—was the only thing that got Gerald out of his chair.

They followed the page—who kept glancing at Gerald's canes with wide eyes—not back to the Great Receiving Room, but to the study where Queen Danya had first confronted Gerald about the need for him to choose a role in the old rescuer/rescuee system.

Omar frowned at the change in venue, but Gerald whispered, "Maybe this is a good sign. They're not trying to intimidate us. Me."

He was less apprehensive, at least, when the steward announced them and bowed them into the room. There was a much shorter distance to cross to reach the queens, who were seated in chairs instead of thrones, on the floor instead of on a raised dais. The intended effect seemed to be one of equality rather than an appeal to authority, and there was another pair of empty chairs across from them—a fact Gerald's bad leg very much appreciated.

Omar bowed and Gerald bobbed his head and Mixte said, "Please, be seated."

Once they settled, she exchanged a long look with Danya while Gerald's stomach clenched with nerves. Finally, Danya nodded stiffly and Mixte started speaking again.

"We would like to discuss this informally, as a family, rather than as monarchs to princes. Your mother and I do love you, Gerald, as hard as it seems to be for you to see that. We do want the best for you. And we can see that, perhaps, as difficult as it may be for *us* to acknowledge it, being here is not the best thing for you."

Gerald's eyes widened. "You can?"

"It's apparent our attempts to ensure your happiness have not worked the way we would have hoped," Mixte said with a regretful look at his canes. "Keeping you here would only cause you to resent us further. No, there's no need to deny it. We know that, for whatever reason, we haven't done as well by you as we have with the others. Even if we can't undo that, there is no point in making things worse."

"However," Danya interrupted. "We do not agree you should abdicate."

Mixte laid a restraining hand on her arm and continued quickly before Gerald could respond. "*Yet*," she said. "We do not agree you should abdicate *yet*. Hear us out, please, Gerald. We will give you our support to found the sanctuary you mentioned in your letter. You will have our full permission to travel as far from Andine as you wish; you will not be summoned back to the capital; you will not be given any diplomatic responsibilities on your travels. We simply don't want to...formalize the arrangement immediately.

"It's not that we don't trust you to know your own mind," she added. "But circumstances change. We don't want to remove any of our options too soon. You can abdicate at any time, after all, but once done...it is not so simple to add you back into the line of succession. This is not a 'no', Gerald. It's a precaution. If, on your twentieth birthday, you are still determined to abdicate, we will give you our blessing. In the meantime...

We hope perhaps a little distance will help us come back together as a family."

Gerald stared at her, at both of his mothers; Mixte, her expression a mixture of love and worry, and Danya, who was as unreadable as ever. It was both more than he ever expected to hear and less than he hoped, but it was enough. It was more than enough.

"Mother?" he said softly, willing Danya to let her expressionless mask slip. "You agree with Mum? You'll let me go, and live my own life, and see how it all plays out?"

"My interventions have not worked as I have wished," she said. "With Mixte taking your side and a dragon in my courtyard, I don't have another choice, do I?"

"Mother..."

"I hope it teaches you a lesson," she said, before brushing off Mixte's arm, standing up, and striding away.

Gerald watched her go, wondering why each new rejection hurt just as much as all the ones before it. Omar reached over and squeezed his hand and Gerald dragged up a wobbly smile. "I just had to press my luck," he said. "She's never approved of me before. I don't know why I thought she would start now."

"You're too alike, the pair of you," Mixte said, a statement that caused Gerald to stare at her in blind astonishment. Not once in his life had anyone suggested he was *anything* like Queen Danya. She saw his expression and smiled gently. "At the core," she said, "you are both stubborn as mules. She knows this is the right thing to do, Gerald. Right for you, right for us, right for Andine. But she can't admit it. Don't hold it against her. I love you, dear, and she does too. She'll come around."

Mixte stood up, gave a surprised Omar a hug, and kissed Gerald on the forehead. "Go on, then. Take your young man and prove her wrong."

He didn't need to be told twice. Omar pulled him to his feet, and hand-in-hand, they went to find the dragon and get started.

About the Author

A. Alex Logan is an asexual, agender librarian from New York state. Always an avid reader, Alex has branched out from reading books to writing them. Alex's other main interest is soccer, which they enjoy watching, playing, and (of course) reading about.

Twitter: @aalexlogan

Website: www.almostalmost.wordpress.com